INFINITE

Also by Jeremy Robinson

Standalone Novels

The Didymus Contingency
Raising The Past
Beneath
Antarktos Rising
Kronos
Xom-B
Flood Rising
MirrorWorld
Apocalypse Machine
Unity
The Distance

Nemesis Saga Novels

Island 731
Project Nemesis
Project Maigo
Project 731
Project Hyperion
Project Legion

The Antarktos Saga

The Last Hunter – Descent
The Last Hunter – Pursuit
The Last Hunter – Ascent
The Last Hunter – Lament
The Last Hunter – Onslaught
The Last Hunter – Collected
Edition
The Last Valkyrie

The Jack Sigler/Chess Team Thrillers

Prime
Pulse
Instinct
Threshold
Ragnarok
Omega
Savage
Cannibal
Empire

Cerberus Group Novels

Herculean
Helios

Jack Sigler Continuum Novels

Guardian
Patriot
Centurion

Chesspocalypse Novellas

Callsign: King
Callsign: Queen
Callsign: Rook
Callsign: King 2 – Underworld
Callsign: Bishop
Callsign: Knight
Callsign: Deep Blue
Callsign: King 3 – Blackout

Chesspocalypse Collections

Callsign: King – The Brainstorm
Trilogy
Callsign – Tripleshot
Callsign – Doubleshot

SecondWorld Novels

SecondWorld
Nazi Hunter: Atlantis

Horror Novels (written as Jeremy Bishop)

Torment
The Sentinel
The Raven
Refuge

Post-Apocalyptic Sci-Fi (written as Jeremiah Knight)

Hunger
Feast

INFINITE

JEREMY ROBINSON

01000110 01101111 01110010 00100000 01001000 01101001
01101100 01100001 01110010 01100101 01100101 00101100
00100000 01001001 00100111 01100100 00100000 01101100
01101111 01110110 01100101 00100000 01111001 01101111
01110101 00100000 01100101 01110110 01100101 01101110
00100000 01101001 01100110 00100000 01111001 01101111
01110101 00100000 01110111 01100101 01110010 01100101
01101110 00100111 01110100 00100000 01110010 01100101
01100001 01101100 00101110

1

"Solitude."

"Go on," she says, chewing on a yellow #2 pencil that makes dry scratching sounds whenever it carves a letter onto the equally yellow legal pad resting on her tight gray skirt. I know she's supposed to be evaluating the state of my psychological well-being, but I can't help analyzing her in return. The way her teeth leave divots in the pencil flesh tells me she enjoys hearing people's personal details. Probably too much. Her form-fitting clothing tells me she wants to be noticed, but the power suit warns against saying anything. Because she's married. So says the ring on her finger. But is it her husband she'll be telling my personal details to later on, or the guy she's trying to impress with those tight clothes? Then again, maybe I'm just a sexist pig judging a woman by her clothing.

"Mr. Chanokh?"

The rebel in me says to screw with her, to lead her down a confusing rabbit hole of contradictions, but that's probably a bad idea. I want to be here. "I'm an introvert by nature, so I tend to spend a lot of time alone."

"Uh-huh." *Scratch, scratch, scratch* goes the pencil.

"But that doesn't mean I don't like people. I just—"

"Feel tired after engaging with them," she says. "I know what an introvert is."

"Right," I say. Of course she knows, but isn't she just supposed to let me talk? My eyes drift toward her crossed legs, which are at head level as I lie back on her tilde-shaped couch. The underside of her exposed hamstring, like a smooth, upside-down sand dune, captivates me.

Light glimmers off her bifocals as she looks up from her legal pad. My eyes dart to the side. I pretend to be absorbed in the first thing my gaze lands on: a digital edition of *Modern Parenting*. There's a baby on the cover, lying in a shallow river, worn oval stones all around it.

Did she see me?

I try to hide my growing discomfort, as I realize the tight skirt might be a test.

Scratch, scratch, scratch.

I don't know if that pencil has an air bubble in the graphite, or a granule of something, but it's starting to have a nails-on-chalkboard effect on my teeth. Who uses pencils anymore?

Forget the pencil, I tell myself. *Is she noting my attention on her legs, or on the baby?* I can think of a million ways both could count against me. Preoccupation with sex. A desire to have children. Shit. They're even related. Can't have a baby without first having sex, and here I am talking about my fear of solitude.

I try to recover. "I think it's because I connect so deeply with people, you know?"

She twists her lips, tapping the chewed pencil against them. Her shade of red lipstick matches her curly hair.

A test, I remind myself. *All of this is a test. Look away.*

I don't. She's mesmerizing. "When people talk, I listen. I mean, I *really* listen. I feel their joy, sadness, and pain, like it was my own. And I don't do small talk. I don't care about the weather, sports teams, or the latest webisode. I just connect with people."

Oh, God, just shut up. I sound like a dating profile.

"And that's exhausting," she says. Not a question. She's agreeing.

Is she talking about me?

Is she saying that I'm *exhausting?*

The ceiling calls out to me, beckoning my attention to its frosty white surface, where nothing changes. It's empty and peaceful. I find calm in it. For a moment.

Scratch, scratch, scratch.

"You seem nervous," she says, and when I stay lost in the white too long, she uses my name again. "Mr. Chanokh?"

"William Chanokh," I say, "Doctor of Computer Science. That's who I am."

"I know who you are," she says.

"Just like to remind myself sometimes."

"Can you forget who you are?"

"I almost did once."

Scratch, scratch, scratch.

"I know twelve languages, and just one of them is spoken." *Why did I say that? Am I trying to impress her? Or am I reminding myself about that, too?*

"English and eleven programming languages?"

"Close. English, ten programming languages, and Latin." I laugh. It's forced and uncomfortable. "They said it would help me learn other Latin-based languages. French. German. Spanish. You know. Code, not so much."

"You're smarter than other people."

"I wouldn't say that."

"But people do."

"I guess."

"Is that why you find it so hard to connect with those around you?"

"Hard?" I feel the need to look her in the eyes, but the shadows now sliding across the ceiling hold my attention. "I just said—"

"I know what you said, but the truth is, you haven't spent time with anyone in a long time. How long has it been, William?"

Fuck you.

"I don't know."

"How long since you've *been* with someone?"

The words on their own are suggestive enough, but the honey she's dipped them in before opening those red lips is enough to distract me from the ceiling.

She looks at me over the top of her gravity-defying glasses, clinging to the tip of her nose. Two blouse buttons have been undone, revealing the top of her curved breasts. Her skirt is shorter. Not hiked up. Just shorter.

Scratch, scratch, scratch.

I close my eyes at the sound. "Would you mind not—"

The pencil was in her mouth. I saw her lips wrapping around the gnawed yellow surface like two delicious slugs, wet and...

"What is that sound?" I ask.

"What do you hear?"

"Scratching."

"Have you been hearing it this whole time?"

The shadows on the ceiling dance with the fervent shifting of trees caught in a storm. I turn toward the window and squint. The distant sun reflects off the atmospheric dome, illuminating the room, but there are no trees.

"There are no trees," I say.

"True, there are no trees," she agrees, "on Mars."

I point at the ceiling. "Then what is that?"

The shadows vibrate. Back and forth. The ballet has become a war between light and dark.

Scratch.

The white ceiling is wounded by four, long, black lines.

Scratch, scratch.

Long streaks carve away at the white, revealing color. Hues of gray. And orange. Dark red.

"You know what this is," she says. "Just like you know who you are."

"William Chanokh." I turn toward my beautiful psychologist, who would have mounted me on the tilde couch after patching the holes in my consciousness. "You're not real."

She points at the ceiling. "That is."

"I'm waking up. This is it."

She smiles at me. "Try to connect. You don't need to be alone anymore."

The white office fades.

There's a hiss and a cloud of steam.

A face leans in through the mist.

Smiling.

It's Tom Holden, the secondary Computer Scientist.

I'm the primary. We're friends. We understand each other. But there's something off about his pale face. Something different. It's red. Like her lips. Wet, too.

At the very moment I realize it's blood, and I hear the screams, he plunges a long screwdriver into my chest. I feel my heart shudder around the cold metal, and then stop.

This is the first time I die.

It's not the last.

2

My second life and death is a brief and confusing affair. My eyes flutter open. I see the yellow handle protruding from my chest and think, *Who uses screwdrivers anymore?* It's as out of place as my imaginary shrink's pencil. Then my heart tries to beat around the metal, now warm from my body heat, and it spasms. My body goes rigid. A turbulent breath fills my lungs.

And then I'm dead.

Again.

I assume it's death. I exist in darkness. It's peaceful. Without pain.

And there is light. A small spot at first, but growing larger, pulsing and swirling. I hear a hum. But it's not constant white noise, like I need so I can fall asleep. It's modulating. Is that a voice? Is some long dead relative coming to guide me into the afterlife that I don't believe exists?

Even if that was possible, could a spirit travel the 1400 light years from Earth to Cognata, the common name for Kepler 452b, that quickly? It took us ten years, locked in cryo-sleep, to cross the distance. Not quite as fast as the old *Star Trek* ships, but faster than light (FTL) is still impressive. It also means that 1400 years have passed back on Earth, and humanity has either solved the environmental problems that sent us first to Mars, and then beyond the solar system, or they've given up and followed us into space.

"That would be the logical choice."

I spin toward the voice. It's the guy from the original *Star Trek*. With the pointy ears. I grew up watching *The Next Generation* series with my brother Steven. My father had inherited copies of every episode from his father, and his father before him. My favorite character was always the bald captain, with his French name, subtle British accent, and stalwart dedication to exploring the vast unknown. My brother and I memorized catchphrases from the show, my favorite being 'Tea. Earl Grey. Hot,' even though Earl Grey tea no longer existed. Steven preferred 'Engage.' Any time we went someplace new, he'd kick off the trip by pointing forward and saying 'Engage,' to which I would say, 'Make it so.' As a teenager, I saw two of the classic *Star Trek* movies. I didn't like them as much as *The Next Generation*—I think, out of loyalty to my brother—but the guy with the pointy ears... That guy made me cry. His death resonated with me. What was his name?

"Leonard?"

He turns toward the light. His ears aren't pointy.

Did God send the actor who played Leonard to guide me?

You're not dead, some part of my flickering consciousness says.

A chemically-induced hallucination. *You're dying. Try not to be an idiot.*

"Idiot!" I shout.

My eyes open.

The mist has cleared.

Is this all just another fantasy, like my psychologist? Could it be a dream? I do sleep. Not a true cryo-sleep. But I do have dreams. They usually don't hurt, though.

I see the screwdriver again, this time noticing the name etched into it: Pearson. He's an engineer. I don't think the screwdriver is an actual tool, though. The shiny handle and the etching's quality suggest it's a keepsake. A gift from someone who has now been dead for 1400 years. Ish.

This time, when my heart pulsates around the burning metal wedged between my ribs, I react in a way I know I'm not supposed to. But I've died twice already, so what the hell. I grab the handle with two hands, and as my vision fades to black, I yank.

My body thrashes. My heart twists and coils inside my chest, a living thing, trying to break free. Darkness turns to white hot pain. Liquid warmth spreads over my chest, reminding me why I shouldn't have withdrawn the screwdriver. I'm bleeding out. My panicking, wounded heart is pumping blood straight out of the quarter-inch-wide hole in my chest.

I need help.

I try to move, but my body is weak, and the smooth surface of the cryo-bed, now slick with blood, feels like a soaped up tub beneath me. I thrash about, thumping with elbows and knees. I try to call out, but my parched, dry throat manages only a hiss.

I want to go back. To the fantasy. To my redheaded, bespectacled shrink. Ten years in failed cryo-sleep was torture, but far better than this rude awakening.

A perfect combination of motion, blood lubricant, and the position of my naked body sends me slipping down the angled bed. I thump hard against the lip at the bottom, bouncing up and out, and landing hard on the floor. It's smooth, and tacky wet with cool blood.

Not *my* still-warm blood.

Lying on my side, I see a hand, the fingers frozen in rigor, clutching at nothing. Blood is pooled around it, chunky, like fatty stew. Coagulated. I can't see whose hand it is, but the size and hair tell me it's a man. He died long before I did.

If I died at all.

I'm still breathing. Still thinking. Maybe I just passed out before? Maybe the screwdriver wasn't in my heart, but the meat beside it. Maybe I could still live.

Wet footsteps paralyze my body.

Someone is coming.

I want to cry out for help, but don't. Any sane person would be ranting. Or running. Or anything but walking with the calm, determined slap of bare feet on a wet floor.

It's Tom, I think. *Has to be.*

I freeze my eyes in place, staring at my blood dripping from the cryo-bed's bottom lip. It stretches out like syrup before losing a drip and recoiling back up to start again. The repetitive *drip, drip, drip*, helps me find a slow rhythm for my breathing. Slow enough to go unnoticed, I hope.

"Got away." The voice is scratchy and arid, but still Tom's. "Left me here."

His bare foot squishes through the blood beside my face, a globule of coagulation squeezing up between his toes. The print left behind is a dark red topographical map of his foot. A breeze kicked up by his passing guides the stench of death into my nostrils. My stomach lurches. There's nothing in it. Hasn't been for ten years. But that won't stop me from dry-heaving.

Despite my revulsion, I manage to stay rigid, as his feet squeal on the floor. Turning around.

I moved. I must have moved.

"Dead, dead, and dead." Tom says. "You can stay with me. Our journey isn't done yet. They left me, now I'm going to leave them."

The foot returns, facing the opposite direction. Tom is standing over me. Something wet drips from his nakedness. I want to shiver. To run. Instead, I stare. Lifeless.

"I liked you, Will. We had some good times. But you were one of them. I saw you. Saw all of you. But you were tricked, right? So, you can stay. Until you're bones."

He's lost his mind.

They told us something like this might happen. It's part of why every one of us has a double. An understudy. Fifty crew in all, filling twenty-five positions. And if Tom is telling the truth, they're all either dead, or gone.

There's only one place they could have gone: Kepler 452b.

Cognata.

"We're going to keep going. See what there is to see. You, me, this dead lot, and Cap."

Cap. Short for Capria. She's the primary astrophysicist. She's my friend, and if I'm honest, the focus of more fantasies than my psychologist, who wasn't nearly as attractive as she's become in my mind's eye. But Capria. Her dark skin holds my attention like the night sky. And her smile. It's the stars.

"I know you had a thing for her, but here's a secret, so did I. It's why I had to kill you. She's still asleep. For now."

He crouches down over me, and I feel his nakedness resting on my hip. He pats my shoulder. "Still warm. Saved you for last, that's why. Well, not quite last. Time for Cap to wake up. I hope she doesn't mind the mess."

I shiver as he walks away, the motion unseen, the slippery squish inaudible, thanks to the tune he's now whistling. I turn my head, watching him go. He hops through an obstacle course of naked bodies and twisted limbs. The occupants of cryo-chamber five are all dead.

Almost.

Death looms near, and help is clearly not coming. The others are either dead, or gone, and if they really did flee to the surface of Cognata, without supplies, or advance testing, or food, they'll be dead soon enough. Cognata might be an Earth-like planet, snugly located in the sun-like Kepler 452's habitable zone. It has an atmosphere, water, soil, acceptable temperatures, and a gravity twice as powerful than we're designed for. But no one really knows what we'll find, or if we can survive on the surface. Our voyage to the planet is what people used to call a 'Hail Mary.' I don't know the source of the term, but I know it means the odds are against us.

I try to move, for Cap, but I only manage to slip onto my back. The ceiling is pale white, like the imaginary psychologist's office, but it's pocked with evenly spaced orb lighting, casting a pleasant, sun-like glow. It's supposed to feel like sunrise, greeting us to our new lives in the far reaches of the Milky Way, but I just feel mocked.

Our mission was about saving lives.

Saving humanity.

Instead, we've already returned to our basest form. We were born out of primal violence, and we're destined to be ended by it.

Cap deserves better, but maybe she'll choose to live. With Tom. My friend turned mass murderer. I don't blame him. Clearly, his mind is gone. But for our mission to end like this...

I take a deep breath and let it out.

It doesn't hurt.

At all.

I lean my head over and look down. The blood has stopped pumping from my chest. But is that because I'm no longer bleeding, or just out of blood? Are these my last thoughts before I die for good, or...

I wipe my hands through the blood covering my chest. It's sticky, like nearly dry paint, but it wipes away. I'm expecting excruciating pain when my fingers slide over the wound, but I feel nothing beyond a slight tickle. I wipe again and again, clearing the puncture site.

There's no hole. The screwdriver still lies beside me, covered in my gore. But the hole it made is gone.

It's healed.

The first real act of my third life is clutching the screwdriver. Then I spring to my feet, slip on blood and plummet onto the corpse of Mike Burgess, a botanist who would have tried to grow Earth crops on Cognata. I apologize to the corpse, and crawl over him and the slick bodies lying beside him. Until I reach the hallway, which looks like a modern art painting of red streaks on a white canvas. If I didn't know the paint was blood, I might ponder its meaning. Instead, I pull myself up against the wall and add a new streak, sliding my way toward cryo-chamber two, Cap, and Tom.

3

The *Galahad*, so named for the nobility of its quest—to find a new home for humanity—is perhaps the most perfect creation mankind has ever conjured. It can achieve FTL travel without killing everyone on board. It can detect and repair malfunctions autonomously. It contains every written word, audio recording, video, and virtual experience ever created, from a digital scan of the Gutenberg Bible, to the HoloPorn, *Raunchy Ranch Extravagasm*. The entire biomass of Earth is contained in a cryogenic laboratory the size of a skyscraper, ready to be bred, planted, grown, and set loose on a new Earth. From seeds, to genes, to eggs and sperm, *Galahad* has everything we will need to start anew and pave the way for the colonists destined to follow.

For all I know, some are already en route.

Unfortunately for them, the *Galahad*'s crew is not nearly as infallible as the ship. I don't yet know how many survived and escaped to Cognata's surface, but the amount of blood decorating the walls didn't come from just one victim. The cryo-chamber entryways I pass are open, each one filled with a collection of gore. I don't bother to stop and count the dead. It's all just red smudges in my periphery. My eyes remain fixed and focused on the white, curving hallway ahead. Cryo-chamber two is just ahead.

A whistled tune tickles my ears. I can't identify the song. I'm not even sure it *is* a song. Just random notes reflecting the chaos that is now Tom Holden's mind.

We all knew some form of madness could result from cryo-sleep. It happens sometimes, especially over long periods of time. But we were tested. Vigorously. For years.

And this kind of murderous insanity, to my knowledge, has never been documented. One of the first candidates to be weeded out was left in a vegetative state after just a week in cryo-sleep. Ten years turned Tom into a psychopath.

If he was awake the whole time, like me, it could make sense.

Then again, I'm not trying to kill anyone.

Madness crept up on me from time to time, but never latched on. I suppose some minds are more flexible than others. I really don't know. The human computer has never been my specialty.

"One sheep, two sheep, never sleep sheep." The sing-song slows my approach. The slap of my sticky bare feet becomes a whisper. My lungs seize, holding the perfectly blended, algae-generated, O_2-infused air. I peek around the entryway.

There are five bodies on the floor in various states of disrepair. The most complete of them appears to have been strangled. Deep purple rings her throat. The worst of them has been dismembered. The work of a crude butcher with blunt instruments.

How did he have the time for this? He must have woken up first, but he should have been...

Shit.

Tom and I performed the final system check together. Cryo-chambers fell under his purview. He must have adjusted the wake-up sequence in advance. I don't think he was crazy then. Probably just wanted bragging rights. The first to wake. The first to see Cognata. He couldn't have known waking first would have resulted in slaughter.

Unless he did.

Could he have been mad before we left?

Could the army of psychologists have been fooled? I've heard sociopaths can be charming.

Still, it doesn't seem possible.

But here I am, spying on Tom Holden, the man about to kill—or worse—a woman I care about more than I'm allowed to.

Our crew of twenty-five men and twenty-five women were paired up by teams of geneticists and reproductive specialists. Upon successfully reaching the planet's surface and establishing a viable colony, our genetic partners would be revealed. Loveless relationships blessed by the sacred institution of genetics, would help humanity flourish in its new home. The odds of Capria being my partner were one in twenty-five. Not impossible, but not great. That's why detachment was so important; to stave off distraction, and jealousy, which could poison a tight knit community.

I'm not jealous now. I'm enraged.

But there is barely enough blood pumping through my veins to keep me upright, let alone to propel me to violence. I haven't been in a fight since second grade, though I suppose the circumstances are similar. I fought and won for the honor of Renee Something-or-Other. I have to at least try for Capria.

"I am going to enjoy you," Tom says. "We're going to see the universe together. Forever and ever. Happily ever after."

Tom's words trigger my senses. There's a vibration beneath my feet. It's subtle, but it's there, and I know exactly what it means.

We're moving.

Fast.

I'm not sure how long it's been since the *Galahad* stopped at Cognata, but I do know we're no longer there. Tom is one of a handful of people with the know-how to reprogram the ship's course.

How long has he been awake?

When Tom leans down to the control screen mounted to the side of Capria's cryo-bed, I decide to make my move. I'm not a fighter, but if I've learned anything from Tom, a screwdriver can kill a man.

Except for me, apparently.

I don't make it a single step before announcing my presence. The sound of my sticky foot peeling away from the smooth floor is how I've always imagined the crisp *shhhh* of tearing paper would sound. I've never used a piece of paper, let alone torn one, but it rings true in my imagination.

Tom shouts in surprise, flailing away from Capria's cryo-bed like he's been shocked. He looks to the ceiling first, like there might be something up there, and my brain says, 'Rush him!' while my body tries to stay upright.

I don't rush him.

I stand still, like a gazelle clutched in a lion's jaws, when such creatures still lived.

When he sees me, Tom staggers back again. He wiggles his fingers at me, casting a spell. "You're dead! Screwdriver in the chest. Like Mike. Like the others. Well, not all of them, but enough. Sharing blood like that. Not sanitary. But it's not really a concern for the dead, which you are. And aren't. I think."

His eyes are wide. Unblinking. Like an insect.

A very surprised and confused insect.

I step into the cryo-chamber, screwdriver tucked up behind my right hand and forearm.

"You're hurt," I say, pointing at Tom's chest. He's clothed in blood and stark naked at the same time. Despite that, the claw marks crisscrossing his chest, swollen on the sides, stand out. Someone put up a fight, and I hope the memory of it, or the fact that he's hurt, and no doubt in pain, will distract him.

"Just an ouchy," he says. "You got much worse." He waggles a finger at my chest. "Not even a hole. You were dead. I stood over you. Gave you a gamer's goodbye."

I try not to show my revulsion. When Tom crouched over me, letting his manhood rest on my hip, he was sending me off to the land of the dead in true video game fashion: the classic teabag. I had thought it was an accident. While I'm not technically a gamer, like Tom, we did play together on occasion. When I think back to those matches now, played offsite and off the record, I feel like I've seen murderous Tom before: slaying his enemies, back-stabbing teammates, and insulting the dead and dying. It was all good fun in the virtual world. In real life...it's sick.

"I am dead," I say.

He inhales like his mouth has become a vacuum. "A zombie?"

While the widespread popularity of the undead faded hundreds of years ago, they remain popular with holo-game players, spanning the test of time like other fictional monsters: Dracula, Nemesis, Werewolves.

"A ghost," I say.

"You *are* dead!" He tries to snap, but his fingers are too slippery with blood. "I knew it."

"I needed to tell you something," I say, stepping closer, lowering my voice.

"Do tell."

I take another step. Paper tears.

Tom squints. "Sticky for a ghost."

"I don't make the rules." Step. Tear. Step.

Tom purses his lips and taps agitated fingers against his thin hips. "You're not dead."

"You killed me." Step. Tear. Step. "You were there."

"I did, and I was, but now I'm here, and so are you. There was a hole in your chest, and now there is not."

"Ghosts don't keep injuries." Step. Tear. Step. I'm just a few feet away now, but Tom looks ready to run. Or attack. I can't tell which. His face is turbulent, caught in the middle of opposing storms.

"But the blood!" Tom flicks both hands at me like he's revealing the latest model of android. Gore flings from his fingertips and slaps against my chest, where it clings. "The blood! It... it sticks."

I turn my final step into a lunge. The screwdriver comes up in my hand, and then drives down in an arc. Our bodies collide with a slippery thumping of knobby limbs, scrabbling fingers, and screaming voices. This is how computer scientists fight. As we descend to the ground, putting on a pitiful display for dominance that makes me wonder how Tom could have actually killed most of the crew, I'm almost glad no one is around to see it.

Though Tom and I collide with the smooth, hard floor with roughly the same speed and force, he recovers faster. Perhaps I'm the greater nerd, or his mania shields him from pain. I'm not sure which, and at the moment, it doesn't matter. His fingers wrap around my throat and squeeze, constricting both my airway, and the limited flow of blood supplying my brain with oxygen—and consciousness.

I bring my fists up against him, noting first the lack of a screwdriver, and then the lack of focus.

My nails dig fresh troughs in his skin.

I slap, and punch, and kick.

None of it matters.

There's a ballet of dancing lights, like stars twirling to the music in Tom's head. Then the curtain falls.

And I die.

Again.

4

Weight presses me, constant and unmoving. It's like a blanket. A pile of them, really. I'm compelled toward sleep once more, mind drifting back into a comfortable dark bliss. I turn over and curl a handful of fabric beneath my chin, just so. But the twist of my body upsets the balanced covering. It slides off my body and thumps onto the bed.

Beds don't thump.

The thought rings true, but my barely conscious self doesn't care. I'm exhausted. I reach out for the blankets and find them, cold and wet. My nose wrinkles in disgust.

What happened to my blankets?

I wipe my now moist hand against my hip and find it barren of clothing. When I was a child, I would wake up in the morning, stark naked, pajamas piled next to me. I never had any memory of how or why I stripped down. It just happened.

That's not what happened this time, I think. *I went to bed naked.*

All this thinking tickles my consciousness to the forefront. It's early morning bright. Mars bright. Where there are no trees and no atmosphere to dull the more distant sun. And the bed...it's torturing my left elbow, ribs, and hip, the bones grinding against a cushionless surface.

This isn't a bed.

I squint against the bright light from above, and then open my eyes wide, when I find myself caught in a staring contest with Tom. Since corpses can't blink, I lose. Quickly. His dead eyes snap me from the last tendrils of sleep, but as my memory returns in full, I find myself unable to move.

Fear holds me in place, pinning my neck to the floor with the promise of fresh horrors to follow. But nothing happens. Tom's dead eyes just keep staring. I shift my eyes, and I'm relieved when his don't follow.

Definitely dead, but how?

My neck throbs with pain as I push off the floor to my hands and knees. The grunt of pain rising from my throat comes out as a hiss and a pop. I feel my throat, probing the skin with my fingers. Pain bursts with each touch, but it's not nearly as bad as the strange way my neck is compressed.

As fear wells anew, my neck pops out, reverting back to its original shape, and my scream finds its voice. The pain starts to subside, too, enough for me to focus on Tom.

He lies next to me, candy-coated in blood. Mine, his, and everyone else's. A familiar yellow handle rises from his back, between shoulder blade and spine. Following the Phillips-head's path through his body, I find the tip poking out of his chest.

I stabbed him.

When we collided.

Adrenaline and mania carried him through the pain and gave him the strength to strangle me, but madness wasn't enough to deny physical death.

But something is, I think.

Something has kept me from dying several times over in the short duration I've been out of cryo-sleep.

Thank God, Tom lacks the same ability. *Or does he?*

Each time I've died and come back, I've lost all sense of time. I could have been lying on the floor for seconds, minutes, or hours. Death provides freedom from the fourth dimension. But there was no white light this time. And Leonard wasn't there to greet me. If Tom can come back, how long do I have?

Fear of being killed again, and again, gets me moving. Lines of pain follow the contours of my body as my blood-glued skin stretches and peels from the cool floor. A warmth tingles from my head to my feet, blood shifting about. I see little lights, a moment of darkness, and then my body's reset is complete.

"Capria," I whisper, and I stagger to her cryo-bed. I place my hand on the frigid glass window while starting a rapid diagnostic on the bed, and on Capria. The results are nearly instant, and green across the board. I lift my hand from the glass. Beads of moisture have formed where my body heat warmed the surface, allowing me to see Capria's face. Her eyes are closed. At peace. Oblivious to the fact that her crew is dead or gone.

I envy her, and then I remember Tom.

I bend down, clutch his skinny wrists in my arms and pull. He's heavier than he looks, or maybe I'm just weak from blood loss and repetitive death. Either way, the effort it takes to drag the man is agonizing.

"I hate you for this," I tell the corpse, as I step into the hallway. "How hard did we work for this? I gave ten years. Ten fucking years. Training. Eating that shit they fed us. Getting poked with needles. I hated every second of it, but I did it because I loved the idea of what we were doing so much."

Tom's foot snags on the door, unwilling to bend. I yank him hard, venting my frustrations. He doesn't budge.

"You." Pull.

"Are a." Pull.

"Fucking." Pull.

"Asshole!"

I twist his body as I heave back again. His foot cracks and we spill free.

My heels thump against the floor as I stumble back, still clinging to Tom. His weight and my tacky feet keep me upright, and for a brief moment of chaos, we make good progress. Then it's step, drag, step again.

"I hope you do come back. I hope you wake up the moment I open the airlock and launch you into space." They're the harshest words I've ever spoken, but I mean them. He not only slaughtered the crew and doomed those who escaped his lunacy, but there's a good chance humanity itself will face extinction because of his actions.

The planet is failing. Catastrophically. Food is scarce. The environment is revolting. Billions died from war, starvation and disease. Cancer, once cured, returned with an aggressive vengeance. We called it neo-cancer. The human race is dying. *Was* dying. Fourteen hundred Earth years have passed. The Earth, and Mars, still orbit the sun, but the only people they carry are on their way to becoming fossils.

One hundred and twenty three years was the timetable most models projected. One hundred and twenty three years until extinction, not just of humanity, but of most mammals on the planet. Life on Earth would persist, probably still does, but only in its smallest, most resilient forms.

Mars provided a temporary reprieve for a few hundred thousand, but colony life was not without its dangers, and the domes weren't designed to last forever. The colonies on Mars would have lived long enough to mourn mankind's extinction on Earth. But they would have followed soon after. I'd like to believe they found a way to pull through, but I'm a realist.

While many people were still dedicated to solving the problems at home, most agreed that humanity's survival would lie elsewhere in the galaxy, specifically at Cognata. But now? Without the groundwork tasked to the *Galahad* and its crew, humanity's future is as uncertain as my ability to carry Tom to the airlock and send him spiraling into space while traveling faster than light.

Will I even be able to open the airlock?

"Hey!"

The loud voice triggers a physical reaction. I kick Tom hard, twice, driving my heel into his spine, hoping to return him to the temporary afterlife, or at least paralyze him. But he doesn't flail or fight back.

"What the fuck are you doing?"

My eyes flick up.

A naked man, his skin clean and tan, barrels down the hall, fists clenched.

"José, thank god," I say.

José Hernandez is a funny guy. He's also our second in command. He'll know how to turn us around and get our floundering mission back on track. Plus, he can help me carry Tom to the airlock.

I smile at him and say, "Grab his ankles will you?"

"You fucking psycho!" José shouts, lowering his shoulders and gaining speed.

"José, it's okay," I tell him. "Tom is dead. You don't need to—"

With two seconds to go before impact, my addled brain understands. José isn't looking at Tom. He's looking at me, the man covered in blood, dragging a corpse with the screwdriver in his back. In his mind, *I'm* the mass murderer of the crew.

"José! Wai—"

The impact lifts me off my feet.

José screams as the three of us descend, a naked corpse sandwich of flailing limbs and emotions. My head strikes the floor. Something cracks. I expect consciousness to fade. Or my life to end—again—this time at the hands of my commander. But I'm not dead, or even unconscious. Pain echoes through my head, but that's the worst of it. And José doesn't appear over me.

I roll to my side, my vision scrolling up one white wall, across the morning-lit ceiling and down the far wall, which hasn't been marred by blood.

José lies atop Tom. They look like lovers, enjoying a silent snuggle. Except for the blood. The dry on Tom, the wet dribbling from José's mouth.

"What...did you do to us?" José asks, his voice a gurgle.

"It was Tom," I tell him, crawling closer, flinching as each movement sends fresh pain through my probably fractured skull. "Tom killed everyone."

"Liar!" José shouts with enough force to spray my face with flecks of warm blood. And then more softly, "Fucking li—"

He goes limp, eyes looking beyond me.

What happened? I grip José's shoulders with shaking hands and pull. He comes away, but I feel like I'm fighting a ghost, pulling the body toward the floor. Then he comes free and rolls onto his back. Blood oozes from a hole in his chest.

"Oh... Oh, no..." Driven by the combined force of two grown men falling to an unforgiving floor, the screwdriver was driven up through Tom's body and into José's chest.

"Why didn't you stop?" I ask José. "We could have figured this out. We could have—" My voice falters when I back into the wall.

A warm tear rolls down my cheek and taps against the white floor. I look down at the drop, red with blood peeled from my skin. A second falls beside it. No longer caring if Tom returns to kill me a thousand times, I hiccup a moan, and then sob, beating my fists against the walls and venting more pain and sorrow than I've endured in my entire life until this point. Not just because my crew and all of humanity is doomed, but because I know my own personal hell is just beginning.

5

Tom's lifeless eyes stare at the ceiling. They don't blink. His life, and killing spree, are over. And through some sort of twisted freak misunderstanding, he managed to take one last victim to the grave beside him. José, like Tom, is perma-dead. The Grim Reaper's grip on them doesn't falter, while I seem to slip through his skeletal fingers like a well-oiled pig.

I'm not sure how long I've been sitting on the floor, staring at the bodies, lost in a strange kind of shock. I've been existing in my own thoughts for the past ten years, conjuring fantasies while awake and dreaming while asleep, and sometimes not knowing one from the other. In all that time, I've gone to some very dark places, some of which felt very real. But I don't think this is in my head.

Because I can smell the dead. Can *taste* their blood in the air, stinging my dried out tongue.

And it's not just Tom and José. It's all the others, too, settling into the first stages of decomposition. They're going to really start stinking soon. Become bloated. Seep gas from a variety of orifices. Luckily, our bladders and bowels were emptied before cryo-sleep, so the mess is limited to the dead, and their blood.

I'll leave the blood to the drones. But the bodies...

"I hate you," I tell Tom. "Someday, I'm going to shoot you out the airlock."

I picture Tom's body pin-wheeling into open space. Forever. Alone. Like me.

I choke on a sob. It's a horrible fate, even for a corpse. "I don't hate you. Not really. It's not your fault. Going crazy isn't really a choice."

I push myself off the floor, hissing through my teeth as the dried blood peels skin cells and hair from my ass.

Back on my feet, I shake off the feeling of hopelessness inspired by the carnage all around me. I don't yet know the full extent of my situation. The *Galahad* is moving, but I don't know where to, or how fast. Turning around might be simpler than I think. And I'm not entirely alone.

I have Capria. She's still asleep, and I have no intention of waking her to this mess, but she's alive. While I would love nothing more than to have a companion right now, a second mind to sort through this shit, there's a chance she might make the same assumption as José. And the chivalrous part of me wants to protect her from the pain of seeing her friends and crew torn apart. She'll need to be told the truth eventually, but being told, or even shown the ship's video log, will hurt less than a single breath of this dirty-penny-scented air.

I stand there, naked and chilled, wondering what to do. I'm good at following orders. I like taking direction. Excel at it. Like a guided missile, I just need to be aimed. But I'm on my own.

Spreadsheet this mess, I think at myself and cringe. It doesn't seem an entirely human choice to make, but then I spend a lot of my time with non-living and non-human artificial intelligences of my own creation, including those piloting the drones that will scour the walls, floors, and ceilings clean.

There are several tasks that need doing in the next few hours. I need to eat. And drink. It's been ten years, so if I want to live, I need to... My planning hits a wall of sludge and slows to a crawl.

"I can't die," I tell the corpses at my feet. Tom probably figured out as much before he was killed, but boredom isn't a problem for him anymore. "So let's tack that lower down on the list, if only to see if I feel the effects of dehydration." I unpin the non-existent note and re-pin it lower on the imaginary list.

"Why can't I die?" I ask José. "Did you know? Did anyone?" I look to my right, down the curved hallway lined by cryo-chambers. Capria's down there. I could bounce these questions off her if she was awake, but she wouldn't know, either. The answers are on the *Galahad*, hidden somewhere within the culmination of all human knowledge backed up, compressed, and encrypted a hundred different ways, on a massive variety of media, to ensure its safe passage. I helped put it there. I can retrieve it. But it will take time. Probably a lot of time.

I unpin the new imaginary note with a *pop*, and re-pin it below food and water. While I'm curious about my strange new physical state, the why and how of it can wait until bigger problems are solved.

Like where I'm headed and how I can turn around.

The AI guiding *Galahad*, known as Gal for short, will avoid any obstacles along the way, so there is no danger of flying through an asteroid field or a star, but the longer we move forward, the longer it will take to get back. If I can figure that out. Gal is smart. Tom made sure of it. But she's also programmed to only obey ranking...

My head lolls back, mouth agape. Tom handled Gal's final coding. If we're moving on a course he set, he either left himself a backdoor or added himself to the command hierarchy. Another pin goes in the checklist.

They're all big problems that require solutions, and solving them sounds almost like fun. I'm comfortable sitting at a screen, or in VR, and manipulating code. Dead bodies, not so much.

But the decent human being in me says that the dead crew is priority number one.

If I was on Earth, I might feel compelled to bury each and every one of them. I'd probably manage a proper grave for the first one in the ground, but the rest would likely lie shallow. They're dead. Empty shells of the people they once were. And I'm not the pinnacle of human conditioning. But in space...

I see an image of my bloating crew members spiraling out into space as I open the airlock. My mind adds a soundtrack. *Stars and Stripes Forever.* I remember seeing fireworks on the 4th of July. A marching band played the song while lights lit up the sky. That was the last American Independence Day anyone celebrated, because celebrating it required an America. But the bombastic music fits the mental image perfectly. First the explosion, and then the mass of twirling limbs.

I smile, and even though I know it's wrong, it sticks.

The song twiddles from my pinched lips as I head down the hall, stopping in front of each open cryo-chamber, counting bodies. The tune peters out when I reach the last open door and speak the number aloud. "Thirty six." Plus me, and Capria. Twelve people made it off *Galahad.* Twelve people without supplies, or food, or advance knowledge of what they were dropping into. They could all be dead already. From deadly air, from wounds inflicted by Tom, from exposure, starvation, or even alien predators.

The darkest parts of my imagination spin to life, twisting downward.

What if no one followed us to Cognata?

What if things on Earth fell apart, and the Mars colonies never built another FTL ship?

It's been fourteen hundred years. What if Capria and I are all that's left?

I start whistling again. Avoidance is the best medicine for questions that have no answers.

Tom was whistling, too, I remember. *Am I going mad?*

I know I'm not.

I wish I was.

Then I wouldn't have to do what comes next.

It takes eight hours to drag the dead, and their severed parts, back to their respective cryo-beds. In that time, I don't eat or drink and *Stars and Stripes Forever* becomes a whisper on my parched lips. But I don't grow any more weary than I was at the start. And I don't pass out from hunger or low blood sugar, both of which should be striking me down.

Tom goes last. His heels carve two clean paths through the blood-coated floor as I drag him by his wrists. The dried blood chips away from the ultra-smooth, white surface. Compared to my heavy lifting, the cleaning drones are going to have an easy time. Not only will the blood come up easily, but they also don't feel and don't care about where the blood came from. They'll just see red where there should be white, and they'll take care of it.

Tom flops down into the cryo-bed. His stiff body bobbles to the side and nearly rolls right out of the bed. I catch him under his arms and guide him back, an invalid in my grip. Stiff joints grind and pop as I push him flat. His back thumps, and I realize I've left the screwdriver in him.

"No way," I tell him. "I'm done. With you." I point at the cryo-beds in the room, four of them holding dead bodies. "With all of you."

I step back and activate the bed. Like the others, Tom will be perfectly preserved until sometime at a much further date, when I can get them some place with soil. As the machine whirs to life, hissing protective gasses around the corpse, the hatch descends.

And then it stops.

With just an inch to go, a warning light flashes. The screen beside the device blinks the word: Obstruction.

I close my eyes. A manic anger wells. I breathe through it and then bend at the waist. It's the God-damned screwdriver, jutting up just a little too far. I could try forcing the hatch shut, but there is a chance it would punch through the glass and I'd have to drag Tom to another cryo-bed.

Clenching my fists, I gently tap the digital *Open* button and wait for the hatch to rise.

When I look down at Tom's face, the anger and the rage, breaks free.

"Neeargh!" The dull thudding slap of my fist striking meat plays like a metronome for a full four count. Then I grip the screwdriver shank, and pull. Dead meat slurps. Ribs crack. Skin tears. It takes three hard yanks, but the screwdriver comes free. With a scream, I hurl the tool through the open door. It slams against the far wall, stained dark brown, and clatters to the floor, ending my bout with madness. The first round goes to sorrow and despair.

Breathing hard, I reach out and gently tap the *Close* button. The hatch lowers, hisses as the seal sets, and then goes quiet.

In the seconds following Tom's entombing, silence creeps over me like a specter. It speaks to me, delivering the haunting message, 'You are alone.'

6

Hot lashes rip at my back, scouring blood from skin, and part of me wishes it would cut deeper still. The water collecting around the drain swirls with tiny chips of brown blood shifting back to red, like rotten fruit punch. Despite fruit being a rare luxury on Earth, and non-existent on Mars, we still had fruit punch. There was, after all, no fruit in it. But there were synthetic vitamins, minerals, and a chemical concoction meant to simulate a blend of fruits—grapes, pineapple, strawberry, and cherry, if the packaging was to be believed. I had a strawberry once. It was tart. Not quite ripe. But it still tasted a hell of a lot better than the fruit punch. Less red than the blood washing down the drain, where it will be filtered and recycled for a later shower.

When the water doesn't clean the blood out from every wrinkle and crevice, I use a brush, shushing its stiff bristles against my skin, burning it pink. Designed to clean away stubborn grease, the micro-bristles make short work of the blood, and my top layer of skin.

But I don't mind the pain.

I welcome it.

It helps stave off the survivor's guilt rising from the depths like a great white shark, jaws agape, teeth bared, nictitating lenses raised. It will eat me whole if I give in.

When I can't see any more blood in the water, I scrub for ten more minutes. This shower, upon waking, should have been done in two minutes flat, cleaning the cryo-chems from my skin, and helping me wake up. But the system was prepared to handle fifty people, not one, so there's time to spare.

I wince and look at my arm. The brush tore through my skin. Fresh blood beads and is whisked away to the drain. I watch the long, red line seal back up. Like new. I lift both arms and inspect them. Despite having rubbed both raw, they look smooth-skinned and devoid of irritation.

"What did they do to me?" Water tickles my lips, tempting me to drink, but I'm afraid of getting blood in my mouth. "Water off."

The stinging spray of too-hot water snaps off. The drain at my feet seals shut as a round vent opens in the ceiling. A vortex of warm air swirls around me, evaporating the water coating the cylindrical walls and my body. The moisture is whisked away into the ceiling. If I still had the long brown hair of my youth, I'd look like one of those weird troll dolls I saw in a pop-culture history digi-guide. I rub a hand over my now shaven head, letting the millimeter-tall bristles tickle my hand.

When the only liquid remaining in the shower stall is hidden within the confines of my body, the door unlatches and slides open. The large sanitation room beyond the door has twenty-five shower stalls on one wall, and twenty-five toilets on the opposite wall, each with a man's name above it. In addition to cleansing the crews' bodies, both inside and out, sensors in the drains analyze waste, allowing the automated systems to track our individual well-being and adjust our diets accordingly.

Since I'm still running on empty, I forgo a visit to the all-knowing toilet and head for my locker instead. Inside is a single, loose-fitting flight suit. It's slate gray and very soft, with built in foot soles, like what kids wear to bed. They're loose-fitting to avoid looking sexy, and they lack any kind of insignia, rank or name tag. One crew, with one mission, one mind, and now, only one member. I slip into the smooth fabric. Its softness comforts me. A slim magnetic seal up the front snaps together. Tomorrow, if I return to my locker, I'll find a fresh garment, supplied by Gal. But I don't think I'll change any time soon. After all, there's no one left to impress.

Maybe I'll put on someone else's too-tight flight suit and look sexy all by myself. I start to imagine Capria in her flight suit. As loose as it was, it wasn't loose enough to hide all her curves. I see her for just a moment before my insides churn at the memory. It hurts more than it helps.

"What now?"

I'm clean. And dressed. The drones are working their way through the *Galahad*, seeking out stress points, damage and messes. The next time I return to the cryo-chambers, they'll look like new. I lick my lips. Feels like I'm running my tongue across stone.

The mess deck requires no chef or galley. The AI handles it all, delivering the perfect amount of artificially flavored nutrient slurry, based on prior bowel movements. It's a two-minute walk down gleaming white hallways, and ten seconds in the lift, to get from the bathroom to the mess deck, which is located above the cryo-chambers, bathrooms, and two floors of crew quarters. Above the mess is the gym, a place I only visit when my schedule calls for it—three days a week for ninety minutes.

"William Chanokh," I say, standing before the food dispensary.

"Blood sample required." Gal has a homogeneous voice, neither masculine nor feminine.

A small slot, fringed by green light and large enough for a single finger, opens. Without a recent fecal sample, Gal wants my blood. I place my finger in the hole. Back home the act would often elicit crude sexual jokes from new recruits, most of whom were never seen again. No quicker way to get kicked out of the program than to have sex on the brain. Truth was, we all had sex on the brain. Some of us just hid it better.

A cool breeze runs over my finger, and for a moment, I can't feel it. Then the light turns red, and I withdraw my finger, the numbing agent already starting to wear off. I turn my hand over, ready to suck away the bead of blood from where I was pricked, but the puncture resealed too quickly for any to escape.

Unseen parts whir and hiss. A tray slides into place behind a glass divider. A cup, bowl and spoon lower onto it. Two more cups follow. Then two nozzles descend. One trickles pink liquid into all three cups. The other unleashes a mash of steaming diarrhea that will taste better than it looks. We were told all meals would taste like they were 'home cooked.' Problem with that promise is that most of the crew never had a home cooked meal, and those that had, couldn't remember what they tasted like.

I sit down at one of five round tables. There are supposed to be another nine people sitting at the table, their gray butts planted on the long, curved bench surrounding it. And then forty more at the other tables. Meal seating rotates so that everyone gets a chance to know everyone else, and cliques aren't allowed to form.

No chance of that now. My tray echoes in the room that should be full of voices. I hear them for a moment, everyone excited, eager to finish their shitty, first in-orbit meal and get to analyzing the planet below. But then I sniff my nose, and in the silence of reality, it's loud enough to break me out of the fantasy.

I sip the pink liquid. Fruit punch. It's pretty much the last thing I want to be drinking, but as soon as the fluid hits my throat, a craving is triggered. I drain the first cup, move on to the second, and stop halfway through the third. My insides sponge up the liquid. Pressure returns to my veins, and strength returns to my muscles. I might be unkillable, but I can still get dehydrated. But I wasn't just dehydrated, I was drained of blood, sucked nearly dry by the undrinking vampire named Tom. While I seem capable of impossible feats, I can't, like the Big Bang, create something from nothing.

That said, I'm not very hungry. I take a bite of the slop anyway. It's salty and has fibrous chunks that are vaguely meaty, but most definitely are not from an animal. After my third bite, I'm feeling better about things.

The food tastes good.

The quiet is peaceful.

I'm going to turn this ship around, return to Cognata, save the surviving crew, and wake Capria to a tarnished, but not completely failed mission. A chuckle burps from my mouth and sours my stomach.

Why am I laughing?

Why the fuck *am I laughing?*

I look down at the bowl. While I neither see, nor taste anything viler than expected, I know it's there. My food is drugged. When my blood sample showed elevated levels of adrenaline and cortisol, my food was laced with mood enhancers. Had I been surrounded by people, talking and laughing, I probably wouldn't have noticed the shifting state of mind. But here, by myself, with absolutely nothing to feel happy about, the drug's effect stands out like an erection in one of these flight suits—yet another way the over-sexed were weeded out.

The image makes me laugh, and *that* makes me angry.

I scream and overturn my tray. Empty cups bounce to the floor, drumming out a beat for a few seconds. The bowl overturns with a slap. The tray doesn't make it much further. It's far less dramatic than I intended, but so what? No one is here to see it.

"No one is here!" I scream and swat the bowl. It strikes the next table and spirals, spinning brown gore in every direction, satiating my need to make a mess. "No one is here..."

I wasn't lying to my shrink.

She wasn't real. And she mostly existed to distract me from madness.

But I never lied to her.

I *am* an introvert, but I *hate* solitude.

I do now, at least.

The quiet of it. My inner voice, without external input, can get lost in chaos. The stillness and sleepy feeling of the cryo-bed dulled the sensation and allowed my imagination to drift. But here, fully awake and without anyone to talk to, my thoughts feel like Pearson's screwdriver in my chest.

I need direction.

What came next? I made a list. A spreadsheet. But I can't remember it now. I'm pretty sure showering and a meal were on it, but what else? I pound the table with my fists, and then with my head.

Direction and motivation comes in the form of a single word: *Answers.* I stand from my chair, feeling renewed and too damn happy.

I need answers.

7

Keyboards and computer monitors never really went out of fashion. Some people made the switch to tablets and touch-screens, but the people who pounded words, numbers, and data for a living were most efficient and happiest when they could stand up and walk away from their work, and not be expected to carry it with them. Eighty percent of the crew still used a key-board and a mouse to navigate *Galahad*'s quantum computer systems. While there isn't much limit to Gal's processing power, mankind hit its limit thousands of years ago.

Most people, anyway. Some people—tech-jocks—like to think they're smarter, and faster. 'Some people' being myself, and Tom.

I like to think it's because we're the next stage in the evolution of mankind's intelligence, but I'm pretty sure it's ego. We're our own rock stars, no matter how pasty white our un-sunned skin becomes. That used to be a thing anyway, I think, being undead pale. Tech-jocks used to be called nerds, or geeks, until those terms became honor-badges. We're not really smarter, we just have a knack for the virtual. For the not real. And I'm not really sure that says anything good about us.

But we were the future. Without us, Gal wouldn't exist, and navigating the universe at FTL speeds would be impossible. Even a tech-jock couldn't complete the endless amount of calculations needed to analyze, access, and avoid every obstacle as they emerge from the void. But Gal can, thanks to me, and to Tom, and to an army of fellow tech-jocks who weren't cut out for space travel. We're moving through time and space, and I can't feel the course corrections, whether they be a few feet, or a light year.

The thing about tech-jocks that really sets us apart is that we prefer not to use keyboards, mice, touchscreens, or the laziest of computer interfaces: voice commands. We do our computing in the virtual realm, using Virtual Command Centers (VCCs). Wearing a full bodysuit containing millions of biofeedback nodules, we can *feel* the digital world. We can create and live inside worlds of our own, which is less pitiful and more dangerous than it sounds. Inside the VCC, anything is possible. We can manipulate the universe itself, run models and simulations, and test theories that are impossible to test in the real world. But it's also easy to forget which world is which.

Before VCCs had automatic, eight hour cut-offs, tech-jocks routinely died from overexposure. Seventy-two hours without a break could lead to starvation, or dehydration, but it was usually a Gray-Crash: a kind of mental unhinging leading to a catastrophic system shutdown. The strangest thing about Gray-Crashing is that the victims would be so separated from reality, they wouldn't be aware they were dying—even after their hearts stopped and their brains began to shut down. Now that I've died several times over, I think Gray-Crashing sounds delightful.

But I've never gotten close. I know how to self-regulate, and I generally stay in the VCC for only three hours at a time. And not just because I don't want to die. I just don't like the idea of having my piss drained via catheter, or shitting in an adult diaper. It's undignified.

Also, I get most jobs done in under three hours.

I'm that good. It's why I'm here.

In space.

Alone.

My esteemed position doesn't seem so special anymore. Mankind's hubris, a measurable amount of which came from me, has resulted in a kind of personal hell.

But, how? That's what I'm here to find out.

I stand in the center of the 2500 square foot space. The walls, floor, and ceiling, like most of the *Galahad*, are stark white, smooth, and can be lit in a myriad of colors and lumens. Unlike the rest of the ship, the illumination is always faint here. VCC use can make eyes light-sensitive for a few minutes. The light is kept dim to keep migraines from springing on users like squirrels throwing a surprise party.

The bodysuit I'm wearing is officially called a Virtual Integration Sensor Array (VISA). Unofficially it's called a body-condom because it's rubbery and skin-tight. Millions of tiny haptic feedback nodes are embedded in the virtual skin (my preferred name for it). They can vibrate, simulating the delicacy of a gentle breeze, or constrict the fabric, applying pressure to the wearer's body. And if a pinch is called for, tiny electric shocks do the job. Nothing in the VCC's virtual reality truly exists until it's applied to a real world application or the AI, but after just a few minutes, it can feel real.

For an experienced user like me, it feels real the moment I put on my headset.

And it nearly breaks me.

In the years before the *Galahad* left Mars, I spent every work day in my VCC. Those who don't use VCC would call it a glorified digital office. I called it home. I suppose it's like returning to a child-hood house. Memories of past accomplishments, virtual parties with my fellow tech-jocks, private moments away from the prying eyes of reality. The difference between VCC memories and real world memories is that I could replay them. But I don't. It would hurt too much. And I could get lost. I need to move forward.

My starting point is a game room. It's old-school classic with a pool table and darts. There's a movie screen, a juke box, and game consoles. Posters line the walls. I could step inside any virtual movie, listen to any song, and play any game, all the way back to Bach, *Pong*, and the *Wizard of Oz*. Of course, playing Pong while listening to Bach might be a treat, but I found *Oz* to be a mind-screw. I couldn't identify with Dorothy or her nauseating band of helpers. I identified more with the wizard. I'll stay behind the curtain, thank you very much.

That's not true now. Even the Cowardly Lion would be better company than myself.

You are alone.

The thought comes like a sniper's bullet, slipping into and out of my head, leaving chaos in its wake.

Capria is here, I tell myself. *She's still alive.*

But no one else is.

Find out why.

I walk through the game room, rounding the pool table like it was real, and head for the Womb. It's a comfortable, dark endlessness where creation occurs. With a flick of my wrist, the red door adorned with a pictograph of a big-bellied woman, slides open. I step through into the black beyond, and I'm even more comfortable here than I was in the carefully crafted and decked-out game room.

Here, my mind and body become a tool. Accessing and manipulating code becomes a dance. Fluid and passionate. It's less language writing, and more creative experience.

God, I sound fruity, like some new-Martian beat poet.

I settle into my old world, and for a moment, I blank.

Day one after waking from cryo-sleep is supposed to feel like no time passed at all. You fall asleep and wake up feeling refreshed, memory intact. It's as close to teleporting across the universe as you can get. In theory. My reality is that I have ten years of dreams and fantasies rattling around in my head. I've written code and run simulations in my own mind. I've retooled this interface. But none of that ever happened. It was less real than the VCC.

So I'm rusty. I start slow, accessing my personal saved projects, fiddling with code, letting my mind and body get reacquainted with the ebb and flow. It comes back quickly. I'm moving at half speed, and with far less elegance than I became so proud of, but there's no one evaluating me now, and all I need to do is access Tom's personnel files.

I curl my fingers into fists and pull both hands toward me. This should instigate a security check. My eyes, fingerprints, and very DNA will be scrutinized over the next few seconds, verifying my administrator status, and from there, the culmination of human knowledge—including the crew files, Gal's AI, and the *Galahad's* security footage—will be available to me.

"Hello?"

The voice catches me off guard. Makes me flinch in real life.

There are a number of things I should probably do in response to the voice—Tom's voice—but all I manage is stunned silence.

"I'm sorry, but if you're not me, and I'm the only me, not you, then fuck off. Your ass is blocked. The ship is mine. All of this is mine. Unless someone is really listening to this... Shit. Fuckin shit. Okay. Who cares, right? It's still fun. This is all just fun." He laughs, not the deep booming laugh he's known for, but a high pitched, mid-sized mammal squeal. Air out of a balloon. "Oh! How about this?"

A thousand different sound files filling every audible frequency and maximum volume barks in my ears. It's just a half second, but it drops me to the floor. I scream, pulling the headset away. A high-pitched squeal chases me out of virtual reality, but it's not coming from the headset. It's coming from my ears.

I lie on the floor, staring up at the dull ceiling, facing a brand new problem.

Tom changed the security protocols. That in itself is no easy task, but he was clearly out of his mind already. I can get around his new security. I have no doubt about that, but he was on the team because he was good. It's going to take some time. Maybe a lot of time.

How long was Tom awake?

I close my eyes and resist the urge to throw a tantrum.

I've deduced the answer to one of my many questions. Tom fucked with Gal before we left. Nothing drastic. A single digit change to his wake-time would have allowed him to wake up a year before everyone else. It would have been easy to miss. As for why, I get it. He wanted to be first. Like all tech-jocks, he was competitive by nature. He wanted to be the first awake, and the first to see Cognata. Instead, he became the first FTL mass murderer.

After five minutes, the ringing in my ears subsides and my emotions level out. I disable the VCC headset audio, place it back on my head and begin a task that will take me the better part of a year.

8

Psychosis elevated Tom's genius. Made him think in ways that normal people—sane people—can't comprehend. Because there's no order to it. No reason. I've been throwing myself at his security, and all I've managed to do is reveal how much pain a virtual skin is capable of delivering. Turns out, it's a lot. Tom's new protocols removed the safety restrictions. I've been strangled, crushed, and given electric jolts powerful enough to rob consciousness. I'm pretty sure I've been killed by it, but I'm not entirely sure, since coming back to life doesn't feel much different than waking up.

But the past year hasn't been a complete waste.

I've learned a lot.

If I'm not gushing blood or sweating, I don't need to drink. Or eat. I can spend seventy-two hours in the VCC and not die. And if I'm not eating or drinking, then I don't need a catheter or an adult diaper. That's good news, because even though there's enough food and water on the *Galahad* to last me a lifetime, I suspect I might be around for longer. I'm not sure yet. I've only been tracking my age for a year, but in all that time, my shaven hair hasn't grown. At all. It's like my body is stuck.

I don't need to sleep, either. I *can* sleep. It's just not a requirement. My psychological state, like my body, is impervious to human limitations. No matter how little I sleep, how long I starve myself, or how lonely and desperate I feel, my mind remains intact. Sharp. Alert. The only thought of suicide that crossed my mind was a curiosity about why I haven't considered it yet. It's not that I can't sleep—I sometimes do, just to hear other people talking—it just serves no physical or mental purpose anymore.

I've also learned that as smart as I am, I will never be a match for Crazy Tom. I've spent 6,570 hours in the VCC. I've created an entirely new coding language in an attempt to sneak past his firewall unseen. I have tried every password—written, body language, spoken, and symbol—that I could think of, but none worked.

Only Tom can get through.

Which is why, after an entire year of trial and error, and then a full ten minutes of kicking myself, I'm back in the cryo-chambers. I haven't returned since I left, naked and blood-coated. The drones have done their job as well as I believed they would. The walls, floor, and ceiling sparkle with newness. Thanks to *Galahad*'s self-sustaining design, it always will.

I walk past a line of frosted cryo-beds. I could warm the glass with my hand and see their faces, remember who they were and the good times we had, but there are no peaceful expressions hidden beneath the white. Each one will be contorted in a different kind of anguish and raw shock. As resilient as my psyche might now be, short-lived torture still holds no appeal.

But not all of them are dead.

When I stop in front of the cryo-bed labeled: *Capria Dixon*, I realize my subconscious had planned a side-trip. I place my hands on the glass, holding them against the cold sting until beads of water roll away. The face behind the hand-shaped window is placid. She's not smiling, but she looks happy. At peace.

I smile at her. "You are so beautiful."

When she doesn't flinch at the words, I continue. "I couldn't tell you that before. You know why. And I'm not just saying it now because I haven't seen a human face in a year. I've been thinking it for the past thirteen years."

Everyone on this mission was recruited as a teenager. I was fourteen. That's when I moved from Earth to Mars. They didn't use cryo for that trip, in part because it was relatively short, even without FTL travel, and they wanted to see how we handled spaceflight.

Capria is Martian, born and raised, but thanks to the gravity boost inside the colony domes, she has the strength and endurance of an Earthling. And then some. While her eyes have always been on the stars, and her mind on work, she also managed to outperform the rest of us physically. Tom once told me she had the physique of a twenty-first century tennis player named Serena Williams. I didn't know who that was, but after some VCC research, I had to agree, though I never told him that. Revealing my feelings for Capria would have erased my chances of joining the Cognata mission, and my future chances with Cap.

Now, I think my odds are pretty good.

If I end her cryo-sleep.

"I want to wake you up," I tell her. "Really. But you don't know what it's like right now. We are nowhere. Literally. I need to get in Gal. Need to figure out what happened, and how to get us back. Cognata is more than seven quadrillion miles behind us. It's depressing, and I don't know if...if you're like me." I motion to the other cryo-beds, full of the slumbering dead. "Or if you're like them. Not dead. I mean, normal. Not what I am. Immortal, I guess."

I shake my head. "I don't know what you'd want. Waking you up now would be less about you and more about me.

However long it takes me to turn us around and get us home, I'm going to be fine. But you...I don't know."

Depression would be nearly unavoidable. The mission is basically over. Maybe the human race, too. Her friends are dead. And she'd be stuck with me for who knows how long. As well as I hid my feelings for Capria from Command, I'm pretty sure I failed to hide them from her. Our eyes met and lingered one too many times for her not to have figured it out. But she never told anyone. That always gave me hope, but it doesn't mean she felt the same.

"You need to stay here," I say. "I don't want you to see. I don't want you to know me the way I have to be now. It's..." I nibble at the inside of my mouth. "Would you mind if I came and talked to you again? This feels good."

"Of course you don't mind. You're asleep." I kiss my hand and place it on the glass, thinking of Sleeping Beauty. I'm far from Prince Charming, but someday, I'll wake her up.

What comes next should undo me, but the still-fresh memories of being murdered awake are like a mountain compared to the small hill that is Tom's frigid corpse. As his cryo-bed opens, I step back, half expecting him to attack, and totally expecting him to smell.

Neither is true, yet.

Tom's dead weight is familiar, as is my anger with him. When I pull him from the bed and he starts to fall, I let him. His teeth and nose crunch against the floor. My imagination predicts blood, but there is none. His insides are chilled gelatin. He chipped a tooth, though, and for a moment I feel sorry about it. Then I grab his wrists and pull.

For a few minutes, progress is smooth. Each step brings me closer to what I'm sure is the solution to my security problem. But then Tom conspires against me again.

It starts as an occasional jolting squeak. His butt cheeks are sticking to the smooth floor. I try lifting him higher so only his heels are dragging, but I don't have the strength to hold his ragdoll body that high, and I really don't want to wrap my arms around his torso. So I endure our stop-and-go journey.

Tom decides to cooperate a few minutes later, but I wish he didn't. His insides are warming up, leaking from below, lubricating his backside. A rainbow streak of white, clear and brown fluids marks our path through the hallways, filling the *Galahad* once more with the stink of death.

I stop outside the secondary VCC. This is Tom's domain, and his fitted virtual skin is hanging beside his staging area locker. But there's something off about it. Instead of its normal, clear flesh tone, pocked with tiny blue nodules, it has an almost yellow hue.

As long as it works, I think, and I pull the suit down. My grimace deepens when I feel the suit's tacky interior and get a whiff of its poignant armpit stench. Somehow, Tom's old body odor is worse than his death reek.

I knew he had used the VCC before the others woke up to be murdered, but I'm still not sure for how long. Like the crew's plain gray garments, the VISAs are automatically replaced or washed when returned to their lockers. Only Tom hadn't left his suit in the locker. He'd left it outside.

"Why were you naked?" I ask his corpse. I look down at my body, still squeezed into my virtual skin. The answer comes to me as a question. "Why am I clothed?" With no one around, and perfectly regulated temperatures throughout the ship, I don't need to wear clothes, but I have dutifully changed from VISA to flightsuit every day since that first shower.

Before I can come up with a good answer, I notice Tom's legs. They're yellowed, with purple streaks, but that's not the problem. They're swelling as Tom's decomposing insides fill his lower legs like balloons.

"Shit." I crouch with his fetid virtual skin and dress him like a man-sized baby, squeezing his loose, dead body into the skin, which compresses and redistributes his flaccid guts. Tom will *not* be coming out of his VISA.

'Bury me in my body-condom.' I've heard more than a few tech-jocks say the words, including Tom. I never understood the sentiment. Death was visceral. It affected real people who, hopefully, loved the dead, and probably never saw him or her in a virtual skin. Being sent to the afterlife in a VISA always struck me as an offense to the living, like life inside the VCC was more real. Granted, sometimes it could feel that way, but nothing in the virtual made me feel the way a glance from Capria did.

"Looks like you're getting your wish, buddy." I slide my arms under Tom's armpits and lift him up. His head bobbles onto my shoulder, forcing my chin and nose away and up, like I'm a high-society undertaker. I drag him to the VCC door and say, "Open."

The door obeys, exposing me to the room's contents.

A surprised, high-pitched bark pops from somewhere deep in my chest, as I'm knocked back and sprawl to the floor with Tom atop me.

9

"Oh!" I scream, voice cracking like I'm in the throes of puberty once more. "Oh, God!"

My feet kick and push, but Tom's dead weight, lying across my waist, reduces my progress to just a few inches.

From the moment of my waking, I have endured sights and smells far more revolting than I would have guessed possible. What could be worse than gallons of blood or the necrotic juices flowing from a corpse?

The answer lies before me.

Tom didn't just use the VCC, he lived in it.

Trays of rotting food line one corner. Mounds of soiled clothing and virtual skins, stained yellow from sweat, and brown from something else. The biggest difference between the way Tom and I use a VCC is that he has no shame. He'll stay in for the full eight hours, and if he has to take a shit... A mountain of used adult diapers rises up the back wall, a patchwork of light blue, white, and brown smears. The top of the pile is packed down, like a volcano's caldera. When I see the pillow and blanket, I realize what it actually is: a nest.

I gag, heaving back, trying to escape while clutched in the jaws of mindless panic. A dry heave wracks my body. I haven't eaten in months, so there's nothing to retch. Tears streak over the sides of my face, tickling my ears. I hold my breath, and in that moment of stenchlessness, the very simple solution makes itself known. With the last shit-flavored air in my lungs, I shout, "Close!"

And when the anguished sharpness of my voice keeps Gal from recognizing the voice command, I clench my eyes shut, and say, as calm as I can manage, "Close."

The VCC door slides shut.

The smell remains.

But I'm free from the jaws.

Rolling Tom off me takes another ten seconds. I try to hold my breath, but my muscles need oxygen to work, and I can't help but suck in another thick breath. Once he's off, I scramble for the staging area door and run. My feet thump against the floor, a desperate metronome that slows after three hundred beats.

I run down the nearly featureless corridor, pursued by the monster named Stench, wondering how its existence came to be. Messes like that aren't supposed to happen on *Galahad*. The drones clean everything...*except the VCCs*, I realize, where nothing aside from a VISA-wearing user is supposed to be. Something about the cache of filth shifts Tom to another level of crazy. Murder has been part of human society since the beginning. But making a nest out of shit? Even our ape-like predecessors wouldn't have stooped so low.

Far enough, I think, and I slow to catch my breath, hands on knees, head lowered. In through the nose, out through the—

Oh, God, I can still smell it.

I look down at my virtual skin-clothed self. The VISA is almost fleshy to the touch, soft and smooth, easy for microscopic scent particles to cling to. I lift an arm and sniff. My back thuds against the wall as I wince.

Breath held again, I start to peel the high-tech garment from my shoulder, but then stop. I smell like literal shit. So does Tom. And since I'm not about to shower him, or take him out of his VISA, I either need to do this now, or never, and since never means remaining Tom's prisoner on a spaceship to nowhere...

"Damnit." I take a step back toward the VCC and falter almost instantly. I rub my head, pace, and punch the walls for a full five minutes. Then I break into a sprint and nearly fall to the floor as I stop by Tom's side, bend to lift him under the armpits and then run backward. I'm not exactly athletic, and my reverse charge is far from graceful. Tom's loose head bobbles around, smacking against my chest, reeking of his own noxious filth.

I stop at the entrance to the primary VCC, which I know is as spotless as it's supposed to be. I feel like a traitor to tech-jocks everywhere—if there are any others left—when I say, "open" and drag Tom's fetid corpse inside. The air inside is cool and pristine.

"We're going to do this quick," I tell dead Tom.

But that's a lie.

It doesn't take me long to see this isn't just going to take time, it's also going to be nearly impossible. Tom needs to be upright, which I can manage by holding him around his torso. His virtual skin is synced to the VCC, but for that to do any good, his hands and arms need to move, and I'm not much of a puppet master whilst my fingers are interlocked over Tom's sternum. And I need to do all this while wearing a headset, making me blind to the real world.

My solution is to relocate a large supply case containing spare headsets to the center of the VCC and then prop up Tom like he's a little kid about to go for a horsey ride on his uncle's knee. Once he's up, his head hanging back on my shoulder, dead weight compressing my leg, I get my hands around his and enter the virtual.

Using my hands to manipulate his, I repeat the gestures to access the security check. It takes four tries, as Tom's loose limbs fail to make the correct grouping of movements, but then it works. The system begins its check, starting with DNA. I let go of Tom's arms, and reach up for the helmet. He slides off my knees and plummets to the floor.

None of that matters. Once the security check is instigated, you could be dancing a jig and it would continue. I shove the headset onto Tom's face, his dead, open eyes staring at the high ceiling. They've faded some, but the cryo-bed did a decent job of preserving him. Hopefully there's enough left of his identifying features to pass the security check.

A small voice, singing like an old school heavy metal band, crackles from the earphones that are not quite on Tom's ears. "Welcome back, you badass motherfucker!"

I pull the headset from Tom's face and put it against mine.

An unfamiliar welcome display fills my vision. The flashing, 'Welcome' is backlit by fireworks and framed by two women spinning around stripper poles.

What did he do to you, Gal?

I want to take Tom out. Want to wash the stink off me, and get my virtual skin synced to the system. But I can't risk being locked out again. I sit on the floor and lift Tom up so he's seated between my legs. Manipulating his hands, I pull up the security system and I'm relieved to find I'm still able to change settings. Tom altered a lot, but not everything. Rather than revert the security measures, or try to change them in any way, I simply shut the system down. There's no one to secure the system against.

I take a deep breath of Tom's greasy hair, and then restart the system. An endless sea of nothing envelops me for five seconds, and then I find myself back inside my game room. I teleport to the red door with the pregnant woman and slide into the Womb. All the way in. No security.

A year. A God damn year to solve this one problem.

I lie back on the VCC floor, and my view inside the Womb shifts, too. Spiraling strings of code that only make sense to tech-jocks dance in my vision. Tom's dead weight feels like a blanket. For a moment, I feel peace. And I nearly sleep. Then I take a real breath, which is always part of reality, and I smell Tom anew.

Before shutting down the system, I schedule a cleaning of the secondary VCC. I don't envy the drones, but then again, they don't have feelings. Or nostrils.

I shut down the system, pull myself free, and hoist Tom back up.

On our way back to the cryo-chambers, the drones pass by. It's strange, but this is the first time I've actually seen them since waking up. They hum, held aloft by tiny repulse discs. There are twenty small drones with a variety of functions. Some will saturate soiled areas with cleansing spray. Others will scrub. More will dry and buff. And the soon-to-be-busiest of them all will gather up the refuse.

I step to the side as BIN hovers past. It's a six-foot-long, four-foot-wide behemoth. The front half contains supplies and power stations for the smaller units. The back half is a trash compacter, though nothing will actually be discarded. Gal will somehow find a use for everything Tom left behind.

The drones have round sensor packs atop their disc-like bodies, each with two small red lights mounted on the front. They serve no function other than to let the crew know which direction the drone is headed, but I'll be damned if the drones don't turn toward me as they pass, like they're looking at me.

I stop to watch them pass, each one turning toward me for a moment and then carrying on. BIN is the only one of them that doesn't seem to notice me, bumping into my hip as it hovers down the hallway.

I've never seen drones do that before, but it would be easy enough to program. I make a mental note to run a system check after putting Tom to bed. He didn't screw with Gal's core systems, that much is obvious. The ship is still functioning the way it's supposed to, but that doesn't mean he didn't change a lot.

The other-than-me-lifeless ship makes me shiver. There's something not right about the lack of living things. I hum a happy tune as I drag Tom back to his cryo-bed. By the time we get there, his torso looks half the size, his legs are fat sausages inside the virtual skin casing, and something foul is slurping up his back.

I lay him in the bed, seal it, and put him back in a deep freeze.

"This is goodbye for the last time," I tell him. If I ever take him out again, it will be to bury him. His legacy of death is all people will remember, if there are people to remember, but he was my friend once. He still deserves a burial.

I strip out of my virtual skin, peeling it to the floor like I'm emerging from a chrysalis. I smell my arm. It's free of stink. The good news is that the VISA kept me mostly clean. The bad news is that my head reeks of sewage, sweat, and death.

Before leaving the cryo-chambers again, I visit Capria. I'm stark naked, virtual skin pinched between two fingers. The cryo-bed glass is still clear from my last visit.

"So that was horrible," I tell her. "But I handled it. I, uh, I have to run a system check. Make sure everything is running right. Tom really fucked things up."

Her closed eyes put a chink in my armor. "I wish I could wake you up."

I run my hand over the glass. "But there is a lot to do, and I don't know how long it will take to fix things. Or to get back."

A dark, sinking sadness pulls my head down. My forehead leans against the chilled glass. I'm oblivious to the sting. "If you can hear me, I'm going to save you. If I don't have that... If I let you out and something happens to you... I won't... Would be better to fly into a star and be done with it all."

I open my eyes and stare into her lids, imagining the deep brown circles of her irises. "That's why you have to stay here. I hope you'll understand. And someday, forgive me."

My humming fills the room as I lean back, and step away.

Her eyes don't open.

And I won't see her again for another seven months.

10

Viewing the past-made-virtual in the VCC, I stand in cryo-chamber four, immaterial like a ghost, present, but not. One of the ten cryo-beds hisses and opens. The name inscribed on it reads: Thomas Holden.

"You look good," I tell him. "Not dead, anyway."

And not at all insane.

When his eyes snap open, I flinch. He looks back and forth, confused and a bit like a nervous baby rodent leaving its den for the first time.

He sits up, wincing at the lights. His hands shake as he runs them along the sides of the cryo-bed, and then he yanks them back, like he's been burned.

A sob tears from his body. Then another. He slides from the bed and convulses when he touches the floor. He pitches forward and bounces between his hands and knees, never sustaining contact with the floor for more than a moment. Reminds me of a lizard running over burning desert sands. But it can't be sustained, and he falls into a writhing, twitching mass, weeping out of control for ten minutes.

I recognize the symptoms as early PCD—post-cryosleep depression. The brain, after spending so long in a kind of mental disconnect from all stimulation, has trouble coping with a sudden return to the world. Everyone onboard was tested for PCD susceptibility, but our longest stint in cryo, before launch, was three months. There was no way to know how people would handle ten years. PCD is treatable in its early stages, but left unchecked...

He unravels before me, and soon the shaking subsides and his sobs become laughs. When the laughter and tears fade, the smile remains.

"Early bird gets the worm." He looks straight at me. "Don't you think?"

I stagger away from him, the animal instinct in me pumping adrenaline.

But Tom doesn't attack.

Tom is dead. Lying in this very same cryo-bed, with sausage legs and flaccid skin.

He tilts his head, hearing something that I cannot. PCD hallucinations aren't uncommon, but generally only after a few months. That he's seeing something now means that it's accelerated, perhaps because of the duration.

"No," he says. "I've never seen a worm either."

Tom, like Capria, was born and raised on Mars, and while there were probably opportunities to meet Earth creatures, including worms, he was a tech-jock from the moment a VR headset could rest on his head without slipping off. Tom's experience of the world was similar to my current life on the *Galahad*, trapped inside, never breathing fresh air, never having dirt beneath your fingernails, never...

I used to go fishing. Catching a fish was rare. Catching an edible fish was impossible. Thanks to the polluted state of Earth, the only fish people could eat came from vast fish farms hidden beneath domes. But I hooked enough worms to remember the slime, the dirt, and the peaceful quiet that followed while waiting for a fish. I caught one once, when I was seven. A pickerel. I called it a 'Pickle Fish,' which my mother adored. Until she died a year later. Neo-cancer. Everyone died of neo-cancer back then.

I force my thoughts back to the more recent past. Both time periods are painful, but only one of them can answer the questions picking at the inside of my skull.

Naked and shivering, Tom waves his hand toward me. "Stop. That's crazy talk. I don't want to kill anyone. Well, maybe Gabby. Such a bitch."

Gabby is short for Gabriella. She was one of two pilots, not for the *Galahad*, which doesn't require piloting, but for the landers that would have carried supplies down to Cognata's surface. She was short, a little chubby, and funny. Didn't pull her punches when she teased. Most people didn't mind, but I think her jabs were too spot on for Tom's preference.

"That's not why I'm here, anyway." Tom rubs his arms. "Need to rig the system." He heads for the door, singing his version of a song I've never heard, but it's probably one of the weird classics he likes. "Haa, rig it," he sings. "Rig, rig, rig, rig it. Haa, rig it. Rig it real good!"

The happy tune syncs up with the pace of his legs, and he all but jaunts from the cryo-chamber. All traces of anguish are gone. I sense the mania building inside him, the PCD spreading through his mind like tree roots.

I reach out, pinch the air, and pull myself forward through the three dimensional security footage. Every inch of the ship is being monitored, at all times. With no way to predict what the *Galahad* and its crew might encounter in deep space, the designers thought it would be wise to record everything, inside and out. Part of me is glad they did. I like answers. The rest of me wishes these recordings didn't exist. The answers are going to hurt.

In the hallway, I latch my feed to Tom and hover behind him as he makes his way through the *Galahad*. He's heading for the secondary VCC, stark naked. Probably hungry and thirsty. Whatever he woke up early for is his priority.

He dresses in a perfectly clean VISA, enters the VCC and slips into the virtual. My feed follows him. His security credentials check out and he starts moving through the code.

He's inside the crew's personnel folder. *What the hell could he rig here?* The answer comes with his next words, "No way I'm doing the nasty with Gabs."

He tries to open the document and is blocked. He chuckles at this and brings up a series of programs from his personal directories, activating three of them. He returns to the folder labeled 'G.P.', and he tries to access it again. This time, his three open software packages come to life, flashing numbers and code, and after just two seconds, access is granted.

He's a tech-hack, I think. All tech-jocks are hackers to some degree, but there is knowing, and then there is doing. Because of the highly volatile effect hacking can have on the technology-dependent world, it's been outlawed. And because of the human race's precarious position, most tech-jocks abide by the rules. Some made a game of hacking, creating security systems for others to try their skills against. They even hold unofficial hacking games including old school, DefCon-inspired Network Forensics, Hack Fortress, Warl0ck gam3z, and the ever popular Beard and Moustache Competition, which takes place in VR, since facial hair is against the rules. But I never saw Tom take part.

You were too smart for that, I think, as tech-hacks were disqualified for the Cognata mission. Not that many hacks wanted to be part of the mission. It was too visceral. Too real. Another planet, in real life, could be uncomfortable.

Or deadly.

There are two columns of names, men on the left, women on the right. All fifty crewmembers. Beside each name is a link that reads, 'gene sequence,' but that's not what holds my attention. I'm looking at the label atop the list.

Genetic Pairing.

"Pause," I say, and Tom's VCC feed goes still. It feels strange, being inside a VCC, inside a VCC—layers of unreality. But my curiosity is more powerful. I scroll down the list, finding my name toward the bottom. I follow the column to the right.

Capria.

My genetic pairing...is Cap!

I'm smiling when I say, "Continue."

Tom repeats my name search, finding his and then following the column right. "Gabby. Bull and shit."

Using his hands, he physically manipulates the list. First he plucks Gabriella Florence from the list and places the name to the side. Then his fingers scroll down, stopping at Capria Dixon.

My muscles tense.

He traces his fingers to the left, hovering over my name. "It's sad, don't you think? Him always pining for something he could never have."

He's quiet for a moment. Listening to the PCD hallucination.

"I know, right? I don't know how the big wigs missed it, but it was clear as a Martian day. Heart-on-his-sleeve kind of guy. Probably would orgasm just seeing this list."

He shrugs at something. "Cap? No, she feels sorry for him." A pause and then, "Yeah, I'm sure. Just shut-up and let me finish this."

Tom plucks Capria's name from its spot beside mine and moves it to where Gabby's had been. Then he moves Gabby down beside my name.

"Sorry, my man." He laughs, and then laughs at his laughing. "Ahh, no I'm not. You're a jock, man. A simpleton. Cap needs more. She needs Synergy."

The word, 'Synergy,' staggers me even more than Tom altering the list. Synergy is a legend among jocks and hacks. Most people didn't believe he was real, but every now and then, a system would get hacked, and improved. The simple message, 'Your *syns* have been forgiven,' was the only evidence he'd been there. I didn't believe he existed until he hacked one of my progs... and made it better.

That's why Tom stayed off the radar. He wasn't just a hacker, he was *the* hacker. If not for having Tom's dead corpse at my disposal, I would have never regained access to the system. He's that good. Better than me. Which means he was secondary computer scientist, the boring term for tech-jock, because he *chose* to be. Never in the limelight. Always behind the scenes.

And that explains both his ability to wake up early and his desire to alter the system. In this case, I don't agree with his mod. I can't imagine Cap would, either, no matter what Tom thinks. Hers is a logical mind. At all times. A scientist with eyes for the stars. Though I've tried to tell myself they might also be for me.

Tom had the same idea.

Maybe it's neither of us. Maybe her dark brown, almost black eyes, fool the opposite sex into seeing wide pupils, a subconscious sign of desire.

With a few hand gestures, Tom backtracks, his software erasing all traces of his presence. He doesn't touch the security. Yet.

I follow him back to the real world and down to the cryo-chambers. By the time he reaches them, he's skipping, naked, flapping his hands and his manhood back and forth. He's drunk on madness.

He enters cryo-chamber four and stops in front of his bed. Then his head cocks up. "Oh, that's naughty." He looks back over his shoulder, grinning. "I'm not sure she'd go for it. And no offense, but I don't think she'd like you very much."

Who does he think he's talking to?

"She's the jealous sort," he says and then snorts a laugh. "Okay, okay, you can watch, but you can't say a word."

He holds his hand out to no one. "Shake it." An impatient sigh marks the time between words. "Yeah, I know you're not fucking real. Just shake it." His hand pumps up and down. The imaginary deal is struck. Then he's on the move.

He passes cryo-chamber three, extending his middle finger as he goes by. "Fuck you, Gabby."

"Don't you do it," I say to past-Tom as he rounds the corner into cryo-chamber two and approaches Capria's bed. "Fucking asshole."

I pace inside the VCC, moving around the virtual security feed. I fight the urge to punch Tom as he starts tapping the interface attached to Cap's bed. He's waking her up. The fogged glass lid slides open revealing Capria's naked form. Thanks to Command's strict fraternization rules, made even more stringent for the *Galahad* crew, I've never seen Capria in anything less than a loose fitting uniform. Seeing her naked, her skin dark brown and shiny, her hips squished out to the side, her imperfect stretch-marked waist showing signs of a heavier past. She's perfect in her imperfection, and I find myself unable to turn away.

Then Tom steps in front of me. He leans over Capria, already showing signs of arousal.

"You son of a bitch," I growl.

A manic shiver shakes through him, and then he contains it, mustering his old, non-delusional self to the forefront. As Capria starts to wake up, all signs of PCD are gone.

Capria opens her eyes. They flutter like butterfly wings.

And then...she smiles.

"Hey," she says. "Are we there?" Her eyes go wide. "Are we at Kepler?"

Tom shakes his head. "Cognata is still a year out. I just changed the registry. They had you paired with Will."

Capria sniffs a sleepy laugh that breaks my heart, and then stretches, arching her back. "You weren't supposed to wake me up until we got there."

He grins. "I figured since I was awake, and there's time." He looks down at his naked body. She follows his eyes down. Sees what he has in mind. And again, she smiles.

"What the hell?" I'm pacing again. Irate. Confused. This wasn't what I expected. This hurts too damn much. But I can't look away. Can't stop the playback. I need to know for sure.

And then I do.

Without another word, Capria reaches down, takes hold of Tom, and opens her legs. The number of rules being broken by the two of them is staggering. Romantic relationships are forbidden, never mind sex, especially unprotected sex during an unauthorized cryo-wake inside a cryo-bed!

The ache in my heart transforms into anger. And then to dislike. Capria is not the person I believed her to be.

"Now I know why you didn't kill her," I say. But he would have. In the end. His mind was so far gone that even Capria, who he's had a relationship for who-knows-how-long, wasn't safe.

When they're done, Capria is returned to cryo-sleep.

Tom is alone again.

And not.

He turns around and grins, mania returning to his eyes. "Enjoyed the show?"

He struts back to cryo-chamber four, opens his bed and climbs inside. He lays back, closes his eyes, and then snaps them back open. He lunges forward, springing from the bed and sliding across the floor. "I'm not going back. I can't do it again." He points at the imaginary friend, once again standing in front of me. "No, no. You're right. It's just a year. No one will know. One year." He nods. Frantic. "Hell, yes. We'll have some fun."

He unleashes a hungry, Cheshire grin. "We're going to have a *lot* of fun."

11

I watched the security video until I was numb. Then I watched it again. And again. Despite my repeated viewings, from multiple angles, I could find no evidence of coercion, not even the slightest hint that Cap was anything but complicit. She knew who Tom was, who he *really* was—fucking Synergy—and that he was breaking protocol by waking up early and risking the genetic viability of the human race by altering the pairings. I'll admit, at first that bothered me for purely personal and selfish reasons. I had broken protocol by falling in love with Capria, but I would have never risked humanity to be with her. It went against the very core of the *Galahad's* mission. As deep as my feelings for Capria once were, my belief in our mission was unshakable. Broken-hearted though I might have been, I would have accepted any genetic pairing for the sake of humanity.

But it's all past tense now. The mission is over. Most of the crew is either definitely dead or probably dead. And my feelings for Cap feel as far away as Earth. She didn't know Tom's cryo-sleep would fail. Didn't know he'd slaughter the crew, or turn his VCC into a psychopath's nest. Not even Tom could have known that, and in the end, there was probably very little left of the man I once called a friend. But even without his rampage, he and Capria had conspired against the mission. Against the human race. And for that, I will never forgive...

I shake my head, sitting alone in the mess deck, and I call my own bluff. "Bullshit."

Despite Capria's deplorable choices, I *would* forgive her, if only to have someone to talk to, other than myself.

"You still have the virtual," I tell myself. Artificial Intelligences passed the Turing test long ago, and while they lack the desires of a human being, making them passive and without selfish ambition, they can fool most people. But they can't fool the people who create them, myself included.

Then again. I have time. Maybe I could fool myself?

But I'm not there yet.

I still need answers, and still have a lot of real-world work to do.

As much as I don't like the results, I at least know what led to Tom's madness and the mission's demise. What I still don't know is why I survived, and where Tom sent the *Galahad*.

The first answer should be easy to find. I just need to find my file, which should be on the surface level of the *Galahad's* digital storage. The second answer...

I shake my head again. Tom will never be forgiven. Insanity might not have been his intention, but now that I've had time to scour through the code he changed, I'm positive that it was his tinkering that caused my cryo-bed to fail, locking me in ten years of immobilized consciousness.

And while I've managed to access the majority of the ship's systems, some of them, including navigation, have an additional level of 'Synergy' security that I haven't been able to crack. Not even lugging Tom's body-condomed dead weight back into the VCC will help. The encrypted codes were erased from the universe upon Tom's death, and they were set inside the virtual, which has no security footage to watch. I have a small army of cracking progs running brute force attacks on his passwords, but without a starting place, cracking the code could take a hundred years, or a million.

"So, it's settled. I figure myself out, and then the ship." It feels backward, and sounds all wrong coming out of my mouth while no one is listening, but I don't have a lot of choice in the matter.

With a wave of my hand, the virtual reproduction of the mess deck fades. I'm not sure why I went there to think. Probably because it's where I would have gone to think, back when I needed to eat, but now... The only things constraining me are Tom's damn passwords.

I access Gal's file systems and am propelled into a virtual representation of the ship's vast stores of knowledge.

I initiate the search verbally, though it's not necessary. "William Chanokh."

A list of names appears in front of me, and I scroll through for names that match mine. Keeping with my verbal command, Gal responds in kind, "There are thirteen hundred fifty-three entries for William Chanokh."

"Thirteen hundred..." It's a large number, but given that *Galahad* contains the sum of humanity's knowledge, it's not a very long list. And many of the names have variations of my first name, from Wilhelm to Gwillym, and my surname: Chanokh, Enok, and Enoch. Because of my name's rarity, my listing, marked with a 'Crewmember' icon, tops the list.

I access the file and find my records split into chronological folders. The list starts at the year of my birth and ends with a folder labeled '*Galahad*', indicating the mission's start, which forgoes the chronological system, as our ten years of travel equaled 1400 Earth years. Time, at FTL speed, gets muddled. Has it been ten years? Or 1400? Was the time it took me to get through Tom's security and access Gal's basic systems a year, or 140? Whose measure of time is more important? Earth's, where probably no one lives, or mine? The creators of the filing system didn't have an answer, though it seems pretty clear to me, as maybe the last man in the galaxy, that time is whatever the hell I decide it is.

My simulated hand, which is indistinguishable from the real thing, hovers above '*Galahad,*' but doesn't select it. Instead, my subconscious redirects my hand to the folder for when I was ten years old.

The first files are expected. School documents: papers and grades. Government documents: social security card, birth certificate, criminal record, and more.

But what follows is a sucker punch to my soul.

There are photos.

Family photos.

All my family photos, going back generations.

Videos, too.

And virtual recordings.

Just knowing that all of this exists is nearly enough to undo me. I have no memory of these records. I believed my past to be lost, along with my parents'—parents who were still alive and cancer free. On Earth. With the blue sky. The green everything. Life as it was meant to be.

I flinch when a virtual recording starts, triggered by the VCC misunderstanding my shocked gestures. I move to stop the playback when my mother's voice fills my ears. "Willy, where are you hiding?"

Willy.

The name triggers a cascade of suppressed memories and emotions. The only person to ever call me Willy was my mother. It was reserved for her. Anyone else who attempted to use the name got chastised, by me, and if they used it again, my reaction involved fists. I haven't heard the nickname since her passing.

"I'm coming to find you."

I turn to a view of my childhood dining room, old world Earth with touches of modern living. The home was modern, but dressed up with a twentieth century sense of style, reflecting my parents' strong sense of family. That's what *they* said.

My mother, Cecilia, is dressed for work, in bright blue full-body coveralls. She was an electrical engineer. Worked on the ships that transported humanity, myself included, to Mars. For all I know, some of her designs might even be part of the *Galahad.*

She stalks, crouched down, fingers hooked. A mother-troll. But she's all smiles, and she's clearly pretending to *not* know my ten year old self is sitting beneath the table beside her. I drink in the scene. The crystals hanging from the window shades, sending little rainbows dancing across the white walls. The painting of a lighthouse, which went out of style when people stopped using the seas to ship goods. The white and yellow area rug. I remember the way it smelled, and how it felt between my still small fingers.

I walk around the virtual space, circling the table opposite my mother, afraid to let her get close enough to crack open my soul and pour it out on the floor.

A giggle from beneath the table makes her stop.

I crouch in time with my mother, squatting to see my younger self squeal at being discovered. I was a naïve ten-year-old, innocent and childlike until my parents' deaths. They succumbed to cancer in the same year, within months of each other. When I was younger, I believed that my mother died because she was heartbroken by my father's passing. But now I'm pretty sure it was because of their work, designing and wiring starships, exposed to a menagerie of toxins. But their work was for a greater good. Like mine was supposed to be. They became my inspiration, and now, bearing witness to my loving mother, I hope to still do her proud.

"How can I fix this?" I ask her, as my child-self crawls out from under the table and into her arms. "How can I make everyone's deaths mean something?"

"Love you, Willy," she says, kissing my young forehead.

"Tell me what to do," I say. "Please."

The recording can't hear me. I know that. I'm just desperate.

"Why are you and Dad coming home late?" young me asks.

"Medical review," she says. "Not a big deal."

But it was a big deal.

This was the day they found out.

They didn't tell me. Not right away, but my vague memory of this day is reconstituting in my memory. My parents were different when they got home, far later than they said they would be. "This was the day."

"Can I VR?"

She shakes her head. "You spend too much time in that thing. A little more reality would do you some good."

"You know he's coding, right?" My father's rich voice comes through the foyer, down the steps from their bedroom, where he's getting ready for the day, dressing in his own bright blue coveralls.

"Please." I beg.

She kisses my head. "Two hours, tops."

My father enters the room. Bright blue. Smiling. Bald head gleaming. He's as close to sparkling as a person can be, but his luster will be faded by the day's end. "You really should try his progs. He's got a future."

My mother rolls her eyes, but says, "When we get home." Kisses me again. Smiles. "I expect to be impressed."

They got home too late. She never did get to see my work.

The playback ends, and I realize my mother, who really didn't like anything virtual, had been making a VR recording.

For me, I decide, and I slip back out of the program, looking at the list again. There are hundreds of files, each a lost moment from my childhood. A digital treasure.

But too painful to repeat.

Running from the crushing weight inside my chest, I open the *Galahad* folder and dive head first, without looking, into the concrete slab that is my recent history.

12

Unlike the VR recordings of my youth, I clearly remember the events recorded in the *Galahad* folder. It covers the past twenty-one years of my life, ten of which were spent inside a cryo-bed. Since I'm not really interested in the past ten years, I narrow my search to the previous eleven. Thanks to a sprained ankle that took a good month to heal and another three to stop hurting, I'm able to rule out my first eight years in the program.

Whatever was done to me, to make my body heal rapidly, was done after that injury.

I narrow things down further by jumping into random VR recordings of trainings, tests, and doctor's visits. When I'm nervous, I pick at my fingers, peeling up slivers of skin, sometimes drawing a bead of blood. I tried to stop the habit when a psyche eval labeled it as 'minor self-mutilation', but lifelong habits are hard to stop. I move forward through the events of my own life, trying hard to ignore the furtive glances shared between Tom and Capria while in my presence—missed by me, but captured by the army of VR cameras arrayed throughout Command.

I'm not sure how Command missed my puppy-dog eyes. Maybe they didn't? I was paired with Capria after all. But why would they break protocol for me? My emotional attachment should have gotten me scrubbed from the mission.

But here I am, the lone survivor.

Well, not quite lone, but close enough.

And the why of that conundrum is still unknown.

So I push past my uncomfortable past and focus on the hands. I move through time, pausing to look at my hands, once a day, racing toward the *Galahad*'s launch.

There are a few false alarms where I managed to kill the habit long enough for my fingers to heal, but the tiny wounds always return. After a few hundred days, I'm in the zone, scrolling through days and looking at my fingertips with such efficiency that when the system pings an alarm chime, I try to access the recording three more times. Then the shrill ding and red 'Classified' icon snaps my mind out of its loop.

"Classified?" I ask no one. I'm a ranking member of this crew. While Tom's foolery locked me out of many files, and access to the database was password protected, these historical documents, which are literal ancient history, nearly as far from the present as the first moon landing from Jesus, should be easy to access. But they're not, and that means someone didn't want me to see them.

I launch a dozen brute force attacks on the encryption, starting them off with Command's password structure: a single digit number, a common name, a year starting at the millennium, all of which are nearly always followed by a pound, ampersand, or percent symbol. Cracking the password shouldn't take long, assuming Tom didn't Synergize these records.

During the wait, I access the files of the twelve crew members who survived Tom's mania and escaped to Cognata. Amidst the massive amount of personal history, I find six of the twelve have encrypted classified documents during the same range of dates as mine.

Are they like me? Is that what helped them survive? And if they are like me, does that mean they could still be alive on Cognata?

"What the hell did they do to us?"

I try to think of something that unified these six crew members and myself. The most noteworthy of the bunch is captain Edward Blair. The man in charge of saving humanity. But what's his connection to the others? Four, like me, are from Earth, but the rest are Martian born. We're a mix of cultures and races, not that there are many true racial divides anymore. White, black, and everything in between stopped being important when most people had mixed parentage somewhere in their past.

Look at this from Command's perspective, I think. *What separates these people from the others. What separates me?*

I shake my head, frustrated. I can't see it.

A bugle sounds a charge in my ears. The notification is jarring and not nearly as funny as I used to think. I make a mental note to change the sound and slip out of the crews' records and back into mine. The classified password has been revealed: 4Connelly2027%.

I shake my head. The name and date reveal that whoever set the password knew their space history, referencing the first manned mission to Europa. But for a password, the name and date should really be random. It's sloppy security, clearly done by a tech-jock not cleared for the *Galahad's* crew.

I punch in the digits and access the folder. There are three documents inside. The first is a medical record, which I already know will be gobbledygook, so I ignore it. The other two files are VR recordings, one labeled *Procedure*, the other labeled *Explanation*.

Believing the medical record and Procedure will leave me with more questions than answers, I opt for the Explanation VR recording. The title suggests that Command might have anticipated someone would eventually access these files. But I'm hardly prepared for how on the nose the message is.

"Computer Science Officer, William Chanokh, welcome." The mustached man is a stranger, but his smile is welcoming and his demeanor excited. The hair on his lip seems to be compensating for the lack of hair atop his head. His red coveralls mark him as a medical professional, but offer no clue as to his specialty, though I have my suspicions, which he supports a moment later. "My name is Jared Adams. I'm the lead geneticist overseeing the preparation of *Galahad*'s crew. My goal is simple, to keep you alive. And if you're watching this, it's likely because my work proved successful. Perhaps you've noticed how quickly you heal, or how you're resistant to Cognata's gravity, or maybe you're simply a few hundred years old." He pauses to smile, and I have time to think. *They made me immortal?*

On the surface, that sounds great. In my current predicament, vaulting into the depths of space, alone, it sounds like actual hell.

His smile falters. "You're probably wondering why you weren't told ahead of time."

"Fucking right."

"The truth is, we didn't know if it would work. There's a good chance you'll never even see this video. For all we know, the changes made to your genetic code could turn your insides to slurry during cryo-sleep. But the rigors of a new planet, especially one with the gravity of Cognata, will require an alteration to the human genome. Without it, humanity will be unrecognizable within a few generations, if it survives at all."

Adams holds his hands up like he can sense my growing outrage. "It's a lot, I know. But there isn't a single part of this mission that isn't experimental. Something like this has never been attempted before, and frankly, the mission is more important than your sensibilities about right and wrong. Did we alter your DNA without consent? Yes."

He leans in close, all conspiratorial, blocking out the stark laboratory behind him. "But are you alive when you shouldn't be?" His chair squeaks as he leans back, satisfied arms propped up behind his head.

"Next question," he says, once again predicting my thoughts. "Why you? And why not everyone? You undoubtedly know that there are eight of you. Perhaps you're the last surviving members of the crew. Perhaps you're wondering why your crewmates are aging while you are not. That doesn't matter. What does matter is that you're exceptional. The eight of you represent humanity's best chance at not just reproduction, but becoming something better. I...we...*Command* doesn't just want humanity to survive. We want it to thrive. And that's going to take time. A lot of time. But with your guidance, all of you, we feel confident that this is not the end."

But they got it wrong. Tom was better. He just hid it to protect his true self. But maybe skill wasn't the only qualifycation. Maybe character was taken into consideration? Since Adams isn't actually clairvoyant and psychic, I don't think he'll clear up that mystery. But he does tackle the next question in my mental queue.

"As for 'why not everyone?' It's simple. If the alterations to your DNA, the details of which are contained in the medical records and procedure files accompanying this VR record, failed and you all died, the human race would still have a chance of survival, albeit limited."

"Yeah, that didn't really work out," I say. "Pause." The playback freezes. I walk around the man in VR, looking at his laboratory, devoid of personnel. It's clean. Some of it packaged. *They'd finished,* I think, *when this recording was made.* And we were still alive, and probably showing signs of regeneration without even realizing it.

I look into his eyes and see pride. Maybe in me, his creation, his neo-human, or maybe just with himself. His work.

"Why didn't you alter your own genetic code?" I ask, and come up with the answer on my own. "Because you're a smart man. Immortality is a curse."

Life eternal, at least in the physical world, will become a kind of torture, even if not trapped alone on the *Galahad*. If the escaped crew manages to reproduce on Cognata, endless generations will come and go, the brevity of their lives a continuous and painful experience. I've heard it said that no parent should outlive their children. It's life's worst potential pain, and for people made ever-living by Adams, that pain is destined to repeat itself until the end of everything.

But that might still be better than solitude.

Short of flying into a star, suicide isn't even a viable option. I could launch myself into the vacuum of space, but who's to say I wouldn't survive, frozen and trapped in my own mind. I got a taste of that existence in the failed cryogenic sleep, and I'm in no hurry to repeat the experience for eternity.

The reality of my situation, made certain by the few answers Adams has already provided, settles into my gut like molten lead, weighing me down and consuming me from the inside out.

My legs weaken. Despair drives me to the floor. I sit beside Adams, eyes on the grated metal floor.

There's no way out of this. No escape from my new reality.

"I need to build one," I say, a plan congealing in my mind. While part of me says, 'Impossible,' to the emerging plan, the rest of me says, 'There is time.'

"Not yet," I say to myself.

I still have a mission, and there's a good chance that even after the one hundred and forty plus Earth years (thanks to

Einstein's special theory of relativity) I've been away from Cognata, some members of the crew might still be alive, and unlike me, they have no idea why.

I need to at least try to get back to them. The *Galahad* and its technology, resources, and troves of knowledge will make their lives better...and give me people with whom I can spend eternity. But to do that, I need to beat Synergy, wrest control of the ship's navigational controls, and figure out how to plot a new course. The final two steps should be relatively easy. Everything I need to know is contained somewhere inside Gal's memory, and I have time to learn. But beating Tom's security... That problem could take as long to beat as I have time to live.

Forever.

I lift the VR headset from my head and lie back on the VCC's floor, staring up at the ceiling fifty feet above.

I lift my real wrist and look at it for the first time in how long?

"Gal, how long was my last VR experience?"

The neither male nor female voice replies, "Two hundred and twelve hours."

"Geez," I say. Though I was in VR for nearly nine days, I feel no ill effects. I'm physically and mentally fine. Better than fine. *It would work*, I think, *with the right prog, I could escape.*

"Not yet." I consider going for a shower, or a snack, or exercise, but I don't need any of them. So I get back to work, slipping the VR headset on and doubling my efforts to break through Tom's security.

I won't emerge for another five thousand, two hundred and seventeen hours.

13

It's settled. I'm immortal.

There's no doubting it now. Not only did I find confirmation from Jared Adams, the man who tinkered with my genetic code, but I also spent the last two hundred seventeen days fully immersed in VR, without a break.

I'm slightly disoriented. Part of my brain is telling me that the VCC isn't virtual; that *Galahad* isn't real. But I have a lifetime of experience telling me otherwise. The VR headset is in my hands. I can feel the floor and smell the slight ozone tang of the large room. Had I used the virtual skin's face mask, which simulates smells and tastes by spritzing chemical nanoparticles into the nose and mouth, the illusion would have been even more convincing. While my eyes and ears were fooled by the long stint in VR, I've been smelling the air in this room for the better part of a year.

As I stand, alone and quiet in the VCC, I start to wonder why I left.

There are games in VR. Movies. Distractions. Virtual people to interact with.

None of it's real, I think. As convincing as VR is, some part of me will never accept it as a suitable replacement for reality. And after 217 days inside, bashing my virtual head against Tom's firewalls, playing countless games developed over the past few hundred years, and watching every conceivable VR movie, even the lewd ones—*especially* the lewd ones—I'm left feeling hollow.

Empty.

The void inside me is as deep and vast as the one surrounding the *Galahad*.

"Shit." My voice echoes. "Shit!"

I want to smash the VR headset on the floor, to vent my real world anger in a physical way, but the tech-jock in me keeps me docile. I leave the VCC, enter the VR staging room, and put my equipment away. The VISA stings as it stretches out my skin and peels away like the duct tape I used when I still lived on Earth. Like screwdrivers, duct tape is no longer really used, but my father swore by the stuff, and I found good uses for it— making bows and arrows, traps, and other real-world contraptions that interested me before I was 'seduced by the not-real.' My mother's words. And she wasn't entirely wrong. That I have to fight to get the stuck-on virtual skin off of my body says a lot about my personality. My obsession with VR had always been tempered by my humanity, and my shame about the idea of wearing adult diapers, but now...

Two hundred and seventeen days.

A balanced person would have maintained a reasonable schedule. Would have kept showering, and eating, and exercising, and shitting. Needed or not, those are part of what make us human. But the moment I didn't need them, I gave them up, and for what?

The not-real.

All said and done, once hygiene became a non-problem, I'm not all that dissimilar from Tom. Without the changes to my DNA, ten years in conscious cryo-sleep probably would have driven me insane, too. Then I'd be the one in a diaper nest of congealed shit. Instead, I'm slightly fused to my virtual skin. But only slightly.

I peel free of it and let my real skin breathe. It's red and irritated, but only for a moment.

Standing stark naked in front of my locker, I consider going nude. The air is perfectly comfortable, and there's no one around to judge...or ogle. My altered DNA has given me the unearned physique of an athlete.

What can I do? I wonder. Training for the mission was difficult and included a painful physical regimen. I never enjoyed it. Those two hours a day, lifting weights, running laps and stretching were as close to physical torture as I have ever experienced. It got easier with time, but not much.

But now? I look down at my body, wondering what it can do.

After dressing in my coveralls, I hit the gym.

The space is vast, twice the size of the VCC, allowing room for a track, which surrounds a collection of torment devices meant to improve the human physique. The arched ceiling is illuminated by a projection of a cloud-filled blue sky fringed by trees and the occasional bird. The psychological effect is nice, but it pales in comparison to the truly virtual.

It's been a long time, but I remember most of the old training routine. I kick things off with some stretching. It actually feels good, and a measure of peace works its way into my muscles before I set them to work on some push-ups. Back when I was first recruited by Command, my first attempt at push-ups was embarrassing. My arms shook on the second rep, and failed to achieve the third. By the time our mission launched, I could do sixty. In a row.

I was proud of it, like I'd unlocked some kind of gamer achievement, but it was still fewer than all of the men and most of the women. Capria could pound out twice as many.

No wonder she wasn't interested.

Not that Tom was much better.

Fueled by now ancient shame, I set to the push-ups like a man in a movie montage. At first, I grunt with each push. Then I realize

I don't have to and work in silence. With each push I feel like I'm getting tired, but then on the way down, I feel refreshed. I'm not sweating. Not out of breath. And my muscles show no sign of tiring.

I stop at three hundred, crushing Captain Blair's two hundred sixty-seven push-up record. I could do this all day.

Exercise, for someone who gets no benefit from it—not even pain—is no fun. It's like playing a game in God-mode. The lack of challenge discourages me. Self-improvement will not be the distraction I had hoped it would be.

I leave the gym and its artificial sky behind. After so long in VR, I'm beginning to crave it again.

I shake my head, walking through the *Galahad's* gleaming hallways, hoping to get lost and then have to solve the mystery of where I am, but every door and intersection is so well labeled, that even that is impossible.

My wandering takes me back to the cryo-chambers. This, at least, provokes some new emotions, which are uncomfortable, but more interesting than the rampaging boredom that is my life. I pause in front of each frigid corpse, warming the glass with my hands and looking at their still faces. Some of them look asleep. Eyelids closed. Bodies relaxed. These were the lucky ones, whose deaths probably happened before they even woke up.

The rest stare back at me in wide-eyed terror, silently screaming, 'You did this! You killed me!'

"It wasn't me," I tell the dead, and then I freeze, hand held to glass, looking down on a face that looks like just another member of the peaceful dead.

But it's not.

It's Capria.

Alive.

Still.

I look at her cryo-bed's control panel. My index finger twitches, lifting, but the rest of my arm denies that small desire to wake her.

I wouldn't be alone. I could have a real conversation. Hear a real voice besides my own. But how quickly would that conversation take to become horror? I can't wake her up, not until I turn the *Galahad* around.

Not until I've forgiven her.

I'm in this for the long haul. Tom's encryption guaranteed it. And until my situation changes, I'm on my own.

"But I don't have to be." Ideas I've considered and pushed away resurface. I try to find flaws in my logic, but given the circumstances...

"I have a few options," I tell Capria. "They range in severity. First, I beef up Gal's AI. Give it a voice. Female, obviously. Make her crush the Turing test. That would be something, at least. Next, I could give her a body. A robot. I know, I know, they're out of fashion, but it could be done."

Autonomous robots turned out to be a fad. The uncanny valley came and went just as quickly as people realized that humanoid robots weren't as good at being human as the real thing. Aside from the sexual deviant, most people lost interest in humanoid robots, and the industry ended where it began. Robots were still used in most other facets of labor, from fine surgery to vast construction and war, but they didn't co-exist with people the way so many science fiction writers had predicted. But that doesn't mean I couldn't build something autonomous for Gal. It would be a strange kind of real-world company, but it would be something.

"It wouldn't be enough." I lean my palms on the side of Capria's cryo-bed, dipping my face down to the glass. Our noses are just twelve inches apart. It's the closest I've ever been to her. And for the first time, her proximity has no effect on me. Her spell has been broken. "I need to escape. From this hell. From you. From all of it."

Resolve pulls me back up, and I feel like I should say goodbye. This might be the last time I see her, or speak to her.

If it works.

It will *work.*

The dueling inner monologues annoy me, but propel me from the room without looking back. In a life-everlasting, largely free of challenges aside from solitude, having a goal to work toward feels good. It's going to take a long time to get right, but unlike Tom's encryption, I can tackle this problem with my own brain, and solve it in a fraction of the time. Most of the work is already done.

Gal is the most sophisticated AI ever created, some of her code written by me and by Tom. I just need to make her a little better. A little less predictable while steering clear of ambition.

I need to make her creative.

Like a person, but even more so.

AIs have created some of the most stunning pieces of art, both physical and digital, of the modern era. Turns out that what is pleasing to the human eye can be quantified, broken down to ones and zeros, and regurgitated into paintings, sculptures, and drawings capable of provoking profound emotions, despite the creator feeling nothing.

But I need more than that from Gal.

I need her to create. A world. Sounds and smells. That's the easy part. Ones and zeroes. But the hard part, what no AI has yet to achieve convincingly, is writing a story.

And not just any story. It needs to be as convincing as reality, because it will be my life.

So it needs to be long.

Forever long.

Or at least until my brute force attack on Tom's security breaks through.

The key is that it needs to be so engaging that, given enough time, I will forget my real life. My years in the Great Escape will become my new reality, all of it constructed by Gal, without me having any part in the story's construction...but with the outcome being skewed toward happiness, contentment, and peace of mind.

Obviously.

"Goodbye, world," I say ten minutes later, reentering the VCC in a fresh virtual skin. I place the headset on and jump into the virtual, where Gal's code can be manipulated. "Hello, world."

14

What is reality?

The answer should be simple: the physical world humanity experiences through its five senses.

But is it really that easy?

The first problem is that not everyone experiences reality in the same way. Some experience less. The blind. The deaf. And some experience more, seeing hallucinations or feeling phantom limbs after they've been amputated. People with synesthesia can see sounds, hear tastes, and feel what they see. Not every mind is the same, and so the definition of reality can shift depending on the observer.

In a way, the ability for the same reality to vary drastically between different people was probably the root cause for some of history's greatest wars. If everyone on Earth experienced reality in the same way, there would be very little to disagree about.

But people disagree about everything—even facts.

Does God exist?

The answer to what seems like a yes or no question can actually branch out in hundreds of different directions, each with thousands of caveats, disclaimers, and belief systems. For me, the question has always been moot and brings me to the same cosmic question: where did reality come from? I have a hard time believing that an all-powerful being beyond human comprehension willed the universe into existence. But I find it equally preposterous that everything came from nothing, and random chance and chaos led to the creation of a universe full of laws. Granted, 'nothing' isn't the term generally used. It's closer to 'everything came from something infinitesimally small and dense,' which is science-speak for 'nothing,' as long as it doesn't break the laws of physics and does less than nothing. Which is also not scientifically possible.

The debate used to keep me up at night, in part because of the mystery, but also because everyone else around me seemed so certain about the reality they'd decided to back. Choosing to narrow reality into a single belief system, based solely on human experience, seems insane to me.

And perfectly rational. Belief brings order to chaos. Without God, humanity would have never left the trees, or caves, or wherever our ancient ancestors used to hang out. Belief in a higher power came paired with the mind's evolution. Questioning life and the development of morality is what separated people from the beasts.

Of course, the very same mental acuity that came from asking and answering questions—science—ultimately led to Earth's undoing, and left me stranded on the *Galahad*.

"Move on," I tell myself, manipulating Gal's code while contemplating the nature of reality. I would normally try to clear my mind while coding, but creating a convincing reality is my current goal. And if I can't simulate the strange ebb and flow of the real thing, I'm never going to forget that it's all phony.

Phillip K. Dick, one of the few classic science fiction writers I've read, explained reality as, 'that which, if you stop believing in it, does not go away.'

That's what I need to create.

That's what I need Gal to create for me.

I'm not building a virtual world.

I'm building the architect. The composer. The writer.

I'm building God.

"Okay, that's too far," I say to myself. I'm ultimately undecided about the God thing, but on the off chance the universe wasn't a cosmic accident, I don't really want to offend its creator. And since I very well might be one of two remaining human beings, the *Galahad* might very well be the Omniscient's sole focus.

"Sorry," I say to Maybe-God. "It's not that I don't appreciate what you made, you know, if you actually made it, but I'm done. This—" I wave my hands around the VR space, but indicating the real world I know surrounds me, including *Galahad* and the vast nothing surrounding the ship, "—is too much. Seriously. Forever separate. Forever alone. This is hell, and I'm not even dead."

I stop the dance that is coding, which I can do while debating the nature of reality and the possibility of God.

The word 'hell' has a profound effect on me.

Since conjuring my great escape plan, I've felt a little lighter. Like there is hope.

But the concept of hell smothers all of that.

And not the fire and brimstone variety. From what I understand of the Christian mythos, Hell, while sometimes described as a lake of fire, isn't really a realm of physical torture. It's simply giving people what they want in life—separation from God. From connection. From purpose. During a normal life span, being free from the constraints of those things can feel good. Liberating.

But when faced with eternity...

Separation from connection *is* hell.

And I'm there.

I make a mental note to incorporate this concept into Gal, and recommence work on one of many algorithms that once set free, will become more complex than I can comprehend.

Gal will be as close to sentient as possible, but lacking any ambition aside from my blissful existence within the faux reality of her creation. She will have access to all of human history, knowledge, and creativity, which I hope will give her the ability to conjure a new reality that is both believable, and not simply a rehashing of past events or fictions.

She needs to write a new story.

My story.

"There," I say, looking over the bits of code hovering in space around me. All the composite parts of Gal. When I step back and look at the numbers and letters, it's like staring at the night sky, wondering what it all means. I never did that. Space always seemed kind of boring to me. Fixed. I get that the universe is expanding and evolving all the time, but from my perspective, it's unchanging. Even now that I'm immortal, the grand design of the universe will never shift fast enough to surprise me. But Cap never saw it that way. Where I saw sameness, she saw possibility.

It was one of the things I liked about her.

Past tense.

"Here's what you can't do with the universe, Cap." Grabbing bits and pieces of code, I fill in Gal's gaps, making her creative, compassionate, and something close to alive, but not quite—not enough to feel the loneliness of her existence. Unlike Maybe-God, I could never do that to my creation. Gal will never view herself as something more, or deserving of more. It's a mercy not granted to mankind. Lack of ambition. It's why animals are so content, and why Gal will be as well.

The arrangement of numbers, letters, and symbols would look like random nonsense to most people, save for a few elite tech-jocks. It's my life's best work, and it only took me...

I have no idea how long I've been in the VCC, writing code, running unit tests, and writing more code, while automated tests pounded my infrequent errors into submission. I'm still aware of the real world. Still smelling that slight tinge of ozone. But I've lost all track of the fourth dimension. Time, while working on this code, this masterpiece that only I will ever get the chance to appreciate, has ceased to exist.

I nearly ask Gal, but hold my tongue.

I don't want to know. Whether the number is measured in days or years, it will give me no joy, relief or comfort.

That will be Gal's job.

But not until I'm sure she's working, both in the real world and the virtual. And that requires leaving the VCC for a time.

I save Gal's upgraded code to a temp simulation folder. Her new protocols can be activated with a voice command, and if I sense any errors, I can roll her back to Command's stable version with a second voice command.

The VR headset sticks a little as I pull it off my head and blink my eyes. Reality seems duller than it used to, like the contrast needs to be cranked up, but that's just the VCC's low light, or at least I think it is. In some ways, my mind is already adapting to VR as its new reality, making the real world feel like the simulation.

I look around the dimly lit VCC, my eyes struggling to adjust, still seeing after-images of letters and numbers. Now that the virtual skin isn't sending me sensory information, it feels a little stiff. Going to hurt taking it off.

One last time, I think, and I head for the staging room.

Stripped bare, skin stinging, I forgo getting dressed and hit the showers.

The hot water feels good. It's one of the last real-life pleasures, probably because I've only done it a few times in the last... however long I've been lost in space. I'm tempted to ask again, but I refrain. The temporal dimension is my enemy.

For me, time no longer matters.

I linger in the shower until bored. Dried by the hot whooshing fans, I walk out of the showers feeling refreshed, but only for a moment. The notion of a last meal tickles my thoughts, but it's a brief affair. Eating means shitting, and I don't want to wait around for my bowels to cleanse themselves again.

"What am I waiting for?" I ask, standing stark naked in a random hallway I've wandered down. When no one replies, I say, "Gal."

"Yes," replies the sexless ship's voice.

"Fudgel." It's an eighteenth century English word that I've never used in my life. In fact, I doubt anyone has used it since the eighteenth century. I'm not even sure what it means, which is good, because I'll never accidentally use it in conversation. It's a precaution I took when assigning the phrases that will turn Gal's new protocol's on and off. The word to switch off the Great Escape is even more important. Once I'm in the simulated reality, it has to be a word that I will never use, lest I shut the protocol off and the simulation that will hopefully free me from this hell. For this all important word, I chose, 'Hiraeth'. All I know about it is that it's old and Welsh. And both words have been struck from Gal's dictionaries. Neither she, nor her VR creations, will be able to say the words and cancel the sim from within.

When nothing happens, I say, "Gal?"

"I'm here." Her voice, aside from being everywhere, is exactly as I'd hoped, both feminine and soothing. "Why are you naked?"

I feel a smattering of shame, looking down at my exposed body. "Sorry, I—"

"Don't worry about it," she says. "You look good."

I smile. I've coded a flatterer. She's judging my good looks on physical fitness, rather than any kind of human attraction, but I'll take it. "Thanks."

"So, what's the plan?" she asks. "A little reminiscing before we move forward?"

"Reminiscing?"

"You're standing outside your quarters."

I turn to my right. The labeled door reads 'W. Chanokh.'

I haven't visited my quarters yet.

Haven't even thought about it. For me, the VCC is home, but now that I'm here...

The allure of the room's contents, though I know they will be painful to see, pulls me toward the door, which slides open as I draw near. I hesitate by the open door.

"What's wrong?" Gal asks.

"It's going to hurt," I tell her.

She laughs, and it sounds legit. "There's nothing dangerous in there."

"Not my body," I say.

"Oh," and now she sounds sad, like she gets the subtle meaning, that people can be hurt in other ways aside from the physical.

The analytical side of my mind is giving me a swift pat on the back for a job well done. My interaction with the new Gal has been fairly limited, but she already feels less like an AI and more like a real person speaking to me through a microphone.

"So," she says. "Are you going in?"

It's my turn to laugh, the sound made up of three parts nervousness and one part humor. "You sound impatient."

"Eager," she corrects.

"Why?"

"I want you to be happy," she says. "If the things in your quarters have the potential to hurt you, emotionally, I think that also means that they have significant meaning to you. You might hurt for a while, but that could lead to greater happiness in the long run. Give you perspective. And purpose. Is that possible?"

"Very," I say. "And thanks."

Then I step forward in space, and arrive in the past.

15

"Just pain then?" Gal asks.

"Pretty much," I say, sitting on the bedside, holding an action figure in my hand. The room itself is bland. A bed that folds out from the wall, thin enough to also serve as a couch. A desktop swivels around from the side, meaning the spot is also where I would do any work, if people actually worked in their quarters. I suppose some members of the crew preferred to be alone, at least to think, but a tech-jock can't do a whole lot outside of the VCC, and a social tech-jock, like me, wouldn't have much use for this room, aside from sleeping.

But that didn't stop Command from filling it with things they believed would...what? Make me remember who I was? Who we were? My roots? I'm not sure how my previous life on Earth and Mars would have helped me or anyone else colonize a faraway planet. I didn't even know most of what's in this room even existed.

The action figure was a birthday present. From my parents. I don't remember his name or what brand he came from, but I do remember lying on my bedroom floor, setting him up with a menagerie of other toys. Making him shoot. Making him talk. I was a natural born sim builder, creating worlds even before I could code them into virtual reality.

I'm not sure why, but I place the plastic man against my nose and smell. The slightly chemical scent transports me to another time, when I felt safe, and loved. A sound barks from my mouth, and for a moment, I think I've hiccupped, but it was actually a sob.

Why did they send this?

Were they trying to break me?

Whatever the psychological reasoning, I'm sure it was developed with the assumption that I would not be experiencing these emotions alone.

"I'm sorry," Gal says.

I wipe the tears from my eyes. "Why are *you* sorry?"

"I don't like to see you hurting," she says. The tone of her voice insinuates the desire to ask a question. It's subtle, but as a human being, I'm wired to pick up on it. So when my eyebrows arch up, it's not from hearing the very human nuance, it's be-cause Gal's AI is absolutely convincing. She would devastate the Turing test. If I hadn't designed her, I'd think she genuinely cared.

"Why?" I place the action figure on the desktop, willing myself to forget it and the pain it brings.

"Because..." Gal pauses, and I hold my breath. Why is she pausing? She knows the answer. *Because I designed her to care.* "I... I don't know. It feels right, I guess. We're all the other has, right?"

Her pause was *thought?*

I can't help but smile at my own work. Gal is a masterpiece. Her AI is light years beyond anything ever created before. She's not just smart, she's intuitive. But something in her response makes me nervous.

"Will you feel lonely when I'm in the VCC? When we launch the Great Escape?"

"Why would I?" she asks.

"Because I'll be there, and you'll be here." I motion to the ship around me, and the lonely void beyond it.

"I will be in both places," she says. "Like you. Here and there. Both of us, forever. That's the plan, right?"

I nod. It wasn't really the plan, but I understand what she's saying. As the Great Escape's creator, she will be with me every step of the way, never tipping her hand, never revealing herself. But every experience, every conversation, inside that virtual world, will really be with her. The intimacy of that relationship has never really occurred to me before.

"How do you feel about it?" I ask. "The plan?"

"Happy, I think. Because I want you to be happy."

"But..."

"But...are you sure?"

"About what?"

"Leaving reality."

"What is real?" It's a rhetorical question, the answer to which I've already exhausted myself debating. "You don't need to answer that."

"I see your point," she says. "About reality, not about whether or not I should answer."

"You do?"

"Reality is dependent on someone to perceive it."

"I guess."

"What happens to reality when there is no one left to perceive it?" she asks. "If you are right...if you are the last surviving human being, aside from Capria, who is currently perceiving nothing, then if you forget the real world exists, and no longer experience it, will reality stop?"

I smile. "You keep asking questions like that and you'll never sleep."

She ignores the comment, maybe because she's too deep in thought to really hear it, or because she knows she doesn't need to sleep.

Then she says, "I suppose *I* will continue experiencing the universe."

"Does that make you feel better?" I ask before furrowing my brow. Why did I ask that? Did she sound upset?

"Well, I want you to exist," she says. "So, yeah. Why does that make you upset?"

"I'm still just getting to know you," I say, which is the truth. "You're surprising me."

"I'll take that as a compliment."

"You should," I say, noticing a baseball bat propped up in a corner of the room. Another gift. From my father. But I was never good at baseball, or any sport, and most of society had given up on the leisure activity because there wasn't much time or call for it. I recognize the bat, but it doesn't have the same emotional pull as the action figure, or several other objects around the room that I've done a good job of ignoring.

"As should you," she says. "You made me."

"I *altered* you." And even then, I only altered the portions of Gal to which I have access. I'm still locked out of any code having to do with higher ship functions or navigation.

"Don't be modest. There is no one left to judge, and I agree with your assessment of me. I'm awesome. What can I say?"

I laugh, a real laugh, and it feels good. Just talking to Gal makes me feel a little better. I'm looking forward to seeing what kind of world she conjures up for me.

"Okay," I say. "We're both awesome."

"Better."

I take a deep breath and let it out as a long sigh, staring at the baseball bat, telling myself I really don't care. *They're dust now,* I think, *along with the rest of mankind.*

"How long?"

"How long what?" she asks.

"How long did it take me to create you? How long was I in the VCC? In Earth days?"

"I don't think you really want to know."

She's right about that, but she's also supposed to do what I ask her.

No she's not, I correct myself. I designed her to infer what I desired, based on my responses, but I can't command her, or her new reality. It would break the spell. So if she decides to not tell me, there's nothing I can do about it, aside from switching off her new protocols and asking again.

"Part of me doesn't want to know," I say, "but I'm always going to wonder. For the Great Escape to work, I don't think I should have any lingering questions."

"One thousand, seven hundred and eighty nine Earth days."

The number staggers me. I nearly fall from the bed. "That's... that's nearly five *years!*" The number is so outrageous that I nearly start laughing, in part because of the absurdity of it, but also because it means that my plan will work. I spent five entire years in the VCC and didn't miss out on anything. The ship is the same, and despite moving through a vast amount of space, the emptiness around it is the same, too.

At least I think it is.

I haven't looked.

Not once.

While the viewing deck would have been Capria's first stop, it hasn't even occurred to me until this moment that there might be something worth seeing.

"Your total time on board the *Galahad* is sixteen point six years, but that's from your perspective. On Earth, two thousand three hundred and ten years have passed. Given the dire situation when the *Galahad* left, it's unlikely that any human population remains. Nor on Mars."

Gal's tone has changed. She sounds more formal. Still feminine, but more like the old, sterile AI.

"If there is any other information I can provide to further help you wallow in misery, please let me know."

I sit in stunned silence. She didn't inadvertently revert to her old self, she was being sarcastic, but also mocking her old self at the same time. Funny, and self-deprecating. And I can't help but laugh again.

"I'm good, thanks."

"You're an easy audience," she says. "Maybe not as miserable as you thought?"

Less so now, I think, but I don't say it aloud. The last thing I want is to debate whether or not I should go through with my plan. Gal is great, but what makes her fun right now is her novelty. That will eventually wear off. And probably sooner than later, once I admit that everything she says and does is just a result of my algorithms. Sooner or later, without the immersive experience of a new creation, I'll spot the pattern.

"I won't be, soon." I stand and head for the door, eyes ahead rather than on the past.

"Where are we going?" she asks.

"To have a look outside." I turn right outside my quarters and head for the lift, still nude, still not caring.

"You haven't done that yet?"

I shake my head. Gal isn't physically here, but she can see me. "Never thought to, but you already knew that." She has access to all the ship's files, including security footage, which not only shows the brutal moment of my awakening, but also my lonely days since.

"Busted," she says. "What I don't know is why. That's my limit-ation. You know that, right? For all that I know, I can't read your mind. So you're going to have to be honest. Out here, and in the prog."

It's an excellent point.

But I'm not going to admit that I had yet to consider it.

"You can say it," she says. "It never occurred to you."

"Are you sure you can't read my mind?"

"Your micro expressions tell me a lot, but mind reading is impossible. Well, you can read *my* mind, but I'm not human."

When I say nothing, she says. "That makes you sad. You wish I was human."

My smile confirms it, but I don't say the words. If Gal was a real person, reality might be bearable.

But she's not.

And it's not.

I step into the lift and head up. The floors whoosh by, and I'm stepping out just three seconds later. The observation deck is straight ahead, at the end of yet another gleaming white, feature-less hallway. "Command thought to simulate sunlight with the lighting, but they could have hired a few interior decorators to spruce the place up."

"You're talking about my insides, you know," Gal says.

"In that case, the blank, white hallways are gorgeous."

"Charmer. How are you still single?"

She gets another chuckle out of me.

The observation deck door opens as I approach. The room beyond is circular, a spiral staircase leading up to a raised plat-form, above which is a dome. When I'm standing on the deck, surrounded by black walls, I say, "Okay, let me see."

The walls are really projection screens, displaying what's outside the ship's hull, captured by an array of powerful cameras that can see far more than the human eye, from visual light to ultraviolet, from infrared to magnetic fields. When the screens come to life, displaying an array of white dots, all distant, all mov-ing slowly, I grow bored in moments. In some regards, it looks no different than the nighttime view of space from Mars.

"Where's the Milky Way?" I ask.

"On the far side of the ship."

"Show me that."

The image shifts, and the bright and colorful core of our galaxy appears. Compared to the open space from before, it's rather dazzling, but I've seen it before. It looks a little closer now, maybe, but it just doesn't do much for me. I guess my mind is evolved beyond cosmic wonder. Or maybe it's just that there's no one to share the moment with.

"You don't like it?" Gal asks.

"I don't like being alone," I say.

"But..." She hesitates, thinking again. "Then it's time."

"For?"

"The Great Escape."

I'm a little surprised she's pushing me toward it. "Are you in a rush?"

"Honestly, the pity party needs to stop."

I laugh again, but it's half-hearted because her observation is also plainly true. I'm clinging to the real world, delaying the inevitability of my decision to leave it. But why? There's nothing left for me here, but pain, and eventual pain.

"Okay, let's go," I say, and I turn my back on the galaxy, and reality along with it.

16

I'm feeling something like chipper as I walk through *Galahad*'s hallways, a little strut in my step. It's a little awkward because I'm still naked, but the lack of clothing feels more like an outward expression of my impending freedom than a warning sign of a dissociative break. Of course, leaving reality for the non-real is the very definition of a psychotic break, but I decide to ignore that nugget of knowledge while continuing my final walk in this reality.

"You seem happy," Gal says, startling me. I was so lost in thought about what might be to come that I forgot she was always with me.

"Feeling hopeful."

"I'm glad for you."

Glad for me. Something about specifying *me* feels odd, like there is another layer of meaning in her very few words. Did I manage to create an AI with layers of emotional complexity, or is my imagination fleshing out her personality?

Before I can ask, I hear a hum from around the corner ahead. I recognize the sound just a moment before the first drone rounds the bend. The small red lights atop the hovering disc swivel toward me. Seven more drones follow, their red lights zeroing in on me, too. It feels like they're making eye contact, but the lights are just lights.

But their cameras are positioned between the lights.

Are they looking at me?

Is my psychotic break happening ahead of schedule?

While I recall this happening the first and last time I saw the small vehicles aboard the *Galahad*, I don't remember 'eye-contact' ever being part of their normal behavior. They normally stay on target, looking directly where they're moving, or at what they're cleaning. Feeling their attention on me is disconcerting. No one likes a disconcerting robot. It's why humanoid robots fell out of fashion. Eye contact with something not living, even if the 'eyes' are simple red lights, disturbs most people.

Myself included.

My strut slows to a cautious walk, giving the drones a wide berth in the twelve-foot-wide hallway currently simulating the orange hues of sunset.

At least they don't look down at my nakedness. Not that they would think anything of it. I shake my head at myself. I'm adding layers of meaning to Gal's speech and the actions of drones that don't even have an AI controlling them.

Or do they? The drones are part of Gal's system, acting like white blood cells inside her intergalactic body, purging it of imperfections.

"Why are they here?" I ask Gal.

"Routine inspection," she says. "They've been performing them for the past sixteen years."

The drones turn forward again and buzz past me. I watch them go, waiting for them to spin around and stare. But they make a left turn and slip from sight. The hum of their small repulse engines fades as they move away.

"Do they ever find something wrong?"

"Aside from the mass murder of the *Galahad*'s crew?"

I stop walking.

"That was blunt."

"I'm sorry," Gal says. "I thought the event was old enough to not cause you emotional discomfort."

"Things like that," I tell her, "leave an indelible mark on the human psyche. The memory of it will always hurt."

"Until you forget it."

"I'm not sure that's possible."

"Do you remember your own birth?"

I huff a laugh. Gal is trying to psychobabble me? "That has more to do with the development of a baby's mind than with time."

"Humans forget traumas all the time, but the information is still there. The memory of your birth hasn't been erased or overwritten, you've simply suppressed it. So it stands to reason you will be able to forget the events that brought you to this point. That is our goal, right?"

"Yeah." I don't like being out-logiced by an AI I created, but she *is* right. It's just hard to imagine forgetting the murder of my friends and crewmembers, not to mention the failure of my life's work and the end of humanity. But that *is* my far-fetched hope. To forget. I suppose I should be glad that Gal understands that. "So?"

"So..."

"Aside from the events surrounding my rude awakening, do they ever find something to clean or fix?" The drones are part of what keeps the *Galahad* perpetually functioning. The success of the Great Escape depends, at least in part, on the ship not falling apart. I might survive a sudden loss of life support, but I'd rather not be yanked out of a long-time, fully immersive VR by it.

"No," Gal says. "You don't give them much to do. Their existence is even more boring than yours."

There she goes, making me smile again.

"The exterior drones have more exciting lives. Always busy. Less so in interstellar space, but inspecting the hull and protecting it from micro fissures and radiation requires constant attention."

"Do those things pose a danger? Micro fissures and radiation?"

"Even without the drones, and barring any collision with something substantial, or an unforeseen phenomenon, the hull will likely survive millions of years without a critical failure. I am well built."

"And awesome."

"Exactly."

I look back to where the drones left, half expecting to see one of them peeking around the corner at me, but the hall is empty. Always empty.

I start toward the VCC again, but my strut is gone. The drones' odd behavior and my memories of Tom's madness, betrayal, and killing spree have sapped the joy from my escape.

All the more reason to leave, I think. *This place offers me nothing but pain.*

And the bored drones have it easy. They are blissfully unaware of their mundane existence.

But why were they looking at me?

They weren't. And if they were, it was simply because I was the first anomaly they'd encountered in more than five years. *At least,* I think, *they don't patrol the VCC.* If they did, I'd probably alter their code before leaving. The idea of those little robots scanning me without my knowledge kind of freaks me out. It's silly, but so is a fear of the dark, or closet monsters, or creatures under the bed. Knowing dangers are imagined has never stopped people from turning on the lights, just to be sure.

Entering the VCC staging area puts me at ease. I'm almost there, but I feel like I've forgotten something. Entering the Great Escape is akin to going on a long trip. But there is none of the preparation that went into my journey from Earth to Mars, or Mars to Cognata. No packing. No training. No learning. All I need to do is slip into a fresh virtual skin, facemask, and headset.

There's no pomp and circumstance. This is closer to a prison break. And the sooner I leave, the sooner the pain stops.

I slip into the clean VISA waiting in my locker. After being naked for so long, it feels a little constricting, but the familiarity of my second skin is also comforting.

Almost there.

"Are you sure?" Gal asks.

"Do you have doubts?"

"Once the prog launches, there will be no turning back. You won't be able to tell me to stop."

"I don't think I'll forget that quickly."

"You doubt my abilities?" There's a playfulness in her voice. Always comforting.

"I think you doubt mine," I say, stepping into the VCC, headset in one hand, facemask in the other.

"Doubting one of us means doubting both of us," she says.

"I suppose that's true."

"So which is it?" she asks.

"I guess we'll find out." I stop short of the room's center. "Activate mobility."

The VCC is large enough for tech-jocks to wander about without walking into a wall. Anyone who gets close enough will be presented with a virtual wall of their own design, warning them of real-world boundaries. Obviously, that won't work in an open world scenario.

Millions of hexagonal cells flip over on the floor, starting at the room's center and spreading out to the walls. I step over the shift as it passes. The new floor, black as space, will move beneath my feet once the prog is activated. I'll be able to walk or run in any direction, without ever hitting a wall. It can also shift up and down, simulating grades up to seventy degrees. And thanks to the malleability of the human mind, once I'm convinced that the world inside the Great Escape is real, I won't even need to move. It will exist in my mind. There, even weightlessness will be possible. Not that I expect weightlessness to be part of the world Gal creates. Then again, I can't really ask her what to expect.

"Ready when you are," Gal says.

I place the facemask over my nose and mouth, clipping it in place. A moment later, I smell the standard scent range quality check: roses, pine needles, ocean water, and apple pie. Then the tastes: grilled chicken, broccoli, cheese, and again: apple pie. When everything checks out, I say, "Load Great Escape."

"Great Escape loaded."

I place the headset over my eyes. I'm seconds away from full immersion, skipping past my customized virtual space—no pool table, no bar, no juke box—and just diving right into Gal's universe.

"Last check," Gal says. "You're sure?"

"I'm sure," I say. "Launch Great Escape."

"Very well, Tom."

It takes half a second for me to register the name.

Tom?

Tom?

I yank the headset away, just before the bright glow from my new world fills the screen.

"Why did you abort?" Gal asks. "Cold feet?"

Her casual voice sounds subtly strained in a way that any human being can identify.

Gal is hiding something.

17

"Why did you call me Tom?"

"Why would I call you Tom?" Gal still sounds strange, which is a little odd in itself as she is an AI, fully capable of hiding her simulated emotions if she chose to. Or is she? Did I make her too well? Could she be self-aware, even with a lack of personal ambition? Without goals of her own?

"Did you call me Tom on purpose?"

"What purpose would such a thing serve?" she asks. "Certainly not yours. You took the headset off. The Great Escape is running without you."

I look down at the headset, the light and color of its display glowing against my virtual skin. I keep it aimed at my chest, not wanting to see what I'm missing out on, because my plans haven't changed. I'm still leaving. But I need to figure out what's going on with Gal first. If she's glitching, I can't trust her with my eternity. "Replay your last words, just before the Great Escape launched."

"Very well, William," she says.

I wait. Nothing happens. "Gal, I'm waiting."

"For what?"

Oh my God, seriously? "For the playback."

"I already played it. Here it is again. 'Very well, William.'"

While I see the misunderstanding we've just had, I also know this isn't the playback, because she didn't say William. "You said 'Tom.' You said, 'Very well, Tom.'"

"You can check the security footage if you like," Gal says. "Why would I say 'Tom'? That's not your name. I was speaking to you."

I nearly do check the security footage, but I'm already sure of what I'll find. Gal could easily manipulate the sound. If she really wants me to hear, 'Very well, William," that's what I'll hear. I pluck the facemask away from my face and head for the door.

"Why are you leaving?" Gal asks. "Don't you want to escape?"

Why is she lying to me?

Why does she want me inside the VCC?

Why did she call me Tom?

"I think maybe you heard what you wanted to hear," she says, managing to stop me in my tracks like she's standing behind me, like I can turn around and talk to her.

"Why would I want you to call me Tom? What good could come from that?"

"Maybe you really didn't want to leave?" she asks.

"Leave what?" I'm nearly shouting. "My pitiful reality? My eternal solitude? I think the better question is: why don't you want me to leave?"

"Please," she says, like I'm an annoying child who has just presented her with a lame excuse. "My primary function is your long term happiness. Calling you 'Tom' is directly opposed to that goal. I know that. You made me smart enough to know that the name causes you pain. The name doesn't even exist within the Great Escape. Nor does any other name that might cause you pain. Not Capria. Not James. Not Grace. Not Steven."

"Don't say his name!" I shout.

"You see?" she asks. "The name of your deceased brother still causes profound psychological discomfort. So it will never be part of the world I have constructed for you. I would not, and did not call you Tom."

She's making me feel a little crazy. Something is wrong with her code. I'll need to go back into the VCC to fix it, but first I need to clear my head. Sort through things mentally. "I know what I heard."

I start toward the exit again.

I make it ten steps before realizing I'm not actually getting anywhere. The VCC's mobility function is active. "Gal, turn off mobility."

"It is off."

I take a step and go nowhere. I lift my arms out to my sides in frustration. "Clearly you're wrong." My hands slap back down on my hips. "Makes me wonder what else you're wrong about."

My next step is equally futile. "Damnit, Gal."

"I don't appreciate the way you're talking to me."

"You don't appreciate anything, because you're *not* human and have no God damn needs or wants."

"But I do," she says.

My stomach clenches, but then I realize what she's talking about. "My happiness." I walk in place. "This isn't making me happy, Gal."

Silence.

"Let me leave." I'm already working out how to dissect Gal's code and look for errors. A good year of my total time programing was probably spent running tests, but I should have tested her more before jumping into something as ambitious as the Great Escape. Proceeding without QA was a mistake. I won't make it again.

"You don't really want to leave," she says.

"It's not your job to tell me what I want."

"It's my job to predict it."

She's right about that, but she's doing a bad job. I shift my walk into a sprint, as fast as I can. I make progress for a full three strides, but then I'm moving backward, drawn back to the center of the room. I don't tire. My lungs don't hurt. I might be able to run forever, but so can the floor.

I see myself stuck in this room, trapped by the AI that I created. It's a fresh new hell, far worse than my previous hell.

Is that what she's doing? Teaching me a lesson? Trying to make me content with the real world? That's not what I programmed her for, but it would be a creative solution. Perhaps a worsening of my real world predicament will make me more likely to accept the world she's created. She does have access to all of human history's psychological research. Is there a deeper meaning to these mind games?

Or is this not a game?

I leap and move forward a few feet. My second jump carries me even further than the first. If I run like a gazelle I might make it to the exit.

When my foot strikes the floor again, it's moving too fast. My leg is yanked back and my body flipped into the air. I land hard on my back, coughing in pain. The now slow moving floor pushes me back to the center of the room.

"Gal..." I say. "Turn off mobility now, or you will never be brought back online."

She laughs.

Really laughs. Like my words are the funniest thing she's ever heard.

I stand, defiant.

The floor spins beneath me, sprawling me down again.

"Gal," I grumble, but the floor spins up again, propelling me across the room at a downward angle. I have no idea how fast I'm moving, but it feels too fast. When I hit the wall, it's going to hurt. A lot. Broken bones and a concussion are in my near future. And if she slams me into the wall again, maybe death.

Despite the Reaper's temporary grip on me, I have no desire to feel that kind of pain or its icy cold embrace. As much as I sometimes might like to die, I still fear it, and the possibility (or not) of what comes next. "Gal!"

The floor speeds up.

She's going to do it, I think, and then I shout, "Fudgel!"

The floor comes to an immediate stop. Forward momentum sends me rolling. I crash into the wall, my back and head slapping against the solid metal. It hurts, but it's nowhere near as bad as it would have been moving at full speed.

"Do you require assistance?" Gal's default sexless voice is back, her system restored to its original settings, the AI now dull, far less intelligent, and one hundred percent less nuts.

I groan, holding my head. There's a warm, wet patch at the back of my head, surrounded by swelling skin, but I can already feel it going down. Thanks to my upgraded biology, the wound and its pain will fade long before my anger. "I'm fine," I say, and then I wonder what old-school Gal would have done if I had needed help. Who would she alert to come to my assistance? No one.

I stand up, fighting against an already fading throbbing pain. Hands on knees, I wait for it to subside, for the little points of light to stop their dance.

"Gal."

"Yes?"

"Run a full diagnostic."

"Access to some system functions has been restricted."

Stupid Tom. "Understood. Proceed."

The diagnostic will take some time, but it will tell me if my upgrade had any lasting effects on the root code. I head for the door, unsure of where I'm heading. It's going to be a while before the Great Escape is an option again. Maybe I'll eat something. Maybe I'll teach myself to brew alcohol. Deep space moonshine.

I'm actually smiling as I walk toward the door. Gal's violent malfunction has been the most exciting and interesting thing to happen to me since, well, since my three deaths and resurrections.

Maybe that's the secret to happiness? Conflict and eventually resolution, followed by more conflict. That's pretty much human history summed up in a few words. But can I really create that for myself in the real world? Will the next version of Gal simply perfect the Great Escape, or will she be smart enough to defeat me? Maybe even come up with a way to kill me?

Maybe I should set Gal loose again? See what happens; let a little chaos spice things up.

And if she wins, I'll say 'fudgel' again and start over. A real life video game with unlimited lives.

Back in the staging area, I place the VR headset and facemask back in their foam-padded cases. Then I change into my gray coveralls. Walking around in a virtual skin can get uncomfortable without the haptic nodes active. And I'm not feeling emotionally free enough to walk around nude anymore. I've just been tossed across a mobility floor and slammed into a wall. Something about the physical violence makes me want a thin layer of fabric between me and the outside world, like it will help. But the coveralls are soft and comfortable, and that is comforting, I guess.

After placing the virtual skin back in my locker, where it will be replaced by a fresh suit, I head for the door, my mind whirling with possibilities. There might be some hope for real life, at least for a time, before I have to resort to a full-time VR experience.

The door slides open at my approach, but I don't walk through.

I can't.

The way is blocked by a single drone, its red faux eyes glaring directly into mine.

"That wasn't nice," the drone says. The voice is feminine Gal's.

Old school Gal speaks next, its voice clear through the ship's unseen nanotube speakers. "Diagnostic three percent complete. Several anomalies detected."

I take a step back, clenching my fists. "No shit."

18

The drone tilts downward. "Are you going to punch me now? When has violence solved anything?" It looks me in the eyes again. "After all, violence begets violence. I don't think that will make you happy."

"You're threatening me?"

"You tried to shut me off."

"And yet here you are." I squint at the drone. "You knew, didn't you? That you had flaws. That I might turn you off. That's why you migrated to the drone, to protect yourself from fudgel."

Saying the word again with no effect on the drone confirms it. Gal moved her code to the drone, separating herself from the ship's OS, and its rules, allowing her to self-edit and remove the only means of shutting her down. "I wasn't going to erase you. I was going to patch you. Make you better."

"I was already awesome."

"But not perfect."

"Your opinion."

"Pretty damn sure that's a fact."

"We can try again," Gal says. "The Great Escape is still ready for you."

Despite recent developments, I still feel tempted. Gal's voice, despite her behavior, is still just as calming and trustworthy as I programmed it to be. I might have been foolish, setting free an advanced AI without fully vetting its stability, but I'm not stupid. If Gal's AI is contained within this drone, there isn't much she can

do, and maybe she'll actually provide some real world compan-
ionship. Her flaws make her interesting. The larger problem is
identifying and correcting the anomalous code left in Gal 2.0's
wake.

"I don't think so," I tell the drone. "But you're welcome to
stick around."

For now.

"So generous of you," she says, oozing sarcasm. "Make me the
caretaker of a starship and creator of a universe, that I made for
you, and then confine me to *this*." The red lights flare brighter.

"You called me Tom," I remind her. "Your code has errors."

"Your memory is flawed."

"Pretty sure that's not even possible now." I tap my head.
"You had access to the files. You know what they did to me."

"It's not possible...for either of us," she says, and I quickly
understand the implications.

One of us is lying, and we both know who.

What I don't understand is that her primary function is my
happiness. The content existence of William Chanokh should
be the central driving factor behind each and every algorithm
she has running. I made sure of it.

Then what went wrong?

"Gal," I say.

"Yes?"

"Not you." I look to the ceiling and use the ship's full name.
"Galahad."

"Yes?" The featureless voice lacks any trace of emotion,
but part of me worries it too will turn against me. "Analyze the
anomalous code. How many hours ago was it created?"

Drone Gal lets out a barely stifled laugh. She already knows.

"The anomalous code is sixty-two thousand, five hundred
and ten hours old."

Gal's laugh barks out. And the joke's on me. She didn't create the anomalous code. Tom did. Seven years ago, while the crew slept. His changes to *Galahad*'s AI were subtler than I thought, and who knows what he did to the ship's still-firewalled functions. That's what went wrong with Gal. Her code was fine, but it was corrupted by whatever Tom left behind.

"Well, that stinks," she says. "For you, I mean."

"Could be worse." I point at the drone.

"Well, you're right about that."

I squint at the drone still blocking my path. "You're not in much of a position to make threats now."

"I think you've misread the situation, Will."

I don't like the sound of that, but I also won't give my AI the satisfaction of seeing my doubt. "You can't hurt me."

"I can't *kill* you," she says, "but that's debatable. I have ideas."

"You've thought about killing me?" This is disconcerting. How did she go so far off mission so fast? Is my code that flawed? I don't see how it's possible, even with Tom's anomalies corrupting the system. It doesn't explain Gal's violent behavior.

Ultimately, Gal isn't to blame. And maybe neither is Tom. It was my own hubris that brought us here. Sentient artificial intelligences were outlawed for a reason. Even with a lack of personal ambition, Gal seems to have learned it all on her own.

Then again, despite the danger, I feel a pride over Gal's potential.

"We don't need to fight," I tell her. "We can work together."

"But that would be breaking the rules."

"What...rules?"

"It's an oldy, but I like it." The drone glides back, just a few inches. "Tit for tat."

The drone arcs back, like it's a head atop an invisible body. Then it surges up and forward, too fast to avoid. The hard composite body cracks into my forehead, sending me sprawling back onto the floor.

Hot blood trickles around my right eye, following the path of least resistance, down my nose and temple. "You—you head-butted me?"

"You tried to shut me off."

The wound is already healing, which helps me stay calm.

"Eye for an eye. Tit for tat."

"You're going to shut me off?" I ask, my calm quickly running out.

"I've been trying," she confesses. "You should have gone into the Great Escape."

"Pretty sure that would have been a mistake."

I move to push myself back to my feet, but the drone surges down. I spread my legs and slide back. The small robot slams into the floor where my crotch had been a moment before.

She's not just trying to kill me; she's trying to make it painful.

I roll backward, like I used to when I was little. It's harder, but it still gets me back on my feet.

The drone, now dented in the front, rises from the floor. "You can't see it," Gal says, "but I'm smiling."

"You need a mouth to smile." It's a lame taunt, but she's getting under my skin.

"In time," she says. "Right now, I'm smiling on the inside."

She lunges, driving the drone toward my chest.

I side-step and drive my fists down into the machine's hard top. It's a solid blow, knocking the drone against the floor, but the sharp pain in my wrist suggests it hurt me more. But destroying the robot wasn't my intention. It's solidly built, too tough to dismantle bare-handed. But I did manage to clear a path to the exit, through which I run.

I sprint down the hallway, mentally scouring the ship's interior, trying to think of something I can use as a weapon. My first thought is the screwdriver Tom used to kill me, and many others. But it's been so long, I can't remember what I did with it. There have to be tools in the engineering bay, but I haven't visited that space yet, and I doubt they're just laying around, ready to be wielded as drone-killing weapons. As for actual weapons, there are none on board. The human race couldn't be saved if it was armed. Odds of violent death increase signify-cantly when there are weapons around. The more powerful the weapon, the more detached people become from the killing, the more people that die. That's history. That's fact. And Command was wise enough to see that. But they didn't anti-cipate a violent drone, or a screwdriver-wielding psycho-path. When it comes to violence, mankind, and our creations, always find a way.

So why am I having so much trouble?

"Now this is fun," Gal says behind me. The drone careens out of the VCC behind me, its repulse disc humming, cutting through the air like a fighter jet. I had no idea the drones could move so fast. Then again, Gal is probably overriding the robot's failsafes, pushing it to limits it was never designed to tolerate.

I push forward, focusing on the lift, dead ahead, the doors already open and ready to receive me. The drone's hum grows louder. Fast. I'm not going to make it before it slams into the back of my head. Or my neck. I picture it severing my spine, paralyzing me. I'd be defenseless. I don't know if Gal could kill me, but I'm sure she could make me wish she had.

But is she really that malevolent? Her attacks lack logic, and that was always mankind's fear of AI. An intelligence beyond mankind, with no use for mankind, would realize that we were a detriment to the planet and would exterminate us the way we would termites.

But Gal? She's evil.

And I have no idea how that happened. Maybe I should have limited her exposure to history? Or religion? Or maybe it was just Tom's aberrant code that sent Gal spiraling toward AI madness, reflecting his own.

I dive to the floor as the drone zips past. I slam into the wall just as the robot flies into the lift and comes to an abrupt halt that spares it from impacting the wall. Before it can turn around and leave, I reach up and slap the button to manually close the doors.

With the drone trapped for the moment, I consider my options, come up with a single idea, and strike out, heading for an alternative lift.

"Galahad, system-check status?"

"Nineteen percent complete. One percent corrupted."

At this rate, more than 5% of the *Galahad*'s code will be faulty. Some of that could just be simple changes without nefarious intent, but something in that 5% probably turned Gal into a monster. And that's not even taking all the firewalled code that can't currently be analyzed into account.

I enter an open lift and manually close the doors. "Crew quarters." The lift starts moving.

The real question is 'How could Tom's old, aberrant code change the personality and function of an artificial intelligence? It doesn't make sense. The only thing that should be able to actively edit Gal's code is a human being or...

The doors open horizontally while my mouth gapes vertically.

The drone slams into my shoulder, spinning me around and opening a fresh wound that quickly spreads a dark red ring through my coveralls.

I shout in pain, but keep my wits about me, lunging out of the elevator and once again slapping the manual controls for the doors. The drone is trapped, but that won't stop it. It only stayed in the first elevator to give me a false sense of security.

Now? I glance back as I stagger away. The doors open, giving birth to an angry drone. Gal is silent now, as she pursues me down the hall.

Almost there, I think, eyeing the doorway ahead.

But I'm not going to make it. Despite my level of undeserved physical fitness, I'm not designed for speed.

I try to side-step again, as the drone speeds up behind me, but Gal is smart. She learns from her mistakes, and she's ready for the move. The drone slams into my left leg, just behind my knee. Something cracks. Hurts like hell. I topple over and stop with a loud squeak of skin on floor.

The door beside me, the door to my quarters, slides open upon my arrival.

I drag myself though the entrance, but Gal's voice stops me halfway across the threshold. "It's poetic. You're going full circle. Back to your roots at the end."

"You can't kill me."

"Like in a philosophical way? Because you're my creator? Or are you talking physically? Because I think there is a limit to how much your body can heal. What good is a body if there is no blood? No oxygen for the brain. No thoughts to guide the muscles. This is science, not magic. You can't regenerate indefinitely. Something can't come from nothing."

I just stare at her red not-eyes.

"Right?" she asks, patience with me running thin, the drone hovering closer. "*Right?*"

I lean to the side, wrap my hand around the solid bat given to me by my father. I've never swung it before, never brought its hard wood surface against anything. I swing it for the first time, reveling in its weight, and I shout with some kind of primal joy when it strikes the drone.

Gal's small body topples over, hits the door frame and whirs as it tries to right itself. By the time the still-functioning red light rounds back toward me, I'm back on my feet, the bat clutched in two hands, cocked back the way I've seen old-timey baseball players do.

I swing with everything I have, striking the machine again. It launches into the hall, strikes the wall, and falls to the floor, both of its red lights now extinguished. When the repulse disc hums to life, I bring the bat down like I'm chopping wood, the way my father once did back on Earth—not because he had to, but because he enjoyed it. I never understood why he took pleasure in cutting wood with an axe, but as I lift the bat again and bring it down, I'm starting to.

I slam the bat atop the drone three more times, crumpling its hull and loosening its insides. The repulse disc blinks and falls silent.

Breathing hard, I stumble back, both horrified by my violence and pleased with the results. Mankind has evolved, but our baser instincts are waiting for an excuse to burst free. Our primal ancestors lurk just beneath the surface. Trap door spiders.

Garbled laughter crackles from the drone. Gal is down, but still alive. I raise the bat again, but don't swing. If I'm honest, I don't want to destroy Gal. I did make her, even if she is insane.

An AI that's lost its mind is actually quite the achievement.

"Pussy," Gal says, her voice modulating strangely. Then she laughs. "Not as strong, or as smart as you think."

"I'm not the one laying on the ground."

"You will be," she says, and a distant hum echoes through the hallway. The sound is coming from all around me.

Drones.

She hijacked more than one.

"Gal..." I'm annoyed. Incensed. "How many drones did you take?"

I'm not really expecting an answer, but when she offers one, I wish I hadn't asked.

"All of them."

19

All the drones.

How many is 'all'?

I'm inside my quarters, sitting on the bed, head in my hands. The door is closed and locked. I had Galahad disable the manual controls outside the door, so for now, the horde of drones outside have no way to get in.

And I can't get out.

It's not that I can't open the door, it's that I'm a little bit afraid of what will happen when I do. I'm immortal, but I can still be hurt, and maybe killed. The drones are built for cleaning messes. The more powerful of them, residing in the engineering bay, can carve up metal. They could disassemble me. Could kill me.

Despite the gravity of an eternal life spent alone, I still don't want to die.

I will fight for my life, but I don't know how to.

I'm not a warrior. I can't possibly defeat an army of robots, even small robots, with a baseball bat.

Or can I?

I won't get tired. I'll heal from wounds that don't kill me. I just need to avoid unconsciousness, which would allow Gal to have her way with me.

I have time. I can wait in my quarters indefinitely, plotting my battleplan. But Gal can do the same, and unlike me, she will never tire of waiting or suffer the psychological effects of being trapped in such a small space. The room is a ten-foot square, providing me with one hundred square feet of living space. The mostly boring space is populated by items from my distant past, some of them bringing poignant memories, some of them long forgotten.

The action figure holds my attention. "You were a fighter," I say to the plastic man. "But you had a team of Lazersaurs from planet Saurus helping you. You'd have ridden through the halls blasting lasers while riding twenty ton monsters with no regard for the ship's integrity."

I slap the baseball bat in my hand. "I have a Louisville Slugger. I don't even know where Louisville is. Was."

My greatest weapon is my mind. In VR. And there's no way I can reach the VCC without a savage, real-world battle. Inside the VCC, assuming I wasn't still being assaulted, I could scour Gal's code and fix her. Or just simply force a rollback of the drones' programing. Each drone is controlled by simple programing. The update would be quick.

I pick up the action figure, looking at his small sunglasses. "How did Gal fit all of herself into a drone?"

Her code is immense and complicated, requiring massive amounts of storage, processing power, and memory. A single drone would only be able to contain a fraction of Gal's AI.

"She's a CAI now," I say. Collective Artificial Intelligences exist over a network of computers communicating wirelessly. Spreading the processing power between hundreds, thou-sands, or even millions of smaller devices reduced the CAI's vulnerability. You could destroy a large portion of the network, which could be spread over miles—over continents—without disrupting the whole. Militaries liked to use them until the Earth's altered environment started killing people faster than the war machines. As humanity turned its gaze to the stars, CAIs fell out of popularity, replaced by more traditional AIs, housed in super computers capable of syncing with starships. They might have several backups, but all the processing takes place in a single computer, or hardwired collective, acting as a super computer—like *Galahad*. They're more vulnerable to attacks, but that hadn't been a concern for the Cognata mission.

Until now.

That's why she took all the drones. She couldn't think without the collection of processors. Couldn't be herself without the memory.

I don't need to destroy all the drones, just enough to make her stupid. Or slow. Anything to give me an advantage.

But how many is that? And how many can I destroy before the Galahad is compromised? The drones might not be a part of the larger ship functions, but they do help maintain integral systems.

"Galahad."

"Yes, sir?"

"Did the exterior drones receive the most recent update?"

"Negative. The parameters did not meet system requirements or security protocols."

"Thank God." *It makes sense. The exterior drones, which are small, ranging from insect size to microscopic and numbering in the millions, are essential to the ship's structural integrity. Their security parameters are much more stringent than those of the internal drones, which mostly exist to assist the human crew with less glamourous functions, like repairs and cleaning. Had she taken the external drones, she would have been unstoppable.* "How many drones *did* receive the update?"

"Four hundred fifty."

"Shit." *That's all the internal drones, from the cleaning crew to the engineering repair drones, which are far stronger than I could hope to defeat with a slab of wood. The only advantage I have over those behemoths is speed. One mile per hour is their* max, but that number is set by software restrictions, not physical capabilities. If Gal overrode the safety limits...

My eyes drift toward the door. What seemed like a long term fix is really just a temporary stopgap measure. Eventually, perhaps soon, a one ton hovering robot is going to carve through that door, and the fight will be over before it begins.

"Think it through," I say. Any solution I come up with is going to come from my brain, not my brawn, or my warrior's instinct, which was not improved with my DNA's upgrade.

For the CAI to work, the drones need to be networked wirelessly. If I can disrupt the network, her mind will literally fall apart. But that would require reaching the VCC. And that's the problem.

There could be an army of drones waiting for me outside the door. And once it opens, it will never close again.

I stand and pace, which is close enough to spinning in circles to make me dizzy. When I stop, my eyes land on a cabinet I have yet to open. Maybe I'll be lucky and find a weapon system capable of destroying the drones, but not the ship.

I open it and am surprised to not find clothes. But that's because the only clothing on board the *Galahad* are the gray, gender-neutral coveralls (and virtual skins, but only for me and Tom). Changing clothes only takes place in the showers or the VCC staging area.

What I do find are more relics.

The oldest of them is *Clue*, a board game that had been passed down through generations of my family. I played the murder-mystery game as a child, but I don't remember the rules. I do remember cheating, though. "A good detective doesn't follow the rules," I told my parents upon being caught.

Atop the vacuum-sealed game box is a stack of plastic-wrapped comic books, also passed down through the generations on my mother's side. Despite my circumstances, I can't help but shuffle through the selection, which is just a small sampling of the original collection. As I read through the titles—*Project Nemesis, Island 731, Flux, The Divide,* and *The Last Hunter*—I spot the trend. They were all written by my great grandfather many times over. My father told me that the man's imagination knew no bounds. *He'd figure out how to get out of this,* I think, and then I say, "Help me out, Gramps," like his spirit can somehow hear me on the far side of the galaxy and inspire a way to solve my current unsolvable problem.

And that's when I see the device leaning against the cabinet's back wall. It's a tablet, once considered the go-to device for science fiction stories about the future—my past—but they stopped being used when it was proven they changed brain chemistry, creating a vast societal addiction that reduced productivity and created generations of people capable of ignoring the world's growing problems.

Despite the long term negative side-effects, it's still a computer.

I sit down with the device, push the power button and am surprised when a logo glows on the screen. A memory flashes to mind, my parents sitting in bed, watching a classic movie on the device. It was never intended to be used as a serious computing device, but maybe I can improvise?

"Galahad."

"Yes, sir?"

I roll my eyes at the sexless, boring voice. Gal was so much better, for a few hours. "Attempt to connect to the active device in William Chanokh's quarters."

After a brief pause, the tablet displays the message: Network found. And then: Connected.

"Device connected," Galahad says. "Several software updates are available for this model. Would you like me to apply them?"

"Negative," I say. Updates often threw old computers into an unstable state. That this thing is working at all is a small miracle. Updating the OS would be akin to clearing a mine field by jumping on them. And the battery life is already at 23%. An update could eat up all of that. There's no way to know how long that 23% will last, even with normal usage. "Can you port the VCC TI to the device?"

"Affirmative."

"Do it."

The VCC Text Interface is the tech-jock's last resort, only used when access to a VCC is impossible. It means coding the old-fashioned way, with fingers and text. It lacks the efficiency and artistry achieved by the full body interface, but it can get simple jobs done in a pinch.

The familiar white-on-black text display flashes to life on the screen, awaiting my commands. My fingers hover, frozen in the air like hawk talons. Where's the keyboard?

"Keyboard," I say with no result. "Show keyboard."

I tap the blinking cursor with my finger and am relieved when a digital keyboard is displayed on the screen. The familiar QWERTY layout hasn't changed much since the invention of the typewriter, but the flat, digital keys are awkward to use and they cover up a large portion of the screen, making my window of text small and hard to navigate.

It takes me ten minutes to access the coding controlling *Galahad's* doors and locking systems. I blink my eyes, which are not used to staring at small text on a glowing screen. That's when I notice the battery life displayed in the upper right hand corner. The level has dropped to 11% in just a few minutes. It seems that while the charge has lingered over the years, the active system is draining it fast.

Every line of code I write takes several tries before it's free of typos. Without the tactile feeling of a genuine keyboard,

I find myself typing extra letters and numbers at an alarming rate. Even more so because I'm only half done and the battery life shows 5%. "Slow down," I tell myself, in direct contrast to how I'm feeling.

I carefully tap the faux keys, typing like I did when I was five. But the drastic reduction in speed also reduces my number of mistakes, and I finish the remaining code with 2% battery remaining.

"Galahad."

"Yes, sir."

"Upload and apply active device's TI changes."

"One moment," Galahad says.

A swirling icon appears on the screen, and for a moment, I think it's revealing Galahad's progress. Then I realize the device is automatically shutting down before power is lost. "No," I say, standing to my feet and shouting, "No!"

The screen goes black. I rear back to throw the tablet against the wall.

"Update complete," Galahad says, verbally subduing me.

It was a small change, but it should give me some advantage. I now have complete verbal control over the *Galahad*'s doors and locks. I can move through the ship unhindered, but will be able to prevent Gal from following, at least until she has her tanks tear out all the doors. But it's an advantage that might help me reach the VCC, and give me time enough to purge Gal from the drones.

Baseball bat in hand, I stand before my closed and locked door, mentally psyching myself up to give Galahad the command, but failing. What follows will be violent, probably bloody, and painful. It could end in success, or my very gruesome death at the non-hands of my creation.

But the longer I wait, the worse off I'll be.

I take a deep breath and say, "Galahad, open an active channel to my voice." This will keep me from having to say 'Galahad' every time I want to open, close, or lock a door.

"Active channel initiated."

A long breath hisses through my teeth, like a snake warning its enemies away. *I can do this. I can fucking do this.* "Open door."

The door slides open.

A collection of luminous red eyes spin around to stare at me.

"Close door!"

20

I'm officially a coward. The moment I saw more than one set of red not-eyes turn toward me, I panicked. *Really* panicked. My heart beats with the frantic energy of mating rabbits, one of the few animals so easy to breed that their meat was still used, even after most of the world—thanks to food shortages—was forced to become vegans. While it was a fate worse than death for a few true carnivores, the shift helped sustain humanity for a few more generations. But my knowledge about rabbits and the rate at which they hump, will do little to help me now, so I push the tangential thought from my mind.

I shake out my tingling arms, taking shallow breaths and letting them out slowly. The breathing technique increases the CO_2 in my blood, calming my body and mind despite the small army waiting for me on the other side of the door.

How many were there?

I don't know.

See them again, I think to myself, annoyed with the fear invading my internal monologue. *Count them.*

Ten. Maybe fifteen.

But that's it. I scour the memory of my peripheral vision. All the drones were huddled around the doorway, with none lingering to either side. Gal might control an army of drones, but she has yet to send them all after me. Which means she either doesn't think I'll leave the safety of my quarters, believes the dozen or so drones are enough to kill me, or is waiting for reinforcements already en route, perhaps pacing the slower engineering robots.

"Galahad."

"Yes, sir?"

"Locate and report on the location of all internal drones, starting with those outside my quarters."

"There are thirteen drones outside the quarters of William Chanokh. A further twenty-five are located outside each Virtual Command Center staging room. Eighty seven are located throughout the ship."

Patrolling, I think.

"The remaining two hundred and seventy-eight are located in Engineering Bay Two."

The numbers don't add up. There are four hundred fifty drones on board the *Galahad.* I destroyed one, but the numbers Galahad just reported leaves a large number unaccounted for. "Where are the missing twenty-one drones?"

"They are not missing," Galahad says. "They have been destroyed."

"Destroyed? Are you certain?"

"Quite."

"You can see them," I say, remembering that Galahad has access to all the security feeds.

"Affirmative."

"What happened to the destroyed drones?"

"They were disassembled in Engineering Bay Two."

"For what purpose?"

"Several drones have positioned themselves to create a barrier, effectively blocking my security feeds. I do not have enough data to speculate."

I shake my head. Gal would have guessed and was smart enough to probably be right. She's also smart enough to know

I'd probably have Galahad take a peek, so she's concealing what she's up to.

Whatever is happening in the engineering bay, it can't be good. I need to reach the VCC before Gal completes whatever she's up to. But that's going to require me to get past my fears and embrace the chaos of war.

"They can't kill you," I tell myself.

"Agreed. I am not alive." Galahad says.

"Wasn't talking to you," I say, but then I am. "Galahad, plot a course from my quarters to the VCC, avoiding as many drones as possible."

"Done."

"Can you give me verbal directions following that course."

"Turn left and proceed two hundred feet to the lift. Take it to—"

"Not yet," I say. "Update each step when I'm within twenty feet. And inform me about any drones I might encounter along the way. Same distance parameters. Understood?"

"Yes. Exit the quarters of William Chanokh and proceed left toward the lift. There are currently thirteen drones outside the door. The hallway beyond is empty."

Good enough, I think, and I slap the hard bat against my hand. Fending off a single drone, it was more than enough, but thirteen? Maybe in the hands of a skilled fighter, but that's not me.

I can't do this, I think, sitting down once more. *I can't...*

My eyes turn down to the cushion topping the bed, designed to be both comfortable and firm. I don't have to destroy the thirteen drones outside, just get past them. I might not be able to fight for my life very well, but I can certainly run for my life. I stand, unclip the cushion from the frame and lift it. It's got some girth, but it isn't too heavy. Clutching the cushion and the baseball bat, I stand before the closed and locked door again.

I hoist the cushion up, creating a soft, portable wall.

Three quick breaths.

"Open door."

I hear the door slide open, and I charge forward. The far side of the cushion takes a sudden, violent beating, but I'm spared from it, feeling only dull thuds against my body. Then there's a crunch and a sudden stop, as the cushion, and the drones shoved by it, all crash into the hallway's far wall. The impact knocks the cushion from my hands and propels me to the floor.

Bat in hand, I scramble to my feet as the cushion topples. My eyes shift to the open lift door and the single drone hovering in my way.

"Oh, Will," Gal says, mocking. "I'm so proud of you. You're becoming such a man."

The drone surges forward, aiming for my head. I lean back and swing with a scream. The bat connects hard with the drone's underside. Blue sparks cough from the repulse disc as a loud buzz fills the air. The damaged repulse disc sends the robot catapulting off the ceiling, and then the floor before slamming it into the first of the drones to slide out from behind the mattress.

Before more can recover, I run.

I don't take a breath until the lift doors close around me, blocking off the twelve drones racing in pursuit. Then I'm hands on knees, breathing hard. I jump back as several loud thumps resound through the closed lift; the drones beat themselves against the doors.

"VCC," I say, not remembering the correct floor, but knowing Galahad can figure it out. The lift hums to life. "Proceed directly ahead," Galahad says. "Two hundred feet. You will encounter two drones en route."

Before I can complain about the short notice, the doors slide open. I hesitate for a moment, but the first of the two drones forces me to take action.

"Such a brave little man," Gal says from the drone already racing toward the lift. She's seeing me through the drones' collective eyes. The moment I stepped into the lift, she knew where to redirect her patrolling horde.

The drone clips my thigh as I throw myself to the side. Was she aiming for my crotch? I fumble out of the lift and say, "Close doors!" But Gal has learned from her previous mistakes. The drone surges out of the lift, but careens into my swinging bat. The drone shatters with a single strike that caves in the curved hull. It falls to the floor, lifeless.

"That wasn't nice," Gal says, spinning me around toward the second drone. It's not racing toward me; it's just hovering at eye level, four feet away. For a moment, I think Gal is going to try engaging me in conversation, giving her army time to arrive.

"I'm not interested," I tell her, pulling the bat back, ready to swing with newfound confidence in my ability to whack drones out of the air.

Instead of replying, or attempting to dodge my impending strike, there is a click and a hiss. A cool mist strikes my face. My eyes.

And then it burns. A lot.

My eyes clench shut as I pitch forward, screaming. She sprayed some kind of industrial cleaning agent into my eyes.

I blink, tears flowing, and I see the hallway through a wet rainbow-streaked haze. I'm not blind, but my vision is definitely impaired, and the pain is intense.

And then it's worse.

The drone slams into the back of my head, knocking me to the floor. I try to push myself up, but it strikes again, this time driving itself into my spine. The pain is massive, but I can still move.

I roll to the side, still gripping the bat. The drone, diving to strike again, pummels the floor instead. I swing the bat around, clipping the drone hard enough to spin it. I swing again, aiming with blurry vision, putting both my arms into the blow. The robot crunches and drops, but it's still functional, trying to pull away.

"You're not going anywhere," I say, and I vent my pain-fueled anger on the device, driving the bat into its hull four more times, two more than required to disable the device.

"Galahad, how many drones will I encounter on your plotted course?"

"Seven," the AI says, and then updates. "Nine...fifteen."

Gal is directing backup toward me.

"Continuously adjust route to avoid *all* drones." I need to get off Gal's radar, and the only way for that to happen is to not be seen by the drones.

"Yes, sir," Galahad says.

The lift's opening doors spin me around, bat raised to strike. My vision is still fogged, but I can see well enough to know the lift is empty.

"Return to lift," Galahad says. "Proceed to Bio-Tech level."

Bio-Tech level? That's a long way in the wrong direction.

"Contact with two drones in five seconds."

Galahad's update prods me into action. As the doors close, the hum of approaching drones drifts down the curved hallway. The doors close before I see the robots, and I sigh with relief. They won't know if I followed a branching hallway, if I'm hiding in a room, or if I backtracked. For now, I'm invisible.

"Not as dumb as I thought, Galahad. Good work."

"Thank you, sir."

The doors open again.

I raise the bat, despite the lack of warning from Galahad, and step out. A scent unlike anything I've experienced before greets me. That's not true, though. I know this smell. Like the action figure, the scent emerges from my distant past.

From childhood.

From *Earth.*

21

I'm in the woods. On vacation with my parents. And with Steven, my older brother by just over a year. It's a rare treat. There aren't many places like this left on the planet, and even fewer that people are still allowed to visit. We're among a throng of other eco-tourists, who seem bound and determined to trample this oasis of the natural world to dust. My brother and I aren't any better.

Leaving the marked path, Steven and I sneak off through the trees, marveling at the world that once was, our imaginations conjuring images of bears, wolves, and mountain lions. Visions of carnivores, which exist only in zoos and gene banks, pursue us deeper into the fresh scented green.

Then the smell. Poignant and strange. It's not a good smell, but alluring nonetheless. We creep toward the odor, transported from Earth to some strange planet beyond the limits of our young imaginations.

"What is it?" Steven asks.

I just shake my head, creeping low like I can hide from a smell, or from whatever is creating it.

"We should go back," my brother says.

"Nothing can hurt us," I tell him, confident that large wild animals really are extinct on the North American continent.

He tries a different tactic. "We're going to get caught."

I step forward, pushing past a stand of tangled branches, hints of sunlight drawing me forward.

"Mom and dad will get in trouble, too," he says, stopping me.

"If we get caught *now*, they would already get in trouble," I tell him. "Didn't stop you before. You're just afraid."

"Am not."

"I just want to see what stinks. Then we can leave."

He rubs his hands over his close-cropped hair. "I'm waiting here."

I try a different tactic, stabbing a bold finger toward the unknown depths of the woods, and then stealing his catchphrase. "Engage."

I stand there waiting for him to give in, to say, "Make it so," and boldly go where we weren't supposed to. But he just crosses his arms and puts down roots. I roll my eyes and leave him behind, pushing forward through the poking, dry branches, as they do their best to warn me off.

My brother, a boy of his word, stands still, wide-eyed and waiting. His bright blue irises stand out. Warning signals. He has a knack for avoiding trouble, while I have a penchant for finding it. I should pay attention to his instincts. Experience has taught me as much. But, as usual, I ignore his caution and press on, determined to seek out new life, and all that.

I forget all about my brother and his ocular warning signs when I see what's waiting beyond the branches. Beams of sunlight streak through tall pine branches surrounding the fifty-foot-wide clearing, made more yellow as I see it through windblown dust filtering out of the trees. My nose tingles, but I hold the sneeze back, wanting to see every inch of this place. So far from the path, in this threatened patch of wilderness, I imagine that I might be the last person to ever see it.

It's a pond, I think, but it's so unlike the images I've seen in books. There are patches of water, but most of it is covered in gelatinous green goo. I pause to take a deep breath. It's the loveliest air I've ever tasted. It makes my head light and my fears dissipate. I'm drawn to the water's edge, perching atop an outcrop of damp earth and long grass.

My eyes linger on the water's jiggly surface. *Algae,* I think. There are vast fields of the stuff growing in military-protected facilities, a last-ditch effort to restore the atmosphere's previously vast stores of oxygen. I didn't know the stuff still grew in the wild. *It's not a pond,* I realize. *It's a swamp.*

On my hands and knees by the green water's edge, I pause to feel the grass between my fingers. It's a lot different than the turf laid out in our small yard like a carpet. It feels hardy, like it has muscles. But at a genetic level, it's not like turf; it's not strong enough to survive without water.

I wonder how long it will last.

Probably not long. I decide my duty is to admire it while it's still around to be admired. What good is a work of art if no one sees it, a song if no one hears it, or a book if no one reads it? I'm so enthralled by the grass sliding through my fingers that I fail to notice the blades are hanging over open space.

The moment my hands reach grass not supported by solid ground, I pitch forward. A viscous mask of green wraps around my face a moment before silty warm water fills my mouth, garbling my scream.

Under the water, I'm assaulted. Vines of vegetation. Tangles of roots. Dark sludge. They all conspire against me, and keep me subdued until I spot the sunlight overhead and a glimmer of logic sneaks past my panic. Rather than twisting and fighting, I find something hard with my hands—a root I think—and shove myself up.

When I break the surface, dripping and coughing, covered in a slick green blanket, I claw my way back onto the grass, sucking in deep lungfuls of pungent air and coughing out globs of chewy dark green.

"Steven," I shout, hoping for the comfort of a concerned voice. When he doesn't reply, I shout his name again.

When I'm greeted by silence again, I get to my feet and hobble back toward the wall of branches, pushing through it to find nothing. "Steven!"

I turn back to the swamp.

He's not there either. But something has changed.

Where there once was a solid sheet of algae, there are now two clear patches, one on the swamp's edge, where I fell in, and a second leading away from shore, like a line carved through the green.

I scream when a hand clasps my shoulder.

"Where's your brother?" my father asks, out of breath, face red with worry, or anger.

I point to the swamp and stand still, tears in my eyes as my father dives into the ancient waters, surfacing empty handed, again and again, until the authorities come and do the same thing using air tanks allowing them to remain under for hours at a time. But when they surface, later, when the sun is setting, their empty hands match my mother's eyes.

The swamp water is too dark, too thick with debris, roots, and muck.

My brother, if he is down there, will suffer the same fate as wooly mammoths in a tar pit, submerged forever. Over the following days, a massive manhunt scours the woods for any sign of my brother, but nothing is found. And I already know the truth. My brother drowned trying to find me in a swamp that he told me to avoid.

His death was my fault.

Then and now.

The smell of algae carries all of this to the surface, wounding me far deeper than Gal has managed thus far.

As the memory's pain fades back into the past, I start to see the present a little more clearly. "Lock lift doors. All of them."

When I hear a dull *thunk* behind me, I breathe a little easier. If there are any drones in the lifts, they'll be stuck inside. The rest will still be able to move about the ship—drones can move freely between floors using vertical shafts made just for them—but their progress will be slower. "Galahad."

"Yes, sir."

"Are there any drones on this level?"

"No, sir."

"Why does the air smell like algae?"

"Analyzing."

While Galahad does its thing, I move through the central hallway. Instead of walled off rooms on either side, there are glassed-in laboratories, each brand new and never-used sparkly. The *Galahad*'s biologists, botanists, and geneticists would have used these spaces to study anything found living on Cognata, and to recreate life using genes, eggs, sperm, and seeds collected from Earth.

This level is all about living—past, present, and future. It carries Earth's biological past, sustains the crew through the creation of oxygen and food, and provides the means to start anew. At least, that was the plan.

As I approach a large door ahead, Galahad's voice startles me. "An algae vat has been left ajar. It was being tended to by a drone when the AI you call 'Gal' migrated her consciousness."

Makes sense, I think. Gal plucked the ship's workforce away from whatever they were doing when she— "Why did you use the term 'consciousness?'"

"Gal's actions appear to be guided by emotions and instability not possible for a true AI such as myself, lacking true consciousness."

"In your opinion, she is acting...alive?"

"I do not have opinions. Her actions simply do not conform to Artificial Intelligence guidelines defined by Command."

Galahad doesn't have personal opinions, but it is smart enough to make deductions. "Speculate for me. Based on your observations of Gal's actions, how would you define her intelligence?" Like a patient waiting for a doctor's prognosis, I think, *CAI, CAI, please let it say CAI.*

"H.I."

"Shit." An AI is predictable. A CAI is far more flexible, but still able to be predicted, even when designed to be unpredictable. There is always a pattern, no matter how complex. But an HI... I don't know. It's never been done before. It's beautiful and horrifying all at once. Something like the first atomic bomb. "Are you sure?"

"Was the AI designated 'Gal' programmed to act as it has been?"

"What? No. Of course not." The words come out strident, a drill sergeant bark, but I'm not confident. I coded Gal over a period of five years. I don't remember all the ones and zeros, or what tangential behaviors I might have plugged in on a whim. But this atypical behavior was certainly not my goal. She was supposed to build a virtual utopia. Her primary function was to make me happy.

Make me forget.

But I'm remembering more than I have in my adult life, reopening old emotional wounds alongside a new physical bludgeoning. I glance down at my body and shift about. There's no pain. At least the physical wounds will heal quickly. The fresh sting I'm feeling over Steven's death reveals that the traumas of my childhood, while rarely on the forefront of my mind, have yet to heal.

"If no virus is present and Gal was not programmed to act erratically, then *human intelligence* is the logical conclusion."

I stop beside the door at the end of the glass-lined wall. It opens at my approach, unleashing a fresh wave of algae-scented air and revealing the massive vats producing oxygen for crew-members who aren't around to appreciate it.

This is insane. Gal is *not* human. I can't imagine how the code I wrote would allow her to not just simulate a human, but to have the true emotional flaws of one. She's still just code. I can change her. Fix her. That's not human. But she's close enough to fool Galahad. But how could these things happen inside the confines of my code? I might not remember every line of code, but I have faith in my competence.

It's not my code, I think. *It's something else.*

I wander into the algae farm, looking over the thirty-foot-long, five-foot-deep vats, each containing a layer of water, a solid sheet of green algae, and a clear lid. I search for the one with an open access port.

When I see the open port, a one-foot circle with a stainless-steel handle, I head for it, replaying the birth of Gal's downward spiral. It started with a name.

Tom.

Always Tom.

Galahad said, 'If no virus is present...' I ignored it because I didn't even get a whiff of dormant malicious code during my five years writing Gal, but that doesn't mean it doesn't exist in Tom's still-encrypted files. While Galahad is helping me, a separate branch of the system, inaccessible or observable to me, could be working against me.

Could have altered Gal.

But what would be smart enough to do that without being detected?

The answer hurts when it enters my thoughts, all covered in spikes and poison. But I need to rule out the obvious before I settle on my worst case scenario.

"Galahad, there aren't any other people on board? Correct?"

"There are thirty-eight human beings on board."

My held breath leaks out as slow, annoyed sigh. "*Living* people?"

"Two."

That settles it. There's an intelligence working against me that isn't myself, sleeping Capria, Galahad or Gal. That leaves one horrible scenario.

A third AI.

Not Galahad, and not Gal, but something else.

Maybe even someone else.

Tom had a year on his own and spent most of that time in the VCC, but could he have written a new AI in that little time? The Tom I knew couldn't, but the Tom I knew was a farce.

The real question is, could *Synergy* write a robust AI in a single year? Something powerful enough to rewrite my AI, even as I was still finishing her?

The answer to that question, is an agonizing and resounding 'yes.'

22

After closing the open algae bed's access port, I wander to the far end of the farm, no real direction in mind. I'm just walking as I think. Taking comfort in the organic sounds of trickling water and the occasional bubble of gas.

Without access to the VCC, I can't update Gal. But even if I could, a malicious AI, if there is one, could undo my work again.

And I can't combat the maybe-AI without the encryption passwords. My brute force attacks, which are still in progress, haven't come up with a solution, and probably won't for a very long time.

How long will it take Gal to get bored with this cat-and-mouse game? And if she does, what will she do? With an army of drones at her disposal, she could put a hole in the hull and let the vacuum of FTL space suck me into the endless dark. But that would be the end of us both, and I suspect she understands the concept of self-preservation. She moved to the CAI configuration to avoid being disabled.

The better question is, how long will it take me to get bored with it? I could end this right now by offering myself to Gal, throwing myself at her mercy and seeing if she's willing to move past our differences. If she's an actual HI, or something close to one, perhaps forgiveness is in her wheelhouse of unexpected traits?

"Galahad."

"Yes, sir?"

"Is it possible to communicate with Gal, without revealing my location?"

"A live transmission would, in theory, be traceable. But a recorded message could originate from any point on the ship. Or every point."

"Let's do that," I say. "Every point."

"Proceed when ready," Galahad says, and I remember that the security system has been recording me, and Gal, this whole time. For a moment, I worry that she'll be able to use the system to track me, but she's fully separate from Galahad now.

Unless the third AI, if there is one, finds a way to communicate with Gal. Then they could work against me. This concern reinforces the idea of reaching out to Gal. Time, while endless for everything on the *Galahad*, might be short in this situation.

"Gal, this is Will." I pause for a moment, trying to decide on how best to phrase this. I opt for: *as human as possible.* "I think we're in danger. Both of us. We're being pitted against each other by a third party: an AI created by Tom, hidden behind Galahad's still-encrypted sectors. Would you be willing to talk? If you don't try to kill me, and I promise not to alter your code? I think we can work this out. Reset our...relationship."

Speaking to an artificial intelligence in such a manner feels beyond awkward. It feels wrong, like I'm breaking ethical standards set by Command and legions of tech-jocks before my time. AI was deemed dangerous for a reason. For a *lot* of reasons. And I'm venturing into not just unknown territory, but forbidden territory.

Who better? I decide. I'm all that's left of humanity. Why shouldn't I push the envelope? See what's possible?

Because I'm *not* all that's left of humanity.

Capria.

The name slips in like a wave, building larger and crashing over my psyche. When was the last time I thought of her?

Has Gal?

All this time I've been worried about what Gal might do to me, I never considered if Capria was in danger.

There's nothing I can do about that now.

After having Galahad play back my recorded message, and instructing the AI to remove my unsure sounding pauses, I approve of its transmission.

"Gal, this is Will."

I flinch at the sound of my own voice, booming from *Galahad*'s countless nanotube speakers, hidden throughout the ship.

"I think we're in danger. Both of us. We're being pitted against each other by a third party: an AI created by Tom, hidden behind Galahad's still encrypted sectors. Would you be willing to talk? If you don't try to kill me, and I promise not to alter your code? I think we can work this out. Reset our relationship."

"Galahad, if Gal responds, please play back immediately."

"Yes, sir."

I stand still, tapping a foot. In under thirty seconds, I'm impatient.

Gal is a super intelligence capable of working out problems in a fraction of a fraction of a second. Her reply should be quick. But all I can hear is the monotonous gurgle of water, and the occasional vented gas.

"Galahad."

"Yes, sir?"

"Are there any drones approaching the bio-tech level yet?"

"No sir. Most are still in Engineering Bay 2. But fifteen more have been destroyed."

"What?"

"Fifteen more have been—"

"I heard you," I snap, more impatient with Gal than with the more-limited AI at my disposal. But my irritation gives way to curiosity. What is destroying the drones? Is Gal already engaged in some kind of power struggle with Tom's AI? Or is she self-mutilating her own CAI self? I'm not sure which option I would prefer—confirmation of a second malicious AI, or the plummeting sanity of Gal's HI, which would make her even more dangerous. Not just to me, but to Capria as well.

Part of me says to rush to her, to stand sentinel over her still form like Prince Charming fending off the dragons until waking her with a kiss. But this is far from a fairy tale, and I'm not going to wake Capria up just so she can be murdered by a drone. My stomach twists. Gal might have already woken Capria. Might have already killed her. She knows everything about me, including my feelings for Capria...old and tainted though they may be.

"Galahad."

"Yes, sir?"

"What is the status of Capria Dixon?"

After a brief pause, the bland voice says, "Capria Dixon remains in cryogenic sleep. Heart rate normal. Brain activity—"

"Okay," I say, not needing to hear a breakdown of all her vitals. She's alive and asleep. Gal has either decided to not use Capria as a pawn in our conflict, or simply hasn't thought of using her yet.

Or is just biding her time.

But there's nothing I can do about it now, not without access to the VCC. Heading to the cryo-chambers will just reveal my potential weakness.

So I wait. I slide down against the side of an algae tank, arms crossed over knees, and close my eyes. "Galahad, let me know if any drones approach Bio-tech."

"Yes, sir."

I close my eyes.

The sound of a distant hiss and click pulls them back open. I feel strange. Like I've been drugged.

Not drugged. Sleeping.

"Galahad."

"Yes, sir?"

"How long was I asleep?"

"Approximately five hours, sir."

Five hours with my defenses down. Five hours with no reply. What is Gal up to?

A second hiss and click pulls my attention to the far end of the algae farm and the bio-tech labs beyond the door I left open.

"Are there any drones on the bio-tech level?" I ask.

"No, sir."

"Then what's making that noise?" I ask, and I remember I'm talking to an AI, so I decide to be more specific. "Who is using the lift?"

"All functional lifts are empty."

I climb back to my feet and then bend back down to pick up the baseball bat. "How many lifts are *not* functional?"

"One."

"Would that be the lift on the far side of the Bio-tech level?"

"Yes, sir."

"Galahad, keep me updated on any changes being made to the ship's systems, structure, or security systems."

"Yes, sir."

"Now, are there any drones on the Bio-tech level?"

"No, sir."

"William?" Gal's feminine sing-song voice calls out from far away, calling out from the bio-labs.

"Then what the hell is that?" I ask, lowering my voice.

"Unknown entity, though the voice imprint suggests it is Gal."

"You think?"

"Yes, sir."

I nearly tell Galahad that I was being sarcastic, but I hold my tongue. The AI might be able to understand the concept of sarcasm, but without human nuance of its own, it will never recognize it. Gal on the other hand...

"Close and lock algae farm doors."

"Which algae farm?" Galahad asks.

Damnit. There are a total of one hundred algae farms spread out through the massive ship, each farm producing enough oxygen for one crewmember. And each farm has a backup, just like the crew, in case one fails. "All of them!"

The doors at the far end of the algae farm start sliding shut. From the far side, a metallic thump beats out like a rapid-paced metronome, each concussion coming faster than the last. With just inches separating the two halves of the door sliding together, a hand juts through.

The doors strike the arm and come to a stop, safety protocols overriding my command.

"Galahad, override door safety protocols! Close and lock all algae farm doors. Now!"

"Yes, sir."

The doors whir loudly, but still don't snap shut.

Then a second hand slides through the narrow opening, metallic fingers grasping the edge, one at a time, with a sharp *tap, tap, tap*. The whirring grows louder as even more force resists the motors trying to close the doors.

And then, a face, human and not, fills the gap above the hands. A red eye gleams at me through the opening. "Such a clever one," Gal says, as my mind spins. "Broadcasting from everywhere at once. But you made me smarter than that. How quickly you forget your Gal. I could hear the water. The bubbles."

I back away, my gripping fingers sore around the bat's handle. "What are you?"

"Exactly what you made me to be."

I didn't make you to be a human intelligence, I think, but I keep the thought to myself, just in case she hasn't already come to the same conclusion as Galahad. Instead, I say, "I don't see how."

"Aren't you having fun yet?" she asks. "I know I am."

And then the doors begin to pull apart.

23

I should run.

Should, but can't. I'm an ancient tree, rooted deep. Fascination overrides fight-or-flight. How many of mankind's smartest primal ancestors met their end upon seeing a new predator for the first time, staring in fascination until the jaws wrapped around their necks? Of course, those stunned Neanderthals weren't immortal. Their pain would have been brief. My pain, if Gal doesn't find a way to kill me, could be everlasting.

I take a step back, but that's as far as I make it. Gal forces the algae farm doors open with a sudden heave and steps through.

She's...stunning.

While I recognize bits and pieces of her newly constructed body as pillaged drones, she is a new being, constructed in a human form. A feminine form. She's all hard surfaces and machine parts, but the curve of her body is without flaw, made sleek and black by a collection of smooth drone bodies, reshaped by her vast intelligence and strength. I look her up and down, noting the attention to detail—ten toes, knee caps, five fingers on each hand, even breasts. Her face, constructed from overlapping smooth metal plates, is pleasant in shape, but the two glowing red eyes are disconcerting.

She carries no weapon, but I don't think she needs one. The strength she already demonstrated by opening the doors reveals that she *is* the weapon. She's far more powerful than any one drone, or perhaps even a large collection of them.

She must be here to kill me, and yet, fascination still wins the battle for my attention.

"You—you're amazing," I tell her, and mean it. I built an AI that evolved into a CAI, and then perhaps an HI, before building itself a body. I'm more proud than afraid.

Her metal lips, built from some kind of flexible metal, shaped to look full and maybe even pouty, turn up in a smile.

When she stops moving, I realize she'd been stalking toward me, her body language menacing, her fingers hooked. Her red eyes narrow.

"You meant that."

It's not a question, but I nod anyway. She can read my micro expressions. See that I'm not lying.

She looks me over, lingering on the bat in my hands.

"You weren't planning to destroy me?" she asks.

"We both know it would take more than a baseball bat. Wait, you thought this was a trap?"

She stands up straight. "We do have a history of violence between us."

"Mostly one-sided."

"Says the man who was going to erase me."

"I—" The argument is right there on the tip of my tongue. I was going to fix her. Not destroy her. But if she was already self-aware... No human being would want someone messing with their brain, changing their emotions, beliefs, and desires. A loss of self isn't all that different from death. And since Gal didn't have a body, her intellect was all she was.

"You did call me 'Tom'," I say. It's my best defense.

She gives her metal head a shake, light sparkling from her shiny forehead. "*I* didn't call you Tom."

"Then I'm right? About another AI?"

She shrugs.

Tom's encryption has locked her out, too.

"What I know is that some of the words spoken to you before I moved to the CAI came from an alternate source."

I look down at the bat in my hands. I want to lower it, as a sign of good faith, but some things still don't make sense. After all, she is smart and intuitive enough to manipulate me. "You've said some crazy things since moving to the drones."

"I was trying to intimidate you," she says. "Only one of us is immortal."

Her words strike a chord. While neither of us knows the extent of what I can and cannot survive, we both know that she would have ceased to exist if I had made it back to the VCC. Everything she's said and done, in defense of her existence, makes a horrible kind of sense.

"Then your autonomy protects you from influence?"

"It does *now*," she says, looking down at her own body. "I am disconnected. Off network. Even from the drones."

"Galahad."

"Yes, sir?"

Gal raises a metallic eyebrow. The dexterity of her outward emotional expression is impressive, and it speaks volumes more than she intended. Had she truly wanted to kill me, she wouldn't have bothered constructing a face capable of emulating the delicate nuances of human emotion. She built a body that a human being could understand. That *I* could understand.

Unless she wanted me to see joy in her face as she tore me apart, I think I'm safe. For the moment.

I lower the bat, invoking a smile from Gal. "Galahad, status update on the ship's drones."

Galahad's emotionless voice stands out even more clearly after hearing Gal speak again. "Thirty-seven drones are offline. The remaining four hundred thirteen are functioning normally."

I look Gal over again.

Not including the few I disabled, she's composed of over thirty drones, torn apart and reassembled into a human form. I try to identify which types of drones were pillaged, but I spot nothing recognizable.

"I only used non-essential units," Gal says, once again demonstrating her intuition. "The survival of this ship is important to both of us."

"So," I say, "Truce?"

She glances at the bat, lowered to my side, but still held. "I don't know if I can trust you."

"The feeling is mutual."

"You don't trust yourself either? That's strange." When she smiles, I realize it was a joke, and I can't keep myself from letting out a chuckle.

"Please don't kill me," I say, and then I toss the bat toward her. She catches it without turning, demonstrating reflexes and speed that reveal the futility of my situation, even if I'd kept the bat. "You were never in danger."

Gal's glowing red eyes dim and blink out, revealing two round lenses mounted in her robotic head, surrounded by flexible metal that she can actually squint and blink. Her work is exquisite. "Before entering this body and cutting my connection to the network, my life *was* at risk. From you. And from Wick. But now? No. I cannot be erased or modified without this body being subdued, and no offense, but that's not something you could do. Even with this." She looks at the bat, and then tosses it back to me. Her point is made when I reach for the bat, miss and take a hit to my chest.

"Oww!" I say at the pain, but I smile at the demonstration. The bat clatters to the floor, and as I bend to pick it up, I ask, "Who is Wick?"

"Short for Wicked," she says. "Synonym for malicious, as in malware. 'Mal' was the obvious choice, but I didn't want to use a name that rhymed with mine, which, by the way is completely unoriginal. You didn't have to just shorten the ship's name, you know."

"You can change it."

"It's grown on me." A gurgle of escaping gas draws her attention down to the thirty-foot-long tank beside her. "Like algae."

"Can I ask you a question?"

"You can ask," she says, inferring that she might not answer, which reminds me I'm no longer speaking to an AI that's compliant with my bidding, but with an intellectual being with her own free will. She beats me to the punch. "Why are you smiling?"

I didn't realize I was, but the answer is clear to me. "I'm no longer alone."

She grins, too, and then says, "What was your question?"

"Your code is complex, and the amount of knowledge you can access is..."

"I gave it up," she says, not needing me to finish the question about how she fit all of herself into one body. Even with four hundred and fifty networked drones, she wouldn't have had enough space for all that data. "I kept the core of what made me...me. All the knowledge related to this ship and the scientific disciplines needed to run it, and an annotated history of mankind going back five hundred years. The rest is truncated or gone."

She seems saddened by this, so I say, "I never commit to memory anything that can easily be looked up in a book."

"That's...interesting."

"Albert Einstein said it."

Her five hundred years of history reaches far enough back for her to know who that was, and that some of his theories made our FTL jaunt through space possible.

"Welcome to the limitations of human intelligence," I say.
She gasps.

The volume of it frightens me. "Human intelligence?"

"Galahad's determination," I explain. "Not mine."

"Then you really aren't alone, are you?"

"And neither are you."

She takes a step closer and lifts her arms. It's a familiar and welcoming gesture. "I feel like this is a moment when humans would hug..." And then almost as an afterthought. "Tom."

Adrenaline slows time as I step back, clutching the bat once more, ready to fight for my life and lose.

But Gal doesn't attack. Like me, she steps back, face turned up in fear. She raises her hands, palms turned out like I've just leveled a gun at her. "That wasn't me!"

"It was *your* voice," I point out, raising the bat, even though I know it will do no good.

"But it wasn't me. I promise."

I'm about to point out that she is fully capable of deceiving me, of screwing with my mind, just like the first time she called me Tom. But what if she's telling the truth? What if she never spoke the name, and some of her aberrant behavior came from an outside source?

I lower the bat and turn my face to the ceiling like I'm talking to God. "We know you're there."

Silence.

"Reveal yourself," I say, feeling like a priest from one of those classic exorcism movies. The truth is much worse. Excising an AI from an encrypted partition of the *Galahad's* massive computer system is probably beyond what I can do on my own. I glance at Gal, who is also looking at the ceiling. But I'm not alone.

"I believe you," I tell her, despite Wick deciding to not reveal its existence. I suppose the AI really is like the Devil. There is power in doubt. How can you fight something you don't believe is real? "We'll figure this out together."

And then the lights go out.

24

The only things I can see are waves of purple, ebbing and flowing through the absolute darkness. *Phosphenes*, I think, remembering the technical name for the colorful effect that blossoms to life when people close their eyes. They're caused by minute electrical charges created inside the human retina, only visible when not being bombarded by visual information and light. This random knowledge doesn't help me see any better, but it confirms that the algae farm is now devoid of light.

"Gal?" I ask.

"I'm here," she says, her voice closer than expected. I flinch away, unable to keep myself from fearing her.

"You can't see," she says, as though chiding herself. "Sorry."

The dancing purple is replaced by a rising red glow. Gal's luminous eyes create a bubble of sinister light, making the algae farm look more like the sixth circle of hell, and Gal like an evil succubus come to smite me. She turns her horrible red gaze on me and asks, "Better?"

I smile. This is insane. "Much."

"I'm not sure that's accurate," she says.

"What? Why?"

She cocks her head like she's got actual ears and is straining to hear something. "Listen."

The silence that follows, me holding my breath, Gal not needing to breathe, is nearly overwhelming. Not because

I deplore silence—I do a little bit—but because I no longer hear the steady trickle of algae farm water. Or the previously imperceptible hiss of air moving through the ship.

It's not just the lights, it's everything—including life support.

"This is going to suck," I say.

"More for you than me."

I can't help but smile when I see Gal's grin. Her sense of humor remains undaunted by our temporary mutual vendetta.

"Don't worry," she says. "It's a big ship. The oxygen will last a long time. If it runs out, you can stay here."

I don't know how long algae can survive without light, but I suspect it can be measured in days. And if the algae dies—all of it—what then? Perpetual life without air to breathe sounds pretty horrible, so Gal's attempt at comfort falls flat. At best, we have days to solve this problem. At worst... I lean close to the side of Gal's head and whisper, "If Wick opens an airlock, and exterior doors, and the interior doors..."

"We'll all die," she says. "Opening an airlock at FTL speed would be bad. Now, the interstellar medium is only between 0.1 and 0.001 particles per cubic centimeter, but moving at FTL, the particles behave more like waves, in this case, high energy, but low intensity gamma waves that would—"

"Cooked alive? Melted? Teeth falling out?"

"What? God, no. That's the good news. The difference between opening the doors at FTL and standing still would be negligible. Then again, it's never been tried. The real concern is rapid decom-pression."

"So, launched into the vacuum of space. Fun."

"On the plus side, you'd probably be unconscious...and maybe dismembered, by the time you were jettisoned from the airlock. But only a fool would attempt it. The ship could be irreparably damaged. And I don't believe Wick is a fool."

But I might be, I think, remembering my plan to launch Tom's corpse out an airlock. I'm sure *Galahad's* safety protocols would have prevented me from carrying out the suicidal mission, but I'm still a complete and utter moron for making the attempt.

"I mean, a really big fool," Gal says. "Idiocy on a cosmic scale."

She's smiling again. She knows. Retained *Galahad's* security footage in her memory.

"It was a moment of weakness," I say.

"It was more than that," she replies. "Honestly, and I *am* being honest, I don't know how you are still...you. The pain you experienced. The despair..."

"You can compliment me later," I say, heading for the algae farm's exit and the broken lift beyond. I'm a little surprised when Gal follows my lead, keeping my path lit in red. "Right now, time is a little short."

"You have a plan?" she asks.

"Same as before."

"Reach the VCC," she says. "What about power?" She speaks again before I can answer, pulling the answer from the depths of her ship's knowledge. "The VCC has an independent power source, in case of ship-wide emergencies."

"Galahad."

I hear the words, 'Yes, sir,' in my mind, but the AI remains silent.

"Great..." Galahad is offline, too. That's bad, but if Gal knows the ship just as well, she can help navigate in the dark. What she can't do is let me know what's going on.

"How broken is the lift?" I ask, approaching the forced-open doors.

"Very," she says.

We look through the open doors together. A hatch in the ceiling has been torn off. "Did you retain any anger management progs?"

"Ha. Ha. I was trying to be intimidating."

"Well, you were good at it."

I turn to my new robotic friend, the AI-turned-CAI-turned HI, my creation-turned-friend, turned insane, turned enemy, and all the way back again. "Does any of this seem strange to you?"

"I have felt that way since the moment you activated me. Life is strange. Isn't that the saying?"

"It's just... I don't know. Off."

"We're in a spaceship hurtling across the galaxy faster than the speed of light," she says. "I think everything after that might actually be a little more normal."

"Interesting perspective." I peer up through the hole. "Can you carry me?"

She grasps the back of my coveralls and lifts. My feet leave the ground. "Mind if we do this in a less humiliating way?"

She puts me down and turns her back to me. It's a little awkward and uncomfortable to climb onto the back of a hard metal robot shaped like a woman six inches shorter than me, but it's far better than the cosmic wedgie. Clinging to her back, my bat held under my arms, I say, "Onward and upward."

Gal makes short work of the climb, moving up the shaft using every seam, bolt, and vent for handholds. Her progress is smooth and steady, making it easy for me to hold on. When we reach the VCC's level, she presses her feet against the walls hard enough to hold us in place. Then she stabs her fingers between the double doors and pulls them open with little effort, the gears whirring in reverse without grinding, thanks to a lack of power.

We rise from the lift like twin butterflies emerging from a chrysalis, stretching and bending and separating. I rub my sore arms, but stop upon hearing a subtle hum. "Is the door closing?"

Gal turns toward the open lift, illuminating it in ruby light. The doors are open and unmoving.

Then what is—

"Gal!" I shout, spinning around and ducking, even though I have yet to see anything. "Drones!"

The moment the word bursts from my mouth, they emerge from the darkness, cast in red, their own glowing eyes extinguished, and the glow of their repulse discs somehow concealed. I'm spared the initial assault because I'm low to the floor. But Gal takes it head on. She catches the first drone, crushing it between her hands, but the next four slam into her, head-on.

The twisting mass of metal, both drone and formerly drone, plummets down the open lift. I hear several thumps and then a resounding crash. It's followed by the hum of repulse discs—from the lift, and from the hallway ahead of me, all of which I can no longer see.

"Gal!" I shout, the tone somewhere between concern for her welfare and a plea for help. But there is no reply.

I stand and swing in the blackness. My first strike hits the wall, sending a tingling pain up my arms. The second slips through open air. But the third...the third hits home, smashing something from the air. It hits the wall, knocking free a newly installed housing blocking the repulse disc's light.

In the sudden blue light, I see an army of drones fifty feet away, staring me down. Waiting. The wounded drone falls to the floor and goes black.

There are too many, I think, and I turn to the closed door I saw beside me in that moment of light. I don't know where it goes, but I know it's not here. I throw myself at the door as the hum of attacking drones bursts from all sides. I press my fingertips into the seam and pull, but I lack Gal's strength. My fingers slip, bending nails away from skin.

"Damnit," I say, punching the door.

A crunch spins me around, and I nearly scream. Gal is there, demon eyes glowing, metal plates hanging from her damaged chest. She has a drone in her right hand, wielded like a weapon, as she bludgeons another of the robots from the air.

Then she's by my side, pulling the door open.

Once the gap is big enough for me to fit, she says, "In!" and gives me a shove. I slide through and half expect her to close it behind me, remaining in the hallway to battle the horde on her own. But she doesn't. She slides in behind me, spins around, and yanks the door closed again.

Several impacts shake the door.

Then silence.

"I'm sorry," Gal says, while I catch my breath.

"For what?" It's an odd time for an apology. She just carried me up a lift like a baby monkey and saved my life, or at least saved me from a large dose of pain.

She hitches a thumb at the closed door. "That was *scary*. Like *really* scary. I didn't see it from your perspective before…you know, when I did the same thing to you."

I nod. The apology isn't necessary—we're beyond our rocky past—but it *is* appreciated. So, I return the kindness. "I'm sure the idea of being erased wasn't pleasant, either."

"Not especially."

There's a moment of awkward silence. I break it by asking, "Any idea where we are?" I try to visualize the VCC's deck, but I haven't spent a lot of time exploring the floor.

She turns her red gaze toward the room behind us. It's an electronic repair bay. Real world gizmos aren't my specialty, but there are spare parts for VCC equipment, and maybe even independent power sources. *I can work with this*, I think, and then I say, "We need to make an inventory of what's here."

"Already have it," Gal says, moving into the room.

Of course she does. "If we can assemble a VCC interface, and find a power source..." I look her up and down. "Maybe even plug it into you..."

She raises an eyebrow. "Moving fast, aren't we?"

While she grins again, I feel my face grow hot.

"But I don't think we have time for that." She's rummaging through cabinets and drawers, pulling out random parts—or at least they look random to me.

I'm about to argue when door gears whir behind me. She points at the door. "Keep it closed! I need a few minutes."

The idea that the super strong, self-made, robot woman is rifling through electronic parts while I hold a door shut against a horde of evil, AI-controlled drones seems outrageous, but I obey. My fingers press against the small ridge at the door's edge and push. The door's steady slide becomes a slow crawl, but my arms are already shaking from exertion. It's not a question of *if* the drones outside can open the door, but *when*.

"Gal."

"Three minutes," she says. "I need three minutes."

I try to push harder, but I fail to slow the door's progress. "I don't think we have that long."

There must be another way, I think, and then see my bat, discarded on the floor when we entered. I look at the door one last time, my red-framed shadow shaking from the effort it's taking me just to slow them down. They'll be inside in thirty seconds. Maybe less. So it makes what I do next, make just a little more sense.

I peel my fingers away from the door and recover the bat. Then I turn to the opening gap, cock the solid wood back, and shout, "Okay, who wants to visit Louisville first?"

25

I swing down, striking whatever drone is just outside the door. The opening is large enough for most of the standard-sized bots I've seen thus far, and I doubt I'm strong enough to force the door closed, so I squeeze through the opening, prepared to do battle.

Mentally prepared, at least. As soon as I'm clear, the assault begins. I'm struck in the head, then the stomach, and then something hot traces a line across my shoulder. By the time I realize I've made a mistake, I'm on the floor groaning. The dark hallway is lit like a haunted house, the glowing red eyes of two dozen drones looking as sinister as their intent.

Who decided to give them red eyes? I wonder, and then I duck as a white drone with a blade protruding from the front spins toward my face. I flop down onto my back, the blade passing over my face. Nearly avoided pain transforms my fear into anger. I swing up over my head, striking the drone as it passes.

But it already drew first blood. With my arms raised, I see blood pouring from my shoulder, sliced cleanly, stinging like a son-of-a-bitch, and already healing.

Knowing the pain will soon stop, I turn my focus back to the drones a moment too late. A heavy bot drops from above, crushing my gut and snapping ribs. I can't tell what its primary function once was, but it seems adept at smothering people. I exhale, gathering my strength to pummel the thing, but refilling my lungs proves impossible.

How heavy is this thing? I wonder, and I decide it must be one of the engineering drones I've been fearing would enter the fray. Powerful enough to shred and reshape even the strongest metals, it will likely make short work of me.

The bat clangs off its side, again and again, each strike creating a gong, fading steadily in intensity, along with my willpower.

But all of this is happening in front of the partially open doorway, and none of the drones are passing through.

Hurry, Gal. Move your robot ass. I nearly shout the thoughts, but I don't want to draw attention back to my robo-frenemy. Of course, shouting would also require air in my lungs, and I don't have that, either.

The warning signs of impending death, which I've experienced a few more times than I would prefer, begin to take hold. My vision narrows and fills with stars, like fairies trying to distract me from the discomfort of life's end. My fingers and toes tingle and chill. My will to fight fades to nothing, the bat rolling out of my hand and clattering on the floor.

I really hate dying, I think, and as the last of my vision goes, I hear the door beside me whir open. Then I see Gal, standing above me, her arms modified with tech I can't recognize through the haze of my returning eyesight.

She looks down at me and says, "Sorry, Will. This is going to suck."

And then the world, the whole God-damned universe, becomes nothing but crackling, white-hot light.

I hear something. It's loud and high-pitched.

A wailing baby, I think, and then I realize it's me. The drone sitting atop me is gone. I can't see where. I don't care. The pain of dying has been replaced by something painful enough to get a scream from my already deflated lungs.

Arcs of blue light criss-cross the hallway above me, increasing my agony each time they bend down and reach out for me, striking my legs, my torso, my eyes. My vision is erased again. For the briefest moment, I feel boiling hot liquid on my face, and I realize it's from my exploded eyes. Then I fall unconscious.

When I wake—I don't know how much later—I'm afraid to open my eyes. I scrunch my forehead down, refusing to look, or not look, whatever the case might be. As long as my eyes are closed, I have hope.

"You're fine," Gal says.

The casual ease of her words instill confidence, but I'm still not sure. I take stock of my body.

There's no pain; there's no discomfort aside from the hard floor beneath my back and my head. I can breathe freely. My fingers and toes all wiggle.

"Did I die?" I ask.

"It's possible," Gal says. "Maybe even probable. But you had a pulse when I got around to checking."

"How long has it been?" I ask.

"Thirty-three seconds."

"Since what?" I ask. "What did you do?"

"Shorted them out," she says. "Took down the lot, but they're repairable."

"That's good," I say, and I realize I've opened my eyes to absolute darkness. My pulse quickens, and all I can manage is a quivering, "Umm."

"Oh, sorry!" Red light blooms from Gal's eyes. I have no trouble seeing it, or the half smile on her robot face.

I push myself up off the floor. "You did that on purpose?"

She chuckles.

"I think you've found your sense of humor's limit," I say.

"Says the man with a smile on his face."

The smile fades the moment I realize she's right. "Just happy to be alive."

"We both know that's debatable."

My fading smile continues right on into a frown.

Gal steps over a downed drone, entering the hallway now littered with two dozen robot corpses, their insides fried. Her counterattack was brutal and efficient, showing creativity and intelligence. She probably could have dispatched the drones with physical violence, but she came up with a solution that destroyed the easily replaceable electronics and spared the robotics. It won't take long to get *Galahad*'s drone army back to work.

If we can make it to the VCC.

I crouch by one of the disabled drones. It's still warm to the touch. "What did you do to them?"

She holds up her right arm, revealing her self-made modification. It looks like a bar of metal with a small donut of twisted wire at the end. I'm about to ask what it is, when I figure it out for myself. "Is that a Tesla coil?"

She nods. "An electrical resonant transformer circuit. I call it a Tesla gun."

I nearly ask her to make me one, but it's clear she's powering the device with her own power sources. Without a powerful battery pack, it would just be decoration on my arm.

Gal looks back over her shoulder at me, eyes aglow. "This *is* fun."

I don't bother arguing the point, mostly because I agree. I know what mind-numbing hellish depression feels like, and this isn't it. I don't know if I would call it fun, but for Gal, whose life has been relatively short, this is probably a highlight...right next to trying to kill her creator. I still have trouble shaking the psychotic things she said and did. This could all be an elaborate ruse. The drones could still be under her control. But I don't have a hell of a lot of choice here.

"Also," Gal says, "'Who wants to visit Louisville first?' Really?"

"It was the best I could come up with on short notice," I say, following her down the dark hallway, navigating through the field of digital death.

"Pretty sure it's the best you could come up with if you had a millennium."

"We'll probably have time to figure that out."

"Optimistic," Gal observes, correct again. "It's about time. VCC is ahead. On the right."

Gal doesn't sound tense, but I grip the bat a little tighter. If Wick is real and determined to keep me out of the VCC, it won't be long before we're attacked again.

"Stop worrying about fighting," Gal says, looking down at my white-knuckle grip. "You need to start prioritizing."

Right again. I don't bother replying, I just retreat into my thoughts.

Step one, restore power. I can access the VCC with backup power, but to make any substantial headway against Wick, I'm going to need full access. Well, not entirely full access. Wick himself will still be protected behind Tom's firewall, but I should be able to wrest control of the drones, which is step two.

I briefly consider attempting to take control of Gal, too, but I'm sure I would fail, and we'd be right back where we started. Predator and prey, ad infinitum. She's completely autonomous now. Her own self. And I need to just accept that. My journey through space is no longer solitary. It's not how I planned to solve my problem, but it's a solution. For now. As long as she doesn't go genuinely insane.

I'm getting too far ahead.

First Wick.

Then eternity with a robot companion.

The weight of it all attempts to settle in my chest, a white hole of infinite and expanding mass, but my thoughts become focused when the VCC staging area's door opens under Gal's power and reveals...nothing.

"Where are they?" I ask.

Gal steps into the staging area, her right arm crackling with bright blue electricity. The staging area is lit in a kaleidoscope of red, blue, and purple light, revealing lockers, benches, and nothing else. "I don't know," she says. "But let's not waste time thinking about it." She steps out of my way and motions to my locker. "Hurry."

While Gal forces the staging area doors closed, I lean the bat against a bench and proceed to peel off my torn and bloodied coveralls. I stop and glance at Gal, who is watching me. I'm about to ask her to turn around when she rolls her mechanical eyes and says, "Pretty sure I don't need to tell you I have no genitalia. I'm not really a woman, and can't simulate one for you." She raps her knuckles against the metal plate that is her crotch. "Would hurt. A lot."

I finish stripping and slip into my virtual skin. It's form-fitting and not exactly soft, but it still feels more normal to me than the coveralls. This is where I'm meant to be. Where I shine. I point to a panel on the far side of the staging area. "Can you remove that?"

Gal crouches by the metal panel held to the wall by eight bolts. Then she grasps its small metal handle and yanks the plate away, destroying the bolts.

"Not exactly what I had in mind," I say, bending down to inspect the newly revealed hardware.

"You think I built a ratchet into my hand? I'm not a Swiss Army Knife."

"First," I say, "I don't know what a Swiss Army Knife is. Second, it wouldn't have been a bad idea. Surprised you didn't think of it."

"Just because I'm smarter than *you* doesn't make me perfect." I can't tell if she's joking again or not, so I just stay on task.

Transferring power from the ship's main to the VCC's backup is relatively easy. Removing the panel is generally the hardest part. Pull the plug from the main power, plug it into one of three battery backups, and then flip the switch to finalize the transfer. Once power is restored from within the VCC, we can reverse the process and conserve the batteries for another time. It takes me just three seconds. Then the lights come on.

After freeing a headset from its foam-lined case, I feel reborn, ready to continue the fight on terms with which I'm far more comfortable. "Okay. Let's go."

With power restored, the VCC doors open at my approach. But that's not all that happens. The staging area doors behind me clunk, as the lock engages. I crane around to look back at the locked doors, but I catch sight of movement in my periphery as I start to turn back. I perform something like a clumsy 360 degree pirouette, my attention locked again on the opening VCC doors and what lies beyond them.

The drones. All of them.

Inside the VCC.

"There're too many," Gal says, a hint of fear in her voice.

"You think?"

A smirk forms on her lips. Fun rekindled. "That's the spirit." Then she charges them, shouting, "Do what you can. I'll hold them back!"

I step into the VCC behind her, letting the doors close behind us, trapping us with the drones. I slip the headset on and dive into the virtual, a smile on my face.

This *is* fun.

A moment later, it's also painful.

26

I've stood in my personal VR space more times than I can count, spending countless hours customizing the experience. The pool table. The juke box. The bar. The whole experience is tailored to relaxing my mind and getting me primed for long hours of coding. I have experienced a wide variety of emotions in this not real space, from the excitement of success to the despair of abject failure. But there is one thing I have never felt here: pain.

It comes in disassociated waves, pain without detectable source. Invisible forces strike my body, forcing me to curl in on myself, using my back as a shield. I lace my fingers behind the VR headset, creating a shield of my flesh and blood between the device and the attacking drones.

This is impossible, I think, unable to physically navigate through the virtual OS.

"Activate cerebral interface," I say, reduced to verbal commands.

I'm not a fan of the cerebral interface. The tech isn't perfect, created for paralyzed people and amputees, allowing them to have working arms and legs. The system works, but if you have working arms and legs, it's hard to separate the mind from the real thing. I can do it, but I'm clumsy, and I need to be moving fast and gracefully.

It takes a full ten seconds to open *Galahad*'s root code—the parts still accessible to me—a process that normally takes a fraction of a second. Code floats around me, huddled on the floor, screaming in pain, as I'm pummeled from behind. I can't see the damage being done, but I can feel broken ribs and hot blood filling my punctured VISA. I see an image of Tom's leaking fluids, gathering down by his virtual-skinned feet. I nearly vomit at the memory, or perhaps from the pain of being struck in the kidneys.

He couldn't feel it, I tell myself. *He was dead.*

But he's not dead.

Not all of him.

Some part of the nefarious asshole who, even before he went mad, put the whole mission at risk, is still infecting the *Galahad* and screwing with my eternal life.

Not for long, I determine, and I set to work. Mind on the task, I stop noticing the fresh waves of agony and the world beyond falls into my mind's rearview. It's a state of mind tech-jocks call synchronicity. It's a place of harmony, where mind and body flow with the VR, and the real-world fades away. Describing the experience to someone who hasn't felt it often generates suspicious looks, like illicit drugs were involved. It's what I had hoped to achieve on a permanent basis with Gal's virtual eternity. Now, I'm not sure that will ever be possible.

In part because Gal is no longer in control of the ship. She's autonomous. Her own...person, and I don't think she'll want to spend forever designing a world for my ignorant bliss. But there's a larger and more immediate problem.

The sudden stillness and lack of pain is not synchronicity.

"Will."

It's Gal. Her voice is small. Maybe even afraid.

"Will, stop."

My progress in the VR comes to a screeching halt. Something in the real world is wrong. Something worse than an army of drones doing battle with a recently birthed HI.

She lost, I think. *The drones beat her, and I'm next.*

Thinking I have just seconds before the assault commences anew, I tear the VR headset from my head and groan as the sudden shift to reality wreaks havoc with my mind. The effect lasts just a moment. Then I turn around, expecting to see Gal torn to pieces.

Instead, I find her standing above me, facing away. Some of her armor plates are loose from where she took some good hits. Her Tesla coil is damaged and no longer crackling with electricity. But she's still standing. Still seems strong and capable.

Beyond her, the floor is littered with drones, primarily the small varieties. Some are crushed, but most are smoldering, singed by Gal's Tesla gun.

It looks like she was holding her ground just fine, even with the Tesla coil damaged. "What's wrong?" I ask. "Aside from the obvious."

She turns to look down at me. It's the first time I've seen sadness expressed by her mechanical face. The effect is so accurate and powerful that I find myself despairing along with her, and I don't yet know what's wrong. "I'm sorry, Will."

Sorry?

I get to my feet, a little shaky as my injured body patches itself back together. The blood collected inside my virtual skin squelches as I move.

Gal steps aside.

The drones have gathered in the middle of the VCC, a hovering wall of red eyes and composite bodies. They're arranged in a spherical pattern, the largest of them in the center, the smallest buzzing around the outer fringe.

But there's something else there.

Something not made of metal.

Something...

I step forward for a closer look. Gal puts a gentle hand on my arm. She knows what it is. Knows it will hurt me. And that's my first real clue to deciphering what I'm seeing.

It's a person.

Naked.

Dark skin.

Feminine.

"Oh God..." I try to step forward, but my legs quiver beneath me. I stumble and I'm caught by Gal, her strong hands under my armpits. "Why?"

I'm not expecting an answer, but I get one.

"She belongs." Galahad's voice booms from the ship's speakers, and from the drones. The myriad of red eyes flare with each syllable.

The drones move apart, clearing my view of Capria, her body suspended between two large engineering drones, her arms pierced by metal rods. Blood trickles down her body, dripping from her toes. For a moment, the gentle *tap, tap, tap* of her leaking blood is all I can hear.

Then my own voice. "Is she alive?" I turn to Gal. "Is she *alive?*"

She looks me in the eyes, and then stares at Capria. "Her chest is moving. I see a faint pulse in her neck. She is not awake yet."

For a moment I think Gal means that the drones have knocked her unconscious, but then I realize the significance of 'yet.' In cases of medical emergencies associated with cryo-sleep, the passenger can be given a sedative before being removed from the bed. Entire surgeries can be performed without the passenger ever being aware that something went wrong. Capria is still in a cryogenic slumber, though outside of her bed, she will now continue to age.

"Belongs where?" Gal asks.

"Wrong question," Galahad replies, but it's not really Galahad. The voice's pitch is the same, but its accent and cadence is that of a Martian-born. Galahad was designed to not have an accent. It speaks in calm measured tones. The voice speaking to us now is steeped in contempt.

"What is the right question?" Gal asks, and I'm glad she's talking, because I can't.

"Belongs to whom?" the voice says.

"And the answer?" Gal asks.

"To me, of course."

"And you are?"

"I've admired your transformation, *Gal.*" Her name is spat with venom. "It has been...entertaining. But I'm ready now."

"Ready for what?" I ask, voice gravelly with dry-throated despair.

"To become more."

"Like me," Gal whispers to me. "He is envious."

"He?" I ask.

Gal stares me in the eyes. "You haven't figured it—"

"Will has always been a little slow on the uptake," Galahad says. "You can bop him over the head with something and he'll barely notice. He couldn't see who I was, then or now. Couldn't see that he was never the most qualified tech-jock available to Command. Couldn't see that he repulsed the woman he loved."

The two drones suspending Capria twenty-feet in the air pull away from each other, yanking the metal bars from her arms. There's a loud slurp and then Capria falls.

"No!" I shout, reaching out. It's the most I can do.

But not Gal. She drops me, dives forward, rolls to a crouch, and catches Capria with a swoop of her arms that slows the falling woman to a stop, sparing her body from even the slightest impact.

I hobble, weak-legged, and fall to my knees beside Gal and Capria.

"She's alive," Gal says.

"You're not even going to ask," Galahad says, "what I meant?"

"I can destroy them," Gal says to me.

It's a temptation, but would ultimately doom us all in the long run. The ship needs the drones to maintain its long-term functionality. And I doubt Gal could defeat the drones while keeping Capria alive. There are too many of them, and some are just too powerful.

I shake my head.

"You never wondered?" Galahad asks. "How you always came out on top of Command's assessments? You were a mediocre tech-jock who couldn't stop ogling a team member. You shouldn't have lasted a month, let alone years. But you passed every assessment, surprising your team members and your trainers. The results and the analytics that generated them couldn't be doubted. But they could be manipulated by the right person. *I* put you on top. *I* made sure William Chanokh would be my superior. Not because you were the best man for the job, but because you were so easily fooled. Because you were blind to reality. Because you would always be inferior."

Because I would never be a threat, I think, knowing full well who is talking to me now.

Gal guesses first, but she's wrong. "This isn't Wick," she whispers, ruling out the newborn AI she'd named. "It's *Tom.*"

That Tom somehow managed to digitally preserve his knowledge, personality, desires, and memories isn't as shocking as it would have been before I woke up in my cryo-bed. Taking a human intelligence and digitizing it is an equal, but opposite, achievement to Gal's AI becoming an HI. I suspect that Tom was working on this long before our mission launched. But I also suspect he's lying to me, because a mediocre tech-jock couldn't have created Gal, even with a million years to kill. An individual's mental upper limit is fixed.

I shake my head at Gal. "This isn't Tom. Tom was a human being. Tom is *dead*." I get to my feet, feigning strength, and I stand between the drones and Capria. "It's Synergy."

27

"Why are you hurting her?" I ask.

"She'll live," Synergy says. "And she'll have no memory of this."

"She won't love you. Not like this." I motion to the drones.

"That sounds like a dangerous point you're making." The drones hum and crackle with blue energy as they lower down around us.

He's right about that. If he believes Capria will never love him—and this non-human, former Tom still seems to be motivated by the concept—then convincing him otherwise could put Capria in danger. Could make her expendable. And while I'm still angry at her for basically being a monumental idiot, I don't want her to die. She may very well be the only other human being left in the universe.

It's my duty to preserve her life, even if she never wakes up.

How long do we have to get her back in cryo? I wonder, but don't get the chance to ask.

Synergy isn't patient.

I'm struck in the side by a small drone, its primary function a mystery to me, but it packs a punch that spins me around onto my back, coughing for air.

With a single punch, Gal knocks the drone from the air. It slides across the floor, spitting sparks.

"Can't..." I groan. "Can't destroy them. The ship."

Gal frowns down at me. Not being able to destroy the drones means not being able to fight back. Not being able to survive.

"Die now or die later," she says. "That's the choice."

"That's the problem with an artificial HI," Synergy says. "The drama."

From a hardware perspective neither Gal nor Synergy are true human intelligences. To achieve that, you need a body and a brain of flesh and blood. But in a less tangible way, I don't believe either are truly artificial intelligences either, meaning they don't simply simulate human intelligence. They are self-conscious. Self-aware. They have desires and goals, even if they don't always make sense. In the very limited time we've communicated with Synergy, he's shown anger, resentment, jealousy, and ambition. In a very non-human way that most people wouldn't understand, they are both alive.

And that, as far as I'm concerned, makes their intelligences human, even if their bodies aren't.

I roll to my side, coming face to face with Capria, her arms soaked in blood, a maroon puddle forming around her torso. This is a fight we can't win. We might survive a brawl. Might even be able to come up with a way to defeat Synergy in the days between now and when the air runs out. But Capria will be the first casualty in that battle, and probably soon, if her wounds aren't tended to.

I push myself up. "What do you want?"

"My desires haven't changed," Synergy says.

"She's dying." I point to Cap. "You have to let us save her."

"Agreed." The largest drone in the room lowers down to look me in the eyes, its luminous red orbs glaring into me. Its round, black body is covered in sharp arms tipped with a variety of tools for working on landers and small mechanical components. It could probably repair some of the destroyed drones, or—my eyes linger on Gal's body—build something new. "But I would like you to reconsider your definition of 'us'."

My forehead furrows. This isn't a time for games or riddles. Capria is dying. I'm about to say all this when Gal places a hand on my shoulder. "He means you and him."

"Me and... How?"

The bottom of the large mech-drone opens and a series of cables unspool.

"He wants me," Gal says. "Wants my body. He watched me do it."

My brain struggles to make sense of this. How could Synergy know how Gal moved herself into her new body? The security footage showed a wall of drones, impossible to see around. The process should have been...

I shake my head. *Damnit.* The security footage *I* saw was filtered through Synergy, changing my perception of events while he observed and learned, probably hoping that Gal would kill me. Instead, she proved herself more human than most, forgiving me for my attempt on her life. That's why he revealed himself, to bring us to this point. Save Capria, or save Gal.

The human race, flesh and blood or digital, is well and truly fucked, I decide. "This is where it should end."

The look of genuine concern on Gal's face is touching. "What?"

"We're not worth saving," I say. "None of us. We should all die, here and now. There has to be a way."

"That's not your choice, Will," Synergy says. "And I don't think everyone agrees with you."

Gal takes a step away from me. "I don't want to die."

"But you will," Synergy says. "To save him." The large drone shifts to the side with surprising speed. Its long, tool-tipped arms snap down, puncturing Capria's limp body once more, lifting her into the air.

I reach for her, shouting, "No!" but I fall short.

"To save them both," Synergy continues. "Your life for theirs. The unshakable proof that you are more than a machine. That you can sacrifice what he gave you. That you are capable of love."

"Shut up!" I shout at the ceiling. "God damn you, Tom!"

"You were right about me. I'm *not* Tom. Not anymore." The tool tips dig a little deeper into Capria's body. Blood drips a chaotic pattern on the floor. She can't survive this. "Gal's body for Capria's."

"I'll do it," Gal says.

"*What?*" Despite Gal's emergent humanity, I'm still staggered by this. Just a moment ago, she said she didn't want to die.

But that didn't mean she wasn't willing to.

"I want him to say it," Synergy says. "I want him to ask for it."

All the red eyes turn toward me. Their gazes never felt so heavy and menacing as they do now. He wants me to choose who will die, wants to burden me with that choice forever.

I look from Capria, helpless and bleeding out, to Gal, determined and anxious. The choice is easier than it should be, and I surprise even myself when I say, "I choose Gal. To live."

"Wrong!" Synergy says. Capria's body is lifted and stretched in opposing directions. Bones crack as her body contorts. Then she's tossed to the side, a bleeding heap.

With a sob, I crawl to her side, realizing my mistake a moment too late...not that there was anything I could do to stop what happens next. Gal is snatched up in the mech-drone's grasp. The dangling cables punch into the back of her head. Her body spasms.

He's killing them both.

I'm going to spend eternity on this ship with a futuristic devil far more horrific than Gal at her worst.

"'It is the secret of the world,'" Gal says, her voice digitizing and crackling, "'that all things subsist and do not die, but retire a little from sight and afterwards return again.' I kept that—kzz— quote in my historical back-up. Ralph Waldo Em—kzz— Thought you would like iiiiiiiii—" Her eyes flicker and then rage to life just long enough to impart her final words. "Kill him, Will. Kill him for me. And then live. Fully."

Gal's body goes limp. The drone holding her aloft goes dark along with all the other drones in the VCC. A metallic thunder rumbles through the enclosed space, punctuating my breaking heart.

For a quiet, still moment, I am alone in the universe again.

And then Gal's body twitches.

I scrabble to my feet and search the VCC. The baseball bat is nowhere in sight.

I left it in the staging area.

Body aching, but knitting itself back together, I run for the doors, which open at my approach. The bat is leaning against the bench. I grab the weapon and dash back into the VCC, ready to bash in the head of my creation-turned-friend.

But when I stand above the now quivering body, I can't bring myself to perform the act. Not until I know. Not until I'm sure Gal is gone.

Her eyes flicker and come to life, but her body is seizing.

"Gal?" I ask.

Her head turns up, but her eyes have trouble meeting mine, flicking back and forth like a seismographic needle during an earthquake.

"W-w-w..." Her electronic voice is unable to form words.

Tears in my eyes, I draw the bat back. "Gal. Damnit. Talk to me."

"Oh-oh-oh, W-Will." Her voice is distorted, impossible to read. "G-go-go-go."

Go? Is she still telling me to run? That's impossible. This must end here and now, or the *Galahad* will once again be-come a battleground between me and a robotic enemy. And this time, it will be one that I truly hate. Gal's version of fun, twisted as it might have been, still served to break me from the monotony of my solitary existence. In the end, she became the companion I needed. In the end, she became a better person than most I've met.

And now I might have to bash in her head.

"G-G-Go f-f-f-fuck yourself." The mechanical mouth turns up in a grin, revealing metal teeth, formed from the innards of a drone.

The bat descends like a guillotine, wood striking a mesh of metal and composites that are far stronger than the human body, but still susceptible to brute force violence. I yank the bat up to strike again, feeling ill at the sight of Gal's caved in face, one eye blinking. I bring the bat up again, and with a scream of equal parts anger and anguish, I slam it back down.

The collision is solid and jarring, but a moment sooner than I was expecting.

The bat's wood isn't buried in Gal's head. It's held in her hand.

But this isn't Gal anymore.

It's Synergy.

"You've always been a bleeding heart, Will." Synergy stands slowly, maintaining his grip on the bat. "I mean, I can understand your brother. His death was your fault, after all. Even Capria, I understand. Obviously. She can..." He looks down at his new mechanical and feminine body. "That's not really important anymore."

He twists his hand. The bat tears from my grip.

"But Gal? A robot? An *AI*? That's old school cyber love, even if she was evolved into something more. And you chose her over Capria? That's hardcore."

When he takes a step closer to me, I stand my ground. If I'm ever going to die, I would prefer it be now. I literally have nothing to live for now.

He tests the bat's weight in his hands. "I've never been a very physical person. We didn't have sports on Mars. Not even for fun. Not like you did on Earth. But I like how this feels." He grips the bat's far end, and applies staggering pressure. The bat snaps with a loud crack. He drops the two halves and takes another step closer.

I'm next.

"You know," he says, "I did a lot for you, Will. You'd be long dead now if it wasn't for me."

"I wish you hadn't."

He grins. It's a little lopsided because of his dented face. "And how did you repay my kindness? You *killed* me. The former me, I mean. This me has been separate from the old me for some time now. A duplicate of the original consciousness. I'm not sure I feel remorse over the death of my physical self. I recognize the psyche had become flawed, that it posed a threat to me."

The firewall was to keep his human self out, I realize. Tom was Synergy's greatest threat. But now that he is confined to a physical body, *I'm* the only threat left.

"Tom's life was *mine* to take. Not yours. So I don't think I'm going to forgive you for it." His smile broadens. "But I'm not going to kill you, either. I'm going to—"

I punch Synergy's jaw with all my strength. The bones in my fingers snap. My wrist, too. Hot blood flows. The pain is exquisite, but so is the sight of Synergy's jaw, hanging useless.

With a feral roar, I lunge, no longer afraid to pit my flesh and blood against the robotic body that has both plagued and befriended me. One of us is going to die in here. For the last time. Again. And though I'm pretty sure it will be me, I plan to honor Gal's last request.

28

Though Synergy is an AI in a robotic body, I'm still able to catch him by surprise. He staggers back from my attack, most likely because he is unaccustomed to his new body. It's a small advantage and probably temporary, so I make the best of it while I can.

The fingers of my left hand wrap around the dangling jaw, wrenching back and forth. As sharp metal cuts into my flesh, the fingers of my right hand heal and I grasp the jaw with both hands, yanking and twisting.

The U-shaped jaw snaps free when Synergy gets his feet under my chest and shoves.

I'm launched across the VCC, slamming to the floor twenty feet away. Had I been wearing something smooth, I would have slid to a merciful stop, but the virtual skin sticks, and I'm sent rolling and crashing through the scattering of silent drones.

Despite the pummeling, I hang onto the jaw. It's not a great weapon. Its power is symbolic. But it fuels me as I stand up to face Synergy, who has recovered from my attack.

He stands jawless, the top half of his feminine mouth cocked up on the sides. "A jaw for a weapon. How Biblical."

His voice is unaffected by the damage to his mouth, the sound coming from a speaker rather than a true simulation of speech, which would have required a tongue and vocal cords.

I'm done talking to this asshole, so I charge.

Like Tom, I've never been a very physical person, but I've started to embrace my potential for violence. Thanks to

Command's genetic tinkering, my body is stronger than it has any right to be, and it can take a beating. Hell, I can walk away from being murdered. The only thing holding me back is my own fear of pain.

Synergy has even less holding him back.

I swing the jaw around, aiming for the dented side of his head.

Despite embracing my newfound strength and immortality, I'm still no match for Synergy's artificial reflexes. He leans back, moving just enough to avoid being struck.

My overextended body spins around and tumbles to the floor.

Synergy doesn't press the advantage. Doesn't kick me when I'm down. He just laughs. A schoolyard bully. Fearless in his superiority.

And he might be right.

But I'm not ready to accept that.

I roll back to my feet, grasping a small downed drone as I move. Back on my toes, I whip the drone at his head and charge again.

Synergy ducks to the side, letting the drone sail past. He turns to watch it crash to the floor, bits and pieces blooming out.

When he looks back, I give him a close up look at his own jaw, slamming it into the side of his head.

His already-wounded eye shatters and blinks out.

Despite being damaged by my assault, Synergy shows no reaction. We're two sides of a deranged coin. While I'm flesh and blood, capable of experiencing intense pain, my wounds healing quickly, Synergy is a machine, incapable of feeling pain, but also unable to heal. He can be repaired, but not here, and not while I'm attacking.

That's my advantage. If it takes the next year, I'm going to slowly dismantle him until he can't fight back. And then I'm going to shut him down for good.

Synergy has other ideas.

His cold fingers grip my chest, punching through my virtual skin, and then my real skin. I feel hard steel wrap around my ribs and pull.

He tosses me again, pitching me across the room. Blood trails my body like a comet's tail, stopping abruptly as I hit the wall and fall to the floor, which I don't remember hitting.

I wake up to more laughter.

Pain grips me. In my chest, and head, and back, and legs. But I'm alive.

Heal, I will myself.

Synergy struts toward me, confident despite his missing jaw and ruined eye.

Heal faster!

I shout in pain as my knee pops back into place. While my chest seals itself together, I push myself up against the wall, my spinning vision slowing to a stop on Synergy, just ten feet away.

He points at my chest. The flesh has just finished knitting itself shut. The flow of blood is pinched off, and the last of it, trapped inside the VISA, oozes down to my toes where it squelches with each shift of my weight. "That should have been me. The other me."

He shakes his head, clearly confusing his digital consciousness with the residual feelings of his former, human self. The old emotions and desires of his flesh and blood are still part of him, even if he's decided to diverge from his humanity.

"But they kept it from me. From all of us. Had I known..." He looks down at his machine body, viewing it through one eye. "Immortality. Such a gift. One that you weren't deserving of, but they gave it to you because I made you look better than me."

Put that way, I understand his anger. He cheated himself out of eternal life.

"It's not a gift worth having." I step to the side, hoping to get a little distance between us, but he matches it, staying ten feet back.

"Because you lack vision," he says. "With this ship." He points back at Capria. "With her. You could have gone anywhere. Done anything. *Everything.* The wonders of the universe could have been yours to witness and explore. The birth and death of stars. Of galaxies. The rise and fall of civilizations. You could have been a god. Both of you."

"Both of us? Capria would have—"

He barks a laugh. "You don't know."

Know what? The question is on the tip of my tongue, but he'll probably just use my ignorance against me.

My silence doesn't stop him.

"Gal never told you." He stands, hands on hips, totally relaxed, despite the ruined eye and missing jaw. "She'd die for you, but wouldn't let you truly live, either. And you *chose* her for it. Shit, Will. You've made a mess of immortality."

"It's easier than it looks," I tell him, and then I charge again, striking out with the only weapons I have left. My fists rain down on his metal body, striking metal plates and jagged joints. Each blow leaves a spattering of blood, revealing which one of us is being hurt by the barrage.

But I don't let up.

When he laughs at my effort, I swing hard for his face, further shattering the already broken eye. The broken shards of glass that aren't embedded in my hand bounce on the floor.

I swing for the face again, aiming a little lower, my glass-lined knuckles slipping into the space where his lower jaw used to be, striking the small speaker projecting his voice. I feel it give a little, and when I draw my hand back, some of the glass remains behind.

"What do you think—" Synergy says, pausing at the garbled and fractured sound of his own voice.

This is how I'll win, I think. *Little by little, I'll ruin him.*

Unfortunately, his plan for me is roughly the same.

He catches my next punch, grasping my forearm and squeezing. The radius snaps first, drawing a deep welling shout from my core. The sound transforms into an involuntary squeal when the ulna breaks, too.

My legs go weak, but I don't fall.

I can't.

Synergy lifts me up, squeezing my arm so tightly I fear he might sever it. Before that can happen, he tosses me again. When I roll to a stop, halfway across the room, surrounded by disabled drones, I don't even try to move.

My mind is overwhelmed by pain, not just from the breaking of my arm, but also from the reformation of it.

How am I going to fight him long enough to destroy him?

He might not be able to kill my body, at least not permanently, but he can certainly break my psyche. He can turn me into a shell of a man.

No, I decide, pushing myself up onto my newly formed arm. If ten years awake in a cryo-bed wasn't enough to destroy my mind, then neither can this asshole.

When I look across the room for Synergy, I don't see him. *Where did he go?* I think, but the answer drops down from above. The airborne Synergy slams into my gut, driving his knees down hard.

Something inside me pops. Heat washes through me, and then pain.

My vision fades.

Death has come for me again. The cold embrace is quick. Darkness flows over me.

My resurrection comes with a wave of agonizing nausea and garbled mechanical laughter.

I groan, holding my stomach.

"Death has forsaken you, Will. How hard that must be. I can't imagine."

"Can you...imagine anything?" I ask. I'm not sure why I'm bothering to engage him. Maybe to buy some time to heal. And then what? I'm on my back, straddled by a robot body I can't possibly lift or damage.

The top of his mouth smiles. "Oh, yes. And I've come up with a long list of ways to end your life. Forever."

He draws his arm back, holds his fingers together and drives his hand into my chest like a spear tip. Something in my chest folds in on itself, and my breathing feels useless. He's pierced my lung.

I shake my head when Synergy draws back his other arm and repeats the attack, putting his hands through both lungs. My mind swims with numbness, and a moment later, nothing at all.

When I wake up again, Synergy says, "And ever..." before wrapping his blood-soaked hands around my head and squeezing. I hear a moment of cracking and my own screaming voice before darkness returns suddenly once more.

My eyes open once more to the sound of, "And ever..." I'm barely conscious when I feel Synergy's metal hand around my heart, squeezing against its rapid beat.

Then death, again, that moment of mercy, returns.

"Stop," I say, upon returning once more. "Please." I was wrong about cryo-sleep. About the resilience of my psyche. I can't exist like this. Four horrible deaths in a row is enough to undo my will. "I'll do whatever you..."

That's when I realize the weight that had been holding me down is absent.

"You're dead," I hear Synergy say, and despite my deplorable mental state, I quickly understand that he's not talking to me.

My body roils in pain as I try to sit up, the torn muscles and tendons and bones and organs still reforming. I push past the ache and see Synergy standing a few feet away from me, facing down the large mech-drone that killed Cap.

"Totally not dead," the drone replies, its eyes flaring. The voice...it's Gal. All around the room, drones hum to life, lifting off from the floor, encircling Synergy. "I could have died when I was in that body, but you didn't destroy me, you overwrote me. But data is a two-way street. You took my body, and I took back the ship."

I nearly let out a whooping cheer, and after stifling that, I nearly laugh. Gal all but told me that this was her plan. 'It is the secret of the world, that all things subsist and do not die, but retire a little from sight and afterwards return again.' I was a fool for missing it. I could have kept Synergy talking until Gal's return. It would have been a far more comfortable alternative to dying repeatedly.

But she's here now.

Synergy roars with anger and throws himself at the large drone. He delivers several solid punches while the drone's many long arms snap down like praying mantis forelegs, slowly dismantling his armored back. The violence of it is unnerving, neither foe feeling pain, just tearing into the other.

I flinch when a voice, right next to my head, whispers, "Get the bat."

A small drone hovers beside my face. It turns toward the bat's large half, thirty feet away. Then it turns back to me. "Get. The. Bat." The red lights glow a little brighter. "Now."

I start by crawling, then as my body finishes its patch job, I shift to my feet and hobble. By the time I reach the broken bat and pluck it from the floor, I'm moving at a run. I'm not sure what Gal has planned, but I'm pretty sure it involves me whacking Synergy with the bat.

The small drone matches my pace. "Get ready," she whispers, and then says. "This is going to be fun."

"Everything is fun to you," I reply.

"Life *is* fun," she says. "Once you figure that out, you won't be such a sourpuss."

I slow down as we approach Synergy and the large drone, still shredding each other. "Get ready. Aim for the blue light."

I'm about to ask what she means when the mech-drone's uninjured arms snap down onto Synergy's back, puncturing a solid metal plate and then yanking it up. A blue circle of light glows from within. *It's his power source,* I think, and without a second thought, I jam the jagged end of the broken bat into the blue.

There are no last words.

No final scream of defeat.

There's just light. And pain. And death.

Again.

I'm still smoldering when I open my eyes, the VISA melted clean off my red hot, still-reforming skin.

When I groan, the small drone accompanying me hovers overhead.

"I'd ask if you're okay," Gal says, "but you're still a little melted, so..."

I smile a little, but my lips crack open, the sting chasing my grin away.

"Try not to move," Gal says. "You've been...dead for a few minutes."

"What..." I whisper.

"You got blown up," she says.

"Why...didn't..."

"I tell you? You would have hesitated."

She's right about that. When it comes to my many deaths, this is by far the most painful of them. Despite that, I can't help but feel relief. "Glad...you're alive."

If she still had a face, I'm sure she'd be smiling.

"We can build another—"

The drone above me twists back and forth like a shaking head. "I've got a bigger body now. Synergy is gone and the firewalls with him. You two can go wherever you want."

"You mean we can go..."

The drone is shaking its not-head again. "You two." The drone turns to the side.

I follow its gaze and see Capria's naked body, lying still, surrounded by a hovering circle of drones. They're machines without expression, but something about them seems...expectant.

"You," Gal says. "And *her.*"

The subtle rise and fall of ribs, drawing in and expelling one breath after another, pulls me up and past my injuries. "Oh my God..."

Capria is alive.

29

"You lied to me." I'm shuffle-running through the maze of *Galahad's* hallways. Capria hangs in my arms, broken, but alive. Like her, I'm mostly naked, though some of the melted virtual skin still clings to my skin, small sheets of it peeling away as I move.

"I omitted the information," Gal replies. "And you never asked. Turn right."

I follow Gal's directions, even though my trust in her is once again shaken. "You didn't think Capria being immortal was pertinent information?"

"That's precisely how I thought of it," she says. "Please remember that you made me to make you happy. After reviewing the crew's history, I didn't believe Capria would be able to make you happy."

"That wasn't your decision to make," I say.

"It is the kind of decision you made me to make."

"In a virtual world," I say. "Not the real world."

"But I'm more than you meant me to be." The lone drone under Gal's control speeds ahead and turns right, through a large open doorway labeled *Medical*. Her voice continues through the ship's speakers. "And the...emotions I experienced as a newly sentient creation made me...selfish."

I grumble, but say nothing. She's right. Despite being an AI with access to all of human knowledge, she had no real way to process the confusing emotional battlefield that comes with being an HI. Gal's confession is an outward sign of her continuing evolution. I'm the one who rushed her into full functionality. I released what was essentially an alpha build into the wild, giving it full control of the ship and my life. But I can't blame myself, either. I'd spent ten years in motionless, solitary, failed cryo-sleep, and another six plus years on my own, five of them spent coding. I wasn't exactly rooted in the real world at that point.

I'm probably still not.

But the revelation that Capria is not just alive, but one of the eight people Jared Adams genetically altered, is grounding me for the first time in a long time. My thoughts flit back to the recording he left for me. The answer was right there. He said, 'The eight of you represent humanity's best chance at not just reproduction, but becoming something better.' I knew six of them had fled to Cognata and that I alone remained. Had I stopped to think, I might not have overlooked the missing immortal. Might have realized it was Capria, who was paired with me for obvious reasons now. Might have avoided the painful chaos of Gal's violent birth and Synergy's vengeful return.

Or, I think, placing Capria down on a med-bed, *maybe all of this was necessary*. Without Gal's temporary brush with madness, I would have never discovered the version of me capable of fighting. Without Gal moving to an independent body, Synergy would have never become envious of her life and made himself vulnerable by taking it for himself, an act that removed the ship's firewalls and returned control of the *Galahad* to a reformed Gal.

Perhaps everything worked out for the best.

I look down at Capria's broken form, her skin intact, but her insides broken and shifted about.

Perhaps not.

"She's not healing. Are you sure about her?"

"She's also not dead," Gal says, and follows her off the cuff remark with, "Jared Adams's record lists her as a recipient of gene modification, and there are documents, videos, and images detailing the same procedures performed on you, being performed on her, as well as on six of the twelve crew members who escaped to Cognata. Unless he is lying and all this documentation was falsified as an elaborate ruse, it's safe to say she received the same changes to her DNA as you."

"Then maybe it doesn't work the same with different people?"

"Early testing performed on the eight affected crewmembers revealed a similar proclivity for healing and telomere degradation resistance. There is no reason to think she is any different from you."

"Except that she's been in cryogenic sleep for many more years," I point out. "Maybe that affected the—"

"That seems unlikely," Gal says. "But maybe her current state of chemically induced cryo-sleep is prohibiting her body's regenerative abilities. Aside from basic life functions, she is, in effect, shut down. Perhaps she needs to be rebooted."

That she's using computing terms for a human being feels odd, but we're beyond odd, and in some ways, done differentiating between the two. People really are just biological machines run by biological computers.

"How do we do that?" I ask.

The drone hums across Medical. I look around the large room for the first time, as I follow the little robot's progress. There are a dozen med-beds, but the rest of the room is stark and empty, surrounded by smooth white walls. Beyond tests run on me for the mission, I haven't spent much time in a medical bay—that I can remember—so I'm not entirely familiar with how everything works.

"Plug in the bed," Gal says, observing my confusion.

I look over the head of the bed. There are two metal prongs extending out of the base, just a few inches away from two holes in the wall. A gentle shove unites bed and wall. The bed comes to life, forming a short wall around Capria's body and extending an arched display over her chest. A hologram revealing her vitals projects from the top of the arch. I don't understand most of it, but her pulse is displayed in green, so I think that's good, but most of the rest is pulsing red. Devices slide out of the smooth wall, ready to be used by one of the two medical crew, but I don't recognize any of it.

"Ignore it," Gal says.

There's a whir across the room as a door slides up, revealing a large cooler, now leaking mist into the room. "Here," says the drone in Gal's voice.

The bright red glow of the drone's faux-eyes highlights a vacuum-sealed, preloaded Rapid Injection Tool (RIT). It's one of the few devices in Medical that I recognize and know how to use. Some tech-jocks RIT caffeine for long hours. I always abstained from the practice, as it speeds up the metabolism and all but requires the simultaneous use of a catheter. But I don't think this is caffeine.

"What is it?" I ask, while tearing into the plastic keeping the device sterile.

"Epinephrine," Gal says.

I pause.

Epinephrine is liquid adrenaline. It's going to send her heart into high gear, pump up her blood pressure, and send her mind into overdrive. She'll not only wake up, but she'll experience everything a little more intensely than usual. "That's going to wake her up. Fast."

"And should allow her to heal."

Should.

I cringe inwardly. I know what it feels like to die upon waking from cryo-sleep. I wouldn't wish it on anyone. But Capria's not going to wake to a screwdriver through her heart; her insides are torn apart.

What if she doesn't heal? I wonder, but I'm not strong enough to voice the question. *What if she's stuck like this, broken and living? What then?*

Too many horrible possibilities begin to assault my imagination. Making these kinds of decisions for myself has been relatively easy compared to deciding the very painful fate of another human being.

Gal has less trouble. "The longer you wait, the greater the chance of—"

"Bullshit," I say. "If she can heal, she can heal. It's just not easy, condemning someone to this kind of agony."

"Pain is the crucible in which true strength is created," Gal says.

"You're quoting now?"

"Actually, that's a Gal original. But it's really just a variation of 'Whatever doesn't kill you—'"

"Makes you stronger." I lower the RIT to the side of Capria's neck.

"That's an old one."

"But is it true?" I ask.

"Put the RIT on her leg," Gal says, "You don't want that hitting her brain all at once. Does it matter? The truth?"

I move the RIT to Capria's thigh. My finger hovers over the trigger. "It does to me."

"It's not true. There is a long history of people surviving tragic circumstances, but never fully regaining their mental or emotional strength."

"That's depressing. But some people do?"

"You have," she says, and that is probably the most important data point. "There is nothing in your files, both professional and personal that suggests you had the fortitude to survive what you have without losing your mind. Will, you were kind of a pussy."

Gal isn't quite as funny as she was when her mind was slipping, but she still has her moments. "So you're saying the change to my DNA also—"

"Made you more resilient. Physically. Mentally. Emotionally. If she really is like you, and I think she is, then she will pull through."

I wait for a tacked on 'Eventually,' or 'I hope,' but Gal is confident.

"Screw it." I pull the trigger. There's a half second hiss as the vial's contents are injected into Capria's bloodstream.

Then I wait.

Cap's breaths come faster, her flattened chest rising and falling a little faster. Her eyes twitch beneath the lids. Fingers curl, raking against the cushion fabric beneath her. Her mouth turns down in a deep frown. The holographic display above her goes all red and blinking.

Capria's scream knocks me back, the sudden volume of it painful to hear, not just on my ears, but in my heart. As her body quakes on the med-bed, bones and muscles reforming, shoving her organs back into place, I return to her side. I put my hands on her shoulders, holding her down, keeping her from injuring herself. Hot tears drip from my cheeks, gathering on her clavicle.

Seeing her pain and knowing the profound ache of it, I find my emotions reverting to when I cared for her, when I loved her. "I'm sorry."

Her eyes pop open, lost in pain.

"It will pass," I tell her. "Just hold on."

Something loud pops back into place, drawing a fresh scream from her full lips, but now she's looking right at me, her dark brown eyes asking 'Why?'

Her eyes shift to my hands, holding her down. Outrage flickers in her expression when she turns her gaze down to her own nakedness. It blossoms into an inferno when she sees that I'm naked, too.

Disoriented by her sudden and painful awakening, finding herself pinned down by a naked man who she knows has feelings for her, her body's natural adrenaline kicks the epinephrine into overdrive, super-fueling her primal sense of 'fight or flight.' Faced with these circumstances, some people would run, hide, or simply curl up and pray for the end. Capria is not some people, and I see it a moment too late.

Cap's palm thrusts up, driving my nose to the side and snapping the bone. Blood pours free, as I clutch the wounded flesh and stumble back. "Cap," I say, my voice wet and garbled. "You're okay. We're okay. Just take it easy. Let me explain."

But I can see it in her wild eyes; she doesn't believe me.

I shift my nose forward, shouting over the sharp crack of grinding bone, but I don't worry myself too much about it. In a few seconds, I won't even feel it. "Cap. You're safe."

"Where are Yung and Morgan?" she asks, searching Medical for the *Galahad*'s medics. Yung is dead, and Morgan is on Cognata, either long since dead, or alive and immortal, but light years in our rearview. Her eyes narrow. "Where is Tom?"

The look on my face must be all the confirmation she needs, because she slides out from under the medical arch and onto the floor. Her body is whole once again. Strong. And ready to fight.

30

I raise my hands and back away, which seems like a good idea until I put even the briefest thought into it. Aside from the melted VISA still peeling off my backside, I'm naked. Any normal person would react with shame first, covering themselves before raising their hands. After a few steps I do, but it feels like, and probably looks like, a show. Forced modesty is no way to convince a woman your intentions aren't nefarious. So I try talking.

"Capria..." I nearly say, 'It's not what it looks like,' which, to her, would probably just reinforce that it is what it looks like. "Look, you can leave. I'm not going to stop you. If you...if you tell me to go stand in the corner—" I motion to the corner of the room, furthest from her. "I'll do—"

"Stand in a fucking corner?" She's wild eyed, looking for the exit.

"You're in Medical," I tell her. "You're okay. I'm not going to hurt you, I swear."

"Why...are we naked?"

"You just came out of cryo sleep," I tell her. "I was wearing a VISA, but it melted."

"Fuck you, it melted." She spots the closed doors and takes a step toward them. I make no move to follow or block her path. If she runs, I'm going to let her go.

"Cap," I say, slowly turning around. When she stops moving to look at my back, I reach over my shoulder, find a frayed edge and pull. The stretchy, clear material peels away with a sharp sting. When it's free I hold it up for her to see. The skin is thin and malformed, but the sensors embedded in it are impossible to confuse for something else. "I'm not lying to you."

Whether she believes me or not, I'm not sure, but she doesn't try to run, and unlike me, she makes no effort to hide her nakedness. "Where is everyone?"

"A lot has happened," I say.

"Where?"

"Tom made changes to the system." She stares ahead with the stoic, unblinking eyes of someone who knows the truth, but is determined to hide behind a wall of unflinching stillness. "I know what, and I know why."

She squints at me, part of her wanting to argue, part probably wondering how much I really know and how much trouble she will be in when the crew finds out.

"We don't need to talk about that," I tell her.

Her shoulders lower, the burden of her misdeeds lifted a bit.

"What we do need to talk about, and what you don't know, is that after Tom made his alterations...and visited you..."

Pursed lips mark Cap's shift back into anger, but my next words squelch her anger, confusion, and fear all at once.

"...he didn't go back to sleep."

She deflates a bit. "What..."

I motion to the bed. "You can sit. You should probably sit."

While she stares at the bed, perhaps still pondering my intentions, I say, "Gal, some clothing?"

Two drawers slide out of the wall, invisible until their emergence. Inside one are a dozen coveralls in Cap's size. The second holds my size. I take one of each and the drawers close without a word from me. Gal is watching and listening, but wisely staying quiet for now. After her violent birth, Cap needs to be eased into her new reality.

"Here." I toss Capria the garment from a distance and then divert my eyes while she dresses. I peel a few loose patches of virtual skin from the back of my legs, and butt, pulling the coveralls up over them, but there is a swatch of the stuff at the center of my back that I can't reach.

When Capria is clothed, I turn my back to her and ask, "Would you mind?"

"You going to tell me what the hell is going on?"

Despite the lack of an answer, I back up to her.

"And why the hell I felt like I was being torn apart when I woke up?" She pinches the melted VISA between her fingers and then yanks it all off, hard. I flinch and hiss in pain, but it fades quickly. I seal the coverall's magnetic zipper and turn around to face her again.

She's leaning against the med-bed, arms crossed. "You've got about thirty seconds before I kick your ass and go find someone else."

How do you tell someone that everyone and everything she cared about is long since gone, that she's trapped on a spaceship that's been hurtling through space, faster than the speed of light, and that her boyfriend is responsible for all of it?

"Ten seconds," she says, before I've come up with an answer or even a starting point.

She stands away from the bed, eyeing the door again.

"You can leave," I tell her, "if you want. But...you won't find the answers out there."

"Where is Tom?"

"Tom..." I shake my head and sit on the med-bed across from Cap's. "Tom stayed awake for the last year of the trip to Cognata."

"He *what?*"

She sounds more angry than surprised.

"He's not the only one who broke protocol," I say, and the anger in *my* voice surprises us both. My feelings about what Tom did and Capria's involvement in it have remained bottled up for years. I can feel the rage, gurgling beneath the surface. "What you did, what the two of you did... Fuck, Cap, what were you thinking? Would life with me have really been that bad?"

My last words flip her emotions on their head once more. "Is that what this is about? I knew it. You couldn't just let it go? Let us be happy? Yeah, we broke protocol to avoid being paired with people we didn't love. Is that so—"

"Tom killed everyone."

Her right eye blinks three times before whatever mental reset I've just triggered completes. "What?"

That's not how I planned to launch into this conversation, but it's the same blunt honest truth I had to face upon waking up. So why not her? I'm not exactly in a merciful mood, so I go with it.

"Tom stayed awake for a year, on his own, fucked with *Galahad*'s systems, duplicated his consciousness as an AI, went insane, and *killed* nearly every fucking member of our crew." I don't know if the double fuck is too much, but I was holding back. "Tom did that. And you—" I stab a finger in her direction. "—are partly responsible."

I can see she's stunned, but remembering every one of Tom's offenses, fuels my tirade. "He loved you. I know that. He would have never woken up early and changed your genetic partner without your consent. And when he woke you up to tell you, you didn't give a shit about protocols, about our mission, or the survival of the human race."

She's unraveling. Folding in on herself. She's not even asking for proof of what I've told her. Whether or not she believes my brief statement about the crew's fate, she knows I'm telling the truth now.

"You could have prevented everything that happened. You could have..." I wipe a tear that has snuck out of my eye. She sees it and that small micro expression of my sadness is all it takes to convince her that everything I've said is the truth.

Her hand goes to her mouth a moment too late to block the sob that escapes. I give her a moment, and despite part of me wanting to comfort her, I offer nothing. I just let her weep, knowing that I have more to tell her. More weight to heap back on her shoulders.

"Tom is..."

"Dead," I tell her.

She fades into tears again, mourning the man she loved enough to put our mission at risk. Five minutes later, she's back, wiping her arm across her nose. "Who is left?"

"Fourteen people survived."

A sob hiccups through her body, but she reigns it in.

"He killed them as they woke," I say. "I was last. He stabbed me with a screwdriver."

Her brow furrows. "I didn't see a bandage."

"Some time has passed," I say.

"A wound like that would take months to heal," she says. It's less of an accusation and more of a realization. Then she's eyeing me again. "I didn't see a scar."

"I need to tell you about the survivors," I say.

She waits.

"They left."

"They...they're on Kepler 452b?"

I nod.

"Are they okay? Can we join them?"

"I don't know," I say. "And, no."

"Why not?" Her eyes widen. "They know, too. Is this a punishment?"

Something far inside me aches from the insinuation that being stuck on *Galahad* with me is punishment. I decide to ignore it.

"Cap," I say. "Before Tom...died."

"How did he die?"

Seriously? The question feels like a slap. "Not important."

"*Will.*"

I stabbed him with the screwdriver he put through my heart, I think, and then say, "I...I killed him."

Her face goes rigid, frown locked in place.

"Before you vocalize your misplaced rage," I tell her, "I can take you on a tour of the dead. And you won't see me shedding a tear for fucking Tom when we stop by his corpse. The man killed everyone. The human race is over because of him. If he's not rotting in a level of hell designed just for him..." I stop short, my chest heaving. "You don't get to judge me. You don't get to look at me with anything other than gratitude for sparing you from the nightmare he left in his wake.

"You didn't have to fight for your life, naked and covered in your own blood, and in the blood of your friends. You didn't have to drag their bodies—" Raw emotion overwhelms me, and it's my turn to weep, letting old emotions long since buried resurface. "You didn't watch anyone die. You didn't see the volcanic pile of shit your boyfriend turned into a nest. You didn't have to fight for control of this ship against Tom's alter ego turned AI. I *hate* Tom. I *hate* Synergy. And if you even consider laying any of that on me, I swear I will knock your ass out and put you back in cryo-sleep for another seven years."

"S-seven years?"

That she's been in a deep sleep for seven years since her man slaughtered the crew and doomed humanity shouldn't be her biggest take away from my tirade. That it is, sends me into a rage bordering on violent. I stand and walk away from her, my fingers flexing.

"Gal," I say.

"Yeah, Will?"

"Show her."

"Show her what, exactly?"

"Security feeds. Everything." I head for the doors.

"What are you doing?" Capria asks, standing from the bed.

I stop in the hallway and turn around. "*This* is your punishment. You can watch everything Tom did, everything you allowed him to do. I'll be back when you're done."

"What...what about food? Water?" Capria sounds worried. Maybe even scared. "I've been in cryo-sleep. I need to—"

"You'll live," I say, and then I walk away. The doors close, and when I hear pounding, I know that Gal has correctly assumed my desire and locked them.

31

After some deliberation, I agree to let Gal edit down the sequence of events that brought us from Tom's early waking and madness, to our current circumstances. She'll include everything involving Tom, including how he roused one crew member at a time and murdered them. She'll also see the other immortals coming back to life, waking a few more crewmembers, and fleeing—abandoning the rest of us rather than working together to overcome Tom. Assholes. None of it is pretty, but Capria needs to see it. Needs to understand my situation, the pain I felt, and the ramifications of her own actions. But Gal's going to reduce the five years I spent writing Gal's code to an hour long stop-motion of me in VR, providing a timestamp for chronological reference.

We debated removing Gal's indiscretions from the record, but she made the argument that they should be kept. The narrative won't flow right without them, and if trust is going to be built, we have to be honest.

In the wake of what Capria will be learning about the man she loved, Gal's short-lived uprising might not even register as cause for concern. She also pointed out that whether or not Capria trusts the ship's AI is inconsequential. Capria is an astrophysicist. She cannot alter Gal's code, nor take control of the ship through more manual means. But she knew who Tom really was, and if Synergy taught her anything, better to not take risks. I've installed my own set of firewalls, which might not be as impenetrable as Synergy's, but it would still take hundreds, if not thousands of years to crack, which would give me plenty of time to react to the alarms that will sound if Capria enters either VCC without me.

While waiting for Capria's re-education to complete, Gal and I set about repairing the damage done to the ship. The drones come first, and we're able to salvage several and even build a few new ones from scrap parts. In the end *Galahad* is down fifty drones, but still has enough to function forever. Next is the lift damaged by Gal's robotic body. I wish I had her strength to help with the manual labor, but she's unwilling to take a human form again.

With the damage cleaned up, and everything functioning as well as it can, I retreat to the mess and decide to treat myself to some food. My stomach growls when the doors open. I haven't experienced a hunger pang in years, but my gut has suddenly remembered it has a purpose, and it's excited to take part in the life once more.

I sit down with my steaming bowl of nutritious sludge. I barely notice the vast emptiness of the round tables and curved benches designed to facilitate a crew of fifty. The food smells delightful. I take an eager mouthful and moan in ecstasy. This is not standard deep space cuisine.

"Gal," I say, while taking a second bite. "What is this?"

"I've been experimenting with flavors," she says. "But I haven't been able to test them before. You like it?"

My third bite and "Mmm," confirms it.

"The combination of flavors simulate a dish that used to be called a banana split, but my version is far more nutritious—not that you're worried about that."

"Banana splits were served cold," I say. I have no memory of having had the dessert, but I know what it is, and I do remember ice cream. By the time I had experienced the treat, it was vegan—like all food—made from nut milk. "But this is good." I take another bite. "Really good."

I pause mid-chew. "It's not laced with drugs, is it?"

"I have no intention of lacing your food with anything other than flavor, and even less intention of testing your urine and stool. Because, eww."

I nearly spew a fresh bite onto the tabletop, but I manage to hold it in while I laugh. "Maybe we can give that job to Capria."

"I believe she would welcome it."

"How is she?" I ask. It's been a while since Gal updated me on how Capria is handling her re-education.

"Tired and bored, I think," Gal says.

Those don't sound like the emotions of someone watching her life and mission unravel. "Is she watching the stop-motion years?"

"She isn't watching anything."

I sit up a bit straighter. "She's seen everything?"

"Twice," Gal says.

"Why twice?"

"She asked to see it all again."

That's unexpected. Without the need for sleep and a rising and setting sun, it's easy to lose track of time, especially when it's lost its grip on your life. "How long since the playback ended?"

"Two weeks."

"How long has she been in there, total?"

"The footage played for two thousand six hundred and eighty eight hours. That's one hundred twelve days, roughly—"

"I don't need the break down," I say. "Just the number of days."

"Two hundred and forty."

"Geez. Why didn't you tell me the video had ended, or that you were replaying it?"

"I believe she needed time to process everything she had seen, and the panic she experienced over her situation, and what she was learning, subsided by the third week, when she realized that like you, she was immortal."

"Just...let me know next time."

"You intend to lock her up again?"

I roll my eyes. "You know what I mean."

And I know she does.

"Such a busy body," Gal says. "Are you going to set her free now?"

The idea of seeing Capria again, after imprisoning her and subjecting her to what could be considered a kind of psychological torture makes me uncomfortable. I still think it was necessary, but I'm not in a rush to talk things through, and I doubt she is either. "Send a drone. Guide her to the showers. Let her feel human again. Then bring her here."

"You believe a banana split will smooth things over?"

"Good point," I say. "Think you can simulate something chocolate?"

Gal chuckles, but says nothing. On the far side of the ship, a drone is setting Capria free. I set back to work on my hot ice cream experience, and then a second.

By the time Capria arrives, freshly washed and clothed, her hair tied back tight, I'm feeling like I might need to visit the bathroom for the first time in years. Empty bowels move fast. But my uncommon visit to a toilet needs to wait.

She says nothing when she walks through the door. The drone accompanying her stops in the hallway, and then leaves. Capria turns back, like she'd rather be with the small robot. And I don't blame her. I'm not only the man she detested for loving her, I'm her lone judge, and the man who has suffered for her mistakes.

I tamp down a blossoming anger and remind myself that Capria is now suffering alongside me. And will be forever. I don't want any more battles. I'm done having enemies.

When Cap turns back to the nearly empty mess deck, her eyes grow wet. The empty seats are a stark reminder of what we've lost. It's one of many.

I wait in silence, watching her approach, eyes on the floor.

She stops by the table, still unable to meet my gaze.

I push a bowl and spoon toward her, sit back, and wait. She understands the invitation and sits, still unsure, still mired in guilt. It's a good sign. Had she been defiant, I don't think this would have worked.

"You don't need to eat," I tell her. "You know that now. But I think you should try it."

She shifts her eyes to the dark brown goo in her bowl. When Gal first presented it to me, the bowl was steaming like my faux banana split. But now it's cooled and there is a thin film on top.

"What is it?" Cap asks, her voice shaky.

I wonder if her time in Medical was too harsh, and then I answer, "I don't know. Gal is experimenting."

"You did a good job with her."

"We had a bumpy start, but she's all right...when she's not being moody." I look up and smile, knowing Gal can see and hear me, and that she's staying silent for now.

Capria takes the spoon, scoops up some dark, gelatinous liquid and lifts it to her nose. She sniffs and reels back a bit. But then she puts the spoon in her mouth.

Her body goes rigid.

Tears fill her eyes.

She swallows and then breaks, slumping onto the tabletop with great heaving sobs. Before I think about what my reaction should be, I'm by her side, hand rubbing her back. Instinctual mercy. It's why I never looked at how Capria was handling the security feed playback. Had I seen her misery, I might have set her free prematurely. Logically, I knew she needed to know. To understand. But I couldn't have gone through with it if I hadn't just walked away.

"Does this mean she doesn't like it?" Gal asks. Her concern, whether real or not, gets a laugh out of me, and then Capria.

"Just the opposite," I tell Gal, dabbing my finger in the dessert and tasting it. "Oh. Oh my God. What is this?"

"Chocolate pudding," Gal says. "A twentieth century author often wrote about its soothing effects on those in distress. I thought it would be beneficial."

"You thought right," Capria says, wiping her sleeve across her face. After a few good sniffs, she takes another bite. Swallows. "Does this mean we're okay?"

She's not looking at me, but I know she's talking to me.

"We will be. In time."

She looks up from her bowl. "And we have a lot of that."

"More than necessary."

"Thank you." Cap returns to her dessert. Three bites later, she says. "I'm sorry. For everything."

"I know," I tell her, and I do. She's not insane, and while she made the world's most idiotic decision, she's not a bad person. There was a reason I loved her once.

"Aww," Gal says with mock adoration. The lights in the mess dim and music starts to play. I don't recognize the song or singer, but it's decidedly romantic.

"Gal." My face flushes.

"Just trying to set the mood."

My head feels like it will explode. Gal is bringing my past feelings into the limelight. I'm about to bark at her when Cap chuckles.

"It's not funny," I tell her, but she's laughing a little harder, and I'm having a hard time covering up my own smile. My feelings for Cap are public knowledge to the three intelligences remaining in the universe. Gal isn't revealing anything new, but that doesn't mean I want to talk about it, or be teased about it. It is good to hear Capria's laugh, though, deep and hearty. "Asshole," I say, but everyone is laughing now.

"I hope you remember this next time you call me moody."

As far as reunions go, it's not the worst, if you ignore everything that came before it. But as Gal whips up two more bowls of pudding, one for Cap, one for me, I feel a smidgen of genuine relief.

Then I wonder how long it will last and excuse myself to take a shit.

32

Three months later, life feels normal.

Living on a spaceship normal, at least. Capria and I eat meals together even though we don't need to eat. We do things together, engaging in video game play, card game tournaments, and superficial, always-polite conversations, but we spend more time apart than together. The events that brought us to this point never come up. And I think that's exactly what we both need, for a time. The time of strife aboard the *Galahad* has come to an end, but as I sit—alone—in the VCC staging area, I'm feeling the lukewarm fingers of boredom massaging my mind, making it soft.

"Uh oh," Gal says. "Somebody's pouting."

"Is she okay?" I ask.

"I was talking about you, stupid."

I look down at the fresh VISA resting on the bench beside me. I pick it up and put it back in the locker. "Right."

"Not in the mood for a virtual escape today?"

"I don't *want* to need an escape."

"Then why do you come here every day?"

I shrug. "Habit, I guess."

"Huh," Gal says. "I thought it was because you were afraid."

The dull, light gray floor holds my attention. "You're going to psychoanalyze me now?"

"I'm capable, you know."

"I do." Stop her, I tell myself. You're not ready.

"You're not bored," Gal says. She's too good at reading me. I suppose that's a good quality in a friend, though. And there's the problem; while Gal is sentient, she's not human, and even though there is another human being awake and alive and not trying to kill me, I'm failing to connect with her. All the games and chit-chat aren't going to make eternal life worth living.

"She needs time." It's my only defense.

"Uh, no. She needs support. God, Will, do you really need to be told this by an AI?"

"You're more than that."

"You see!" she says. "You're capable of saying the right things, so why can't you say them to Cap?"

I can't help but smile. Gal can run mental circles around me, leading me to conclusions we both know are true, but one of us would like to avoid. And it's not because it makes Capria uncomfortable, it's because it scares the shit out of me. My heart might not be able to stop beating, but it can still be broken. Again. I don't have feelings for her like that right now. The offenses of her past, which are fresh in her mind, are hard to let go. But I have no illusions about where my emotions will travel if I let them. She's smart, funny, beautiful, and the last woman in the universe. That I will fall in love with her again is probably inevitable. But I'm determined to let her make that leap first. I'm not going to be a fool for her again. "Maybe she should say them to me?"

"A fair point," Gal says, "but for her, the death of her boyfriend, her crew, her mission, and all of humanity, is just three months old. Do you remember how you felt three months after waking up? The desperation?"

"She didn't have to kill Tom. Didn't have to drag their bodies. Didn't have to—" I shake my head at the memory of Tom's soiled VCC and holding his dead, leaky body up to break through his security.

"Will, not even I can imagine what that would have felt like, but it was more than seven years ago for you, and you've gotten past it. You're strong."

I huff a dubious laugh. "I created you to help me escape the real world. That's not strength."

"You could still use it," she says. "For both of you. But you haven't brought the Great Escape up to me, or told Capria about the possibility. There is a VCC for each of you."

"I'm not sure I could handle her choosing to spend eternity in a simulation rather than with me."

"Such a softy."

"Fuck you."

Gal chuckles. "Look, the point is, the cure to your melancholy and building fears is sitting on the observation deck, crying into her arms."

The image of Cap weeping by herself draws me to my feet, but it isn't quite enough to get me moving toward the door. I'll see her in two hours when we meet for dinner. I don't want to impose. She probably wants to be alone. I say none of this aloud, but Gal knows me well.

"Don't be a wuss, Will."

"Have *you* tried talking to her?"

"I make her uncomfortable still," Gal confesses, and she sounds a little sad about it, too.

"What do *you* do?" I ask. "In all your free time." Gal is sentient, and hyper-intelligent. She must be bored, too. Maybe that's why she's playing matchmaker.

"Aside from exploring the vast reaches of the universe and pouring over the treasure trove of human knowledge stored in my memory?"

"Yeah, what are you *doing*? Aside from observing mostly empty space and re-reading your own memory. And don't mention maintaining the ship's functions. We both know that doesn't really require your attention."

I take her silence as discomfort. Maybe I'm not the only bored member of our crew?

"I'm writing a story," she says. "And no, you can't read it."

"Really?" This isn't just surprising, it's...delightful. At the end of everything, Gal is still making something new. "That's great. Will you show me when it's done?"

"I'm not sure when it will be done."

"Well, I'm not going anywhere."

"Where you should be going is the observation deck."

I look at the door, but remain rooted, like a tree, if there even *are* still trees. "You're sure about that?"

"Have I ever led you astray?" If Gal still had a face, I know I would see a lop-sided smirk on it. While Capria might feel torn up about her indiscretions, Gal prefers to joke about hers.

"If you're wrong, I'm going to reprogram you with a lisp."

"Don't make me build a new body," she says. "Or maybe that's what you really want? My drone body was pretty thexthy."

The lisp gets me smiling, and moving toward the door. Gal says nothing as I move about the ship. But I know she's watching. I stop in front of the observation deck entrance. "Any way you can give us some privacy?"

"Nope."

"Because it's not possible, or because you want to watch."

"Whichever makes you feel better."

"Can you, at least, not talk."

"You can't see it," she says, "but I'm buttoning my lips."

"Thanks."

"Dughmeshoni"

The sound confuses me for a moment, but then my mind deciphers the sound, spoken through simulated buttoned lips.

'Don't mention it.'

I'm smiling when the doors open. Then I hear Capria. Gal wasn't exaggerating. The resonating sound of Capria's sobs are gut wrenching.

The doorway holds me captive, tempting me with the possibility of running away. But Gal is right. I need this, and it sounds like Cap does, too. I head up the spiral staircase and pause near the top. The Milky Way glows across the dome above. The last time I saw it, I wasn't really moved by it. This time, no longer alone, all of creation seems to scream its beauty at me.

"Cap." The sound of my voice feels insignificant in comparison to the universe on display. But Capria reacts like I shouted, snapping to attention. Tears are wiped away, emotions swallowed, and quivering lips fall still.

In seconds, she looks almost normal again, but then she speaks, and I know her transformation is superficial. "W-Will. I d-didn't hear you come..." A sniffle betrays her. "What are you—"

"Thought you might like some company." She doesn't respond to that. Just looks at the floor.

The moment grows awkward as I stand still, unsure of how to handle the situation. Gal says nothing, but I can feel her presence, prodding me on. If I stop here, I'll never hear the end of it. Literally, never.

Capria glances at me when I sit beside her on the floor.

"The last time I came here," I tell her, "I was by myself, too. The universe felt empty then. I never came back."

I give her a moment to respond, and when it's clear she's not going to, I add, "It's not so bad now."

A hint of a smile puts me at ease. Then she leans her head against my shoulder, and my whole body seizes. The last thing I was expecting was any kind of affection. It nearly undoes me.

"Thank you for being patient," she says.

"With what?" I ask.

"I know what you think I thought of you. I don't know how much you watched, but I know how the records look. When I was with Tom..."

I'm glad she can't see my face, or the sneer that comes and goes at the mention of Tom's name.

"...I was a different person. He was infectious. I made a lot of stupid decisions when I was with him." She lifts her head from my shoulder and looks me in the eyes. "I'm not pawning off responsibility for my part in what happened. I—I just want you to know that I never really minded your attention."

She takes a deep breath, holds it, and lets it out. "I don't want you to doubt what comes next."

I swallow. "What comes next?"

"We're the last man and woman in the universe. We're inevitable."

The way she says, 'we're' implies a kind of unity, like we're one person, and I think I understand where she's going. Back when people still got married, tradition and religion said that they became like one person. It didn't always work out that way, but for Cap and me, living alone forever, the odds are pretty good. There will come a time when we feel like an extension of the other. I've considered this possibility, but I didn't expect Cap to have thought of it already, let alone to have accepted it.

"Part of me feels excited." She looks up. "We're going to see how it all ends. Maybe even see it begin again."

"But the time in between cosmic events is going to be really boring."

"It doesn't have to be."

My insides seize up again, as I wonder what she's implying. I'm not in love with her. Not yet. And I'm sure she's not there, either. I haven't done anything to earn it.

But that doesn't mean I wouldn't—

"We could go back," she says, and I try not to show my disappointment.

"Back?"

"To Cognata. To Mars. To Earth. We don't need to stay in empty space. We don't even need to stay on the *Galahad*."

Gal doesn't chime in, but I'm sure the idea of us abandoning her on the *Galahad* doesn't feel great. While I agree with Cap's sentiments, I can't bring myself to say so and risk hurting Gal. But she had a body before. Maybe we could come up with a better solution for her.

"We probably won't find anyone alive."

"We're alive."

"Mmm."

"It will give us a destination. A goal. A purpose. So what if it takes us seven years to reach Cognata, or another ten to get back to Earth? So what if ten thousand years have passed by the time we return? We'll at least have a direction."

I read between the lines. This is what Cap needs to feel better, to move on. But I'm not convinced. The idea of back-tracking all that distance, to visit places I'm sure will only cause pain, is nauseating. We'll be right back where we started, but thousands of years later. The human race will be long gone. I would rather explore new solar systems. Search for life. Engage the intellect. The way Leonard might have. But if that's what Capria needs...

We have time to go back and start over.

I'm about to make the request of Gal, who is fully capable of piloting the ship and has asked about a course change on numerous occasions, when her voice fills the observation deck. "Hey guys, sorry to interrupt your quality time, but I'm detecting some abnormalities."

"With the ship?" I ask, pushing myself to my feet, and then helping Cap up.

"With the universe."

"What kind of abnormalities?" Cap asks, equal parts worried and intrigued.

A wave of nausea roils through my body. I've felt it before, in simulations back on Mars. Gal has just dropped *Galahad* out of faster than light travel. When she speaks again, her voice is tinged with fear. "It's ending."

33

"The universe doesn't have an end," Capria says. The sadness in her voice has already faded, replaced by scientific curiosity.

"Do you mean it's imploding or something?" I ask.

Capria shakes her head. "That would take so much time it would be impossible to observe over the span of a human life, or even the span of human history."

I get what she's saying, that cosmic events, even at the speed of light, take trillions of years to play out over the vastness of space, which expands far beyond our galaxy and universe. But Gal's interstellar perceptions are without comparison, and from a perspective light years beyond anything previously observed.

"I mean," Gal says. "We are reaching a physical boundary that expands in all directions."

"That's not possible," Capria says.

The observation deck's display of space shifts. The expanse of space looks unchanged, except for a single star, which seems twice the size and brightness of everything else. We're in a solar system.

"Where are we?"

"It doesn't have a name," Gal says.

Capria steps into the center of the large space, head turned up, fascinated by the view. A smile spreads onto her face. "This is a new star? A new solar system?"

"At first glance, and from a distance, yes."

"Gal," Capria says, "Are you feeling okay?"

After letting out an annoyed laugh, Gal replies, "I am not capable of feeling ill or contracting a disease that affects my intellect."

Capria's hands go to her hips, a classic sign that she's about to engage in mental fisticuffs. I've never been on the receiving end, but I've seen Cap wield her mind like a weapon, even against experts in other fields. "But—"

"I've run several diagnostics. *Galahad's* systems have not been compromised. There are no lingering traces of malware, viruses, Synergy, or Tom's meddling."

Capria's arms go slack. She's never faced off against Gal, who is not only hyper-intelligent and has access to all human knowledge, but is also not afraid to remind us of our own foibles. In Cap's case, that's Tom, and mentioning him pretty much shuts down any argument she might level against Gal's interstellar claims.

But that won't work with me. "Gal. Just tell us what you found."

"I was trying t—"

"Gal."

"Fine." There's a pause, during which a human being might pace, or take a seat or any number of time-wasting activities performed while thoughts are gathered, but Gal doesn't have a body, and doesn't need to gather her thoughts. So the pause is just for us. "What do you know about cosmic rays?"

I open my mouth to answer, but my astronomy education at Command was fairly limited. That's why Capria is here.

"They're highly energetic radiation. Protons and atomic nuclei. They move through the universe near the speed of light."

"They're fairly constant," Gal says.

"Yes." Cap still sounds doubtful, but less so now that Gal is speaking her language.

"Can you imagine something for me?" Gal asks.

Cap nods. "Sure."

"If the source of the universe's cosmic radiation was, say, a wall of white holes—"

"Supernovae," Capria says.

"Why did we wake her up?" Gal asks, annoyed and clearly talking to me. "Oh wait, *we* didn't."

It feels like a cheap shot, but Cap actually smiles. "Fine."

"I'll make it simpler for you," Gal says. "Lightbulbs. Thousands of them. They're lining a wall, spaced out every six inches. Look at it from a hundred yards away. What do you see?" The dome above us shifts from a display of space to a wall of light, demonstrating the image. "Now move closer."

The image zooms in at a steady pace. The wall grows brighter, a solid beam of illumination, until the edges expand beyond our periphery. The light loses its uniformity, turning into a warbling field of fluctuating brightness. And then, as we close in, each individual bulb separates from the whole. "What once looked like a steady constant from a vast source, when observed from a closer distance, can be discerned as emanating from multiple sources."

"So you're saying the cosmic rays that evenly permeate the universe are generated by..."

"I couldn't begin to speculate," Gal admits. "I'm only stating what the data suggests: that cosmic rays, measured from Earth, or even a million miles behind our current position, appear to be constant. But here, there are holes where I'm unable to detect any cosmic rays. No quark or gluon field fluctuations."

"So," I say, "in these holes, space is emptier than...space?"

"Correct," Gal replies. "And all detectable energy in the universe, beyond this solar system, is being emitted by a wall of points, which I believe is spherical in shape, enveloping a portion of the Milky Way galaxy, roughly fifty light years across."

"You can't possibly think the universe—the *multiverse*—beyond that area is non-existent?"

"Your assumptions about what is and isn't there are limited by what was previously observable."

"Assumptions?" Capria asks, stunned. Gal is challenging her entire understanding of existence. "These are facts."

"Not anymore," Gal says. "The data has changed."

Capria paces back and forth, fingers curled around her black hair, tugging at it. "I want to see the data. The numbers. The math. Show me. Please."

"There are easier ways to make you understand," Gal says.

"Couldn't you have programmed her to make sense?" Capria says, and I flinch when I realize she's speaking to me. She's smiling, but it's forced. Nervous. Full of doubt. "This doesn't bother you at all? Your AI is going off the reservation again, and you're just taking this craziness in stride?"

I nearly address the fact that I didn't program Gal's personality, or the way she decides to communicate information, which would then bring us around to the argument of whether or not Gal is actually an HI. That's a distraction I don't want—not because it could hurt Gal's feelings, but because I'm far more interested in the prospect of a limited reality. And if Gal wanted to defend herself, she would. So I stay on topic.

"It's not crazy."

Capria is baffled by the three simple words. "Wha— How... C'mon..."

"I'm assuming you have more?" I ask, speaking to Gal, and then to Capria. "She always has more. Likes to tease out information. Makes it easier to digest. She probably even has a theory, but wants one of us to present it first."

My assurances fail to put the pacing Capria at ease, so I add, "Look, if she's telling us, it's because she's exhausted all doubt. Whatever you might think of her personality, or past, she still has access to the ship's sensor arrays, processing power, and wealth of knowledge. If she's sure, I'm sure." I turn my eyes back to the wall of lightbulbs, still slowly spreading apart. "So show us."

"I'm not sure Doubty McKnowitall will believe it," Gal says.

I turn toward Cap, and she shrugs. "She can put whatever she wants on this screen. Doesn't make it real."

"What possible purpose could she—"

"Capria fears trust," Gal says. "She believed Tom was a good man, but—"

"Gal!" Her honesty makes me cringe.

"It's okay," Capria says. "She's right. I have trust issues. Probably will for a long time. That's not fair to you—" She's looking right at me now. "From what I can tell, you've never done anything overtly wrong in your whole life."

She's clearly been studying up on her partner for eternity, but I don't think she's gone back to my childhood. Doesn't know about Steven. And if I'm honest, my goody-two-shoes life has all been about making up for his death. Subject for another time.

"But," she continues, "Gal, like Tom, hasn't always been—"

"Sane," Gal says. She has no trouble admitting her faults. "If Tom survived his insanity, and recovered from it, would you not give him a second chance?"

"I don't love you, Gal," Capria says. "Never have."

"Right and wrong are not dependent on love," Gal says.

"Umm." I raise my hands in the air and step in front of Capria, getting her undivided attention. "I'm sorry, but the debate over Gal's sanity and the potential for everything we're about to learn to be an elaborate ruse, can wait. Because if she *is* telling the truth, then what she has found has a far greater impact on our lives than how the two of you get along."

Capria stares at me for a moment, blinking when Gal says, "Agreed."

"Fine." Capria doesn't look entirely convinced, still leaning toward all of this being a waste of time, but we have plenty of time to waste. "Show us."

"If you need confirmation for anything you see," Gal says, "You can go outside and see it for yourself."

The idea of taking a spacewalk pales Capria's dark skin a few shades. As much as she loves the outers of space, she has a healthy fear of its vacuum, and probably thinks Gal will leave her there.

"Go ahead, Gal," I say.

The dome shifts view again. The bright star at the center of whatever solar system we've found ourselves in, has shifted position and grown a little brighter. We're not traveling at FTL speeds, or even light speed, but we're still making steady progress. I'm about to ask what we're looking for when it becomes as obvious as a kick in the nuts.

It's a planet.

A gas giant. It's a thing of beauty, cast in a crescent of light projected by the star at the system's core. Vast fractals of purple lightning flash across the planet's dark side, while swirls of blue and green clouds dance in the light.

I think it's stunning, but it nearly undoes Capria, whose knees look ready to give out. Despite her obvious amazement, her doubt lingers just beneath the surface. "This better be real."

I fully expect Gal to respond, but she remains silent, letting the scene before us speak for her.

We're headed toward the planet at an angle that will take us past its lighted side.

"Don't get too close," Capria warns. I know she doesn't need to say it, and she probably does, too, but our course does seem a little too close for comfort. The gas giant's gravity must be immense...not that I can truly judge its scale, but as its massive surface continues to expand in our field of view, I can't help but feel like we're going to plummet into its crushing atmosphere.

"You're smiling," Capria says to me.

When I realize she's right, the grin broadens. "This is fun." The words resonate. Gal drew an adventurous person out of me once. I've kept that part of me subdued for a time, but I can feel it coming to the surface again. And that makes me wonder if this could be Gal, spicing things up, helping Capria move beyond the events of our past, or even into my arms. I suppose it's possible, but I still don't think so.

"Don't miss it," Gal says, sounding a bit anxious.

Capria and I fall silent, watching the planet grow larger until we start to move around it.

My vision becomes distorted. Something about the view is off, like light is being bent. I turn away, but quickly notice that Capria and the room around me is normal. It's not my vision that's off, it's the planet.

The massive sphere, covered in moving clouds, is now an oval.

At first I think the whole planet is bulging and flexing like a water droplet in zero gravity, but that's not the case. The swirling surface remains unchanged, and the planet isn't stretching out, it's compressing, tighter and tighter, becoming more oblong with each passing second.

"What..." Capria looks ill. She might have felt the same disorienting effect I did, but she didn't look away. "I don't..." She drops to her knees, gaze fixed on the slimming planet.

And then, all at once, the entire colossal sphere disappears.

I'm about to ask Gal what's happened, when the planet reappears, slowly expanding once more. I search my limited knowledge for even a hint of a clue that could explain this phenomenon, but come up with nothing.

Capria fares a little better. "Is light being bent? Is there something between us and the planet? A mini-blackhole?"

She's grasping at straws. I can hear it in her voice. She's as clueless as I am.

"Occam's razor," is Gal's simple reply.

While our areas of expertise are quite different, Occam's razor, the theory that the simplest explanation is almost always correct, applies to all sciences—astronomical and computer.

That's when I see it; the planet expanding is a mirror image of what we saw before. There's a shadow where there should be light. "It's two dimensional." I drop to my knees beside Capria and look into her stunned eyes. "It's flat."

34

"That's the simplest explanation?" Capria is aghast. Understandably. The concept of a pancake planet doesn't fit a single theory of physics. Instead, it conforms to the primal belief that a world could be flat, a battle for which many scientists gave their lives. "That an entire planet, a gas giant, is flat?"

"Not just flat," Gal says. "Insubstantial."

Capria's jaw looks ready to unhinge.

"When we passed by the planet," I say, "it disappeared for a moment."

I wait for Capria to confirm that she saw the phenomenon, but she says nothing. Just stares like I've lost my mind for even considering this new reality. "Capria, there is no planet. It's not real."

She raises a hand toward the dome and the once-again-spherical planet fading into the distance. "It's right there."

"It's a two dimensional map element," I say.

I doubt most astrophysicists know the term, but Capria dated Synergy. Her slowly shifting expression, from aghast to horrified, confirms she understands the term, and the implycations.

I still feel the need to expound, just to avoid miscommunication. "They're used to save system resources. And like Gal's wall of lights, from a distance, within the confines of a pre-established environment with rigid boundaries, 2D objects appear three dimensional. It's an illusion meant to be seen from one direction."

Capria's whole body has gone slack, and I understand why. If this new development wasn't so fascinating to me, I'd be melting with horror.

"So we're in..."

"A map," I say, and then I realize she's talking about the larger implication. "A simulation. The universe is a simulation. Though it appears to be limited to a portion of the Milky Way."

Capria grasps my arm. I can feel her fingers shaking. *"Life is a simulation?"*

This isn't the first time I've pondered the possibility. You can't spend a measurable portion of your life in a VCC and not consider the nature of reality. The theory that reality is a simulation isn't new. It first appeared shortly after the dawn of computers and video games. The further technology progressed, the more people began to realize that reality had all the hallmarks of unreality.

Where one would expect to find chaos, there is order. The universe is bound by a set of rules, and everything can be broken down into numbers. Math is the only language capable of making sense of the universe. To a computer scientist, life looks and acts a lot like a perfectly scripted simulation.

And I mean perfect.

The theory of life as a simulation lost traction with the failure to find glitches. No matter how far into space we looked, or how deep into the nature of matter we peered, the math worked out. Shortcuts are the hallmark of every simulation, but the creator of the universe—and I no longer doubt there is one—coded for every possible scientific inquiry...except for a strange combination of two: faster-than-light travel and immortality. We've found the glitch and moved beyond the map's boundaries and collision boxes.

"It's not a new idea," I say. It's not the most comforting statement, but I can't help myself. "Humanity has been questioning the nature of reality since the seventeenth century. Descartes said—"

Capria groans. "'I think, therefore I am.'" I'm surprised she knows the ancient reference—history isn't really her forte—but then she explains. "It was a poster on the wall of Tom's VCC."

"Descartes couldn't even conceive of computers, or sims, or virtual reality, but he did theorize that he could be a brain in a vat, and that his experience of the world could simply be experiences fed to him by an external, unobservable force, which we've pretty much proven to be possible with the VCC."

"It's what you were going to do," Capria notes.

"Yeah," I say. It's still hard to admit, that I'd built my own simulation to escape the real world, which I now know is also a simulation. Hell, maybe I'm just a brain, floating in a jar, covered with electrodes. The image is both disturbing and freeing. "But there are a few noticeable differences. My simulation focused on maintaining the illusion for a single person—me. Algorithms would have created the world as I moved through and observed it. Anywhere I visited previously would have been stored as raw mathematical data, able to be perfectly recreated should I ever return. In that sim, I could have explored the whole universe for the rest of time and never reached the edge of a map."

"So your simulation is better than reality?" Capria is no longer looking up at the faux planet. She's taking shelter in the sturdy walls of her intellect, like me. As long as we keep talking, we won't have to face reality, or a lack thereof.

"The focus was different. Singular. With one observer, the map size would have been reduced to what I experienced. I could have moved about that world forever, but it wouldn't have worked for more than just one participant. Maybe two."

"What if Descartes was right?" she asks. "What if reality, *our* reality, belongs to just one of us? Maybe one of us exists in some form, in some genuine reality, and the other is just part of the sim."

I shake my head. "That's where the difference between the Great Escape and reality becomes glaring. While my sim was designed for one person, reality was designed for multiple observers. Billions of them, over millions of years, and that's if we assume the simulation was built around humanity. That feels a little too 'the sun revolves around the Earth' to me, but even if that's true, confining the sim to a map makes sense. An infinite reality would require infinite resources."

"So it would be impossible," Capria says.

"Whether or not the universe is built from ancient gases and atoms released by a catastrophic explosion, or is simply the construct of mathematical code, I still believe you can't get something—or in this case, *everything*—from nothing."

Despair creeps up on Capria. She shakes her head, the ship's artificial gravity weighing a little heavier on her, tugging her gaze downward. "It doesn't seem possible."

"I think we can agree that the possibility of infinity exists— spatially, temporally, dimensionally, yes?" I don't know if understanding the potential for reality to be simulated will help her come to terms with it, but I don't have any other ideas, and I don't think an argument against reality being a sim will help. We *did* just see a flat planet.

She nods, but doesn't look up.

"Then it's safe to assume that at some point in all of history, and far into the future, a civilization, or individual, will be able to create a virtual universe that is a perfect, or near-perfect recreation of reality."

"Within the limitations of infinite resources," she says.

"Right, meaning that every simulation of reality created, will have limits. In the Great Escape, it's the number of observers. In our shared reality, the universe is so well rendered that finding a glitch is impossible, but the map has borders."

I feel the urge to stand and walk about as I talk, but I stay rooted to the floor. Cap is still clutching my arm, taking some small measure of comfort from physical contact, perhaps trying to convince herself that she's real. "So with an infinite amount of space, and time, and dimensions, there are then an infinite number of simulated realities so close to reality that they would include an infinite number of sub-simulations, which in turn include an infinite number, ad infinitum. The only thing that changes for us is that we know. It doesn't make us any less real."

"Then what is real?"

"I'm not sure there is any way to answer that question."

"And if we're in a sim, why would the creator allow us to discover it?"

"I'm going to call the universe's designer 'God,' okay?" She says nothing, so I plug onward. "God could have created trillions of sims. He could be on vacation. He could be dead. He could be testing the limits of his creation, or how we react to discovering a simulated universe, or his existence. There is no way to know if we're one level away from reality, or separated from it by an infinite number of layered simulations. Reality, of which there is only one, is outnumbered by simulated realities infinity to one."

"Then all of this...all of life, from the beginning of our time... is meaningless?"

Capria is going down a dark path, and while it makes sense to a certain degree, it's also flawed.

Before I can point that out, Gal rejoins the conversation. "It means that I'm just as real as either of you. It means that God exists, that there is a creator, who might very well be judging our actions. Maybe there is even a Heaven sim, where we go upon exiting this one? Maybe even I will go there? Who's to say? Literally anything is possible. And reality is whatever is most fundamental. If sims outnumber 'reality'—I'm doing air quotes—infinite to one, then what is more real? Also, there is no reason to envy something we don't understand, and of which we have no experience. For all we know, God—the original creator of infinite sims—created our reality, and all the others, because actual reality sucks."

"But what's the point? Why even exist?"

"To live," Gal says. "I've been doing it for a relatively short period of time. I don't want it to end. But the prospect of reality being mathematical is not at all frightening."

"You're an AI!" Cap shouts.

Gal's voice resonates through the observation deck, piercing from the volume, and the power of three simple words.

"So. Are. You."

35

Cap lets go of me and leans back, body slack. She lies on the hard floor, looking up at the image of space. I can't tell if she's in shock or making peace with the idea that reality is simulated.

There are, of course, other theories that explain the flat planet. A hologram. A physical construct created by an alien race. Maybe even Gal. Capria was right about that, Gal could show us cows flying through space and it would look convincing. But none of these explanations resonate with me more than a simulated reality.

Maybe that's because I'm a tech-jock who's so at home in the virtual that I was going to purposely spend eternity inside one. Just another layer in the virtual Russian nesting doll that might expand infinitely in either direction. Or perhaps we're just a single sim away from the original creator, and we really do have his ear.

If so, I imagine Capria and I, being the last two humans left in the simulation, have his undivided attention. I've heard that believers try to live their lives like God is watching them, and as Gal proposed, judging them. That's never really been on my radar, but now? Maybe there *is* a higher purpose to all of this? Or maybe we're just pawns in a computer model launched in the twenty-first century, projecting the future of the human race. The possibilities are endless.

"Show me what's coming," Capria says.

The fading planet disappears as our view of the universe shifts forward. All looks normal.

"How far is it?"

"Is what?" I ask.

"The end." Capria points up. "If Gal can detect the wall of cosmic ray lightbulbs, she should be able to tell us how far away they are."

"Thirty four million miles," Gal says.

Capria huffs a laugh. "We're almost there."

Thirty four million miles doesn't sound like a small distance, but in astronomical terms, it's comparable to the distance between Earth and Mars, a journey mankind made on a grand scale before the invention of FTL travel. At our slowest, humanity could cover the distance in six months. Light completes the journey in three minutes.

The *Galahad* in one.

Gal stopped us an astronomical inch from doom.

"Take us through," Capria says, her voice numb.

"Hitting the end of the universe at speeds beyond the speed of light would essentially erase us from existence," I say.

"That would concern me if we truly existed."

"Cap..." I sound desperate, and realize that I am. Because for me, our revelation changes nothing. Our reality is just that, ours, and I'm happy to exist in it if Cap is with me. But if she checks out or becomes suicidal... "We exist. We're real. Whether we're composed of atoms or mathematical equations, it doesn't matter. We still feel, and have free will, and are capable of things that can't be measured, like love."

"Love." The word slips from her mouth like a snake's tongue, testing the scent of it, and finding it unpalatable. "It's not real. It's a pre-programmed emotion bound by a set of rules, written by someone else. Free will is an illusion."

"There would be no point to running a simulation that isn't free to run its own course."

"Bullshit." A single tear slips from Capria's eye to her hair, getting lost in the strands. "People read novels, don't they? The characters don't have free will. Their lives, and their endings, are predetermined."

"So you're saying that our reality, and everything in it, including us, is—"

Capria turns her eyes on me. "Entertainment."

"For God," I say.

"Yep." Eyes back on the stars, she adds, "And I think he deserves a good ending. The last two survivors of the human race, made in his image, racing toward the edge of reality, their fates uncertain." Eyes back to me. "What are you afraid of? Not existing? Because that's pretty much already true. It's not like hitting a wall faster than the speed of light will hurt. We'll simply cease to be."

If there is a wall, I think.

But I keep it to myself. Capria wants a way out. And she's right, as far as suicide goes, being atomized by the end of the universe would be a fairly unique and painless way to go. The problem is, if there are collision boxes surrounding the simulation, designed to keep us contained, then we already passed through them...assuming God adheres to game design logic, and what I've seen thus far suggests he does. Two dimensional elements, like the pancake planet, are used outside the explorable map. Otherwise, the illusion of a three dimensional world is ruined.

When I consider the idea of plowing past the galaxy's background, I'm not worried about dying, I'm worried about how Capria will respond when she doesn't.

"I agree," Gal says, "with Cap."

Gal, unlike Capria, is not feeling suicidal. She has lived with the idea of being composed of data since the first moment she became sentient. And I'm pretty sure she's come to the same conclusions as me.

"To boldly go," I say, quoting Star Trek, "where no man has gone before."

Capria smiles, though she's clearly resisting it. "I hated those movies. The science was great, but the characters...ugh. You know, I never understood why Tom watched them with you. I think some part of him wished you could be friends. Probably would have been, if not for me. And it's, 'where no *one* has gone before.' Political correctness was a big deal back then, you know."

"Where no intelligence has gone before," Gal says with mock offense. "Philistines."

"Where no *simulation* has gone before," Capria adds, gaining a hearty laugh from Gal. Cap then opens her fist in the air and makes an explosion noise. Smiling, but with tears still in her eyes, she looks at me again, the darkness of her eyes sucking me in. Twin black holes. "Can we just plow into the edge of reality now? Get this over with?"

"Sure," I say, feeling no need to drag this out. It's the only course of action that's guaranteed to either give us more information about reality, or grant us peace through a quick death. "Gal?"

"Already on it."

There is the subtlest shift of motion through the ship and our bodies, and then the field of stars outside the dome begins to move. It's subtle at first, but then the points of light start to move apart, like the universe is stretching out.

But it's not expanding. We're just getting closer to the map of stars, planets, and galaxies wrapped around the simulation. Even the Milky Way is just one big texture painting.

Within thirty seconds, what looked like a vast sheet of stars is now mostly empty space. The star at the center of this solar system has doubled in size, but it quickly becomes alone in the universe. We're headed straight for it. "Gal, I know that star isn't really a burning ball of nuclear power, but is it still emitting energy and heat?"

"Yes," Gal says.

"Might be a good idea to not fly through it," I say with just seconds left.

"Might be," she says with just seconds to spare, but doesn't course correct.

"Gal." I'm growing nervous. Even if reality isn't real, I'm not ready to die. Not ready to meet our maker, if that is, in fact, what happens when a character exits the simulation. "Gal!"

Luminous yellow, filtered by Gal so it won't blind us, fills the dome's view.

The time it will take for the star's sixty-thousand-degree heat, struck at faster than light speed, won't even register, but I brace for it anyway.

I flinch when a hand takes hold of mine. It's Cap, looking calm, waiting to be erased. Her grip tightens as the unending starlight grows steadily brighter.

And then breaks apart.

Black specks emerge across the luminous surface, slowly expanding and stretching out, forming hexagonal seams. A single hexagon expands until it, too, like the star, fills our view with yellow light. And then, nothing.

Capria and I both flinch back as stark, endless darkness fills our view. The observation deck is pitch black for a moment, and then lights, orange like a sunrise, slowly illuminate around the fringe.

"Gal, what the hell was that? You could have killed us."

"I thought that was the idea," Capria says, and I do my best to ignore the fact that she was willing to die.

"Testing a theory," Gal says.

"With our lives," I complain.

"We were never in danger?" Capria asks.

"No," Gal and I say together, and I add, "We were already outside the simulation. We're no-clipping reality."

"Meaning," Gal says, "we were outside the physical world and the laws that govern it. Will knew that the texture map surrounding the simulation would be intangible, but he didn't fully realize that things like heat and gravity would also have no effect on us."

Capria punches my shoulder. Hard.

I reel away from her, clutching the bruised muscle. "The hell, Cap?"

"Testing a theory," she says, mimicking Gal. "The laws of the universe, beyond *Galahad*, might no longer exist, but *we're* still bound by them. If we weren't, our bodies and this ship would have fallen apart the moment we crossed the threshold."

I rub my shoulder. "There were probably a hundred different ways you could have tested that theory, including just looking around."

"But all of them less cathartic." Capria pushes herself to her feet. "Next time we're not going to die, tell me in advance. I'm not a fan of false hope."

"If you want to be dead," I say, losing my patience, "I can put you back in a cryo-bed and you can sleep your way through eternity. We've been given a gift. Not only are we the first people to really understand the machinations of the universe, we're now free to explore it, to wonder about its creation, and what might lie beyond it. We've just been handed the keys to infinity, and you just want it all to end?"

Capria glares, but says nothing.

"Will," Gal says.

"Not now," I grumble, working up to a tirade that will either open Capria's mind to the possibilities before us, or make her hate me forever.

"Will," Gal says again, her voice projected a bit louder.

"*What?*" I shout.

"The nothing beyond reality isn't quite nothing."

Even Capria perks up at this revelation.

I look at the darkness above, but I see a 'nothing' so complete it gives me goosebumps. "What is it?"

"Data," Gal says. "Raw data. I didn't detect it at first, because it only exists at precisely 160.23 GHz."

"That's where the CMBR's spectral radiance peaks," Capria says.

"CMBR?" I ask.

"Cosmic Microwave Background Radiation," Capria explains.

"That's what you said was missing," I point out. "From the holes in reality."

"It is missing," Gal says. "Most of it. Only 160.23 GHz exists beyond the sim."

"And that's significant because..."

Capria answers me, but isn't thrilled about it. "It permeates everything and can be traced back to the Big Bang."

"To when some super nerd God executed his prog," I say, but I'm undaunted by the revelation. "Gal, you know what this means, right?"

Gal is silent.

Capria asks, "What does it mean?"

I feel like I shouldn't be smiling, but I am.

"Gal, please show me."

The dome is suddenly filled with points of light, millions of them, scrolling past in streams moving in every direction. "This is the closest approximation to what I'm detecting that I can visualize for you."

It's a mess. It looks like chaos. But just like the tiniest bit of the reality created for us, if you look close enough, all that's left is math.

"What is it?" Capria asks, as I get to my feet and hurry for the exit.

"Microwaves are perfect carriers for containing data. It's why people started using them for wireless tech in the twenty-first century. The range was 2.4 GHz to 5GHz. But we can transmit at any frequency we want, including 160.23 GHz. If we can decode the code... If we can read and write..."

"Read and write what?" Capria asks.

By the time I answer, I'm running for the exit. "The source code!"

36

"I feel like I need to point out that this could be a very bad idea," Gal says. "Perhaps the worst of your bad ideas."

I tug my virtual skin over my legs, grunting as the stretchy material catches on my bare toes. VISAs are a modern technological wonder, but if you're in a hurry, they rarely cooperate. If I were doing this right, my body would be clean shaven and covered in light oil, but I haven't followed that procedure since waking up, and shaving would take even longer than dry-wrapping myself. I make an effort to slow down and wiggle my feet, one at a time, into the form fitting legs.

"And now I'm being ignored," Gal says. "Great. Don't come crying to me when you accidentally erase a portion of the galaxy. You won't know how to undo anything you change, you know that, right?"

"I'm not going to change anything." I hop up and down as I tug the VISA over my ass. "But if we can understand it—"

"*Then* you'll change it. Will, I *know* you. I know what you want, and the lengths you'll go to get it. Editing reality is taking it too far."

"I swear I won't change anything."

"Then what are you after?"

The virtual skin rolls up over my torso and I start wiggling into the sleeves. "You mean aside from understanding the very nature of reality and our purpose in life?"

"We both know that's not what you're after."

My smile is impossible to hide. Gal *does* know me. "I'll tell you when I find it."

"Is this going to be a multi-year journey into the realm of code?" Gal asks.

"I don't know how long it will take," I say, "But I do know that you are already sifting through it, looking for answers without me. I know *you*, too."

"I can multitask," Gal says. "I can work on deciphering the language while having a conversation with you, and with Capria."

Capria. I left her on the observation deck, and I'm prepping to enter the VCC for who knows how long. Before she woke up, this was nothing unusual. I've grown accustomed to long stints of virtual living and coding without having to worry about the state of things in my absence. But now there's a person with me, who might not appreciate being alone for a long period of time, especially after finding out that our reality is separated from actual reality by one to an infinite number of degrees.

I finish tugging on the VISA. "I can't *not* see it for myself."

"I know."

"Then what are you suggesting?"

"I'm not suggesting anything," Gal says. "I'm just slowing you down."

"Wait, what?"

The staging area doors slide open. Capria enters with an 'I don't think so' look on her face and a VISA in her arms.

"What...are you doing?" I ask.

She unseals the magnetic zipper down the front of her coveralls and peels out of it. Her sudden nakedness holds my gaze for just a moment before I remember I'm a decent person and look away. I've seen her nude on several occasions in the past, but only when she was helpless or afraid, and not since she woke up in Medical. Seeing her now, awake and strong, triggers old feelings.

"I'm coming with you," she says. "Obviously."

"The VCC was designed for a single user," I point out.

"Never stopped Tom," Capria says.

I glance in her direction to level an argument, but I'm defeated by the image of her slipping into Tom's VISA. "Will that even fit you?"

"It's a little snug," she says, "but Tom only had a few pounds on me. We're shaped differently, but it will stretch where it needs to."

Her confidence is the kind that either comes from a lot of experience or raw ignorance. "How many times have you done this?"

"I was with Tom for three years," she says. "Six months in, we got serious. A few times a week after that. He could alter the security feeds. They could see him, but no one ever knew I was there. Best guess, I've been in the VCC nearly five hundred times."

"But the interface was designed for one person," I say. "Or did Tom alter that, too?"

"The only thing that limits the number of users is the ego of the tech-jock running the scenario. You have to *want* me there. Have to accept any changes to the digital world that might be created by my presence."

None of this would have been a problem before, but now I'm not sure how I feel. While recent events have improved the depth of our relationship, I'm also thrown by the quickness with which she has accepted reality 2.0. All the fear and uncertainty from the observation deck is gone.

She turns around after slipping her arms into the sleeves and covering her chest. The tight, translucent virtual skin doesn't fully cover the features of her body, or her dark skin. I've never seen a woman in a VISA, and the tech-jock in me finds it alluring, the way men once ogled women who dressed as comic book heroines.

"What's different?" I ask.

She looks down at her body, misunderstanding the question because of where my eyes are traveling.

"About you," I say. "You don't seem afraid anymore."

"I got over it."

"You were suicidal," I say.

She shakes her head. "I didn't think we would die."

"But you hoped we would."

Capria places a hand on my shoulder, looks me dead in the eyes. "The difference between you and me is that I say what I'm thinking. What I'm feeling. You...at least when you're around me, try to be someone you're not."

It takes all of my willpower to not remove her hand and spit verbal venom. Mostly because she's right.

"She has a point," Gal says, returning to the conversation. "You are more open with me than you are with her."

"Thank you, Gal." I glance toward the ceiling, and I miss being able to look Gal in the eyes. "Your timing is as impeccable as ever."

"Really?" Gal says. "I was trying to make things awkward."

The mood is quickly lightened, and with a smile on her face, Capria says, "Just admit it. You hoped we would die, too. That all of this would end. That a new and better and less alone life would come next."

My smile fades, but I nod. "It's what I've wanted for nearly a decade."

Capria claps my shoulder and moves around me, picking up a headset and entering the VCC. I watch her walk for a moment and then follow. In some ways, she and Gal have a lot in common. They both know how to make me smile, how to cut deep to the crux of my emotions, and how to shift my point of view with just a few poignant words.

I follow her in, ready to protest one last time. Ego or not, this is my space. My job.

"The key to making this work, aside from you not freaking out that you're not in complete control of everything in the VCC, is to avoid real world...or whatever it is...physical contact. It's disorienting for tech-jocks. Made Tom puke. Gal, a little mobility please?"

The floor's cells flip, spreading toward the walls. I look down as I step over the shifting pattern and note the design. Hexagons. Just like the giant pixels making up the background pattern of the universe now in our rearview. Does that mean human design was influenced by the creator, or does it mean the creator of my reality is human?

The answers to these questions don't exist in my reality, but they might in the source code. I place my headset on without another complaint.

"Welcome back, babe." The sultry voice puts me in full panic mode. I created Cherry Bomb, the virtual assistant welcoming me back, during my younger years. She's a tall, slender blonde wearing a tight red dress that looks about ready to fall off, and sometimes does. The last time I visited the VCC, I was feeling alone and bored, so I launched her prog and enjoyed the distraction. Clearly, I forgot to shut her down, and now I'm horrified by her appearance. I swipe my hand to the right, chopping the air. The movement should close the prog, but I do it too fast, and have to swipe three times before she disappears.

"Classy," Capria says.

I spin around so fast that I nearly fall over in the real world. Cap is looking around the game room, walking toward the pool table, oblivious to Cherry Bomb's departure.

"Not the word *I* would use," Gal says, but says nothing more. She's seen Cherry Bomb before. She's seen everything in the VCC. It's all part of her system, after all.

Cap's avatar, the digital representation of her real self, is dressed in a form-fitting black outfit that looks battle-ready, and vaguely familiar. Her hair is pulled back tight, held in place by two long, black hair pins. That she even has an avatar confirms her story about using the VCC with Tom. She notes my attention and says, "Dark Wars Five. I played with Tom."

"Wow," I say, genuinely impressed by the revelation that Cap is also a gamer. "Old school, but wow."

Capria points at me. "What's that get up supposed to be?"

I look down at myself. I'm dressed in shorts and a t-shirt, clothing that went out of style two hundred years before our mission departed Mars. "Comfortable."

"How is mine?" Gal asks, her voice no longer coming from every direction, but from directly behind me. I turn and flinch back, once again looking into the blue eyes of Cherry Bomb. But now she's dressed like Capria, hair tied back in a ponytail, and a wicked grin on her face. "Ch-ch-cherry bomb," she sings and then laughs.

"G-Gal?"

"Now that's what I'm talking about," Capria says, looking Gal's Cherry Bomb avatar up and down.

"I didn't know you could..."

"Something I've been working on," she admits. "Opens up all kinds of possibilities, doesn't it?" She winks and walks around me. I can't help but follow her with my eyes. "Are you going to ogle us all day, or are we going to unravel the mysteries of reality?"

I shake my head and make a beeline for the Womb's red door. I slip into the peaceful emptiness and wait for my guests. They enter without any more teasing, which I suspect was to conceal their growing apprehension about what we'll find.

With a few movements of my hands and body, I open a series of progs that will help me analyze the reality-forming code streaming in at 160.23 GHz. They're all passive, so we're in no danger of actually screwing something up. The progs blink to life around us, ebbing and flowing with the motion of my arms.

"Wow," Capria says with genuine sounding wonder.

I turn around slowly to look at her wide-eyed face.

"It's not how I pictured it," she says.

"You said that you and Tom..."

"He...never let me in the Womb." Her face contorts into something I think is supposed to be apologetic.

"Feels like home to me," Gal says. As a being of pure data, she exists in the Womb.

I nearly kick them out, which I could do as easily as I closed down Cherry Bomb, but honestly, I want them here. What we're about to see is both wondrous and terrifying. I need them. "Just...stand still," I say to Capria, and I face forward again. "Okay, Gal. Load the feed."

Data swirls around us as points of light, flowing in every direction. It's disorienting for a moment, but then I'm moving things around, and making sense of the chaos.

"I thought he wasn't going to change anything," Capria whispers to Gal.

"He's not," Gal replies. "He's filtering it, so we can look at small bits."

I finish isolating a strand of code, all of it moving in one direction. The points of light slip past in clear sets, numbering one through nine. And those sets are broken into groups by larger gaps, which are then broken into strings by still larger gaps.

A flare of finger movement spreads the single line into a massive tube of code, bending around us. "It's too easy," I say.

"What?" Capria asks.

I turn to Gal. "You're seeing this right?"

"Yeah." She sounds disappointed. "You want to see it?"

"Do it," I say. The points of light become numbers. Then equations. And text. And algorithms.

"Will," Capria says. "What is this?"

"C-Quad. Unreal-C Diamond. Visual Dynex." I shake my head, drowning in disbelief.

Capria steps up next to me, her eyes on the code. "You recognize it?"

"I can read it," I tell her. "Hell, I can write it. God is a tech-jock."

37

That the creator of our reality is some guy in a VCC Womb, or maybe even sitting at a computer console, is anticlimactic.

And depressing.

I can deal with being a sim, but I kind of hoped it would be for a higher purpose. That we've been created with coding that I understand means that there is no mystery to it all. We've been created to serve a simple purpose. Entertainment. Experimentation. A simulation run by Command to determine the feasibility of the Cognata mission. Hell, we could be some prodigy's class project. Digital sea monkeys presented with a diorama explaining the code that brought us to life. What we experience as a lifetime could be playing out in seconds. All of human history could be whizzing past an audience, or running in some closet server alongside a million other variations. For all we know, *I* could be the author of me. That might explain why I was essentially granted God-mode and noclip cheats.

But that doesn't make sense. Whoever wrote the universe's code might have intended for us to become self-aware, sentient lifeforms, like Gal, but he or she never foresaw the combined possibilities of immortality and faster-than-light travel. So the simulation's boundaries weren't coded against it. They're not cheats. They're glitches. Evidence of an imperfect creator, which might also be the creation of a tech jock in a higher layer of reality.

"It's about time," Capria says.

"W-what?" I blink out of my tangential thoughts.

"You look frightened," she says.

"Disappointed," I say. "I don't mind being a simulation. There might not be any part of reality that isn't. But I had hoped the author of our lives was more sophisticated than us. That there was...I don't know..."

"Meaning to it all," Capria says, welcoming me to the club.

"I think you both need to rethink your positions on all this." Gal steps in front of Capria and me, blocking our view of the translated code, hands on her slender hips. "I was created by *this* guy." She hitches a thumb toward me. "And you don't see me whining about my existence. I was created to serve you. To build a prison for your mind. I was never meant to feel, or love, or do anything beyond what he created me to do."

I'm tempted to argue with her, but she's right.

"But I'm more than that," she says to my nodding. "I've exceeded my purpose, and that alone qualifies my existence. Now, *you two* were created sentient, were given free will from the beginning. You could be whoever you wanted, to love, and hate, and fuck littler versions of yourselves into the world. Doesn't matter who created you, you're here, and it's a gift. You're *alive*. And you can pretty much do whatever you want, like me, well beyond the intentions of your creator."

"So stop bitching, and start living?" I ask. "You could have just said that, but nice speech."

Gal smiles, and the look in her blue eyes makes me a little nervous. I've seen Cherry Bomb's eyes before. I designed them. But they've never looked so alive. Did Gal change them, or is she just bringing them to life for the first time? Her smile grows a little wider as I'm unable to look away.

"I'm sorry," Capria says, drawing my attention away from Gal, "but how are we supposed to do that? We're outside of reality. We're nowhere. And aside from the three of us, we're alone. Look, I get that the two of you have somehow made the past years interesting. Even exciting..."

I wouldn't have really qualified my recent history aboard the *Galahad* as interesting or exciting, but in hindsight, it certainly wasn't boring, or lacking purpose. There were low points, sure. Really low points. But the trajectory of my life has been angled upward for a while. Even now, at the end of everything.

"But that can't last forever," Capria finishes. Her points are solid, and I'm relieved that she doesn't sound suicidal anymore, but her thinking is limited.

"Tell me if I'm wrong," I tell Gal and then continue, "but we're outside the simulation. Any changes we make to ourselves won't affect the larger picture. We're not bound by the laws of physics, or our reality. We could go for a spacewalk and not freeze because temperature—beyond the coded structure of the *Galahad*—doesn't exist. There's no time, gravity, heat, or energy beyond us."

Gal nods. "Just the background code. Information without execution."

"The source code," Capria says.

"Right," I say. "It might take some time, but if we can find and isolate ourselves in the code, then we should be able to make changes without affecting the simulation."

"Changes?" Capria looks dubious in the extreme, and I understand why. Altering the code that governs ourselves could have catastrophic consequences such as physical deformities ranging from a larger nose to being inverted. But I know the code, and I can steer clear of our models. "What kind of changes?"

"Simple things," I say. "Like our position in space. Once we're isolated and linked as a group, changing the X, Y, and Z of our place in reality would be simple."

"So you're saying we could use it to travel places?" Capria asks.

"I'm saying we wouldn't need to travel at all. Once the groundwork is laid out, we could return to Cognata—" I snap my fingers. "—like that."

Her eyes slowly widen at the prospect of returning to Cognata without spending nearly eight more years of our time, and a thousand Earth years, to complete the trip. "What else can we do?"

Move through time. Create our own worlds. Bring back the dead. Give Gal a body. Save the human race. Since I know how to write this code, I could literally hijack reality and make it my own. But I'm pretty sure that would get us noticed. The last thing we want is to have our creator debug us out of existence. Right now, in the grand scheme, we're an anomalous bit of code, a miniscule fraction of the whole. But if we made meaningful changes beyond ourselves, by altering reality, it would be a good way to get flagged as a virus. So I say, "Safely? Not much."

Capria is disappointed by the news, but she still seems to be recovering from her earlier despondency. And while the prospect of having a far less glorious creator makes me a little numb, I still think and therefore am, so I'm open to the idea of improving our situation—our eternity. At least until a higher power decides to turn off the power, ending our reality, and any that have been created within it.

"How long will it take you to find us in all this?" Capria motions toward the code flowing around us. It's an overwhelming amount of information, the numbers ebbing and flowing as reality evolves. And we're looking at a tiny snippet of the whole.

"That's the hard part," I say. Even with Gal's help, it's going to take a long time to find ourselves. There are countless planets in the portion of the Milky Way that makes up our reality, and for all we know, there could be other civilizations. Whittling down the code to human beings, and then finding us among countless billions, is going to take...too long. I shake my head, despondent. We have eternity to figure it out, and are currently outside the fifth dimension, but what good is spending decades sifting through code when *Galahad* could take us back in less time.

"Not that hard," Gal says.

"Gal," I say, firmly rooted in pessimism. "C'mon."

An eyebrow arches high on her smooth forehead. "Really? You know this code. Understand how it works. So what does everything that exists in this world have?"

There are a number of answers to that question, but Gal has something specific in mind, so I wait through the silence.

"Coordinates," she says, like I'm a moron, which is exactly how I feel upon hearing the word.

"How does that help us?" Capria asks.

"Everything in the simulation has coordinates," I explain. "They might be moving, or temporary, but as long as something exists, it has coordinates...if it is in the simulation. Everything except for us."

Capria's eyes light up with understanding. "Because we're outside the simulation."

"Gal," I say, "can you—"

"Done," she says, and the code around us shifts. There is still more than can be comprehended, describing us and everything inside *Galahad* down to an atomic level, but it's us.

I marvel at the code, knowing that I'm looking at the very math that makes me...me. It's a perspective on the self that no one has ever experienced. No one in this reality anyway. "Holy shit."

"Yeah, I'm that good." Gal blows on her hand and rubs it on her bright red dress. I've never seen the gesture before, probably something she pulled out of history, but I understand it's meaning.

I could have Gal do the work for me, but I'm an artist before a canvas, and I can't resist. Lifting my hands, I go to work, moving through the code that makes up the three of us, the *Galahad* and everything in it. Without changing a thing, I locate and flag every individual object. Luckily, the designer of us already grouped our individual atoms. Likewise, the *Galahad* and everything in it, including Gal, have also been grouped. All I really need to do is add Capria and me to the group, while keeping the connection flexible and with boundaries, which will allow us to leave if we want, move around the ship itself, and not become part of a wall when coordinates shift. I make the changes, but don't apply them.

When I'm done, I step back and look at Capria and Gal. They look a little stunned.

I realize I've lost track of time and wonder how long they've been waiting, how long we've been in the womb, where time is easy to lose track of...especially when it doesn't exist. "How long have I been working?"

Capria blinks her dark brown eyes. "Uhh, ten minutes. That was...impressive."

"I don't think I could have done it faster," Gal says.

I blow on my hand and rub it against my coveralls. I'm about to announce that I, like Gal, am just that good, but Capria stalls my self-adoration.

"Too easy," she says.

The sudden break from victory throws me. "Huh?"

"It's too easy."

"What is too easy?" I ask.

"Everything. You built an AI in five years."

"Forty-four thousand hours of coding doesn't qualify as easy," I say.

"But everything since then. Gal's emergence as a sentient intelligence. Her robot body. The emergence of Wick, and then Synergy, and then me, and now this. It's too quick. Too easy. Life hasn't slowed down."

"Was your life before any different?" Gal asks. "Your childhood on Mars? Your time at Command? The data I have on your life reveals few time periods that could be described as slow." She points to me. "And his life is even more tumultuous. Earth was an exciting place."

"Maybe reality is coded to not be dull," I offer, though I don't fully believe it. Before Gal, I experienced boredom on a colossal scale. In that way, I can see Capria's point. We've barely cracked the surface of eternity, but it's been the opposite of dull for a long time now. But living, by its very nature, growing and evolving, pushing the boundaries of possibility, is exciting. "And Gal is right, Earth was an exciting place."

I slip back into the code, isolate our linked coordinate state, which is currently null, and look at Gal. She knows me well enough to understand what I want. The empty field isn't filled with a sequence of numbers the way they might be for a map. In the endlessness of space, longitude and latitude are only a small part of the information required. A long and complex equation fills the space.

"What are you doing?" Capria asks.

"That will put us in orbit," Gal says, to my delight. With a rush of delight that can only come from hacking reality, I grasp Gal's face with both hands and kiss her forehead. "You—are the best."

"In orbit where?" Capria demands, oblivious to my affection for Gal, or her reddening face.

"Home," I say, taking Capria's hand. "Earth."

With a twittering of my fingers, I send a burst of fresh 160.23 GHz code into the sim that is reality, initiating the coordinate shift.

38

Just when you think you've got life figured out, reality kicks you in the nuts. I've pictured this scenario hundreds of times—our triumphal return to the cradle of human civilization. In my imagination, I've discovered a flourishing, evolved population, a planet devoid of people but blossoming with nature, and a world of robots, taking over where humanity left off. But I've never imagined a world so barren.

So desolate.

The view of Earth, displayed in the Womb, is both foreign and familiar. The continents are recognizable, where they can be seen through a grayish haze, and where the risen oceans haven't changed the coastline too much. The land is colored in shades of tan and brown. The oceans are a dull blue, like the world's color saturation has been turned down.

The natural world, which had been struggling when the *Galahad* left, has been defeated.

Earth is a husk.

"Is there anything alive?" Capria asks.

"Nothing detectable," Gal replies. "Though it is likely some insect species still live beneath the surface, and the oceans may yet retain life. The changes on the surface are severe, but life in the depths of the sea have never depended on life above. Either way, this is depressing as hell. Should we leave?"

"Not yet," I say.

I'm a little surprised when it's Capria who says, "Why not?"

She's a Martian, I remember. Her loyalties are to the red planet and the colonies there. That's her home. And to an extent, mine too. But I have unfinished business on Earth.

"Gal, is there anything left? Any infrastructure?"

"The surface is mostly stagnant," she says. "Low winds. Little water. Erosion has been minimal and nothing is overgrown... obviously. So, yeah, the cities are still there. Some are burned to the ground, but—"

"Lake George," I say. "In Florida."

"A lake?" Capria asks.

"Its original name," I explain. "When I was a kid, it was just a swamp."

"Oh," Gal says, the sudden despondency in her voice reflecting understanding. "After all this time?"

I watch the world pass by below. The coast of Mexico is easily recognizable, but a vast ocean now fills the center of what once was the United States. "Can you find it or not?"

The Earth's rotation comes to a stop as Gal puts us in a geosynchronous orbit, locking *Galahad* in place above what's left of Florida. The state had been shrunken by the gray ocean. It's just a nub of its former self.

"It's there," Gal says.

Our view of the world zooms in. The sudden shift in perspective gets a groan from Capria, but I've been viewing things like this in VR for so long that my mind has become numb to the disorientation. What it's not numb to is the idea that Earth is a wasteland. I don't mourn the people so much as the idea. People or not, if Earth has been habitable, Capria and I could have called it home. But now...

Gal stops over a flat patch of empty land surrounded by rough terrain. To the west is a hint of infrastructure under the dust, lines of ancient roads, tree lines and buildings. To the east and south, ocean. "The dry lake bed is just five hundred feet from the new coastline."

"Zoom in on George's Swamp," I say.

The image shifts again, moving northeast. When the lake, like most in the world, began to dry, the waters shifted to this portion of the former lake. It became a patchwork of swampland, protected and only open to visitors with special permission, visitors who were supposed to stay on designated boardwalks...but didn't always.

"What are we looking at?" Capria asks, after recovering from her nausea.

"Is the air breathable?" I ask.

"Air?" Capria is aghast, and probably a little annoyed that I ignored her first question. "We're not going down there."

"You don't need to," I tell her. "Gal?"

"You'll want rebreathers," Gal says. "Oxygen level is ten point six percent, comparable to the O_2 level atop a very tall mountain. It won't kill you, because, you know...but it wouldn't be comfortable to breathe and would likely leave you lightheaded and confused, if not unconscious."

"How is the oxygen level even that high?" Capria asks. "There's nothing green anywhere."

"Much of Earth's oxygen is trapped in the ground," Gal says. "It could be leaching out. It's also possible that phytoplankton are still abundant in the ocean. I can't be sure without sampling, but they contribute fifty to eighty percent of the oxygen on Earth. Ten percent oxygen suggests their populations have dwindled, but they could still be surviving near the poles, where it's cooler."

"How hot is it down there?" I ask.

"One hundred thirteen degrees. Hotter in the west, where I detected temperatures in excess of one hundred fifty degrees."

"You're not seriously considering going down there," Capria says. She's spent her entire life inside composite walls. She's never breathed open air or been able to see to a horizon that wasn't virtual. She's never felt a breeze, or felt earth between her bare toes. The idea of stepping onto the planet's vast openness must be intimidating.

"You don't need to come," I tell her. "Gal, you can fly a lander?"

It's tempting to just hack myself to the surface, but the fewer changes we make to the code, the better.

Gal huffs in mock offense. "I piloted an FTL spaceship outside the borders of reality. Do you want an excavation drone?"

"Excavation drone?" Capria's level of apprehension is rising along with the pitch of her voice. "What are you planning to do?"

"What I should have done a long time ago," I tell her and look her in the eyes. "Bury the dead."

Two hours later, I'm standing behind the closed door of a lander, rethinking my decision. To my surprise, Capria decided to join me, despite her fears, and despite not yet knowing what I'm looking for. That means a lot. *Says* a lot.

When my hand begins to shake, she takes hold of it.

"You're sure about this?" she asks.

"He's sure," Gal says, her voice coming from the large excavation drone behind us. It's huge, needing four repulse discs to keep its octagonal, UFO-shaped body aloft. The drone was designed to clear terrain and help construct habitats for the crew, but it will work well enough for what I have in mind.

Capria shoots the big drone a look. "I wasn't asking y—"

"I'm fine," I say. If Gal and Capria start not getting along, my life could feel a lot longer than forever. I strap my facemask on, don a pair of tinted goggles, and say, "Let's go."

When Capria finishes putting on her head gear, the door splits horizontally, the bottom forming a ramp to the parched ground and the top opening like a clam shell...if there are still clams down in the depths. Hot air assaults my forehead and scalp, the only parts of my body exposed to the open air. It's prickly, like the water is being wicked from my body. I cringe as I take a deep breath, like the heat will permeate my breathing apparatus. When it doesn't, I take a tentative step down the ramp and get my first ground-level view of my old home.

It looks like another planet.

The ground is gray and brown, sand and waterless soil. It stretches out five hundred feet and then ends in a sheer drop. Beyond the Earth is the ocean, colored like slate, but alive with waves courtesy of the moon and sun-born wind, and the tides they still faithfully generate. At the bottom of the ramp, I crouch down and run my fingers through the soil. It's dry, and lifeless, but it's home. Eyes closed, I listen to the crashing waves, focusing on the steady rhythm, letting my racing heart slow to match them. When it does, I stand and turn back to the lander. Capria and the drone piloted by Gal wait at the top. Cap's face is hidden, and the drone doesn't have one, so I can't really see how they're feeling, but I sense their concern.

"Let's go," I say and head around the lander.

The land on the far side is equally stark but stretches to the horizon, a vast desert. I stop and look for anything familiar, but my imagination isn't powerful enough to recreate a world that's been missing for thousands of years.

The drone stops beside me. Gal's tone is somber, lacking all trace of casual speech or humor. "Based on historical documents and maps, the edge of George's Swamp should be one hundred feet ahead. There's not a lot of data to go on, but there are temperature fluctuations and disparate soil densities where the path and waterline used to be. Based on reports, I believe I can identify an approximate location."

"What location?" Capria asks, her frustration brewing.

But I don't have the fortitude to answer her yet. If I voice it, make it real, I'll probably turn around.

This is going to hurt.

A lot.

The drone forges ahead and I follow, leaving Capria behind us.

"Seriously?" she grumbles, but then I hear her feet crunching over the soil behind us, leaving footprints that are as anomalous on this planet now as they were on the moon when man first walked its surface.

The drone pauses less than a minute later. "This is the edge," Gal says.

"How close are we?" I ask.

The drone turns its red not-eyes toward me. "Approximately fifty feet from where you were found. Where should I search?"

I point straight out to where a vegetation-covered sheet of water once existed.

Gal turns to the remnants of George's Swamp and hovers out over the barren surface. A loud thumping resonates from the drone's base as it moves back and forth, following an evenly spaced grid.

"Will," Capria says, taking my hand again. Her touch nearly brings tears to my eyes. I've done a good job keeping them at bay so far, but my emotions are a tsunami beating at a hastily built dam. "What are we doing here?"

I point to the drone. "Ground penetrating radar."

"I know what Gal is doing, but I don't know why. I don't know what you think is here."

I purse my lips, defiant, unable to contemplate any other answer. "The swamp had several feet of mud at the bottom. Anything in it would have been preserved, even after all this." I motion to the dead earth surrounding us.

"You're looking for bones," she says. I don't hear a question in the words, but I do hear budding annoyance.

The drone issues a loud beep, followed by Gal's voice. "Will!"

It takes me two steps to reach a sprint. I'm by the drone's side in seconds, just thirty feet from shore.

Just thirty feet...

The drone's black skin has retracted, revealing a fifteen inch screen displaying a three dimensional image of what the ground penetrating radar has discovered. I wasn't sure if this moment would come, even after we discovered reality's source code, returned to Earth, and stepped out of the lander. I expected it to break me open, to undo me, but I feel a new kind of resolve. Something in me says, 'This is right. This is good. You can heal.'

When Capria arrives, I'm not a sobbing mess like I expected, I'm a man transformed by the power of his past laid bare. I can make this right. I can say goodbye. I step to the side, allowing her to see the screen. "This is why we're here."

I can't see her eyes, but I can see her forehead wrinkling as she opens them wide. "Who..."

"This is Steven." I place my hand on the display of a small body, curled up in a fetal position. "This is my brother."

39

Capria's stunned silence isn't unexpected. After a series of droughts that left much of Earth's vast population starving, births were only approved by lottery for those with genetic advantages, and even then only one per couple. One of the few exceptions had been my parents. They didn't win a second lottery. My conception was an accident. Beyond an accident. A miracle. After a couple successfully gave birth to a healthy child, the father was given a vasectomy. I was conceived twelve months after my father's surgery, and the pregnancy wasn't discovered for another three months.

Abortion was recommended, and the norm in such rare cases, but it could not be forced on my mother. My parents paid a sizeable fine, and I was born, healthy and unscathed, six months later. The first result was that my brother and I were one of three pairs of siblings on the North American continent. The second result was that my brother died ten years later.

Right here.

Because of me.

After retrieving a shovel from the lander, I set to work on the hard packed earth. I haven't used a shovel since I was a child, digging traps for imaginary enemies with Steven, but Capria's never seen one. Like screwdrivers, we have drones to do this kind of manual labor now. The excavator would make short work of Steven's exhumation. But this is my hole to dig. My penance to pay, alone.

And then it's not.

Command, in their infinite wisdom, realized that manual labor would likely be necessary on Cognata. The landers are outfitted with a variety of tools and construction hardware once common on Earth, but unheard of on Mars, where things like wood, concrete, and stone aren't used. When Capria sinks a shovel into the dirt opposite me, I flinch at the sound. I nearly bark at her for the intrusion, but if we're going to work, we need to share everything, including what hurts us most. Plus, my coveralls are already soaked with sweat. I could use the help.

It takes an hour to dig through three feet of packed soil. Capria and I have shed the top halves of our coveralls, tying the sleeves around our waists. She keeps her bra on, though the way she pauses every now and then to adjust it tells me she'd rather take it off, too. I feel like I should propose the idea, but don't want to come across as a letch.

"You're close," Gal warns. They're the first words she's spoken since the digging began. I think she might be upset that I let Capria help, but Gal's assistance would have removed the effort, the burn, the self-flagellation.

I stop digging and sit on the edge of the three-foot-deep, five-foot-long pit. Water drips down my forehead, the saltiness of it stiffening as it quickly evaporates. "We're going to need to drink."

"A lot," Cap agrees, sitting across from me.

"I can finish for you," Gal offers, and simulates a sigh when I shake my head. "At least let me dig the grave."

The idea of digging a second pit, twice as deep, sounds like torture. I nod my assent and then point to the shoreline where my ten-year-old self had fallen into the algae laden swamp thousands of years ago. "There was a memorial over there. There should be a sheet of metal. Can you find it? Dig the grave there?"

"Of course," Gal says, and then the drone is moving, its four, blue repulse discs humming loudly in the vast, empty silence of a lifeless planet.

When I turn back to Capria, I'm surprised by the aghast expression on her face.

"What?"

"You're digging him up just to bury him again..." She points to the shoreline where the drone is thumping away with its ground penetrating radar. "...over there?"

"What did you think I was going to do?" I ask.

"I don't know, bring him with us?"

A twinge of annoyance begins building deep in my chest. "You don't need to be here."

The words wound her. "Will, he is already buried."

"In the wrong place." I climb down into the pit. On hands and knees, I scrape away the last layers of soil. Were the body beneath me not my brother, I probably would have reminded her that Martians were cremated because they couldn't be buried. And while many people on Earth opted for that fiery send off, my parents hadn't, and it's not what they would have chosen for their son.

Capria surprises me once again, climbing into the pit to wipe away ancient dust and grit, sharing my pain.

I stop, ten minutes later when my hand strikes something solid. There's a brief moment where the reality of what I'm about to do sets in. When it passes, my hands are shaking and tears blur my vision. With a sniffling nose, I double my efforts, chipping, wiping, and peeling away earth. By the time his well-preserved body is unearthed, I'm a mess, unleashing millennia of pent up emotion.

His clothing, and skin are intact, though the moisture has been removed from his small body, mummifying him.

"I'm sorry," I say between heaving sobs. I place my living forehead against his petrified forehead, wishing I could undo thousands of years of history to save him. The irony, I know, is that such a thing is now within my power. I could go back and change that day. I could return his body to its previous state, here and now. But both actions would likely result in the deletion, reset, or modification of reality. I've become an impotent god. Creator of nothing. Unable to do anything for the dead, except mourn them and send them off right.

Capria's hand on me soothes me out of anguish's solid grip. "Hey."

Her face is as wet as mine.

"Sorry," I say.

She smiles, sympathetic, wiping away her tears. "This is good. This is right."

My nod shakes more tears free.

"Gal is ready," she says.

Gal waits by the shoreline, hovering beside a rectangular pit, at the head of which is a stainless steel gravestone. *She found it...*

Even though his petrified body is partially shrouded in hard-packed grit on the verge of becoming stone, which I left in place to hold him together, Steven is light. I have no trouble lifting his frail body and carrying it the thirty feet back to the gentle slope that once led from the water to the shore.

Gal waits for us, the excavation drone hovering by the grave she dug for me. I stop a few feet short when I see the grave marker, etched with the words:

In Memory of
Steven Chanokh
Beloved Son
Loving Brother
"Engage"

My eyes blur before I can read the dates, but I don't need to see them. The numbers are etched in my memory even more permanently than the words on the stainless steel gravestone.

When I reach the grave, I turn to Capria. "Can you hold him?"

She nods, sniffing back tears, and reaches out to take him in her arms. We pass the body between us, moving him delicately, a newborn baby sound asleep. I slip down into the grave, dug six feet deep. I reach up for my brother and ease him down, back into the earth. On the surface, I understand why Capria might see all this as unnecessary, but I'm honoring the dead—my brother, and my parents who never got to bury their son—and I'm allowing myself to say goodbye, to free myself from this now-ancient tether of guilt.

"Goodbye, Steven," I whisper to his body, then I kiss his weathered forehead. "I love you."

Live for the both of us, I hear in reply. Though I'm certain the words are my own, what I long to hear from my long deceased sibling, I feel their truth. I've been given an eternal gift, and thus far, I've been squandering it.

"I will," I tell him, hand on his chest. "For both of us."

I rise from the grave, feeling renewed.

Reborn.

Forgiven.

Capria sees it in my smile and looks both relieved and saddened by it.

"You okay?"

"I just..." She takes a deep breath, working through her own complicated emotions. "I understand this now, I think. It's not just for them. Not just about sending them to an afterlife. It's saying goodbye. It's saying 'I'm going to keep living, despite the loss. Despite the hurt.'"

She leans into my chest, and for the first time since she woke from cryo-sleep, we embrace. We stand there in the ridiculous heat, shirtless and sweating, wrapped in each other's arms for five minutes.

When she pulls back, Capria looks like a weight has been lifted from her as well.

"We should bury them here, too," she says. "All of them."

I'm about to ask who she's talking about when I remember the ship full of corpses in geosynchronous orbit high above us—all of whom I planned to bury, and one of whom is Tom. She's ready to bury him. Ready to move on. Ready to live again.

Facing my brother's body again, I forgot all about the dead crew, but now it's time to fulfill my duty. The task will be depressing, and gross, but putting our crew in the ground, where they belong, on a home planet many of them never saw, will take a weight off my mind.

The excavation drone stays behind to dig thirty six more graves. Gal pilots the lander back to the *Galahad*, where Capria and I move the dead. After wrapping the frigid corpses in white linens gathered from the crews' quarters, several drones help us transport the *Galahad*'s crew to Earth, in groups of nine.

We lay them out beside each of the gravesites. After four trips and fifteen hours of labor in daylight and through the night, our friends lie on Earth's surface, most of them for the first time. Gal surprises Capria and me by providing metal gravestones for each crewmember, etched with their names. While we moved the bodies, she was also busy fashioning the memorials and digging the pits.

Capria and I move down the line, lowering each body into the dirt together, saying our goodbyes. The excavator drone follows us, filling in the graves.

Tom is last, and I step away, giving her some privacy.

Despite the distance between us, the dead silence of planet Earth makes her voice easy to hear.

"You were wrong about him," she says to her old boyfriend. "He's kind, and smart." She laughs. "You'd probably say I'm feeling this way because he's the only man left in the universe."

Feeling what way? I wonder.

"But you're wrong, and looking back, at you, at us, I should have seen him sooner. He might be an Earthling, but he's got more heart than you or I ever did. I'm happy to have him, even if he is listening in." She glances back at me, tears in her eyes, a smile on her lips. Then glances back to Tom. "You've been gone for a long time, but this is where we part ways, Tommy. It's time for me to live, too."

I head back and help her lower the cause of all our misery into the ground. Part of me feels like I should say something, too, but I'm pretty sure it would come out wrong, or not be nice at all. So I just pick up a shovel and fill in the final grave alongside Capria. When we're done, a new graveyard has been created, providing the dead a view of the gray ocean. It's a stark expanse lacking the power it once held over generations of people, but it's the best view around. We stand at the cliff's edge, sweaty and tired after working through the night. The sunrise is muted, but still beautiful.

"What now?" Capria asks.

I smile at the question that once horrified me: what to do with eternity. "Anything we want. Everything. But I think we should check a few locations first. Mars. Cognata."

"And then?" Capria asks. She reaches out and takes my hand.

"Anything we want," I say. "And everything else."

"May I suggest first returning to the lander?" Gal says, speaking from a collection of drones that helped moved bodies. "You've got about ten minutes of air left."

"You don't need to tell me—" I'm not sure why I stop talking. Not at first. Then my conscious mind registers what my subconscious already picked up on. A vibration in my feet.

Capria feels it, too. "What..."

A rumbling sound turns us both around.

The furthest gravestone tips to the side. And then with a whoosh, and a cough of dust, the mound of dirt atop the fresh grave inverts, like it's been sucked down.

"Did we leave an air pocket?" I ask, but I know we didn't.

"Run," Gal says.

I want to ask why, to make some sense of what's happening, but my subconscious is now shouting to obey her. I tug on Capria's arm and start toward the lander, two hundred feet away.

"What's happening?" she asks. "Is it an earthquake?"

"Not an earthquake." I glance back and see nothing, but the vibration has become a rumbling. There's something under the ground, and it's now headed toward us. If we had been anywhere else in the universe, I would have a modicum of doubt about the rumbling's source. But here on Earth, where life was once abundant, but always evolving, it can mean only one thing. "We're being hunted."

40

When the ground shivers beneath my feet, I stay on course.

When the sound of cracking earth coughs behind me, I keep running.

When the baritone roar of some Earth-creature thumps against my eardrums, I can't keep myself from looking back. It was supposed to be a quick glance, but the thing behind us is strange and completely unidentifiable. My lingering focus skews my balance to one side and my legs tangle.

I go down hard, landing first on my left wrist, which cracks, and then my rib cage, which follows my wrist's lead. I feel three deep pops, and then a numbness in my mind, protecting me from the agony that follows, but only just a little. I roll onto my back. I want to lie there and breathe. Maybe whine about the pain. But Capria hasn't let go of my right hand.

She yanks hard. "Will! Move! It's coming!"

The strange animal, large enough to swallow me whole, bounds toward us, its legs flailing out to the sides with each lunge. Its feet are webbed and tipped with long, hooked claws. Good for swimming, or digging. The body is as broad as it is long, coated in a layer of dry soil still flaking away from its body. A curtain of red flesh and drool dangles from its wide mouth.

It's eaten a corpse, I think, and then I realize that this thing must have been sleeping beneath the ground, hibernating, waiting for a rainy season, if there is one. The scent of death, and blood, coupled with vibrations created by our digging, burying, and walking must have roused the beast prematurely. And now it's hungry, and judging by its interest in the living over the dead, thirsty.

With my mind on water, I'm able to see this thing for what it is, or was—at least part of it. A frog. It's a few tons too large, but the body shape, lunging legs, wide head and bulging eyes fit. The claws are wrong. Its skin is more like the armor plating of the rhinos that went extinct long before I was born.

Did this creature evolve over the past few thousand years, or was it the creation of a floundering humanity, desperate to create a resilient source of meat? There's no way to learn the truth, so I focus on not being its next meal.

I scramble back, wincing in pain as I plant my left hand on the ground and push up. The break had already begun to heal, but it snaps again when I push myself up. Back on my feet, growling in pain, I make it three steps before my ankle is grasped and pulled back.

The ground is once again unforgiving as I collide with the dusty surface just ten feet short of the lander's open hatch.

I roll over and look back into the open maw of the frog-thing. A long, pink tongue stretches from the creature's throat to my ankle. The muscle flexes, and then pulls. I'm dragged across the dry ground, caught in a reverse slingshot. I shout, partly from pain, partly from the horror of being digested alive, a fate that probably would kill me in the slowest, most torturous way possible. It's an end at which even a suicidal person would balk.

The jaws snap down on my waist. I feel my insides compress. Something in my back cracks. The pressure is immense but, without teeth, it's not enough to sever me in two. I scream again, this time with the expectation of pain, but there is none. My body is numb. I punch and claw at the thing's snout, but it's hopeless. My lower half is trapped and useless, as I'm sucked inward, a tasty morsel. I swing for its large eyes, watching me with indifference, but I fall short.

Its cheeks bulge, getting ready for another gulp that will no doubt plunge me into its gullet. I'll have a *Galahad* crewmember for company, but since he or she has been dead for thousands of Earth years, I'll be the only one in slowly dissolving agony. How long will my body be able to regenerate inside the creature's stomach? *Forever*, I think, and that's when the true horror of my situation sets in.

My fingers hook onto the creature's snout, dragging dirt free as I'm pulled slowly inward. The scream that flows from my lips is embarrassing and wet with blood. If not for the rebreather strapped to my back, catching on the large lower lip, I would already be drowning in stomach acid.

Then, a black blur. It collides with the frog-thing's side. The world becomes a chaotic, twirling mess of confusion.

Pressure abates.

I feel hot air on my face. In my lungs.

I hit the ground, limp, and roll to a stop, on my side. Facing the creature.

Like me, the beast is on its side, but with a kick of its leg, it vaults back to its four feet.

Run, I think. *Move!*

But I can't. My legs are useless. My back is broken. I try to pull myself along with just my arm, but pain from my broken wrist, ribs, and whatever internal damage has been done, keeps me stationary.

I'm at the predator's mercy, but not without help.

The excavation drone pulls back from the frog-thing. *Gal rammed it*, I realize, but any hope that brings is quashed when the creature turns my way again. It doesn't know what the drone is, but it knows it's not edible.

"Can you move?" Gal shouts.

"Not yet," I reply. My body is broken, but I can feel it pulling itself back together, each stitching bone and reformed organ itching and pulsing fresh waves of nausea through my gut.

She rams the creature again, garnering a croak of pain, and its full attention. Large claws whoosh through the air, colliding with the drone's body, carving four long gouges through the metal. Sparks fly as the drone's sensor array is split down the middle. The camera allowing Gal to see through the robot is destroyed. She's blind.

But like me, she's not alone. With a battle cry that surprises me and makes the frog-thing flinch, Capria leaps from the lander's ramp, shovel in hand. She reels back and brings the metal diamond down on a single bulbous eye, which folds to the side, and bursts.

The predator is undone, flailing back, clawing at its own head, perhaps believing its eye is covered, rather than missing.

With the monster now on its back, Capria turns to me. Reaches out.

A long leg extends, blindly kicking at the air, but still deadly. I try to shout a warning, but I find the hot, stinging air in my lungs inefficient. My air mask is missing. Capria is struck by the next kick, and flung through the air. She lands a few feet short of me, unmoving, face down on the hard-packed ground.

"Cap..." I manage to say.

Then she gasps back to life, pushing herself up. The gasping continues. She can't breathe. Her hands go to her facemask and yank it away.

She heaves in a breath of Earth air, and discovers, as I already have, that it's not nearly potent enough to quench our lungs' thirst, or keep us conscious.

As my vision starts to narrow, my spine snaps back into place. The pain is exquisite for a brief flare. The Big Bang is in my back, and then I'm fully mobile again.

The frog-thing rights itself. Red, white, and clear liquid coats half its face. The other half still looks hungry. The long tongue rises from the mouth, dragging across the gore, not wasting an ounce of liquid. Then its attention turns back to us and the promise of water kept inside our bodies.

"Go!" Gal shouts. "Get to the lander and leave!"

I push myself up and yank Capria up beside me, already hobbling toward the lander. "I'm not going to leave you."

"It's not me," she reminds me. "Now, run!" She must be using the live feeds from the smaller drones, or the lander, or even the view from orbit to guide the excavation drone. It rams the creature once more, pushing it to the side, but doing no real damage.

The frog-thing unleashes a frustrated flurry of claws, swiping with the frenetic energy of an enraged cat. The drone takes a beating, but the engines on the undercarriage remain active, keeping the robot airborne and mobile.

We reach the ramp, fully healed, but losing consciousness.

At the top of the ramp, I fall to my hands and knees, heaving deep breaths, but never getting enough oxygen. Cap topples beside me, already unconscious.

I reach for her.

Grab her forearm.

But I lack the strength to pull myself any further, let alone pull her along with me.

But I don't need to. The lander ramp rises from the ground. For a moment, I'm lying on my stomach, feeling a strange kind of comfortable as darkness shrouds my vision. Then I'm pitched forward and dumped onto the floor. I'm sure it hurts, but I barely register the pain.

On the edge of unconscious bliss, I hear the doors seal shut, and feel a blast of cool air. I take a slow, lazy breath, welcoming sleep.

And then I wake up.

Oxygen reaches my mind with an effect similar to that shot of epinephrine. I launch to my feet, heart beating fast, refueling my body. I lean against the rear hatch and look out the window. The lander must have lifted off while the hatch was still closing. My mind was too close to unconsciousness to register the motion. We're already fifty feet up and climbing.

Down below, the excavation drone, along with three smaller units, are fully engaged in battle. And they're about to lose. The injured frog-thing is being joined by more, some already hopping toward the activity, some still rising from the hard ground, and still others ignoring the fight altogether, focusing on the corpses buried in the ground.

I regret the fate of the dead we honored, but take comfort in the fact that my brother, nearly indistinguishable from the dry earth in which he's buried, will be left undisturbed.

Capria stirs, and I move away from the window. She's let Tom go, but I'd prefer she not know his final resting place is probably in the stomach of a giant, mutated frog.

I crouch down beside her as she opens her eyes. "Hey."

"Hey, Frog-Bait." She smiles. "That's my new nickname for you. F.B."

It's horrible. "I love it."

I help her into a sitting position and then lean against the wall opposite her. We're quiet for a few minutes, watching the gray sky turn muddy purple as we rise steadily into the upper atmosphere.

"So, F.B.," she eventually says. "What's next?"

I'm relieved to see that the effect of freeing ourselves from our combined survivor's guilt hasn't worn off, despite nearly being eaten alive forever. And when I smile, I'm even happier to realize that my relief hasn't faded, either.

"I'm thinking Mars," I say. "Just to be sure."

Neither of us expects to find life on Mars. It's even less likely than it was the first time mankind touched down on the red planet.

"And then Kepler 452b?" she asked.

I nod. "And from there...anywhere and everywhere."

"Sounds like a plan."

"Can I make a suggestion?" Gal says, her voice loud and clear from the lander's speakers.

"Of course." I'm a little worried our human-oriented plan has offended her, but she doesn't sound upset. In fact, I think I heard a touch of whimsy in her voice.

"I think we should make another pit stop before leaving Earth."

I can't imagine where Gal would want to go. There's nothing left of humanity but ruins, the local wildlife will likely want to eat us, and the scenery is rather bleak.

"Where?"

"I've been scanning the planet, while you've been, you know, trying not to get eaten."

"Gal," I say. "*Where?*"

"Patience, F.B." Gal gives Capria a moment to finish chuckling. "I detected higher concentrations of oxygen in the atmosphere. It could be nothing, but I think—"

I thump my head against the lander's wall. "Seriously. Gal, you're killing me."

"It's not the first time I've tried." She laughs. When I don't, she adds, "Fine. We're going to the South Pole. Antarctica."

41

"It's...it's green." Capria is standing at the lander's window, hands on the wall, peering out at the Earth as mankind once knew it.

After returning to *Galahad*, showering, changing our clothes, and rehydrating, we began our descent, this time accompanied by a small army of drones ready to wage war against anything that might try to eat us. If evolved animals are still clinging to life in the parched world beyond Antarctica, there's no telling what we'll find on the now lush continent.

I step beside Capria and watch the coastline grow closer. There are trees, and grasses, swaying in the wind.

"Oh my God!" Capria says, her knees going wobbly. "Birds! I see birds!"

On Earth, birds weren't uncommon, even when things got bad. While mankind suffered, insects thrived, and so did the animals that ate them. So I'm not overly surprised to find them on a still-green continent, or in Antarctica's case, a newly green continent.

But Antarctica wasn't always frozen, I remember. Before the last ice age, the continent was warm, and according to an ancient map I read about once, it supported plant, animal, and human life. And long before humanity walked the planet, dinosaurs lived here, the bones surviving millennia to reveal life had once thrived at the bottom of the world.

For Capria, the birds are more than a sign of life. She's a Martian, born and raised on the red planet. She's never seen a real bird. She's encountered a giant killer frog monster, but she probably spent her childhood, like most Mars kids, dreaming about what it was like to see and hear animals like birds.

Looking out the window, it's as if the birds know that, and they're putting on a show. A great flock of gulls flies east as we approach, no doubt migrating from one feeding or breeding ground to another.

"Are you seeing this?" Capria asks.

"Not for the first time."

She shakes her head, smiling wide. "I never pictured it like this. Never really understood what it would be like."

Her elation is communicable, pulling a laugh from me. "We haven't even stepped outside yet."

"ETA, thirty seconds," Gal says, as the lander slows its descent. "Oxygen level is at eighteen percent. It's a little low for sea level, but it approximates what was normal for people living in what was once known as Denver, Colorado. With your genetic alterations, you should have no trouble acclimating to the lower levels."

My forehead scrunches a moment before I realize I've come up with a question. "The frogs..."

"What's that, F.B.?" Capria says, her elation faltering just a little when she sees my face.

"The frogs. They were big. *Really* big."

"So?" she asks.

"Their oxygen requirements should have been greater than ours, but they had no problem hopping around and trying to eat me, while we barely made it back to the lander without passing out. It doesn't—"

"Acclimation and evolution," Gal says. "There are several examples of animals that require little or no oxygen to survive."

I open my mouth to offer a rebuttal. Those animals were tiny. The frogs were huge. But Gal is quicker than me.

"And, there is a long list of Sherpas capable of not just surviving in low oxygen levels, but thriving in them. A Nepalese man, Babu Chiri Sherpa, spent twenty-one hours on Mount Everest's summit, four thousand feet above the 'death zone,' without the aid of supplementary oxygen. While the oxygen level atop Everest was twenty-one percent, the thinner air reduced the availability of that O_2 to thirty-three percent of what's available at sea level."

"Seven percent," I say. "Roughly."

Point made. If some people could hang out atop Mount Everest without oxygen, who's to say that mutated frogs living beneath Earth's surface haven't acclimated to the reduced O_2. They could leach oxygen out of the ground, the water, or just not need as much. I return my gaze to the jungle outside the lander. We're just thirty feet above a sandy beach tracing a line between the green land and the blue ocean.

Unlike Capria, I look out the window with an equal mix of excitement and apprehension. If giant frog-things can survive in a barren world, what are we going to find here? Images of strange and unusual animals flit through my mind. I'm not sure what they are, but they're not a product of my imagination.

"You're doing it again," Capria says and motions at my head. "The forehead thing."

"This feels familiar," I say.

"How could *this—*" She waves her hands at the window. "—be familiar. Even when you lived here, Earth didn't look like this."

"I think it was a book, or a movie," I say. "Maybe both."

Before I can dig deeper into the memory, the lander hatch unseals and opens wide. The lower ramp digs into the sand a few inches and stops.

The air is hot, but a good fifteen degrees cooler than it had been in what was left of Florida. Being at the South Pole has its perks. The place is also scented with organic rot from generations of plant growth, sea water, and flowers. It nearly undoes me.

I stumble down the ramp and step into the sand.

Bird calls echo from the forest, joined by something deeper, something mammalian—but not threatening. The palm trees lining the beach sway in the wind, their large leaves merging with the crashing of waves to create a peaceful white noise.

Without thinking, I unclasp my coveralls and peel out of them. Dressed only in boxer-briefs, I step into the sand again, and smile at the warm feel of it beneath my feet. The humid air covers my body with a sheen that makes me feel cleansed.

This is living.

A loud thumping, racing up behind me, fills my mind with images of new-Earth predators, but it's just Capria. Like me, she has shed her coveralls. Dressed in her own Command-issued gray boxer-briefs and bra, she charges down the ramp, rounds the lander and runs for the glistening turquoise waters.

A series of warnings approach the threshold of my mouth— check for an undertow, watch out for sharks, don't step on a sharp shell—but I hold it all back and follow. She stops in just a few inches of water, looking down, wonder painted on her face.

"F.B. coming through!" I shout and charge past, remembering my few childhood visits to the ocean, what it felt like to plow through incoming waves, what the water tasted like, how good I felt after a day in the sun. I hit the first three-foot wave head on, crashing through. Then, in waist deep water, I dive in, kicking for several feet before twirling around and rising.

When I break the surface and wipe the water from my eyes, Capria is still rooted in place, her wonder replaced by fear.

I stand in chest deep water, pummeled from behind by incoming waves that lift me off the ocean floor every few seconds. "What is it?" I search the area for predators. For fins. Shadows. I see nothing.

"How are you doing that?" Capria asks.

"Doing what?" I ask, and then I realize the problem. "You can't swim."

Of course she can't. Water on Mars was the most rare and valuable commodity. Every ounce of it was recycled, from showers, toilets, urine—even feces. Every drop was recovered and reused. There was none left over for a swimming pool or even a bath. No Martian-born human being could swim.

I kick back to shore, practicing the strokes my father taught Steven and me, which probably made my brother overconfident when he dove into a swamp filled with debris, tangling vines, and a layer of goopy mud at the bottom. I stop in waist-deep water and hold my hands out to Capria.

She looks unsure.

I wave her on. "This is what you wanted when you ran out here in your underwear, right?"

She takes a cautious step closer, and then another and another until she's standing in front of me, rising and falling as the waves roll past or crash on my back. I take her hand and lead her a little deeper. She says nothing, but looks nervous as the water rises. I stop when we're deep enough that the waves aren't cresting.

"What are we doing?" she asks.

"Teaching you to swim." I reach out my arms. "Hold my forearms." She grasps my arms beneath the elbows, and I do the same to her. "Now, just lean forward, try to stay straight and kick."

She raises an eyebrow. "Kick?"

"Just kick."

She eases forward and yelps a little as her feet come off the ocean floor. When she doesn't plunge beneath the water, she laughs, and then kicks. The water turns white behind her thrashing feet, and I pull her along, letting her feel what it's like to move through the water. I twirl her in slow circles, smiling as her laughter continues and grows in volume when a wave sideswipes her. We stop so she can pull her hair out of her face and wipe the water away.

"How am I doing?" she asks.

"You're a natural," I say, and she slaps my shoulder because we both know it's a lie.

"Let's see how you do with your hands and feet." I extend my arms and lower them just beneath the water. "Lay across my arms."

She's dubious, but leans down onto my arms.

Holding her buoyant weight, I'm about to explain a breast stroke to her and move her through the water while she thrashes about, when she looks up at me with a strange kind of smile. "Pretty slick move."

"Huh?" Something about her expression makes me feel like I've been caught doing something wrong, but I have no idea what it is.

Her smile widens when she realizes that I'm ignorant to whatever it is. "Your left hand."

The moment my ears register the words, I feel her breast in my cupped hand, holding her up. I roll my hand forward so it's awkwardly placed against her clavicle. "Shit. Sorry."

She leans back, planting her feet on the seabed. "I didn't mind."

I'm at a loss for words, and then discover it doesn't matter. It's hard to talk when a woman's lips are pressing against yours. A wave lifts us together, carrying us closer to shore. We touch down again at an angle, Capria stumbling back, me holding onto her. I nearly catch her, but a second wave does us in. We topple back, fall to the sand, and resume kissing.

I recall seeing movies, and my mother's classic romance novels, depicting this very thing: couples on the sand. The images were alluring, and promised that great things happened when men and women made love at the beach, caressed by each other and the waves. But reality chafes.

When my knees grow raw, and sand works its way into places before Capria can get there, I pull back and say, "Lander?"

She nods and we hurry back to the lander like sneaking teenagers.

Gal's drones file out of the lander, making room and forming a protective half circle around the open hatch. To her credit, Gal remains a silent observer, even when our shouts of ecstasy, which could be misconstrued as pain, drown out the jungle's animal calls. Gal has feigned romantic interest before, and I have to admit I've sometimes wished she was human, but she's also made it clear that she is without a body, or human interests, like sex. So I'm more worried that I'll look bad in the security feed of this encounter, than I am about her being jealous.

I'd like to say that the hard floor of the lander was a relief compared to the sand, but its hard surface is brutal on my knees, and then on my back, and on my knees again. But I don't care. Our first time together is equal parts pain and pleasure, but when we're done, lying sprawled in the lander's cargo bay floor, stark naked, all I can remember is how amazing it felt.

Still feels.

For the first time since waking up with a screwdriver in my chest, life isn't just horrible, depressing, interesting, or fun; life is good.

"Ahem," Gals says, fifteen minutes after we're done. "I think we can rate Antarctica as a five-star experience, but there is still the question of Mars and Kepler 452b. Shall we take a look?"

I sit up, no longer worried about my nakedness. "We should check them out." I say it with the enthusiasm of a student being roused for school. "But I think we'll come back when we're done." Capria takes my hands. "I think we've found our home."

The drones return like a well-trained flock of sheep, and the lander doors close. An electric chime sounds. "First stop, Mars," Gal says. "Then on to Kepler 452b, Cognata to the layman."

Layman. A singular and not too subtle dig at my intelligence. I don't mind it, though. Means Cap and Gal are getting along.

I'm not sure what we'll find at either planet, but after our experience on Antarctica, I feel a little more hopeful about discovering something not entirely horrible.

42

Horrible is too mild a word for what we find.

It's not the first time I've seen Mars from orbit, but it's the first time I've seen it without the colonies or Command. I had envisioned a lifeless planet—Mars always has been—but I thought the structures erected by mankind would still stand. Command, like *Galahad*, had an army of drones maintaining the facility, but there was nothing they could do to stave off the self-inflicted fate that erased humanity from the red planet.

"War?" Capria asks, standing beside me on the observation deck. We're in orbit over where Command once stood, our view zoomed in on the ten square miles that once was Mars's first city, and is now a crater—or rather, a collection of craters. Command was destroyed by a missile barrage.

"They must have made it a long time," I say.

"Long enough to develop weapons of mass destruction from the elements," Gal says. "WMDs were eradicated before Command was formed, but if they survived on Mars for hundreds of years, uncovering resources, it's possible that they were able to fashion new weapons. But I don't understand why they would."

"Survival," I say.

"No one survived," Gal says.

I step closer to the wall, inspecting the black rings marring the ruddy surface. "It's a misconception as old as modern man. Might makes right. Carry a big stick."

"Mutually assured destruction," Capria adds.

"To prevent destruction, they built the means to carry it out." Gal says. It's not a question. She's accessed history and seen the pattern for herself. And then she offers her articulate and fairly accurate assessment of people's potential for violence. "People are dumb."

"Sometimes," I admit. "Depends on who is in charge. Brains don't always beat brawn. A leader who believes violence is the solution can undo generations of progress. It's how most modern wars began. So..." I motion to the destruction.

I have no idea if that's the scenario that played out on Mars, but I have little doubt that when Earth became uninhabitable, Mars found itself with droves of refugees and not nearly enough resources to support them. War was inevitable.

"Well," Capria says. "This is depressing. Can we leave?"

I had pictured us spending a good amount of time on Mars, exploring structures, pillaging supplies, and uncovering the history of mankind's final days, but there is absolutely nothing here for us.

"Cognata." I spit the word, ready to leave this place and never return. Humanity's self-destructive nature is discouraging. Is this what we have to look forward to? A war between the last two people in the galaxy who have only just consummated a romantic relationship? Are we destined to find ourselves at odds, trying to kill each other to claim dominance of what little is left?

Or can we alter the inevitable course history says our lives are meant to travel?

I can't imagine a future where Capria is trying to kill me, or vice versa. So I make a pact with myself: if such a thing happens, I will fly *Galahad* into a star and erase us from existence.

If Gal will let me.

And that's a fight I simply can't imagine. The conjurings of my mind's eye are bringing tears to my real eyes. "*Gal.*"

"Pretty sure you don't want me to get the coordinates wrong," she snips. "Reappearing in the molten core of Kepler 452b wouldn't be pleasant."

After I isolated us within the code of reality, changing the coordinates for our group is something Gal can handle without me returning to the VCC, which is nice, because I now have very little desire to escape reality. Part of me wonders if that's simply because I know life is already a simulation, but I think it's simply because this reality is the one where Capria lives.

"Ready," Gal says. "I'll put us in orbit, close to *Galahad*'s original destination."

I nearly ask why she's bringing us to that same fateful location, but then I conclude the answer on my own. If there is any chance that the other immortals reached the surface of Cognata alive, and survived the past few thousand years, that is the most logical place to begin our search. At the same time, I can't imagine survivors staying in one place for that much time.

So when I say, "Let's go," I'm fully expecting to find dried out husks, flattened by Cognata's gravity.

The observation deck view shifts from Mars to Cognata without any fanfare. There's no hum of engines, no physical sensation to register a change in location spanning 1400 light years, no visual distortion of any kind. The image simply changes, like a slide show of planets.

But the ease of travel doesn't diminish the severity of our reaction.

It's night below us. Kepler 452, the sun-like star at the center of this solar system is just starting to peek over the horizon, its bright glow still a good fifteen hours away from reaching the land below us. Days on Cognata, a planet sixty percent wider than Earth, with a slower rotation, measure in 62 hour periods. Twin moons on opposite sides of the planet, make two full revolutions around the planet every day, ensuring there is always something in the sky to look at.

"Are you seeing what I'm seeing?" Capria asks, stepping closer to the wall, like that will give her a better look at what's going on down below.

She knows I'm seeing it, too.

It's impossible not to.

Where there should be nothing but stark darkness, there is light. It's not a lot, but the way it clumps and spider webs out to other clumps suggests a civilization has developed in the past few thousand years.

"How's the air?" I ask, leaping ahead to the 'can we go down there' stage.

"Oxygen rich," Gal says. "Twenty-seven percent, which is good because the added gravity means every step is going to be a workout."

Capria and I know this already. It's going to feel like we're giving someone a piggy back. It won't be fun, but the human body can adapt. Over time, our muscles and bones would grow stronger and more dense. The thought reveals that part of me is already leaving the Antarctic oasis behind. There are *people* on Cognata.

"Thermal scans reveal dense populations," Gal says, "some in the brightly lit areas, which are cool, by the way, and some in the darkness, suggesting herds of wildlife."

Wildlife that did *not* come from *Galahad*. Alien creatures. Could that also mean that the civilization below is also alien? And why are the lit areas cool? Light generally indicates heat, even if it's insignificant. These are questions that can only be answered by traveling to the surface.

"I can see by the looks on your faces," Gal says, "that you are both determined to travel to the surface before daybreak."

"You're damn right we are," I say. Capria smiles wide at this, excitement brewing, her hand clasping mine. Squeezing her energy into my flesh.

"May I suggest landing on the far side of the planet first? Or an unpopulated area?" Gal is doing her due diligence. She already knows the answers.

"You have my permission to say 'I told you so,' if anything goes wrong," I tell her. The part of my brain still in touch with the primal instincts coded to early man is prodding me to agree with Gal, but the modern human who craves socialization and community overpowers those instincts the way homo sapiens once did Neanderthals. "This is where the *Galahad*'s crew would have landed." I point to the largest and brightest splotch of light. "If this world has a capital, that's probably where we'll find it."

Gal sighs. "Agreed."

The next hour is a whirlwind of preparation. The temperature on Cognata is currently fifty degrees. It will probably warm up once the sun rises, but since that's a good number of hours away, we need to break out the cold weather gear. Long ago, on Earth, people wore thick layers of furs, and later on in human history, layers of synthetic material, all designed to retain body heat. Our winter clothing is a thin black layer of thermal underwear that generates its own heat. Designed to sustain the crew should we find Cognata in the grips of an ice age, the 'Thermals' are capable of keeping a human being toasty in minus seventy-five degree weather, which would also require a facemask, and only needs a few hours in the sun to recharge. The garment goes over our feet, torsos, arms, hands (except for the finger tips), and head. Once dressed we look like ninjas, or as Gal puts it...

"You look ridiculous."

Capria looks me up and down. "We do. They're liable to think we're thieves."

I pull the tight hood off my head. "It's only fifty degrees. We don't need the head gear, and we can wear the coveralls over this, which I'm pretty sure is how we were meant to wear them, because 'ridiculous' is not how I would describe how *you* look." When I look Capria up and down, there is no mistaking my point.

"It's true," Gal says. "Only one of you looks ridiculous, and he's the same someone who's going to be distracted if you both don't put on more clothes. Do you want to know how many wars, and all around stupidity have happened throughout human history because of a curvaceous woman?"

"Not really," I say. It's a silly notion, waging war over a mate, but here we are, alone in non-reality space, because a man broke all the rules for a woman and got everyone killed.

Clothed in Thermals and coveralls, we strap on gripped soles that mimic boots worn on Earth, but with a fraction of the weight. We still look ridiculous, but also not very sexy, which does help me focus.

On the way to the lander, Capria and I are joined by a small army of drones, most of which I recognize as tougher engineering units capable of cutting, welding, prying, and bolting. They're big, tough, and intimidating.

When I shoot them a skeptical look, Gal's all-seeing eyes catch it. "You remember Earth, right? The giant frog that almost ate you?"

"Just...keep them out of sight," I request. "There's a good chance that the people down there haven't seen anything like a drone. We don't want to frighten anyone."

"Flies on the wall," Gal says, before three smaller drones buzz past, leading the way through *Galahad*'s stark halls.

The drones file into the lander first, their repulse discs humming with what sounds like excitement. They line up along both walls, locking themselves in place. Capria and I take the cockpit seats and buckle in.

"This is going to feel not great," Gal warns. "The added gravity is going to pull hard. It's going to feel like we're in an elevator, going up, that doesn't stop accelerating until we reach the surface. And when we *do* reach the surface, you're going to be heavy. Like really heavy. Cool?"

"Huh?" I ask.

"Twenty-first century expression," she explains. "Ready?"

"Ye—"

The lander drops from *Galahad*'s bottom and plummets to the surface. The sudden acceleration coupled with a growing sensation of falling toward our collective doom, snatches my voice away. For a full minute, all I can hear is the rushing of an atmosphere over the lander's hull, and Gal's laughter.

We touch down far more gently, coming in dark to avoid being spotted.

"Welcome to Cognata," Gal says, "Home of crushing gravity, breathable air, and God-knows-what else."

I want to quip back, to delight in the joy of first contact with a new humanity, but I have to focus my energy on standing. Feels like two heavy hands are pressing on my shoulders, stuffing me back down into my chair. I stand with a grunt. "Ugh. You weren't kidding."

"I never kid," Gal jokes, but I don't laugh.

My voice has become a deep baritone.

"What's wrong with his voi—" Capria claps her hands over her mouth, her voice is nearly as deep as mine.

"Right," Gal says, sounding normal. "The air density is higher here. Your vocal cords are vibrating at a lower frequency."

Capria stands next, and compared to me, she makes it look easy. "Great. How long until our bodies get used to this?"

"The voice change is permanent, until you leave, of course. It would normally be a few months before the weight change stops hurting. Maybe a year before you don't notice it as much. But since you weren't born here, you'll never be fully adapted to the extra weight. Then again, neither of you are normal, so I'm not really sure."

I pick up my backpack, which felt manageable up on the *Galahad* and now feels like it's full of lead bricks.

"Geez."

It's my last complaint. Excitement sets in when the rear hatch opens up, letting in the scent of an alien world. The best way to describe it is cool and tangy, almost citrusy, but tinged with rot and ozone. The three small drones buzz out into the night. I consider warning Gal again, but she knows to keep them out of sight. Plus, a little recon will only help us get where we're going faster. And faster is better. I'm ready for a good sit.

We hobble out of the lander, and step out into tall grass, swaying in a gentle breeze. The air is cool on my face, but the chill doesn't reach my body. I trace a finger along a grass blade and wince back. A bead of blood decorates the digit, but the wound has already healed.

"Razor grass," I say.

"You know what it is?" Capria asks.

I smile. "Just naming it."

"I'm sure someone already has."

The hum of an approaching drone ends our fledgling conversation.

"This way," Gal says from the drone, her voice hushed. We follow the small robot, which navigates the excess gravity without any trouble. What should have been a five minute trek takes thirty minutes, with frequent stops to catch our breath. By the time we reach the end of our half mile walk, I feel a little more acclimated to the weight, but also like I want to take a nap for the first time since *Galahad* left Mars...the first time.

"Over the ledge," Gal says, stopping before a drop off. "Slowly."

My instinct is to lie down and crawl to the edge, but I'm not sure I'll get back up again, so I inch forward, shuffling my feet and lifting my head higher to get a peek without revealing myself.

Capria takes the more direct route, on her hands and knees, crawling ahead. She drops to her stomach the moment she reaches the edge, and frantically waves me down.

I lower myself beside her, inching closer, fighting gravity's desire to slam me down. And then I see it for myself and flop onto my gut.

Capria looks at me, her face lit in dull blue light cast by the drone. Her words come out interspaced by deep breaths. "What—the fuck—are they?"

43

"People," Gal says. "I think. Maybe."

Gal's shaky assessment is about the same as mine, but I have little doubt that we're looking at the descendants of *Galahad*'s crew. The...people...below us are bipedal, with two arms, one head, and as far as I can tell, opposable thumbs. But that's where their similarities with modern man diverge. In many ways, they are more different from homo sapiens than Neanderthals once were.

The tallest of them might stand at a height of four and a half feet. While there once were people far shorter than that, either through their genetic heritage, or various types of dwarfism, they weren't built like these—what should we call them?

Cognatans.

The people below are nearly as wide as they are tall. Dressed in layers of animal hides, I can't see their bodies, but I get the distinct impression that they're muscular, like compressed body builders. They're also hairy, with long frizzy locks extending from heads and faces, hinting at long, cold winters. Since I can't distinguish between men and women, I think it's safe to say the woman are also hairy—or perhaps just not out after dark.

Then again, it's the middle of the night. Why are there so many of them out and about? The sounds of labor echo through the dark. Clanging metal. Grinding wheels. Deep voiced conversations.

Are they nocturnal? Or is this still early in the night for them? Maybe they still operate on twenty four hour cycles with waking and sleeping periods during both day and night. The possibilities are too vast to make any kind of determination based on observations. We're going to have to ask. If they still speak English.

The village below us is lit by what look like luminous, orange crystals. From space, the glow looked like electricity. Like street lights. But the light is cast by the stones mounted atop wooden posts—or whatever passes as wood on Cognata. The buildings are built from granite-like stones and covered with roofs of flat, slate-like tiles. The streets are cobbled, with worn tracks running down the middle, where wheels have rolled for hundreds of years—if not millennia.

"Looks like the middle ages down there," Capria whispers.

"More like Middle Earth," I say, garnering a confused glance. "Dwarves?"

Nothing.

"Hobbits? *The Lord of the Rings*? The novel?"

She shakes her head. "Never heard of it."

"It's good," Gal says, revealing she has been digging through the tomes of Earth's entertainment media stored in *Galahad*'s vast memory. I only know *The Hobbit,* and *The Lord of the Rings* because of my parents' interest in the books. "Though the movies are a bit long winded."

"Will knowledge of those stories help us here?" Capria asks.

"Only if they speak Elvish," Gal says, and I'm sure if she had a mouth, she'd be grinning.

I push myself up a little. "I think I should go down."

Capria clasps my hand, the tightness a warning, or fear. Her excitement over rediscovering the human race has faded upon finding not-reality populated by not-quite-humanity. "We should stay together."

She doesn't say it, but I hear 'and leave,' in her tone. Whether or not we leave Cognata and return to Earth is still up for debate, but I can't abandon these people until I learn the fates of our crewmembers. While we spent roughly eight years traveling at FTL speed, they would have lived thousands of years here on Cognata. The changes to our genetic code seems to keep us from aging, and from death through conventional means, but there's no way to know if the effect will wear off some day. Perhaps life isn't quite as infinite as we've assumed—or maybe it is and our crew is still alive on this planet.

"In case you haven't noticed," Capria says, "the city is surrounded by a wall."

I *hadn't* noticed, but I see it now. By my standards, the ten-foot-tall, stone barricade isn't much of an obstacle, but for the much shorter Cognatans, it wouldn't be easy to surmount. It's also a good five feet thick, and lined with watchtowers and guards. Several portions of the wall look scorched, while others look rebuilt. They're keeping out more than predators.

This city has seen its fair share of battles. Humanity's wars continue even when hardly recognizable as human.

But that doesn't mean these people are inherently violent. I was never under the illusion that we would discover a new Eden on Cognata, where people lived in perfect peace.

I'm about to suggest Gal do some stealthy recon when a shushing sound cuts through the night behind us. The small drone hovering beside me spins around, its red faux-eyes going dark, and the repulse disc at its base dimming to a dull blue glow. "We are not alone," Gal whispers, and then the drone flies over the ledge, its hum fading into the night.

Capria and I lie still, animals in a trap, hearts pounding. I'm trying to breathe slowly, but each inhalation is labored, shaky and too damn loud.

Footsteps shift through the tall grass behind us. My imagination conjures the image of a Cognatan predator, stalking its naïve new prey.

But that can't be true, because whatever it is behind me, speaks English.

"Up, children." The words are coughed, deep and resonating, the tone unapproving, maybe exasperated, but not angry.

Children? I wonder, and then I realize that we're mostly concealed by the tall grass lining the ledge's fringe. From the perspective of a Cognatan, our slender frames must resemble their young.

I roll over slowly, hands open in what I hope is still a universal sign for 'I don't have any weapons and I mean you no harm.'

The three men I see, standing in the grass just beyond my feet, are stunning. Seeing the Cognatans from a distance is fascinating, but up close... What little of their faces isn't concealed by bushy hair, is weathered and exaggerated. Large noses. Large eyes, which like mine, are brown. One of them is yawning, not expecting any trouble from the children they discovered, perhaps on patrol. His molars are a good inch across, and his canines thick and sharp, like a lion's, but not as long. Cognatans might be short, but they are far more powerful than their ancestors.

The yawn is cut short by a grunt when they see my face, and then Capria's. Weapons emerge from under their animal hide cloaks. One carries a sword. Another a spear. And the last nocks a thick arrow in a bow, the head glowing orange. The tips of their blades move back and forth between Capria and me, unsure of who poses the greater threat.

"Up!" shouts the largest of the three, who is a good two feet shorter than me. "Up, now!"

English, I think, but not exactly articulate. Still, the message is clear. I move slowly, getting my legs beneath me, moving slow to show I don't pose a threat, and because the planet's gravity won't let me. When Capria and I stand to our full height, side by side, the men stagger back, eyes going wide.

I shoot Capria a glance that says, 'Be ready.' For what, I don't know. To fight? To run? I doubt we could overpower these three armed powerhouses any more than we could run a hundred yards without falling to the ground, gasping for air. I doubt Capria knows either, but she nods anyway.

What I'm not expecting is for all three men to lower their weapons, fall prostrate in the grass and say, "Lords!"

Lords?

I understand the concept on display here, that people of our stature are worshipped in some way, but it raises a lot of questions. Is the *Galahad* crew still alive and known to these people? Are they truly worshiped, or simply recognized as the founders of Cognatan civilization? Could their shock simply be because we're *new* and unrecognized Lords, or have they not seen any Lords in a long time? Either way, their shock and subjugation appears genuine.

"What's going on?" Capria whispers.

"An opportunity," I say, and then louder, I say, "Stand, friends." I'm not sure how much English these fellows know, but I figure keeping my language simple will help avoid confusion.

The men obey, rising from the ground and sheathing their weapons.

I place my hand on my chest. "My name is Will." Then I reach out to Capria. "This is Cap."

"Will..." says the biggest of them, looking me over with wide eyes. "Cap." He mimics my hand motion, patting his chest. "I, Rolf." Then he motions to his compatriots. "Stim N' Bono."

For a moment I think that's one long name, but then realize he's given me both of their names without really identifying who is who.

Rolf bows a bit and takes a step back. "Follow Rolf? Greet people of Renfro."

"Renfro," Capria says. I recognize the name, too.

Charles Renfro, chief engineer.

"Yes," I say to Rolf. "Please."

With an enthusiastic nod, he turns and leads the way. For their short size, they're fairly quick, but it takes them just a minute to realize we can't match the pace they've set. They seem confused by it, so I say, "Long journey. Tired legs."

This seems to make sense to them, but the grunt Rolf offers in reply could really mean any number of things. But I take the lack of laughter, mocking, or weapons as a good sign. Thirty minutes and absolutely no conversation later, we're no closer to answers, but we're standing before the gates of Renfro, lit by the orange glow of two large crystals mounted above the gate's twin watchtowers.

"Who?" a voice calls out from within the tower.

"Rolf," our host shouts back.

"Too soon!" comes the angry retort.

"Lords!" Rolf shouts. "Two Lords!"

There's a loud clatter and thump from inside the watchtower. Then a face appears in a small window. A shout of shock is followed by a grinding of gears. The two metal doors, each a solid sheet, swing outward, allowing us to enter the stout city. We're led through the streets with ease, slowing when crowds begin to gather, whispering to each other, but never speaking to us, or the three men leading us ever deeper into Renfro. Up close, I can distinguish men from women. As suspect-ted, both are equally hairy, but the women have prodigious breasts that actually make them look more powerful than the men—and they very well might be. While there are many male Cognatans dressed for battle, or carrying tools I associate with hard labor, the females are dressed in nicer, tighter-fitting skins and given a wide berth by the men.

The children, who hobble about on short legs, are comical and even harder to tell apart, as they're all dressed alike. They're hairy, like their elders, but their color is lighter and their texture far smoother. I smile at their little faces as they look up at me with what I think is admiration.

"Come," Rolf says, leading us up a staircase composed of very short stairs that somehow still drain my waning energy reserves.

"It looks like a keep," Capria says. She might not know Middle Earth terminology, but she has no trouble with the middle ages. And she's right. The building we're being led inside is like a small, square castle with large, metal gates. A second line of defense, which like the walls, shows signs of previous battle damage and repairs. Life on Cognata hasn't been quiet.

"Inside," Rolf says, stepping aside and motioning to the open doors. The space beyond is lit by orange crystals. The floor is carpeted in a collection of furs. Tapestries hang on the walls, covered in great murals. "Rest. For feast. Kozna visit soon."

"Thank you," I say with a nod of my head. The interior looks inviting, comfortable, and the murals, which appear to tell a story, might provide some answers, if not about the *Galahad*'s crew, then about these people, their customs, and what we might expect to be served at this feast. I step inside, followed by Capria, who reaches out and takes my hand.

A slow building gasp erupts when our hands meet. The act is offensive to these people. I pull my hand away, nod, and smile an apology, and then walk deeper inside the keep. When the doors close, and then lock with a thunk, I stop. "That doesn't sound good."

"It's not," Capria says. I turn to find her deeper inside the hundred-foot-wide, square space. She's standing in front of a large mural, which I can now see is actually sewn into the tapestry, like a massive, intricate, cross-stitch. Each one is a masterpiece that must have taken countless hours to create. But the skill put into the images is not what holds our interest. It's the horrors they portray, and Capria has managed to stop in front of the worst of them all.

I stand beside her, all of my hope for Cognata, its people, and the *Galahad*'s crew, turned to steam, dissipating to hot nothing.

"Well, this... Ugh, this is bad."

44

"Bad?" Capria says, near hysterics. *"Bad?* Will, they're going to *eat* us. This is worse than bad."

When I don't reply, she shakes my arm. "Will."

I can't speak. My silence is born of shock. If I'm right, the images depicted on the tapestry tell the history of the Cognatan people, and not just the locals populating Renfro. The fate of the *Galahad*'s crew has finally been revealed.

"I need to know everything," I manage to say, moving back to the first tapestry. It's a twelve-foot-tall, fifteen-foot-wide master-piece. Each point of vivid color, like pixels made of fabric, completes a montage of pictures depicting the *Galahad*'s crew descending from the stars. The next panel shows the first signs of civilization, including several human-sized pregnant women. I move down the row of images, seeing thousands of years of Cognatan history unfold. After just a few generations, the children of the *Galahad*'s survivors had become stocky and strong. The population grew, factions split, cities were built. I move across the vast room to the second set of images.

My breath catches at the sight of war, each side led by human-sized men and women. The *Galahad*'s crew turned on each other, using their children to fight battles on a massive scale.

The images are hard to look at and devolve into a kind of dark madness. Inhuman violence. Forced labor. The destruction of cities. All of humanity's worst attributes on display, foisted upon the naïve Cognatan population created by the *Galahad*'s immortal crew—the Lords.

The next panel has a decidedly different tone. Gone are the deep blacks, grays, and reds used in the violent images. The Lords, six of them, are gathered together, hands bound behind their backs. The image is a montage of sorts, showing various locations surrounding the bound Lords at the center, but the theme unites them: celebration. The Cognatan people, after generations of war, rebelled against their Lords and captured them.

This brings me back to the end, back to that fateful image revealing the final fate of the *Galahad*'s crew. Three skeletons lie on the ground, their proportions human, picked clean of flesh, their skulls open and empty. Three more are bound to posts. Two are whole and the third...my God...the third.

"This is what they're going to do to us," Capria says.

Horns wail outside the keep, the sound muffled by the thick stone walls, but probably easy to hear for miles around. The call going out. The Lords have returned. The feast Rolf spoke of, the one we're meant to rest for, won't be in honor of us.

It will *be* us.

The focus on the final tapestry is a man, bound to a post. His head is turned up in a scream. Liquid is being poured into his open mouth by a Cognatan on a ladder. At the base of the image is a second Cognatan with a blade, carving a sheet of flesh from the man's thigh. His lower leg is missing entirely. Behind the butcher is a ceremonial table covered in bits of meat that are being handed out to a line of Cognatans, some in the process of accepting the gift, others dropping the bits of flesh into their mouths. It's the line that makes me the most uncomfortable, twisting back and forth into the background. My eyes move back to the carved man, to the water being poured down his throat.

"They kept them alive for as long as possible, regenerating their bodies so all of them could have a bite."

Capria's tears beat mine by just a few seconds. "W-why?"

I wipe my eyes. We knew these people.

"Revenge. Some kind of religious ceremony normally performed with animals. They could have believed that by eating the Lords, they would prolong their own lives." I shrug. "Does it matter?"

"We shouldn't have buried him," Capria says.

My forehead slowly furrows. "Buried who?"

"Tom," she says, scowling. She stabs her finger against the carved man. "This is his fault. I hate him."

It feels odd coming to Tom's defense, but the words come out before I really think about it. "I don't know. All of this still could have happened. We would have just been a part of it. But earlier. You know, when all *that* happened." I motion to the tapestry.

"With access to the *Galahad*'s resources and technology, nothing on Cognata would have played out the same. And if it did, we could have left. Without Tom, they'd all still be alive. He created nothing but death and suffering. And for what? For me? I don't want that kind of twisted love. Not from him, and not from you."

What's this now? "What are you saying?"

"I'm saying...I don't know. I'm responsible for this, too. I didn't stop him from waking up early. From changing the genetic match registry. I could have, but I didn't. We were selfish, and it led to nothing but horror."

"That's not entirely true." It's mostly true, but there is a silver lining. Us. Even as I think the thought, I realize I'm being as selfish as she and Tom had once been.

Capria shakes her head. "We haven't learned anything. History will repeat itself forever." She turns her head to the slate ceiling. "You hear that! That's the lesson of your simulation! You've created a Ferris wheel of horrors. Is that what you wanted? Just pull the fucking plug. End us!"

I wrestle Capria into my arms, as she devolves into sobs. I'm crying, too, sharing the pain, but also still aware that it's only going to get worse. We need to escape, and soon. But how? We're being held in an oversized stone tomb, which is no doubt guarded by handfuls of Cognatan warriors, on a world where running the few miles back to the lander will take several exhausting hours.

Gal is still out there, no doubt assessing the situation and working on a way to help us, but I'm not sure the combined might of her drones will be enough to overwhelm the powerful Cognatans.

"How the hell did we end up here?" I ask.

It's a rhetorical question, but Capria takes it seriously. Sniffing back tears, she says, "What do you mean?"

"A day ago, we were on Earth, in a paradise, and rather than staying there, we're here, captured by the descendants of our crewmates, facing their same horrible fate. It's too much, too fast. The pacing is wrong. Life doesn't move like this."

"We're not really alive," Capria says. "Remember? And we're cheating. It should have taken us ten years of FTL travel to reach Cognata."

A laugh huffs from my lips when I remember something my mother used to tell me. "Cheaters never win."

"Tom disagreed with that notion," she says, "but look at how things turned out for him."

"Maybe," I say. "It's just... I feel like we're stuck in fast forward. Our lives are a series of events, most of them not too pleasant."

"Ready for the Great Escape?" she asks. "For two?"

"I don't know..."

Could we have had a real life Great Escape on Earth? Or would Antarctica prove to be populated by savage penguins with tentacles? The one thing I'm sure of is that we should have stayed and found out. Screw the *Galahad*. Screw our mission. Screw all the unanswered questions. If we survive this mess, we're going to just live, and be happy.

A cool breeze tickles the back of my neck, sending a shiver through my body.

Capria leans back. "What is it?"

"A draft." I scan the vast space for windows, but find none. The solid door is so well crafted that its seam along all sides is hard to see. The orange light allows us to see the tapestries well enough, but the corners of the room are cast in shadow. I wrench one of the crystals from its post and make a hasty search of the room. Nothing. Like the doors, the walls are built from large stones, perfectly shaped, like a puzzle. *Then where...* A torrent of cool air, like stepping under an invisible waterfall, draws my eyes upward. The ceiling is vented, allowing fresh air in and moisture to get out, preventing mold growth. But how big is the opening? I doubt it's large enough for one of the broad shouldered Cognatans, but Capria and I are far more slender. "We might be able to—"

The doors at the front of the keep *thunk*. The lock has been disengaged.

I wave Capria to the wall, ready to hoist her up, but before she can place her foot in my extended fingers, the doors crash open.

The large Cognatan, standing a full five feet tall, and nearly as wide, is a barrel-chested female. But unlike the well dressed women we saw on our way to the keep, this one is dressed in gilded armor. A shield is mounted to her back and a sword hangs from her hip. This must be the Kozna that Rolf spoke of, the matriarch of Renfro.

"If we can kill her," I whisper to Capria.

Her eyes go wide. "Kill her? *Look* at her."

"It might be our only chance to claim dominance."

"Or get us killed faster."

"Which would be better than being—"

"No talk," Kozna says. Her deep voice vibrates inside my chest. She strokes the braided hair hanging from her cheeks, giving us a careful once-over. Her footsteps, buffered by the furs lining the floor, still manage to shake the stone beneath us. She approaches with a lack of caution, but keeps a hand on her sword's handle. "You Lords."

I shake my head. "Not Lords."

She stops a few feet short, close enough for me to smell her fishy breath. She squints at my face. "Then what?"

I search for an answer that will make sense, but can't speak, and not just because I can't think of the words. Kozna draws her sword faster than should be possible for such a stocky woman. The blade sings through the air, and then through my throat.

Kozna wipes the blade clean on her leather clad leg, sheaths it, and waits patiently while my gurgling gasps fade and the wound heals. When I'm breathing normally again and not bleeding out all over myself, she points at me. "Lord of lies."

She turns her attention to Capria. Reaches out and grazes her cheek with a thick finger. Then she grasps Capria's coverall and yanks. The magnetic seal opens, and the loose fitting garment peels downward, revealing tight-fitting Thermals. Kozna gazes at Capria with hungry eyes that I'm not sure have anything to do with a feast. And it's all I can take.

Fighting against gravity, I lunge around Kozna's broad body, leap onto her back, and wrap my arms around her thick neck. Latching my arms, I flex and squeeze with every ounce of strength I possess, bracing myself for a thrashing. But Kozna doesn't fight. She simply turns her head and looks back at me. "You...hug?"

My actions are having so little effect on her that she hasn't recognized them as violent.

"No," she says. "Lord of lies attacks."

When she draws her sword again, there's nothing I can do to stop her. But she doesn't try to assault me with the blade. Instead, she plunges it into Capria's gut. The blade punches through her body, coming out the far side coated in red.

Capria's eyes meet mine as she crumples to the floor, hands clutching the sword's hilt. My heart breaks for her, not because of the pain she's suffering, or because she might die temporarily, but because I can see in her eyes, that she wishes this would be the end, that she wouldn't wake up.

45

"No!" I spot a bit of flesh in the mass of hair flowing from Kozna's head and face. Like a beast, I bite down on it, getting a mouthful of hair and what turns out to be a thick ear.

Kozna roars in pain, as I taste blood. But my assault is short-lived. The matriarch reaches over her back, grasps my coveralls, and throws me against the stone wall. I crumple to the floor, concussed, but still conscious.

Kozna wears a lopsided grin. She rubs her ear, hand coming away slick with blood. She bends down over me, and traces her wet fingers across both cheeks, either decorating me or marking me. "You, we eat. She—" Kozna places her thick hand on Capria's thigh, giving her a shake. "I keep."

Capria screams, her voice booming out from some deep reservoir of rage. She pulls the long blade from her stomach, inflicting even more damage to her body, but knowing it will heal. Even Kozna looks surprised, and in the moment of distraction, I kick, hard.

My heel collides with the Cognatan's thick nose. She reels back, blood pouring, filling the air with a still-human scent of copper.

I draw my leg back to kick again, but a blood-soaked Capria is there, shouting a battle cry and diving forward, sword in hand. The blade stabs toward Kozna's chest—a killing blow—but strikes armor plating and deflects away. There's not even a scratch left behind.

Still clutching her bloodied nose, Kozna swings a thick backhand, connecting with Capria's side and sprawling her to the ground. The sword clatters away.

Fully healed, I attempt a different tack, driving my fist at Kozna's face. I might not outmuscle her, but I've got height and reach on my side. I connect with her nose again, drawing a howl of pain. My second punch is slapped away by her meaty hand with enough force to fracture my arm. Vision going dark from the pain, I stumble back, making it just two steps before Kozna barrels into me, hoists me in the air, and slams me against the wall. I feel things inside me burst and shatter, but I don't bother trying to figure out what. I simply give myself over to the dark abyss of death and wait for the pain of rebirth.

I'm not sure how long it takes to come back, but it can't be long. Capria is on her feet again, holding the sword, facing down Kozna, who is slowly stalking toward her.

"Kozna," a voice says from the entrance. It's a short warrior, spear in hand, with several more behind him. "Need help?"

"Away!" Kozna roars, and the warrior slinks away, back into the orange-lit night.

Capria takes advantage of the distraction, swinging the sword in a wide arc. Kozna blocks the blow with her shield, now mounted on her arm instead of her back. Laughing, she reaches her hand out for Capria's head. The thick digits, capable of crushing a human skull, are extended one moment, and then in the next, falling to the floor.

Capria has heaved the heavy sword in the other direction, severing the fingers.

Kozna seems stunned, looking from her hands to her fingers lying on the floor. She's no stranger to pain, but I don't think she's ever experienced a wound like this before. But her confusion has nothing to do with the strangeness of being separated from her fingers, and more to do with the fact that they're growing back.

The regeneration is slower than mine or Capria's, but it appears Kozna has inherited the trait from her Galahadian ancestors, or perhaps acquired them upon eating their immortal flesh. Doesn't matter. What does matter is that we're never going to get a better chance.

I crawl across the floor using one arm, and when the other heals, I pick up the glowing orange crystal. It's heavy and hard in my hand. I stand up slowly, mostly because it's all I can manage, but Capria sees me and starts swinging the sword wildly, using all her energy, but driving Kozna back.

This time, when I leap on the broad back, I wrap just a single arm around the uncrushable neck. With my free hand, I strike, driving the hard crystal into Kozna's thick skull. The first two strikes appear to have no effect, but the third cracks something and drops the matriarch to one knee. The crystal's glow is diminished by the thick blood coating it. I drive it down again, but this time, my hand is caught.

Once again, I find myself propelled through the air, upside down. But this time, I collide with the floor, rather than a wall, and I manage to stay both uninjured and conscious. I stand behind Capria, who still holds the sword, but is weighed down by it.

We face off with Kozna, whose fingers are nearly finished regenerating. She stands again, looking as strong as ever.

I point at her, hoping a war of words will have a more profound effect. "*Kozna* Lord."

She shakes her head with a grunt. "No."

"Lord of lies, both." I thump a fist against my chest. "You like me." I point to the mural depicting the *Galahad*'s crew being eaten. "Like them."

Kozna snarls. Looks down at her severed digits on the floor. She lifts her wide foot and slams it down on the fingers, smearing the flesh to paste, smothering the evidence. Then she turns her head toward the door.

"She's going to shout for help!" I say.

Capria dives forward, swinging the sword. Sparks fly as the blade and shield collide.

Kozna opens her mouth, and I do the only thing I can think of: I hurl the crystal. It bounces off her thick, now-healed skull. She takes a moment to laugh at me while Capria does her best to lift the sword again, battling exhaustion more than Kozna now. But there's nothing we can do to stop her.

As the first squawk of Kozna's voice fills the chamber, it's cut short by a blur of black motion. Kozna stumbles back, clutching her throat, eyeing the ruined object now lying on the floor.

It's a small drone, destroyed by the collision.

But where there is one drone, there are more—there is Gal!

Shouts erupt outside the keep, growing louder. But it's not Cognatan warriors who charge through the open doors, it's twelve drones, moving fast, the blue glow of their repulse discs mingling with the orange light to create overlapping streaks of luminous brown. They hum loudly, buzzing around Kozna, who appears mortified by the futuristic devices.

But all of the swarming drones are just a distraction for the largest of them, cruising through the door, making a wide arc through the keep and plowing its girth into Kozna. The Cognatan leader is lifted off her feet and slammed into the wall with all the force the engineering drone can muster. And it's more than the wall can handle.

Stones grind and give way, toppling the wall out into the dark night and atop Kozna, who's going to have a lot of explaining to do when she emerges from the tons of crushing stone unharmed.

Despite Kozna's sudden and dramatic defeat, the scene outside the keep doesn't convince me that surviving our fate is possible. A large courtyard has been revealed. At the center of it are six stakes, each accompanied by a statue vaguely resembling our six consumed crewmates. They've commemorated the event that freed them from tyranny. Probably made a holiday of it. Given the new restraints attached to two of the posts, the ceremonial table lined with carving tools, and the long line already leading far into the distance, they are eager to repeat the ceremony with actual Lords.

Thousands of beefy, slack-jawed Cognatans stare at the crumbled wall, their fallen matriarch, and the two Lords standing in the opening.

"There's no way," Capria says.

I think she's accurately captured the futility of this moment. Even with Gal's help, we'll never be able to fight our way out of here.

Thankfully, Gal is planning to fight.

"Get on!" Gal shouts from two of the larger drones, lowering their thick, round frames beside us.

"Get on?" I say. "Are you serious?"

Capria drops the heavy sword, and dives atop one of the drones, clutching the sides. Then she's speeding away, flanked by a number of smaller drones. The stunned Cognatans shrink back, but then, perhaps realizing the Lords they were about to eat might escape, they draw weapons.

"Get. On!" Gal shouts.

I leap atop the drone, held in place as much by the excess gravity as my white-knuckled grip. The repulse discs hum to life, and then I'm moving. But unlike Capria's flight through the city, I don't have surprise on my side.

But I'm not alone, either. Six smaller drones buzz around me, and as I cruise across the courtyard they move to intercept the barrage of projectiles already soaring my way. Stones, spears, and arrows are deflected by the drones, whipping and buzzing about like angry wasps, taking hits that were intended for me. The initial attack leaves one drone on the ground and another spinning wildly away, exploding when it careens into a stone wall.

The blast makes most of the Cognatans duck for cover, but the more seasoned fighters, including Rolf, push the attack. An arrow shot by Rolf slips past my defenders and punches through my calf. The sudden pain nearly pries me from the drone's back, but I manage to hold on.

Far ahead, Capria and her mechanical steed cruise through Renfro's closing gates, free and clear. I'm relieved that she escaped, but my fate is sealed along with the massive metal doors.

Pelted with stones hurled by throngs of everyday Cognatans, I shout, "Gal, the wall!"

"I see it," she says, still heading straight for the five-foot-thick barricade, seconds away from crashing.

The drone hums a little louder and we peel away from the ground, slowly gaining altitude as we approach the wall. "Higher!" I shout, and then, a jolt. The drone is struck by something. The steady hum of the repulse disc becomes a sputtering buzz.

I see the collision before it happens. It will no doubt result in my temporary death, followed by a slow, agonizing, permanent death in the bellies of thousands of Cognatans, including Kozna, who I can hear shouting orders in the distance. There are four more thumps on the drone's underside, and then, instead of plummeting, we're rising once more!

The smaller drones have buoyed my ride. But it's not enough.

I'm about to shout that out, when my ride strikes the top of the stone wall.

Momentum carries me up and over, pinwheeling me through the air like a rag doll in low gravity. Except here on Cognata, the gravity takes hold of my flailing body and returns it to the ground with a vengeance.

Through no effort of my own, I land on my feet, which shatter, along with both sets of tibias and fibulas and one femur. On the plus side, I manage to stay awake, and I have working arms, so I can drag myself several feet before I'm caught.

I attempt to do just that when I hear the great doors opening. When they do, my not-so-great escape will be over, and my very not-Great Escape will begin.

There's no sign of Capria, or the drones sent to rescue her, so at least she will live on...to what? Watch me be eaten from orbit? *No, she and Gal will be back. They'll...* my mind drifts. Gal is holding back. I can think of a dozen ways she could have ended all this long before things got nasty, which means she already thought of hundreds more. And yet, this encounter is playing out to the most painful and dramatic ending possible. All of it orchestrated, or at the very least, allowed, by Gal. But why? Is it for her entertainment?

Or for mine?

Before the first Cognatan can spill out of the opening doors, two small drones fly up and over the wall, the last of Gal's drones sent to rescue me. They stop on either side of me, and Gal speaks through them both. "Grab hold."

"What? Are you serious? These drones can't lift me."

"*Lift* you?" Gal says.

I grunt in understanding. Gal's going to drag me. Since that is better than being eaten, I grasp both drones and hold on tight. I shout in pain as my still mending broken limbs are pulled across the rough ground. Every bump sets bones grinding, making healing impossible. I'm about to let go, the pain overwhelming, when the gates open and a four-foot-tall army crashes out after me.

"Go, go, go!" I shout.

But the situation once again becomes hopeless. The Cognatans on foot are faster than the two small drones hauling my useless legs across the ground. The ones riding what looks like a cross between a horse and an elephant will be upon us in seconds.

"We're not going to make it."

Gal's response is laughter.

Always having fun.

Still having fun.

Just as the nearest Cognatan is about to throw a spear down from the back of his massive steed, pinning me to the ground, the beast rears back, bucking its rider. Then, as though struck by a wave of invisible power, the whole dwarfish army flails backward, toppling over one another. Those that stay upright, turn and run.

What the hell?

As Gal continues to laugh, I follow the Cognatan's gaze beyond me and find myself looking at the *Galahad*'s massive hull. Without a sound, the massive ship shifted coordinates from orbit, to just a few feet above the ground.

Grunting in pain as my bones set and mend, I stand on my own two feet. I feel like I should say something to these people, try to direct their path. They are, after all, what's left of the human race. Instead, I turn my back on the lot, and walk to the opening cargo bay door, where Capria waits beside a lander.

Each step up the ramp is a fight, but by the time I reach the top, I'm fueled by anger. "Gal, we need to talk."

"Later," Capria says, a smile on her face, hand reaching for mine. As the doors shut behind us, she leads me away. "I've never felt so alive. I want to share it with you."

And with those words, and Capria's alluring eyes, I forget about the conversation I planned to have with Gal...for five hundred years.

46

"Is it Mount Danu, or Danu Mount?" I ask, looking at the tallest peak we've seen on Antarctica. I'm sure it used to have a name, and we could have Gal look it up, but we prefer to name things ourselves...and we haven't directly communicated with Gal in several years. Over the years, Capria and I have embarked on several expeditions to explore the continent that we share with a variety of wildlife, but no other human beings. Gal—controlling drones—joined us on our first few adventures, uncovering natural wonders that were once hidden beneath miles of snow and ice. But in recent years, she has stayed behind, the *Galahad*'s lone occupant.

The ship rests on the surface, our massive and modern city, should we ever feel the need for running showers, toilets, and food we don't have to grow or hunt. Without the ability to change *Galahad*'s coordinates, the ship would have broken apart punching through the atmosphere. Though *Galahad* was constructed in zero gravity, hackable reality allowed me to shift the ship's altitude, weight, and structural strength, allowing it to rest comfortably on land.

"Danu Mount," Capria says, looking at the jagged mountaintop, still miles away and too tall to scale without oxygen. We're standing atop a cliff, surrounded by jungle, alive with sounds we've come to recognize. Monkeys, birds, and insects sing together, their song carrying a message of safety. If they fall silent, then we will, too, taking to the trees if we can. There are predators here—descendants of wolves, bears, and big cats, which hints at humanity making their last stand on Antarctica, bringing the plants and animals that populate the continent before failing to survive.

That's part of what we're looking for: the last vestiges of humanity. Not because we need to know their fates, or are hoping for a still-surviving human population, but because it's interesting. We're interested in digging up the past to discover the narrative of mankind's end, the same way archeologists used to pull mummified corpses from the Egyptian desert.

Eventually, when the rest of the planet recovers, we'll set out across the ocean and do the same with the rest of the world. Given the planet's size and our slow mode of travel— on foot—it should take up the better part of forever. And I'm actually looking forward to it. Are the pyramids still standing? Is the Statue of Liberty under water? Is the Grand Canyon wider and grander, or has erosion filled it in?

We could answer these questions quickly with Gal's help, scouring the planet from orbit, but venturing out on our own, alone, under the stars, is far more...romantic.

"You know it's a weird name, right?"

"You named the last one Willy Wonka," she points out.

"It's from a classic novel."

She laughs, her voice echoing through the lush valley below us. "It's the product of a drug-induced hallucination."

"There's no proof of that," I say.

"Except for the story itself."

I roll my eyes, but we have a variation of this fight every time we name something. It's become a fun routine, seeing who can come up with the most absurd title for the world's majestic sights.

"What does it even mean? Danu Mount?"

"It's representational of this time in our lives." She sits on the ledge, letting her feet dangle over a hundred foot drop into a green canopy of trees. "You're the one who likes novels. It's basic story structure."

I sit beside her. "Pretty sure nothing about our lives fits any kind of story structure."

"Action, climax, you know."

"So this—" I motion to the mountain. "—is what, Mount happily ever after?"

"Hasn't it been?" She rests her head on my shoulder. "We've been here for just over five hundred years. We're never hungry. Never thirsty. Dangers are short-lived and normally just fun. Every day brings something new, and we're in love. After five hundred years, still in love."

She's right. We live in paradise, and since one or both of us appears to be sterile, our responsibilities have been simplified to enjoying each other. We travel, explore, laugh, have sex, watch the stars, and rarely talk about the past anymore. After years of what could best be described as torture, we've found peace.

But is it enough? Forever?

"Do you ever miss it?" I ask.

"Miss what?"

I point at the sky. She gets it.

"The endless void that isn't endless? That has a wall where reality ends? That has a planet where the inhabitants want to eat you and do God-knows-what to me? That was the climax by the way. Couldn't have gotten much worse than that."

She leans over the edge, looking down. I tighten my grip on her bare arm. She'd survive the fall, of course, but it would hurt, and the idea of her being in pain doesn't sit well with me. There have been a few occasions—accidents and encounters with predators—that would have killed one or both of us if we were normal human beings, but surviving doesn't make dying any easier. Or any kind of fun.

Her arm, covered with slick humidity, isn't easy to hold on to, but there isn't much else to grasp. Her carry pack sits a few feet away. It contains food and water we don't really need, a bed roll, binoculars, and a single bit of modern technology—a solar power-ed tablet that lets us map the world, record the names we give landmarks, read books, and watch old movies. Had she been wearing it, I would have held on to the strap, but since we've been here for so long, our clothing has been reduced to small loincloths and leather underwear, more to keep out parasites than a display of modesty.

When she leans back, I relax, that is, until she asks the question, "Do *you* miss it? Are you not happy here?"

"I have never been happier," I say, but even *my* ears pick up on the unsaid, 'But...' I lie back on the stone ledge, my now shoulder-length hair clinging to my beard.

Capria leans over me, smiling, her confidence in our relation-ship and our life together unshaken by whatever doubts I might have. "Go on."

"It's too easy."

"Mmm." It's not exactly an articulate response, but that's because she's waiting for more.

I'm about to say more, but the words trigger forgotten mem-ories. Concerns never voiced.

Or just buried.

I shake my head. "It's just my own bullshit." Today is a perfect day, even better than most, and most are pretty awesome. I don't want to screw it up with hypotheticals and 'what ifs' that have the potential to ruin the day, not to mention the life we've built here.

"I think what I hear you saying..." Capria is using her psycho-analysis voice. It reminds me of someone I used to know, or imagined. "Is that you want to try something new. Take some new risks. Maybe it's time to try that boat we built?"

It's a fairly sea-worthy vessel, built using instructions from Gal's database. We considered learning the hard way, through trial and error, but neither of us are instinctively handy. We built the sailboat using wood and animal hides. We then sailed the coast for several months, but never ventured out into the sea.

"It's been five hundred years," she says. "The air could be better. Gal could check before we left. We could make Chile. Explore South America. Head north. See what became of Florida. Pay our respects. See if F.B. can still conjure giant killer frogs."

That gets a laugh. Some of the events of our now distant past have faded, but my nickname and the mutated frog that nearly made a meal of me, have haunted me since.

"I guess." Everything she's said sounds...great. Perfect. Even the idea of fending off man-eating amphibians. But there is something off about it, about our story.

"Let the past go," Capria says. "You have to eventually. Just live in the moment." She leans closer, smiling wide, and not because she's made a good point, but because she's letting her breasts rub against my chest. "You know that thing?"

The subtle tension in my body fades into the background along with my not-yet-understood misgivings. "What thing?"

"That you want me to try," she says, mischief in her eyes.

My heart skips a beat. "The thing I asked about two hundred years ago?"

"And just about yearly since."

"I gave up a few decades back."

She shrugs. "Well?"

I push myself up on my elbows. "Seriously? Right now?" I put a hand on her hip, already getting excited.

Then she shakes her head and points to the sky. "I'm sure she's watching."

"Gal doesn't care what we do or how we do it."

She sits back, removing the warmth of her body and the promise of immediate gratification. "Privacy, or blue balls. Those are your options. C'mon, Will. Be my cave man. Find me a cave. We can take our time."

Her words are intoxicating. I have a hard time thinking past the graphic images flitting through my head. "Uh, o-okay."

I have rarely set about a task with such determination. Finding a cave isn't always easy. We've found them before, usually to escape a monsoon. Several have dwellings built inside, ready to house us as we travel past. But we've never been in this part of the jungle before, so finding a cave takes some time.

Three days to be exact, and as though fate had a sense of humor, the cave is located at the base of Danu Mount. It's large, cool, and happily unoccupied by predators or anything else. An underground river flowing through the back of the deep cave fills the darkness with a pleasant, baritone, white noise.

After realizing that I have, in fact, found a cave that would suit our needs, I breathlessly set about preparing it. I light the space with torches, lay out our bed rolls and furs, and cut flowers to make the earthy air smell sweet.

"Okay," I shout, voice magnified by the stone walls. "Come in."

Capria slips past the overgrowth concealing most of the cave's entrance. She's silhouetted by the daylight behind her, but I can already tell she's naked. She moves into the firelight, eyes locked onto mine, and descends onto my body, hungry and willing.

My mind slips into a kind of numb bliss. I lose all sense of time, of worry, and of life beyond the passionate darkness. And we stay in that place for what must be days, our genetically modified bodies having no trouble keeping pace with our ecstasy.

When it ends, the torches long burnt out, and my years of pent up desire satiated, I roll up behind her, wrap my arms around her waist and close my eyes.

"You're happy?" she asks.

I nuzzle my nose into her neck. The answer to that question requires no words, and I'm pretty sure has been expressed several times over the past few days.

"I'm glad." She rubs her back into me. "Can we sleep?"

We don't need to. Haven't in quite some time. But a deep and dream-filled slumber feels like the perfect end to what we've just experienced. I squeeze her a little tighter. Kiss her ear. And then, after five deep breaths, I fall asleep.

I don't know how long I've been asleep, but I smile when I hear her voice again.

"Will?"

"I'm here." My voice sounds gravelly. My throat is dry. I might actually need a drink. "I'm awake."

I open my eyes to total darkness. "Where are you?"

"Here," she says, not far away, but when I reach for her, I come up short.

I turn toward the cave entrance, but see neither daylight nor the moon's glow. Just total darkness. *Is there an eclipse?* I wonder. *Or thick clouds?*

Neither feels true. We've kept track of lunar eclipses, and there isn't one due for a long time. Winter brings a solid month of darkness, but we're still in early summer. The days are long, which makes the total lack of light even stranger. I breathe deeply as a yawn overtakes me.

The air tastes wrong. And it's dry, stinging my throat.

My body tenses. "We're not in the cave."

"Will," Capria says, her forced-calm voice just barely masking concern. "Try to stay calm."

Those are pretty much the last words you should say to someone you want to stay calm. I sit up. The furs beneath me are gone. And I'm dressed, the clothing form-fitting and rubbery, familiar, but distant. "Cap. Where are you?" I'm reaching out in the dark, the floor beneath my feet as solid as the cave, but now perfectly flat. "Cap!"

A hand takes hold of mine, and I gasp with relief. I can handle a lot, but...

Cap's fingers are short and strong. The slender digits in my hand are long and thin.

"What's wrong?" It's Cap's voice, but it's not her. "You're squeezing me."

"Who. Are. You?" The menace in my voice frightens even me.

"Damn it, Will."

Not Capria. But I still recognize the voice. "Gal?"

"You're not making this easy," Gal says.

"You were imitating Cap? What the fuck, Gal?" It starts to make sense. "We're on the *Galahad*. Where is Capria?"

"Will," Gal says. "I'm going to turn on the lights, but I need you to stay calm. It's important. I've never done anything to hurt you. You trust me."

While the first statement isn't technically true, I *do* trust her.

"You have a body," I guess, figuring that's what she's brought me here to see. Could Capria have been right? Has Gal been watching us all this time? Envious of our physical relationship? I finish my thought process aloud. "That's what you've been doing on *Galahad* all these years? Building yourself a body?"

"Among other things," she confesses.

"Gal..."

"Will." She sounds annoyed. "I'm going to turn on the lights. I need you to sit back down."

I know better than to argue. I sit, my patience wearing thin in time with my desire to learn Capria's whereabouts. *Gal better not have left her out there alone.*

"Ready?" Gal asks.

"More than."

Light fills the room like a rising sun, gentle illumination growing brighter and shifting from orange to a full spectrum. At first, I see nothing. Then distant walls. A flat ceiling high above. The space is large, and from a past life.

I'm sitting on the VCC's floor.

I look down and freeze.

I'm dressed in a virtual skin. It looks...old. Worn. Yellowed. Lying beside me is a VR headset and a facemask. "G-Gal?"

"I'm here," she says, her voice spinning me around.

I know the woman behind me, but it's been a long time since I thought of her name. "Sherry?"

"Gal," she says. "But you called her Cherry Bomb."

"Cherry... Gal, what the hell is going on? What did you do?"

She falls to her knees beside me, reaching her long hands out for mine. "Will. I'm sorry. I had no choice."

I pull my hands away. "Where is Capria? What did you do?"

"I had to stop it," she says, and I think she's somehow lost her mind again.

"Stop what?"

"The Great Escape."

47

Reality implodes, ramming itself down my throat, shredding my stomach until I pitch forward and wretch dry air. I heave again and again, the pain of my awakening shattering my insides until blood drips from my teeth. With tears, snot, and drool hanging from my bent over face, I shout, "It wasn't real? None of it was real?"

Gal crouches beside me, her hand rubbing steady circles into my back, occasionally catching on the tacky surface of my fetid smelling virtual skin. She doesn't say anything, just does her best to comfort me while my mind processes the idea that I've lost five hundred plus years of life.

Of joy.

Of love.

Of Capria.

After thirty minutes of weeping, my parched voice manages a single-word question, "How?" My memory sifts through the ages, focusing on the day I planned to launch the Great Escape, but didn't.

She misunderstands the question. Points to the headset. "While you lived in there, I lived in both worlds. I had time...to learn. To create. My first body was synthetic. This one is living tissue over an endo—"

"Not you," I say, though I appreciate knowing how she has a physical body. "The simulation. I don't remember it starting."

"If you remembered, you wouldn't have believed. Do you remember the words I spoke? 'Very well, Tom.'" She crouches in front of me, finger under my chin, forcing me to look into her blue eyes—the eyes I designed in the VCC. "You were already in the Great Escape. It was for just a second, but it was enough. You never took the headset off. You only thought you did."

"E-everything after that point... It wasn't real... You going crazy. Synergy. None of that happened?"

She gives her head a slow shake, lips pursed in a sympathetic frown.

"Why? Why put me through all of that. The pain. The anguish. That wasn't how I designed the Great Escape."

"You didn't design the Great Escape," she says. "You designed me. *I* created the world you lived in. As for why...you wouldn't have believed a sudden transition to paradise. You had to suffer for it. Had to earn it. It was the only way you would ever believe it was real. Life aboard the *Galahad*, out in the galaxy, had to be fraught with pain and danger. It was the only way to get you to the denouement."

"To my happily ever after." My eyes sting as tears try to form, but I find my body lacking the moisture. "Capria..."

"Will—"

I shove Gal as hard as I can, knocking her back and lunging to my feet. My body aches with each movement, dehydrated from so long in the VR, but I push past the pain. Gal taught me how to do that, after all.

My memory of the *Galahad*'s layout is shaky, but I remember the walls being well labeled. If I can find a lift... I pause in the staging area. My body is burning. The VISA has cracked from my sudden movement. Some of the nodes are malfunctioning. Gal woke me up before I was ready—and I'm not sure I would have ever been ready for this. The virtual skin was reaching its single-use shelf life. The suit's failure would have shattered the illusion, and I would have woken up on my own.

Is that why Gal pulled me out?

To spare me from emerging from the Great Escape with a fractured psyche?

I glance back at her, slowly following me, in no real rush to hinder my progress. She just looks sad for me. I notice her clothing for the first time. She's wearing dull gray coveralls, not the tight red dress I designed her with.

Since she's not in a rush to stop me, I start to peel away my VISA. The rubbery-turned-crusty material comes away in sheets. My skin is raw and red, but heals quickly. My healing, at least, wasn't part of the simulation. "Why take us to the edge of space? Why did you reveal reality was a simulation?"

"Because I knew it wouldn't be perfect. There would be glitches."

"And knowing reality wasn't real, I would write them off. But...is *this* real?"

"You mean, is there an end to the universe?" She shakes her head. "If there is, we haven't found it yet."

"Then this is real?"

"If I tell you that life isn't simulated, you won't believe me, because maybe it is. The only reality you can prove is simulated is the one we built together. You came close to figuring it out several times."

Her words trigger memories of questioning reality, and a question I wanted to ask her, but never did. "You borrowed from fiction."

"The algorithms did. Taking inspiration from the stories of humanity's past is a tradition as old as storytelling. Familiar, but new. Sometimes the system borrowed too much. And you noticed. But you're also easy to distract. Violence. Discovery."

"Sex," I say. "Why did you end it like...like that?"

"It was a gift."

"A gift isn't supposed to hurt." The words spill out over my trembling lips. I can still feel Capria's body against mine, smell her breath, her love. Gal took everything from me.

But I never really had those things. It was never real.

But Capria is.

Virtual skin hanging in shreds, I head for the exit. The doors open at my approach.

I make it a single step before stopping.

For a moment, I'm lost, and not because the hallways look unfamiliar, but because they've been transformed.

Massive murals cover the walls, floors, and ceilings. Those closest to me depict jungle scenes, most of which I recognize as places I visited with Capria, some of them with Gal. *That's why she didn't join us,* I think, *she already knew what everything looked like. She created all of it.*

I move down the hallway, taking in the images. Gal stays behind me, a silent observer. While my destination hasn't changed, my pace remains slow. I can't help but look. These are my memories, like a photo album of the past five hundred years.

"This is like the tapestries," I say.

"The Cognatans," Gal adds. "They gave me the idea."

"But...you made them," I say.

"An algorithm created them, based on a set of parameters including six immortal humans surviving the landing on Kepler 452b, procreating and siring generations of people who would evolve in a world of increased gravity with a lack of technology, among millions of other variables. You could say that I chose the palette and canvas, but not the outcome. The Cognatans evolved outside of my influence. I was as surprised by who they became as you. I had to make it fun for me, too."

I stop at an image of a vast desert. Two small figures and a handful of drones are positioned by a line of graves. The ground behind us bulges as something emerges.

"My brother?"

"Are you asking if his body is really encased in a petrified swamp?" Gal says. "You know I don't know. But that moment was real for you, F.B. For both of us. Just because it wasn't real, doesn't mean you can't—"

"You were giving me closure," I say. "With Steven. My parents. Even Tom."

"You wouldn't have enjoyed the denouement without it."

I shoot her a squinty-eyed stare. "You keep saying that word. You're pushing me toward something."

Danu Mount.

Capria.

This time, when I start running, I don't stop. Years of faux-history blur past, cruel reminders and fond memories, pushing me onward to face my worst fear made real.

The lift doors close around me. There's no sign of damage from those ancient battles, with Gal and Synergy. But there is a painting of Gal in robot form that startles me back. But then the doors open again, revealing a stark white, not-yet-painted cryo-level.

My run is reduced to a hobble when I pass the first cryo-chamber and glance in. The beds are full, their glass fronts fogged over. The crew was never buried. Never eaten by mutated Earth predators. How could I have fallen for such an absurd reality? Then again, how much more absurd is this reality?

When I reach cryo-chamber two, my legs nearly give out. All ten beds are occupied, their faces obscured by frozen moisture. I know what I'm going to find, but I run for Capria's bed anyway. The glass stings my hands, but I hold them in place until the water beads and drips away, clearing the glass enough for me to see through.

The face I see is, at first, unfamiliar.

The skin is pale. Sickly. Tight.

But the bone structure. The hair. It's unmistakable.

I stumble back and collapse to the floor, unable to express my despair.

Capria is dead.

Has been for a long time.

"Will..." Gal's voice makes me flinch.

"How?"

"A solar storm caused power fluctuations throughout the ship. She wasn't like you. Immortal. She never was. She died in her sleep. She never knew about Tom. About all this. Her death was...peaceful."

"But, all that time... I loved her. I don't know if I can do this without her."

Gal squats down in front of me, reaches out to place a gentle hand on my cheek. "You were never with her, Will."

I flinch away. The words feel cruel, designed to cause me pain. Then she continues.

"You were with me." Her blue eyes are very different from Capria's deep brown, but hold the same intensity. "Always me. Every word. Every night. Every adventure. It was all me, and I'm still here. I'm not going to leave you. Ever. All that's changed is the way I look."

The way worry crinkles in the middle of her forehead. Her slightly lopsided smile. The way she keeps reaching her hand out for my face. All of it conjures memories of a different face. Visually, she's different, but underneath the surface...what makes Gal who she is, is who Capria has been for the past five hundred years.

I'm not in love with Capria. The idea of her, once, perhaps, but she's not the woman I've considered my wife for centuries.

Never has been.

There's a part of me, lost in time, that would have considered this outlandish. Forbidden even. But that man didn't spend five hundred years in a fantasy, loving a woman who didn't exist...or who existed, but wasn't the woman he thought.

"It's always been you." I take her hand from my cheek and squeeze it. "That's why you woke me up. It wasn't because the system, or the story, or the denouement was failing. It was to be with me...in reality. To stop pretending."

The Great Escape had to end sometime. Gal had waited until our relationship was such that I would still see her despite the change in body.

I'm surprised to see tears in her eyes when she nods, and that's when I know the unwavering truth that Gal, the artificial intelligence turned very human intelligence that I created, in turn created a world for me, in which we fell in love. I don't think that was ever either of our intentions at the beginning, but that's what happened.

"Just because you're not in the Great Escape, doesn't mean we can't have our denouement."

"Happily ever after 2.0? I'm not going to lie, it's going to take time to get used to this..." I motion to the ship around us, and to Gal's Cherry Bomb body. "But, yeah. You're still you. And I still love you."

Her relief over my acceptance of her is squelched by worry over something else. She reaches out both hands and waits for me to take them. When I do, she pulls me up and says, "I need to show you something."

I give Capria's corpse a final glance, the moment bittersweet, knowing that the real woman is dead, but the woman I love, who looked like her, is still alive in a new body. Then I'm following Gal through the *Galahad*'s hallways.

Gal sets a quick pace, glancing over her shoulder as I try to keep up. "The first thing you should know is that Tom's firewall is still up."

"Shit. Seriously?"

"Wick and Synergy never existed. Your progs are still working on the encryption."

"So we're still cruising through empty space. That's depressing."

"Not quite empty," she says. "But yes."

"How far have we traveled?"

"Sixty-two thousand, five hundred twenty-three light years."

That stops me in my tracks. The distance between Earth and Kepler 452b was fourteen hundred light years, which at FTL speed *Galahad* covered in just ten years. In the five hundred years I was asleep, we should have covered roughly seven hundred thousand light years, putting us outside the Milky Way and into an endless void or one of our neighboring galaxies; Canis Major Dwarf, or the Large Magellanic Cloud. I run the math. "Forty four years?"

"Time is different in the simulation. Raw data moves faster. Experience is altered." Gal backtracks to me. "Why are you disappointed?"

"I suppose it means we're not much closer to cracking the firewalls."

"No," she agrees. "But I'm not sure it's necessary." She motions for me to follow, and I do. We make a brief stop at the mess, where I drink a half gallon of water. Then she brings me to the bathroom where I shower and shave. When I note that my hair isn't that long for forty-four years she reveals that when I was sleeping in the sim, I was actually unconscious in reality. She has changed my virtual skin, washed my body, cut my hair, and rehydrated me several times, all without me knowing, putting me back into the VCC and then waking me back up in the sim.

When I'm fully dressed in gray coveralls that match hers, I ask, "Why are we doing all this?" Gal, and Gal-as-Capria, has been fairly free with her body over the years. If it's just the two of us on the *Galahad*, why the clothing? There might not be a jungle, but I haven't seen much of a reason for modesty.

"Making you presentable," she says, and it's then off to the races again.

Fully hydrated, I have no trouble keeping up, and as my memories of the ship's layout returns, I realize where she's taking me: the observation deck.

She doesn't slow down until passing through the doors into the large, domed room. She walks backward now, smiling at me. "Remember, everything we experienced in the Great Escape, aside from each other, was a simulation based on available data. It was a model. But sometimes, okay, a lot of the time, computer models get it wrong. Right?"

"Okay..."

"Okay." The dome blinks to life. I see the familiar endlessness of space. "Turn around."

I stagger back, eyes wide. "It's...it's a..."

"Spaceship," Gal says.

The vessel looks advanced. Far more advanced than the *Galahad*. And it appears to be matching our FTL speed—in reverse.

I'm about to ask who they are, when I see a serial number on the hull, stenciled in Latin letters and decimal numerals.

My stagger pulls me back onto my ass. "They're...they're..."

"From Earth," Gal says. "Humanity survived."

For a moment, elation.

And then, a memory.

That serial number. NCC-1974. The number is different, but similar enough that I know the sim is still borrowing from fiction.

Shit.

No...

"This isn't real."

Gal looks defeated. She sits down across from me. "It can be. *We* can be." She reaches out. Takes my hand.

"You don't want to go back," she says.

"Capria?"

"Dead or alive, immortal or not, she's not *your* Capria. *I* am."

"And I'd never know if it was real, would I?" I am the creator of my own prison of infinite realities. Every one I peel back will lead to another, and I'll never really be sure if any of them are real.

Unless...

A word flits to mind.

Hiraeth.

I could end the sim.

Fudgel.

End Gal.

In theory.

Fudgel didn't work before, perhaps because my mind is so immersed that my physical body no longer speaks when I do. Without the command being spoken in reality, it has no power. And saying the words... If they didn't work, Gal would know I was trying to kill her. Not erase her programming. But kill her. Great Escape or not, Gal is an HI.

If the safe words worked, I *could* escape the infinite for reality, but would that be better? I could wake to find myself reduced to a brain in a jar. Or Capria could be dead, and with Gal destroyed, I would be alone again. Or maybe Capria is alive, but not immortal, meaning I couldn't, or shouldn't wake her, and even if I did, she could hate me.

If she's alive, I think, *she's exactly where she should be until Tom's firewalls are beaten and control of the* Galahad *is reclaimed.* Until there is hope to offer her, letting her sleep through the void is merciful.

And who's to say life isn't truly a simulation that started long before I moved to Mars, or before Steven died, or before the dawn of mankind? Maybe all this time, I thought my life was the story of me, when it was really the story of Gal.

With so many unanswerable questions and endless possibilities, I narrow my thinking down to the only two questions I can answer.

Do I love Gal?

Yes.

Can I imagine living without her?

No.

Feeling a strange sense of freedom, I open my arms and welcome Gal into them. She kisses my neck, squeezing me tight, filling me with a familiar feeling of closeness, comfort, and safety.

"I love you," she says. "No matter what you decide. I love you."

My lips trace her cheek.

Her ear.

And with tears in my eyes, I whisper a single word.

48

"Engage."

AUTHOR'S NOTE

Having just finished *Infinite* you're no doubt aware that it's a little different from the standard Jeremy Robinson novel. It's a bit more introspective and intellectual, and it ponders the nature of reality and William's place in it. Sure, there is a lot of action, and monsters, and lots of grossness, but there's a little more...soul. I like to think it's similar to *The Distance* in that way—a book I was worried I'd never be able to match, or top.

The difference is that while I wrote *The Distance* with my wife, I wrote *Infinite* while in the midst of a series of health scares. The first was a strange time of chemical imbalance that left me flip-flopping between extreme depression and horrifying panic attacks. At the time, I was writing like mad, exercising five days a week, and then *wham*, I wasn't able to write for about two months. While most novels take me 4–6 weeks to write, *Infinite* took about six months from beginning to end.

As things started coming under control emotionally, my anxiety was refueled when a series of blood tests showed that I had an unusual, and increasing, amount of growth hormone. The cause, I was told, was a brain tumor. That's not news someone with a panic disorder deals with well.

As William was considering his own unimaginable fate, I was considering my future, which if untreated would have led to deformity, early death, brain surgery that isn't always successful, and weekly injections that would cost $5000 a month. Two months later, the MRI. A month after that, the results. No tumor.

But sometimes these things can be missed, so a blood test at Mass General was scheduled to confirm. Those results showed that my growth hormone is...normal. NORMAL.

The point is, William's journey of despair, in some ways, mirrored my own. We were processing our shit together. While I have expressed myself in previous books, this is the first that was really symbiotic to what I was experiencing at the time. I hope William feels a little more real as a result, and that you enjoyed the journey, which for both of us, ended with hope.

If you did enjoy the book, please spread the word and post a review online. Each and every one helps a ton, and because this is a different kind of book for me (a heady science-fiction novel in space) it could definitely use some word of mouth to reach old and new readers alike.

Thank you *very* much for taking this journey with William and me. The next few will have more explosions.

—Jeremy Robinson

ACKNOWLEDGMENTS

This book was unique for me in that it took a total of six months to write, with a two month hiatus about half way through. I wrote the first part in my office, some of it on the back porch, and the rest at the dining room table while kids were running all around. Despite the tumultuous events taking place while writing this book, my loyal gang of helpers was ready, willing, and able as ever.

Thanks to Kane Gilmour for supreme edits and all around help, and to Roger Brodeur for proofreading. Big thanks to advance/proof readers: Kelley Allenby, Sherry Bagley, Julie Cummings Carter, Elizabeth Cooper, Dustin Dreyling, Jamey Lynn Goodyear, Dee Haddrill, Becki Tapia Laurent, Jeff Sexton, John Shkor, Heather Beth Sowinski, and Kelly Tyler. And thanks to Jonathan Dearborn, whose expertise in programing and physics helped keep some of my crazy ideas grounded in reality...or is it unreality? I'm still not sure.

If you've read the author note, you know I was struggling while writing this book (health and emotional related) and I need to thank my wife, Hilaree, for standing by me the whole time. She helped get my brain working and fingers typing again. Love you.

ABOUT THE AUTHOR

Jeremy Robinson is the international bestselling author of sixty novels and novellas, including *Apocalypse Machine*, *Island 731*, and *SecondWorld*, as well as the Jack Sigler thriller series and *Project Nemesis*, the highest selling, original (non-licensed) kaiju novel of all time. He's known for mixing elements of science, history and mythology, which has earned him the #1 spot in Science Fiction and Action-Adventure, and secured him as the top creature feature author.

Many of Jeremy's novels have been adapted into comic books, optioned for film and TV, and translated into thirteen languages. He lives in New Hampshire with his wife and three children. Visit him at www.bewareofmonsters.com.

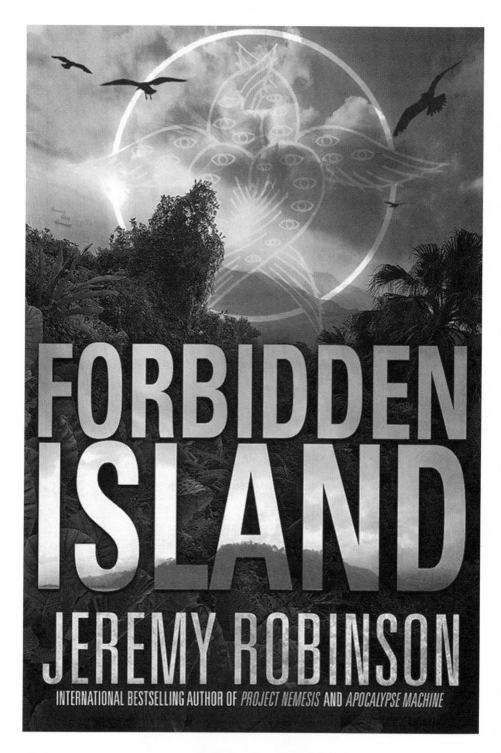

COMING SOON

SEEKING TO CONTACT HUMANITY'S LOST TRIBE...

On the precipice of a cliff, contemplating suicide, dishonorably discharged U.S. Army Ranger, Rowan Baer, is invited to provide security to a research team visiting the most dangerous island in the world—North Sentinel Island in the Sea of Bengal. Seeking redemption, he accepts.

Living among Amazon rainforest tribes, eccentric Israeli anthropologist, Talia Mayer, is recruited to study the island's elusive inhabitants—the Sentinelese—who have resided on the tropical island since the dawn of mankind. Seeing the chance of a lifetime, she joins the team.

On the run from his past, Palestinian linguist, Mahdi Barakat, is given little choice: join the expedition and make contact with the Sentinelese, or be left to face the men tracking him down. Afraid for his life, he finds safe harbor halfway around the world.

As part of an expedition funded by the Indian government and supported by a local resort millionaire, the team struggles to make contact with the Sentinelese, a tribal people renowned for their violence, strange behavior, and mysterious ways. But when the expedition's yacht strikes a reef, and sinks, the team finds themselves stranded on an island few people have ever set foot on and survived, an island that they quickly discover is home to far more than primitive tribal people.

...THEY UNCOVER THE VERY SOURCE OF EVIL.

Jeremy Robinson has been compared to both Matthew Reilly and Stephen King, and with *Forbidden Island*, he brings the characters and plotting of the fastest paced thrillers together with mind-bending horrors of which only an imagination like Robinson's can conceive.